DECEPTION OF DREAMS

CARA BLAINE

Vinci Books

vinci-books.com

Published by Vinci Books Ltd in 2026

1

A CIP catalogue record for this book is available from the British Library.
Paperback ISBN: 9781036733797
The EU GPSR authorised representative is Logos Europe, 9 rue Nicolas Poussion, 17000 La Rochelle, France contact@logoseurope.eu

By Cara Blaine

Stories of the Seven

Deception of Dreams

Venandi Venator

Token of a Wolf

Promise of a Bruja

Luxe's Lullaby Trilogy

Luxe in Between

Luxe in Quest

Luxe in Arms

The World of the Seven

Seven Kingdoms, Seven Patron Gods & Goddesses:

Revas

- Sonos, God of Dreams and Nightmares
- Capital: Sonos City

Kaosuda

- Kaelith, Goddess of Chaos and Order
- Capital: Kaelora

Orakolas

- Orix, God of Prophecy and Ignorance
- Capital: Thalorin

Libeverro

- Veyra, Goddess of Truth and Lies
- Capital: Veyrin

Milpacio

- Zerath, God of War and Peace
- Capital: Paxeris

Kompatos

- Selyne, Goddess of Mercy and Vengeance
- Capital: Selvaris

Bonsanco

- Tavros, God of Fortune and Ruin
- Capital: Bast Tavra

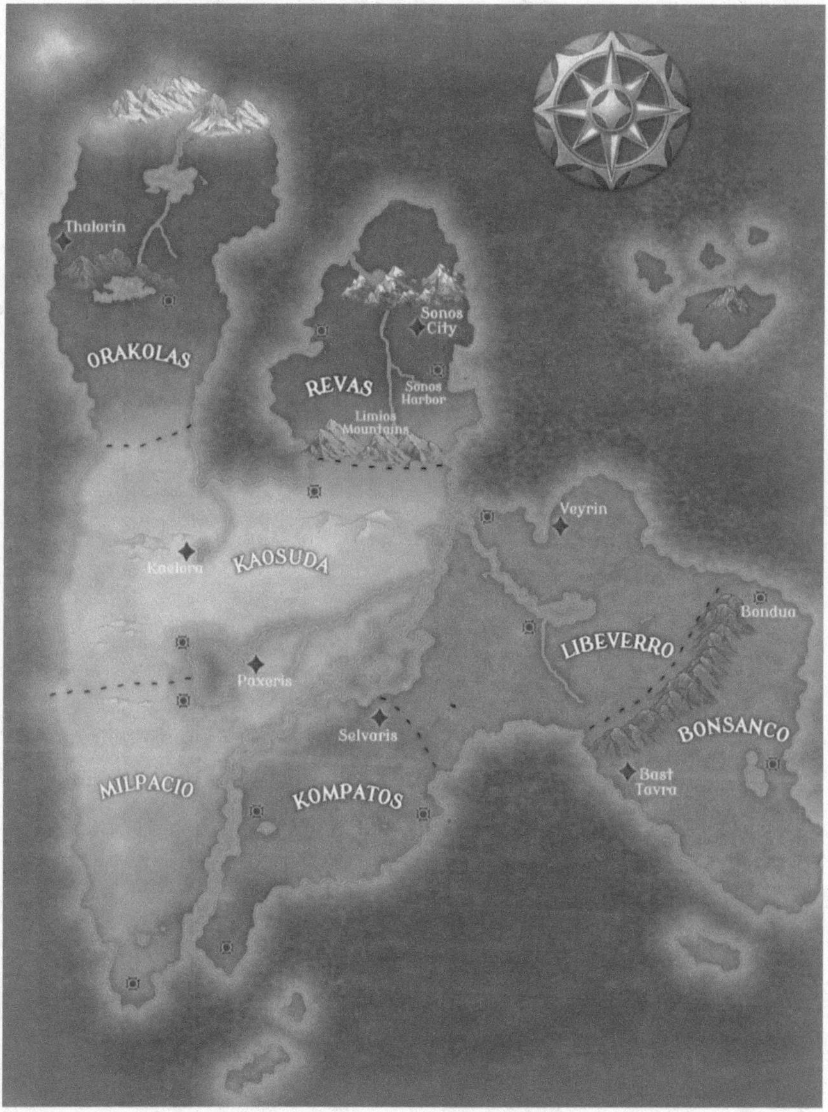

Thalorin
ORAKOLAS
Sonos City
REVAS
Sonos Harbor
Limios Mountains
Veyrin
KAOSUDA
Bondua
LIBEVERRO
Paxeris
Selvaris
BONSANCO
Bast Tavra
MILPACIO
KOMPATOS

Chapter One

MILOS

Milos was awake, but he pretended not to be. It was less awkward that way. The lumpy, straw-filled mattress shifted as the woman next to him stood up. The quiet fumbling as she dressed was quickly followed by the creak of the door opening, and then the soft thump as it shut.

He sighed in relief as he rolled over, stretching and blinking at the early morning rays, which snuck past the edges of the sun-bleached yet grungy curtains. It wasn't that he hadn't liked the young woman. She was pleasant enough, even more experienced than he anticipated, since the town was too small to have a brothel. But they both knew they'd likely never see each other again, so why expend the energy on small talk and fake pretenses?

Even if she did hope to spend more time with him, he couldn’t risk her discovering his true identity. Milos smiled at the thought. How might the pretty little Kaosudan kitchen maid react if she knew she had shared an intimate night with the prince of Revas? The idea amused him, but he wasn't about to tell her.

The fact was, he preferred traveling in disguise. He presented himself at the various courts as expected, but on the road? He was just a regular man. Well, a wealthy one, admittedly. He couldn't exactly pretend his retinue of guards and servants didn't exist. But many of the wealthiest nobles boasted similar, and his people were loyal enough to keep their mouths shut.

One of his guards, an older man named Bristio who had guarded Milos for many years and taken a fatherly interest in the prince, had expressed concern at one point because he imagined Milos was impregnating women across the continent. Milos would never be so irresponsible. There was plenty of fun to be had without coating a lady's womb with his seed, and he wasn't his father. He refused to be. In addition to not allowing himself to come inside a woman, he took contraceptive herbs regularly.

Not that most people knew of Tirano's illegitimate gits … but his mother did, and once he was grown and started to travel on his own, Anela told Milos as well. If his mother had one goal in raising him, it was to ensure he'd be nothing like his father.

He couldn't blame her.

Milos wondered about the others his father had sired, though. He couldn't help his curiosity. His mother never told him any details, other than she knew of two for certain —twins—and had reason to suspect a couple of others. The twins were a boy and a girl. Milos would have liked to have siblings, although he understood why his mother chose not to bear more children. These half-siblings would be a few years older than Milos, but he wouldn't recognize either of them if they walked up to him in the street. He stretched his arms out to either side, yawning as he tried to picture them.

A disturbing thought occurred to him and he swallowed

hard. What if one of the many young women he had been intimate with... No, he couldn't complete the thought. The Seven wouldn't allow such a horror to happen, surely. Besides, being in her late twenties, his half-sister was likely married. Still, perhaps he should ask his mother if she knew what the woman looked like. He shuddered and coaxed his thoughts to wander different avenues.

As he lounged, uninterested in actually getting up for the day, a knock sounded at the door. A resigned breath hissed through his teeth before he responded. "Yes?"

"We must make haste, my lord." Milos recognized Bristio's voice as the door cracked open. "I'm coming in."

Milos ensured the linens covered him adequately as the guard ducked his head to pass through the door before shutting it behind him. All of the doorways in Kaosuda were too short for his guard, and for Milos as well; the desert denizens tended to be shorter on average.

Despite the early hour, the old man's silver-threaded brown hair was pulled back, his appearance clean and neat.

"Apologies, Your Highness," Bristio murmured, his jaw tight as he loomed over the bed. Wide shouldered and battle scarred, his intimidating appearance made him even more effective as a royal guard. "We must leave at once."

Milos sat up, alarmed. "Why? What happened?" He ran a hand through his wavy dark hair in an attempt to tame it after a night of sex and sleep.

"I received intelligence that Kaosudan forces are preparing to launch an attack at the Revas border. We need to cross before the battle grows too large for safe passage."

Damn. Milos didn't especially want to return home yet. He rose, still clutching a sheet to cover his nude state, and glanced around the small room to locate his clothes. "But they know I'm here. I'm supposed to attend a diplomatic meeting at the Kaosudan court in three days' time. Are you sure the rumor is accurate?"

"As certain as I can be. I suspect the idea was to entrap you, perhaps hold you as a hostage, based on the timing. It's not worth the risk." Bristio shifted, obviously impatient and ready to be on the road. He took his job seriously; he'd do anything necessary to protect the heir to the throne of Revas.

Milos scrubbed his hands over his face. "Fuck. All right. I'll meet you at the stables shortly."

Bristio gave a single sharp nod and departed, allowing the prince to ready himself in privacy.

Milos mounted his horse in the bustling innyard just outside the worn down stables, glad he always refused to travel in a carriage. He was something of a horseman and enjoyed riding and the outdoors too much to stay cooped up in that manner. The other advantage was their party could cross the terrain more quickly without the wheeled contraption forcing them to stay on the roads.

The town was small, and their party of eight left behind the squat, dust-colored buildings in no time. Palm leaves waved in their wake as they drew away from the oasis.

Instead of heading west to continue their journey toward the capital, they raced for the north. Their usual travel pace would bring them to the border within two days, but Bristio insisted they continue.

"We should keep going. We can't truly rest until we're on our own soil," Bristio said as the sun sank below the horizon, prompting groans from all. No doubt they wished to wash the grit from their eyes and hair. Milos understood why Kaosudans often traveled with their faces covered—it was a smart solution when one lived among sand dunes.

Milos pulled up alongside the grizzled soldier when they slowed to give the horses a break. "Any ideas on what prompted this attack?" It could have been anything; Tirano and the Kaosudan king had an ongoing feud of sorts. While neither had ever openly declared war, their dislike of each other was common knowledge. And now Milos couldn't even attempt to repair the relations, as was the original plan. "Why does Kaosuda seek violence in the midst of an attempt at diplomacy?"

Bristio raised and dropped one massive shoulder. "Would that I knew, Your Highness. It's always possible that it was unprovoked."

The alternative hung between them like an invisible anvil. Bristio would never criticize Tirano openly, yet both of them knew that Milos's father had likely made some move to instigate the current drama.

Milos's other question was one he didn't voice. Did Tirano remember that Milos was supposed to meet with the Kaosudan ruler and his advisors … and then did something to cause this conflict anyway? "I wonder if my mother is aware."

Bristio shook his head. "Hard to say. She has her ways of gleaning intelligence, but the king…"

Milos understood. His mother tried to rein in some of the king's questionable whims, although often with little success. If she knew Milos was in danger, she would be a thorn in her husband's side. It wasn't impossible that the king would at least try to keep her in the dark, to make his own life easier.

After all, that appeared to be the chief motivation behind most of his decisions.

They rode late into the night before finally stopping to camp for a few hours, mainly to allow the animals to rest. They were out of the dunes now, passing through the plains and entering the sparse forests near the border. Bristio chose the most secluded spot he could, although it wasn't as effective for hiding as the dense forests in Revas. But then again, no one wished to be in *those* woods overnight.

Propped up against his pack, Milos thanked the Seven that it was summer, so going without a fire wasn't much of a hardship. He soon drifted into a light, uneasy sleep.

He woke to the eerie light that preceded dawn. Bristio gripped his shoulder, and as soon as Milos blinked his eyes open, the man brought a finger to his lips in warning.

Then Milos heard it: the sounds of a large group traveling on the nearby road. As the others in their party led the horses farther from the thoroughfare to hide behind the rise of a small hill, he and Bristio remained in place, crouching behind the brush, gazes trained in the direction of the noise.

A few minutes later, Kaosudan soldiers marched around a corner and entered into their view. They were unmistakable; their uniforms differed greatly from those of Revasian soldiers, who always proudly paraded in the kingdom's colors of purple and blue. Kaosudans wore light brown fabrics and leathers the color of desert sand, no doubt to blend in with the miles and miles of dunes and arid land. Some still wore a swath of cloth over the bottom half of their faces despite being beyond the sand.

Bristio cursed under his breath and Milos silently echoed the sentiment. The knife at his belt suddenly felt small and inadequate, and Milos was eager to find the others in their party and have his sword at his side.

The two men eased away from their hiding place,

staying low. The grass and mulch cushioned and silenced their footsteps. Once they reached the others, Bristio proposed a plan.

"We can't use the road, obviously, as we don't know if more soldiers will be coming from behind. We need to move farther east and then to the north to avoid the main travel routes."

"Sir, we'll run into the Limios," one soldier pointed out, referencing the mountain range just north of the border. "There is no pass to the east, is there?"

Bristio inclined his head in acknowledgement. "We will. You're correct, there's no pass sufficient to move armies, which is why it should work. We can make our way through on the horses, and they aren't likely to follow."

Another soldier shifted uncomfortably, rubbing his hand over a grizzled jaw. "What about the Diona?"

Bristio shrugged. "What about them? We won't bother them, so they'll probably leave us be. If they're even still around."

Everyone knew the magic folk, while longer lived than humans, struggled to produce offspring. Eventually, they might die out, but the kingdom still engaged in trade with some of the Diona, so they hadn't disappeared quite yet. Milos assumed it was only a matter of time, unfortunately. He had never met a member of their race; their interactions with humans were rare ever since the Sundering hundreds of years ago. Prior to that, the two races had lived in harmony, according to the historical texts. He had always been curious about them, although never curious enough to risk seeking them out in their mountain territories.

"The whole reason we use the other pass is because the Diona demanded it all those years ago," Milos pointed out. He wasn't eager to trespass against the reclusive folk with their impressive magic. Leaving them in peace was part of the ancient agreement. Aside from that, however, he'd take any excuse not to journey through the treacherous mountains. The Diona weren't the only danger; nightmarish beasts roamed as well, and rock slides weren't uncommon.

Bristio's voice grew hard. "It's our best option."

Milos swallowed a groan, even as he heard others give resigned sighs. He had to try to dissuade Bristio. Ultimately, Milos was the final decision maker, but he typically bowed to Bristio's decades of experience in these matters.

"We can move much faster than those soldiers. Most of them are on foot. I think we can head north from here and remain out of sight of the road. We'll certainly be able to cross before that group catches up to us. Then we'll have the protection of our own units as well as access to the pass."

A few of the others gave faint nods as their gazes darted back and forth between the head guard and the prince.

Bristio chewed the inside of his cheek as he considered Milos. "These woods are not as dense as I would like for such a scheme. With the horses, they're likely to spot us."

"We'll be fine if we don't bunch up. We'll ride single file with some space between, and stay behind cover as best we can." The more Milos considered it, the less he desired to prolong their journey for weeks in uncomfortable conditions. Comfort aside, it didn't sit well with him to avoid the conflict; as future king, he should attempt to join his father's army and speak with the commanding officer, if nothing else.

Bristio narrowed his eyes, then released a breath. "All right, Your Highness. As you say." His reluctance was apparent, and Milos was surprised he gave in so easily. "You should remember, though, that if it does not go well, it was your order, and you'll have to answer to the king for it."

Milos barely suppressed his scowl. So that's how Bristio would play this? He wasn't a child, so the implied "I'm going to tell your father" threat left an acrid taste in his mouth, especially since Bristio knew Milos's relationship with the king ranged from deeply strained to tepidly neutral at best. "I am always accountable for my own actions, sir," he said stiffly.

Without further discussion, he strode over to his horse, which someone had readied for him, and mounted. The rest of the party scrambled about, grabbing any remaining items from the forest floor and hurrying for their horses.

Milos rode north until he could fully see past the hill. He could still hear the soldiers, but he could no longer see them, and so he continued, leading his retinue through the woods.

Chapter Two

VERANA

Ana detested going to the weekly market, but at least it was a fine summer day. Shopping and trading in the bitter cold was far worse. While the surrounding forest remained dark and foreboding year-round, the villagers fared better in the summer and thus were far less likely to take out their hardships on their neighbors. She hefted her basket more securely over her arm, and the jars of goat milk she had brought to trade clinked together.

Gray and white fur streaked by the corner of her eye, and she glanced to see Cecil racing back toward the tree line. He hated the market too, but he would find her later. Ever since she had rescued him as a kitten from freezing in the snow years before, he never left her side for long. She silently wished him happy hunting as she reached the edge of the village.

Carts and makeshift tables lined the square, while the wood structures of homes and small businesses lurked behind the temporary market. Folks called out to sell their wares and Ana flinched at the onslaught of raucous voices.

"The freshest of fish!" one man yelled. "Get your fresh fish here."

A small smile lifted the corners of her mouth despite the noise. Everyone's fish was always fresh here, as they were only a few miles from the coast. Fishing was one of the primary occupations for the inhabitants of this village, as well as the population of Sonos Harbor, a slightly bigger town situated at the ocean's edge.

Harried mothers tugged their children along. "No, don't you dare touch that!" one woman scolded, causing the toddler to wail. Apparently he was desperate to run his grubby hands over the soft skeins of yarn for sale. Ana eyed the display of blues and yellows and greens enviously; she didn't blame him, it was very tempting.

The local templekeeper, Pastro Emilio, stood on a wooden crate, delivering the messages of the god Sonos. Ana didn't stop to listen; she had heard it all before, when her mother used to insist on the entire family attending services. The message was always the same: honor thy king as thy god, for Sonos favors the good King Tirano; sacrifice for the good of your kingdom; that type of thing. Ana had always wondered why Her Majesty Queen Anela was never mentioned. She was, after all, a royal too, which meant she was favored and gifted by the gods. Ana never had the courage to ask.

Her mother, Halia, was properly devout. Ana, on the other hand, had inherited her father's skepticism. Her father wasn't born and raised in Revas as Halia had been; he hailed from Libeverro, a country to the south. Ana had never been, but she knew the Libeverrans worshiped a different deity. Still one of the Seven, of course: Veyra, the goddess of truth and lies.

However, if her father remained devout to the goddess

of his homeland, he kept it to himself. Ana rather suspected her father had no use for any of the gods.

She reached the spot where the vendor she sought was usually set up, but he wasn't there. Frowning, she glanced from side to side with no luck. Annoyed, because she wanted to finish as quickly as she could, she chose not to go randomly searching. Instead, she turned her focus inward, listening to the tug in her gut that would tell her which way to go. It was an odd skill, one she had kept secret since she was a small child for fear of judgement. She was already considered *different*, being half Libeverran and not ladylike or devout enough to please the villagers. She had no desire to fuel the gossip, or to catch the attention of the pastros.

Her cheeks burned, remembering the last time she was subject to both, only a year prior. She had been with a young man, Gino, from Sonos Harbor at the time; they were only kissing when caught, but she hadn't realized he was already engaged to be married. Nor did she expect to be on the receiving end of so much judgement—more so than he, which was hardly fair. She wasn't the one who was engaged. She counted herself fortunate that no one had found them in the woods the day prior, doing far more than kissing.

She shook off the lingering shame and embarrassment, focusing again on her inner guide. This knack she harbored was quite useful. Her innate sense led her across the square to the exact man she sought. She stepped into the line. He was busy with other customers, and Ana couldn't help hearing the conversation. The two men speaking with the vendor had strange accents, which intrigued her. Most travelers and traders visited Sonos Harbor or the capital, or both; not many ventured into her village. She wished she could ask where they were from, and what it was like there, but she knew it would be considered too forward of her to initiate a chat with two male strangers. She let the thought go with a sigh.

When it was her turn, she traded goat milk and mushrooms for a length of cream-colored fabric. Her older brother Ameleo had outgrown his shirts once again. The blue or green would suit him, but dyed fabrics were too expensive for everyday clothing.

Several transactions and vendors later, as she finished up, she heard, "Ana!" Turning, she smiled to see her younger brother, Aldo, making his way toward her through the throng. She waited patiently as he stopped to talk with at least two different people on his way.

"Hey, Alleycat," she said when he finally approached. He had always been friendly—their father joked that Aldo had never met a stranger—and her affectionate nickname for him reflected that. He was just like an alleycat in the capital, following people around for any possible scrap—of attention, in Aldo's case, while it was more often about food for the cats. He didn't mind the teasing, as he knew well enough that she adored him. "What are you doing here?"

He lifted and dropped a shoulder. "I finished my chores. Mama told me you'd be here. Want to go foraging when you're finished?"

Ana was a skilled forager, thanks to her unique ability. She nodded. The more food they could store away over the summer, the better winter would be. "Yes, let's. I'm finished here. We can empty this at home"—she held up the woven basket—"then take a walk in the woods. It's too early for apples. We may find some berries or mushrooms though."

When they arrived at their cabin, which was in a small clearing at the edge of the woods, about a ten-minute walk outside the village, they found their mother Halia laundering the bedclothes near the small front porch of their two room home.

"We're almost out of soap," was Halia's greeting as she wiped sweat from her brow and pushed loose strands of wavy blonde hair behind her ears. Grabbing the paddle again, she asked, "Did you get more lye?"

Ana cringed. She had forgotten.

Her mother glanced at her and frowned at the expression on Ana's face. "Verana Elisa, did you forget one of only five things I asked for you to fetch?"

Ana sighed and nodded. "Yes, Mama. I'm sorry. I can go back, the market isn't over yet."

Her mother huffed. "You'd forget your own head if it wasn't attached. Never mind, I'll go myself. Get these hung up to dry." She pointed to the wet fabric.

"Yes, Mama," Aldo said.

Halia fetched her coin purse inside as Ana and Aldo began the tedious process of emptying the tub and hanging the linens.

Half an hour later, Aldo and Ana entered the forest behind their home to forage as planned, leaving the goods from the market at home. With some luck, they might fill the empty basket to the brim.

Despite the danger, Ana had always felt drawn to the quiet dark of the woods. Even so, she knew not to enter the forest at night, when unfriendly beasts and other strange creatures roamed the shadows. Some said the Diona kept the creatures in check during the day, allowing them to roam at night, but those were only stories.

Others said the Diona were as dangerous as the creatures they allowed to roam under the stars; they claimed the fair folk held an extreme prejudice against humans. The

Sundering had taken place so long ago that the true history had dissolved into folktales and rumors.

The stories didn't diminish the quiet peace of the woods, and they had several hours of daylight yet. It was too early in the season to gather much, but in truth, Ana and Aldo loved any excuse to spend time together.

Their mother birthed Aldo much earlier than anticipated, and both mother and babe struggled for several months afterward. Ana was responsible for much of Aldo's care, as well as nursing Halia as she recovered, while Leo and their father worked on farms and fishing boats, and then did all the chores Ana and her mother would typically do. The circumstances around Aldo's birth established a deep bond between brother and sister, which persisted in all the years after. She had never been as close to Leo. They tended to butt heads, both equally as obstinate as any goat she'd ever seen.

Still, she'd always remember the time he defended her when one of the village boys tried to … take something she wasn't offering. The boy had gone home with a black eye and other scrapes and bruises. No matter how much they argued, Ana knew Ameleo cared for her.

Her thoughts turned to the two foreigners from the market. "Do you ever think about traveling?" Ana asked as they strolled through the shaded wood. She breathed in the scents of damp summer grass and evergreen trees as she called upon the feeling inside that would tell her if they drew close to anything edible.

"To the capital?" Aldo stooped to inspect a patch of dandelions, knobby knees straining against the fabric of his britches. Earlier that year, when he turned fourteen, he had sprouted up as quickly as the plant he examined. His height now matched Ana's, but he was still gangly as a newborn colt.

"It's past time for those. Once they flower, they're too bitter," Ana advised. "No, not the capital. To other countries. Wouldn't it be something to be able to say that you've visited all seven nations?"

Aldo shrugged, eyes scanning the tree roots and brush. "I suppose. But we don't have enough money for something like that."

Ana swallowed her sigh. He was right, but it didn't stop her from daydreaming. "Pretend we did. Where would you go first?"

He ran a hand through the wavy blonde hair he inherited from Halia as he considered. "Probably Libeverro. Where Father is from."

Ana smiled. "Good choice. I would do the same. Maybe we can save up enough, eventually, and visit Libeverro together."

"Just you and me, right?" Aldo asked.

"Definitely. Just the two of us. Mother, Father, and Leo wouldn't want to go, anyway."

That evening at supper, it started to rain. Fortunately, they had already brought in the bed linens, but Ana realized the goats were still out. She stood, mid-meal, to go persuade the animals into their shed for the night. Aldo stood as well.

"I can help." He smiled at her, gesturing at the back door.

She looked at his plate. "You've barely eaten; go ahead and finish. I'll be back in just a minute."

"I'm not hungry tonight anyway. Come on, let's go before it gets any worse out there."

Leo interjected, "If you don't want it, can I have it? I could eat two more suppers, easy." He gestured to his plate, which only had a few crumbs scattered over the smooth wood.

“No you will not, you’ve already had seconds and Aldo needs to eat! He’s skin and bones,” their mother scolded.

“Mama is right, leave his food alone and don’t be greedy,” Ana said. Aldo had always been thin and a light eater, despite his mother’s best efforts. His recent growth had emphasized it.

“I wasn’t asking you, Ana, was I? You should mind yourself, it’s not your food,” Leo argued. Ana took a breath to respond, but Aldo, ever the peacemaker, held up his hand as he moved toward the back door.

“It’s fine, Mama, Ana. I’m really not hungry. I ate a lot at breakfast, and Leo is always hungry. Right, brother? You could eat more than all of us put together. "

Leo grinned at this. “I'm still filling out. It's not my fault.” He wasn’t wrong. He’d gone through the phase Aldo was in years ago, but now his shoulders were busting out of his current shirts, which is why Ana had just purchased fabric for a new one.

“Go ahead, it’s yours.” Aldo gestured at his food.

Ana shook her head, giving up. The two ran out into the yard and managed to coax the goats into the shed, with a little trouble.

“Aldo, help me corner her,” Ana said of the last nanny goat still out in the rain. Aldo crept closer and to the left, opposite of his sister, to try to cut off any escape attempt. They worked well together, no matter the task. She managed to dart in and grab the goat, and Aldo slipped a lead around its neck. They shut her in the shed with the others.

“These goats don’t know what’s good for them. You silly, ridiculous things!" Ana huffed as they closed the gate.

"We're soaked now, and muddy to the knees, you stubborn twits!"

"Tell them all about it, Ana. I'm sure they'll see sense and apologize," Aldo teased.

Ana laughed. "You never know. If I taught you manners, perhaps I can teach the goats as well," she said, raising her eyebrows at him. Aldo could always cheer her up when she was frustrated or sad. "Thanks for your help, Alleycat."

He smiled. "You're going to call me that until I'm in my grave, aren't you?" he asked.

"I certainly am," Ana responded. "And I'm not sorry." They ran back toward the cozy warmth of their home, laughing.

After supper, their father took out his instrument. He had played it frequently when the children were small, but he rarely did so anymore. Once he tuned the strings, they sang together in front of the fire. They danced to the last couple of songs, Ana paired with Aldo and their mother with Leo.

In the months to come, Ana would think back on this night with great longing.

Chapter Three

ANELA

Tempting aromas drifted from her sitting room as Anela emerged from her sleeping chamber. The small dining table, its reddish-brown hue polished to shining, held a tray laden with breakfast and tea.

As the kitchen maid departed with a murmured, "Good morning, Your Majesty," and a hasty curtsy, Henriella entered. The corners of Anela's mouth automatically lifted in a genuine smile as she sat and waited for Hen to join her. Outside of spending time with Milos or losing herself in the oblivion of sleep, the routine of breaking her fast with her closest friend was the best part of each day.

"My queen," Hen murmured with a bob of her blonde head. Anela envied her golden tresses; they hardly showed the silver creeping in, whereas her own dark copper hair loudly proclaimed that specific sign of aging.

Anela rolled her eyes. "We're alone, Hen. The servants all left."

Hen glanced around to confirm before her blue-satin-clad shoulders relaxed and she grinned. "Ah, good."

The two proceeded to dig into the various platters, adding portions of eggs, sausage, fruit, and toasted bread to their plates.

"Have you heard from Milos? Will he be home soon?" Henriella spread butter on her toast, the movements precise and proper. Even when no one else was watching, the mannerisms of court were deeply ingrained in both women, especially so in Henriella. Anela often had the thought that Hen should have been a queen rather than herself; her friend had always been better at abiding the plethora of rules, the proper etiquette seemingly second nature to her. But then again, producing an heir would have presented a problem for her oldest friend.

Anela shook her head as she swallowed a bite of egg. "Nothing yet. I think it will be at least a month before he's home."

"If he doesn't return engaged to the Kaosudan princess, Tirano won't be pleased." Henriella's tone was shrewd.

Anela let out a very unqueenly snort as she reached for her juice. "No, but when is he ever?" She deepened her voice, wrinkling her brow into a stern look to mimic the king. "He has evaded his duties long enough. By the Seven, Anela, he should be married and here by my side, learning how to rule." Hen chuckled.

It wasn't his duties that Milos evaded, it was his father, and at his mother's behest. When the prince was young, she traveled with him as much as possible, using diplomatic relations as an excuse. Now that he was grown, he was less interested in traveling with his mother, but she encouraged him to continue the habit all the same. Milos was kind and compassionate, as she had hoped ... and she doubted he would be so if he had been in close proximity to his father all these years.

Anela often wondered what life would be like if she could go back in time to when she first met her husband, Tirano, the then-prince of Revas. Might she refuse to marry him if she had another chance?

She pondered this as she abandoned the juice to sip her tea, then reached the usual conclusion. Yes, she would still marry him—how could she not, when he gave her Milos? But surely she could have done ... *something* differently. Alas, she had no power over the past; she shoved the thoughts down, knowing they were pointless.

As they finished their meal, a knock sounded at the double-door entrance to her quarters. She called out her permission and a palace guard stepped into the room. "His Majesty requests your presence in his quarters, Your Majesty. Immediately."

Anela groaned to herself. It was too early to deal with Tirano. And she especially dreaded private meetings; he was much more unpredictable in those circumstances. Yet, while she had openly defied him in the past, she had learned to choose those battles carefully. She could be more effective if she pretended to be dutiful to him and kept her defiance covert.

"Yes, I'll attend him shortly. Thank you."

A servant entered to clear the table and Anela bid goodbye to Henriella. "If I have time, I'll find you later for a walk in the gardens."

Her friend forced a smile, dark blue eyes troubled. "Of course."

Anela made her way through the shadowed, stone-walled corridors, smiling and nodding to acknowledge people bowing or dropping curtsies. She had grown accustomed to the gloominess of the castle over the years, yet she still felt a sharp pang of homesickness at times, a yearning for the seaside palace of her youth: bright and airy, built of light-colored stone, marble, and sea glass, with windows galore to take advantage of the coastal view.

She fingered the pendant on her chest, one of the few thoughtful gifts from her husband when they were courting: a gilded seashell. She wore it often, not for his sake, but because it felt like carrying a little piece of home near her heart.

Slowing as she grew closer to her destination, she allowed herself a moment to take a deep breath and straightened her shoulders.

The guards outside the king's quarters nodded at her, expressions stoic, before opening a door to announce her presence. "Her Majesty, the Queen."

She swept in and the door clicked shut behind her. Tirano occupied the spot behind his gilded dark wood desk toward the right side of his sitting room. His looks no longer affected Anela as they once had, though he was handsome as ever, with silver threaded black hair, a strong jaw, and tawny skin.

He didn't stand when she entered, as was polite, but she was accustomed to his disdain. Striding to him, she stopped in front of the desk, which was covered in all manner of writing utensils and papers. A strained smile fixed on her lips as she clasped her hands in front of her, resting them atop the flounced leaf-green skirt of her dress.

"You summoned me, my king?"

His dark brown eyes studied her. Finally, he responded, "Yes. Sit." He gestured to a chair on her left side. She lowered onto it, stiff backed, the expectant expression fixed on her countenance.

He blew out an explosive breath as he leaned back in his chair, hands gripping the leather covered arms. "I didn't wish to speak with you about this matter, but I have few options. So, tell me, have you been experiencing any ... changes ... with your abilities?"

Anela fought to keep her reaction neutral. This was indeed an odd question. Although he wasn't specific, she knew he was speaking about her "gift" of prophecy. All royals in the seven kingdoms inherited gods-given magic, the specific powers dependent on which god or goddess was patron to that nation. She originated from the royal family of Orakolas, and the patron deity of their kingdom was Orix, god of prophecy—and ignorance, as all gods represented a duality. Light and dark. Good and evil. They encompassed both, as did the humans and Diona they created.

"Well," she said, hesitant. "As you know, my *abilities* are quite different from yours. I don't use them regularly. I have less control in summoning my magic than you do; it has a mind of its own." He stared at her, apparently unmoved, waiting. "But no, I haven't noticed any changes."

She chewed the inside of her mouth, unsure what answer he was hoping for. He narrowed his eyes and leaned forward. "You haven't noticed a ... weakening? A fading of strength?"

A helpless shrug accompanied her answer. "No." She paused, debating. It was reckless to question him in return, yet she was dying to know what instigated this and took the risk, asking, "Have you noticed something of the sort with your own gift, my king?"

His ponderous expression morphed into a scowl. "We are finished here. You are dismissed."

It had been worth a try. Lips pressed together, she gave a sharp nod and stood, hurrying out of the room. The abrupt dismissal reminded her of an argument they'd had long ago, when she had accused him of treating her like a dog.

One night when Milos was about seven weeks old, Anela was woken by someone climbing into bed with her. She quickly realized it was Tirano.

"What are you doing?" she asked, half awake. He had not come to her in such a manner since before she told him she was with child. It had been at least a year.

"Visiting my wife," he said. She could tell he was drunk.

"To what purpose?" she replied in an icy tone. "I was asleep."

He tried to kiss her, but she ducked away from him. He sat up, a confused, owlish expression on his face. "You are healed from the birth, are you not?"

"I am."

"Then why do you push me away?"

She was speechless for several moments. She sat up as well so she could meet his gaze in the low light of the dying fire. Tendrils of hair strayed from her plait; she tucked the escaped pieces behind her ears.

"You ask me why? Why have you treated me as little more than an acquaintance for the last year? You only speak to me if you can't avoid it, or to criticize. You spend no time with me except what is absolutely necessary, and never alone. Why is that, husband*?"*

"And now here I am trying to spend time with you, alone. This is the reception I get. How can you blame me for not seeking you out?"

"Do not turn this around on me. I asked you a question. Why have you treated me like this? Why did you think I would welcome you to my bed when you have been entirely disinterested in me? Cruel, even?"

"I did not seek your company because pregnancy made you overly emotional and entirely irrational, and I had no desire to bear the brunt of that nonsense. As for your second question: because I am your husband, and it is your duty." He sounded more sober now, and angry.

She crossed her arms and shook her head, her mouth pressed into a thin, hard line. "I did my duty. I produced a male heir, healthy and whole, and I care for him day and night. I owe you nothing more." It was true; everyone in the castle thought her extraordinarily odd because she didn't wish to hand the babe over to a nursemaid. But Anela had little love in this place, and she wasn't about to give up the love of her son to a stranger.

"I am the future king. You owe me obedience just as every citizen of Revas does."

"Obedience? Is that what you want, for me to come when you call, like a dog? Sit, Anela. Stay, Anela. Please me, Anela!" Her voice rose; she uncrossed her arms, her hands balled into fists. "I tried to give you my heart and you were not interested. You dropped it under your boot, and you crushed it. But now you expect obedience*." She said the last as though it were a foul word.*

He attempted to untangle himself from the bedclothes so he could stand.

"You are an ungrateful wretch," he spat as he got to his feet. "I was giving you another chance."

She barked a laugh. "Another chance? For what? To open my heart to you once more, so that you may trample what's left of it? You are correct. I feel no gratitude for another chance with you. And that is no one's fault but your own."

Anger darkened his eyes as his chest heaved. He opened his mouth to respond, but their yelling had woken the baby, who started to wail.

Anela rose and fetched Milos out of the bassinet, cradling him. His cries quieted to an insistent whine.

"If you will excuse me, Your Majesty. I need to tend to our son." She turned her back on him and walked away.

Anela ground her teeth at the memory and barely noticed her surroundings on the walk back to her quarters. She forced herself to return her focus to their more recent conversation.

What had that been about? Was something wrong with

Tirano's magic? Sonos, the god of dreams and nightmares, was the patron god of Revas. If Tirano's powers were fading, had he lost favor with Sonos? At least now it made sense why he had to ask *her*; as the only royals at the palace currently, no one else nearby had a gods-given gift. Nor would Tirano ever consider asking such a question of a monarch from a different kingdom. They might make the same assumption as she, and he would never show a potential weakness to another ruler. Briefly, she thought of the prophecy that had plagued her for decades, wondering if it could be related to the present situation.

She changed direction, her curiosity choosing her path. It carried her out of the castle, to the temple situated nearby on the grounds. There were several in the capital city of Sonos outside the castle gates as well, but the royalty and nobility couldn't be expected to worship with the masses. Anela had always thought the tradition silly. Back in Orakolas, the nobles and royalty celebrated holy days alongside all of the citizens, for they believed that while the gods had gifted the royal family power, that power was to be used to the benefit of the people. It was the gods' way of ensuring everyone was looked after, even though the gods themselves no longer walked among them. Therefore the royals weren't above other people, they simply had a larger responsibility to ensure the kingdom prospered.

Entering the cool, dark space of the holy building, she paused to allow her eyes to adjust. Diona-made lanterns, the same as in the castle corridors, hung evenly spaced throughout, but they barely made a dent in the windowless gloom. She stopped when she reached the row of benches nearest the door, glancing around in search of a templekeeper.

One approached from her left, bowing low and speaking with a mild, quiet voice. "Your Majesty. May I help you with anything?" The man was in his late middle years, blue robes billowing about his portly frame. She typically only came to the temple when she was obligated at the equinox or solstice, and she didn't recognize him; perhaps he had transferred from another temple.

"Yes. I wish to peruse the temple's collection of written works." She smiled warmly. "Can you lead me to them?" Only the religious texts were kept in the temple rather than the library. She had never had reason to seek them out, but she knew they were under lock and key.

He bowed once more. "As you wish, Your Majesty." He hesitated. "I am also happy to answer any questions you have, if you'd rather not dig through old, dusty texts?"

"I appreciate it, but I'm not even sure where I'd begin," she lied. "I'd rather browse and do my own research." The questions she had… If she asked them aloud, who knows what he might think. What rumors might spread. It could complicate things unnecessarily.

Mild confusion and perhaps a touch of wariness was evident in his expression, yet he couldn't deny her. "As you wish, Your Majesty. If you'll follow me?"

"Thank you."

He led her deeper into the temple and they passed through a door before reaching a staircase. The narrow passage was lit with the same Diona-made lights. "The books are held underground, where they're better protected from sunlight and extreme temperatures," he explained.

"I see. Please, lead the way." A few beats later, she asked, "What word from our god Sonos of late?" She kept her tone casual, as though she was simply making small talk. "Has he sent any dreams of interest?"

The man stumbled, gripping the railing to right himself.

"Oh, well, I..." He cleared his throat, continuing down the stairs. "Why do you ask?"

"Is it a difficult question to answer?" she returned, her curiosity spiking at his evasiveness.

He glanced back at her; she kept her expression neutral. "Truthfully, it's been fairly ... quiet on that front. I thought maybe you had heard something of it, as some pastros have been expressing concern."

"No, I've heard no rumors," she reassured him. "I'm sure there's nothing to be worried about. As they say, no news is good news." Her tone was still light, but her heart sped up. If Tirano wasn't sending dreams to the pastros...

The templekeeper grunted, neither affirmation nor denial.

They reached the bottom and walked down a narrow hallway. The pastro stopped at a door and pulled a ring of keys from his pocket, unlocking it and leading her inside.

The room wasn't overly large, and it was packed with books and scrolls. Shelves reaching the ceiling covered every wall, with a few separate bookcases standing in the middle of the room near a table and several chairs.

The pastro briefly explained the organization system. "I'll leave you to it, unless you'd like me to wait?"

Anela assured him she was fine by herself. "I'll find one of you and let you know when I'm finished so you can lock up again."

He left with a swirl of blue robes, shutting the door gently behind him. She selected several texts she thought may have the information she sought, and settled into one of the shabby armchairs to read.

Several hours later, neck aching and sight blurry, she replaced the final scroll. Despite her physical discomfort, she was extremely pleased with her discoveries.

A royal's gods-given gift could weaken, or disappear altogether. It didn't happen often, but there were recorded incidents throughout the history of the seven kingdoms.

It could happen if a monarch was very ill of body. If the person was healthy, it was generally seen as evidence of the king or queen falling out of favor with the gods. Again, this wasn't common, yet there were records of royals losing their power—and usually their crown along with it.

Anela returned to the ground level of the temple almost in a daze and let the pastro know she was finished. As she walked back out into the sunlight, an emotion surged inside of her. She didn't recognize it initially, but after absorbing it for several beats, she realized what it was: hope.

Chapter Four

MILOS

Milos, Bristio, and the rest of the retinue managed to overtake the unit of Kaosudan soldiers, successfully sneaking past them through the thickening trees, just as Milos had hoped. As darkness fell, they continued on, determined to reach Revas as soon as possible.

When the moon was high overhead, Bristio called them to a halt. He held up a finger, listening. Milos heard nothing.

The older man kept his voice low as he jerked a chin at one of the other guards. "You. Scout up ahead. We'll wait here."

Milos shifted in the saddle, tired and sore from the relentless travel, as they waited. The only sound was the whisper of a breeze through branches. Half an hour later, the guard returned.

"The Kaosudan army is encamped that way. The soldiers we saw must have been a second wave. There was no sign of battle, but..." He waved a hand. "The camp stretches a good distance in both directions. I'm not sure how far afield we might need to go to circumvent it. We could run out of supplies in the attempt."

Milos silently cursed. His gamble wasn't going to pay off after all. But on the other hand, it sounded like Bristio's plan may not have worked either. "You don't think they'll let us pass? I doubt anyone would recognize me on sight."

Bristio leveled a stare at him in the moonlight. "They'll suspect, regardless. I'm sure they're informed that you were visiting, and you're obviously neither Kaosudan nor a peasant. They'll know we're Revasian from our accents alone."

Milos pressed his lips together as he considered. Bristio wasn't wrong. All of the seven kingdoms spoke the common tongue, with accents and dialects varied according to region. "How much gold do we have?"

Bristio shrugged. "A decent bit. What are you thinking?"

Milos smiled as he lifted an eyebrow. "Bribery. We could try to bribe a sentry to provide us safe passage through the camp."

The others murmured their support of the idea. Bristio heaved a sigh. "It *might* work. But it's a risk."

Impatience flashed through Milos as sarcasm laced his tone. "We could plan to fight our way through, if you'd rather." It frustrated him when Bristio stomped on all of his ideas without presenting any alternatives.

Twenty more minutes of discussion didn't produce any new possible plans. They would attempt to bribe their way through the enemy camp.

As they neared the grouping of tents, a sentry spotted them, like they assumed would happen. "Who goes there?"

At Bristio's signal, they halted as he called back, "Weary travelers, sir, on our way home. May we pass?"

The sentry appeared out of the dark on horseback, pointing a nocked arrow at them. "Have you weapons?"

Bristio held up his hands and nodded to the rest of their party to do the same. "Yes, but they're not drawn. We simply wish to ride through."

"You're Revasian." It wasn't a question.

"We are. We visited Kaosuda to trade."

"Keep your hands where I can see them." They complied as the soldier drew closer, only slightly lowering the weapon. "We are on the eve of a battle with your countrymen, sir. I assume you weren't aware."

"Indeed not," Bristio lied.

"So I cannot let you pass. You may surrender and remain under guard in the camp." The unspoken words were clear: the second option involved bloodshed.

"Sir, I understand your position, but we want nothing to do with this battle. If you'll allow me to reach for my purse, I can show you exactly how much we'd appreciate your aid."

Milos noted that no other sentries appeared to be nearby. They must be somewhat spread out, or perhaps simply concentrated on the opposite side, nearer to the border. If necessary, they could deal with the lone soldier and retreat to determine a new plan. He kept his hands in view while lowering them enough that he could reach a knife more quickly if need be.

The sentry glanced over his shoulder, then returned his attention to Bristio, considering. But then one hand moved from the bow and went to his belt, where an alarm horn hung.

He grasped it. Milos whipped his dagger out, took aim, and a breath later the man cried out as the blade sunk into his shoulder before he could lift the horn to his mouth.

Milos cursed. He had been trying for the throat. Bristio was already surging forward, sword drawn. The sentry dropped his bow, which he couldn't use with only one hand, fumbling for the knife at his belt.

Bristio slashed his throat, nearly taking off his head, as his hand touched the hilt. Blood sprayed and his horse reared, toppling him onto the ground.

Milos and the others gathered around the old guard. "Now what?" Milos asked, breathless, as his heart pounded in the confines of his chest.

"Now, we retreat, and—" Bristio started.

"Timio, that you?" a voice called from a distance. "Timio, confirm!"

They were out of time. Milos's mind raced. If they turned around, the other sentry may still see them and pursue, bringing more soldiers with him, and they'd be no closer to home.

"We have the element of surprise. Draw your weapons; we ride for the border." Milos urged Bruna into a gallop, barely hearing Bristio calling his name. But he was already gone, leaving the others no choice but to follow.

The camp was settled for the night, with most of the soldiers inside their tents and a few gathered around fires throughout. Milos thanked the Seven for that luck—especially Tavros, the god of good fortune and ruin. Tavros was the patron god of Bonsanco, not Revas or Kaosuda, but Milos figured it couldn't hurt.

They raced past tents, fires, and soldiers alike, Milos doing his best not to draw too close to any of the Kaosudans and their wicked, curved blades. Shouts sounded around them and pounding feet pursued them. The alarm horn finally sounded, and it wasn't long before Milos heard arrows whistling through the air. Fortunately, aiming at moving targets in the dark proved challenging. One struck his saddlebag, and Bruna increased her speed.

Moments later, they left the tents behind, although Milos thought they still had pursuers. The winking lights of many campfires in the distance broke through the darkness. The Revasian army.

The sounds of the Kaosudan soldiers behind them faded. As they drew closer to the Revasian camp, Bristio alerted their own sentries. "Make way for the prince of Revas!"

They slowed at the edge of the tents. Milos dismounted to walk Bruna after their sprint. He leaned against her, catching his breath and willing his heart to slow, then patted her on the flank. "Swift as the wind, as always. Thank you, girl." He inspected the arrow to ensure it hadn't injured her. Fortunately, the only damage was to the saddlebag. He yanked it out of the leather, tossing it to the ground.

The camp had erupted into action at their arrival, and Milos hadn't walked twenty feet before he was approached by a sleepy looking young man, his dark purple tunic wrinkled and askew. With a bow, he said, "Your Highness. Apologies, we did not anticipate your arrival. May I take your horse?"

"No apology necessary. I didn't anticipate it either." Milos winked at the boy. "No, thank you. I'll tend to her myself."

The camp was organized in the way Milos was accustomed to. He had never been in an actual battle, but he had visited army camps before to confer with the general, relay messages from his father, and boost morale. He made his way to what functioned as the stables and took care of Bruna and the tack.

As he finished, another soldier found him. "Ah, Your Highness, there you are. General Casio requests your presence, if it's not too much trouble."

Milos exhaled heavily. "Yes, very well." He followed the soldier across the camp to the general's tent. The man pushed aside the flap, which was decorated with an image of a white moon and star above a purple mountain, all on a background of dark blue: the emblem of Revas. Milos caught a glance of the general pacing within the canvas structure.

The soldier announced the prince and left. General Casio faced Milos and bowed, with a murmured, "Your Highness." His body was rigid, jaw clenched.

"General," Milos responded. He stood straight, hands behind his back, and waited.

The older man released a breath. "May I have permission to speak freely, Your Highness?"

A corner of Milos's mouth twitched at the general's efforts to appear calm. He was livid, and Milos wasn't surprised. The commanding officer couldn't punish Milos for his recklessness, outside of the inevitable lecture, but Milos could at least give him that much.

He inclined his head. "Yes, you have my permission."

General Casio waved a hand, still agitated. "What in the world were you thinking? I know this escapade wasn't Bristio's idea."

Milos shook his head. "You're right, it wasn't. He should not be disciplined in any way." He waited for Casio's nod, then continued. "I was simply trying to get my retinue across the border before the battle. And we succeeded."

"But why were you even *there*?" The general spread his arms to either side.

Milos frowned. "I was in Kaosuda for a diplomatic tour. My father was aware of my location."

It was the general's turn to frown. "Are you certain of that, Your Highness?"

"Yes, quite. I had specific instructions from him concerning the meeting I was supposed to attend at the Kaosudan court. When Bristio caught wind of an imminent battle at the border, he insisted we depart prior to the meeting."

Casio looked entirely deflated. "Indeed. Well, yes, that makes sense. Who knows what could have happened had you attended? You might be a hostage as we speak." He almost seemed to be talking to himself.

"That was Bristio's logic as well. But by the time we neared the border, the Kaosudan camp already blocked our way. Bristio wished to go east and then through the mountains. It was ultimately at my insistence that we take a more direct route." Milos shifted his weight, feeling both antsy and exhausted as the excitement from their mad dash drained away.

"Your father did not inform us of your visit in Kaosuda." The general shook his head. "I can't imagine why."

Milos pressed his lips into a thin line. He wasn't close with Casio like he was with Bristio, but Bristio trusted and respected the man, so Milos was inclined to as well. "If I may speak frankly, sir, assuming our conversation won't leave this tent?"

The general nodded. "Please do, Your Highness."

"You know of the decades-long hostility between the two kingdoms. My father abhors the king of Kaosuda. If I was taken hostage, do you think this simple border skirmish would remain just that?"

Casio tilted his head. "Our own prince as hostage would equate to a call for war. King Tirano would most likely order us to invade."

Milos inclined his head in affirmation. "Exactly." He didn't think he needed to spell out all the implications. "If that's all, General, I'm rather tired and would like to find a tent of my own."

The general rubbed his chin, brow wrinkled. "Aye. One of the captains vacated his tent for you, but if you'd prefer mine..."

Milos smiled. "That's not necessary. Any tent is fine with me." He would rest tonight. The following day, he planned to depart for the city. The king surely assumed Milos was still in Kaosuda, likely taken hostage. What would his father say when Milos walked into the castle, unexpected and unharmed? He was eager to see the look on Tirano's face when he realized his scheming had failed, despite knowing his father would find a way to punish him for it.

Chapter Five

VERANA

As the weeks of summer slipped by, Ana grew more and more determined to save up all the coin she could to make their dreams of travel a reality. Aldo had a natural talent for drawing, so she encouraged him to use any scraps of parchment he could find, in the hopes they might sell some of his drawings at the market. If not in the village, maybe they would visit the capital and try their luck there.

Meanwhile, Ana took advantage of the long days to forage as much as she could. The harvest from their home garden was needed to feed the family, but some of the extra bits she foraged could be sold. So she gathered much more than they could preserve or store and attended the dreaded market every week.

Leo wasn't exactly encouraging when he discovered their plans. One late afternoon, the boat he worked on that week came back into port. Ana and Aldo were nearby, and once Leo finished unloading, he gathered his own share of the fish and walked down the dock. The two caught up with him to walk home.

"What are you two doing here?" Leo asked as they turned toward the village.

"We finished our chores early," Ana explained. "And Aldo wanted to come see the trade ships."

"Someday, Ana and I will go on a voyage on a ship like that." He pointed back over his shoulder to the biggest of the vessels.

"Oh really?" Leo arched a dark eyebrow in amusement. "How will you manage that?"

"We're selling extra at the market," Aldo explained. "And saving most of the coin we earn."

Leo only smiled and shook his head. "If you say so, little brother."

Ana bristled at his condescending tone. Leo always thought he knew better just because he was the oldest. "Why couldn't we? People go on sea voyages all the time."

"That's true," Leo agreed. "But do those people live in our village? I've never known anyone around here to do anything like that."

"You don't know everything," Ana retorted.

"We don't need to argue about it," Aldo interrupted. "Leo can think what he wants. And someday, he'll be waving on the docks as we sail away. Don't worry, we won't forget you while we're having our adventures, brother. We'll bring you back some sort of treasure from a foreign land."

Leo snorted but didn't argue further. They walked in silence until they made it through the village.

"Since *I* caught these," Leo said, holding up his string of fish, "That means one of *you* has to clean them, right?"

"No, thank you!" Ana immediately replied. She hated cleaning fish; the scales got everywhere.

"I don't want to either," Aldo protested. "Last one to the

house has to do it!" He broke into a run, Leo and Ana on his heels.

Leo had the longest legs and quickly overtook both of them. Ana and Aldo had a close race, being virtually the same height, but Ana won. As they tripped up to the cabin, breathing hard and laughing, Halia opened the door. Ana could tell by the look on her face that she must have been watching from the window. She fought to catch her breath and reached a self-conscious hand to her hair; running had jostled some curls loose from her plait.

Halia scowled at her. "Racing your brothers, Ana? When are you going to grow up? At twenty, you should know better. In fact, you should be considering marriage by now, not traipsing around like a child. And the state of your hair!" Ana had inherited both her tawny skin and her curls from her father; the chaotic tendencies of the latter had always frustrated her mother, whose pale hair fell naturally into lovely soft waves when she wore it down.

"It was just some fun, Mama," Aldo defended.

Halia shot a look of warning at her youngest. "This is not your concern. Go tend to those fish."

Leo and Aldo dispersed as Halia continued to lecture Ana. It wasn't the first time, and Ana typically tried to remain quiet except for the occasional "Yes Mama," or "I'm sorry, Mama." Her patience for the admonishments grew thin, however, when her mother returned to the subject of marriage.

"Mama, you know I don't *wish* to marry right now." Ana attempted to keep her tone steady and calm.

"And what does wishing have to do with it? Does wishing keep a roof over your head? Your father and I won't be here forever." Her mother waved a wooden spoon for emphasis.

"I can take care of myself," Ana mumbled, turning her gaze downward to study the swept stone floor beneath her sandaled feet. She didn't trust herself to school her expression enough to not further anger Halia.

"Don't be so naive, daughter. And what about children? Do you not wish to be a mother?"

Ana shrugged, not voicing her true thoughts: her own mother didn't seem to enjoy her role much of the time. "Maybe. But I have plenty of time. You didn't have Aldo until you were twenty-eight."

Halia huffed in disbelief. "Yes, and it almost killed me, or don't you remember?"

Ana's teeth ground together as her head whipped up to give her mother a look of reproach. "Of course I remember. I learned how to take care of a babe at six years old. Besides, you don't *know* that the difficulties with Aldo's birth had anything to do with your age."

Halia's chest rose and fell as she breathed deeply, obviously attempting to rein in her emotions. "My concern comes from my love for you, daughter. Sonos knows all and sees all, even our thoughts when we sleep, and he speaks through the king to help our kingdom prosper. You are not following the path laid out by Sonos and the rest of the Seven, nor our good king. Perhaps if you started attending service at temple once more—"

The front door opened, and Ana's father ducked his head to fit under the frame as he shuffled inside. He had been helping a neighboring farm in the fields that week; he sat on the nearby stool to remove his muddy boots as Halia closed the door behind him. Glancing between the two women, his brow wrinkled in concern. "How are my girls today?"

"I'm fine, Papa," Ana answered with a forced smile.

Halia spoke over her. “Your daughter is being obstinate and shortsighted.”

Luciano winced. “Ana, why don't you check on the goats while I speak with your mother?”

“Yes, Papa.” Ana, relieved, refused to meet her mother's gaze. She stooped to kiss her father on the cheek before she hurried out the back door.

She found Aldo in the yard, sitting on a stump and cleaning the fish. Leo was nowhere to be seen. After she dutifully checked on the goats—who were munching away on a patch of clover—she joined Aldo, upturning a wooden bucket to use as her seat.

Aldo's smile was soft. “I'm sorry Mama is so hard on you.”

Ana shrugged this off. “Papa is talking to her. He's the only one who can reason with her when she's like that.”

Aldo chuckled.

“Where's Leo?” Ana glanced around, but her older brother hadn't appeared. She squinted to inspect the forest at the edge of the clearing to see if he had maybe ventured into the woods for kindling, yet she detected no movement among the trees.

“He washed up and went back to the docks.” Aldo tossed the cleaned, gutted fish into a separate bowl and picked up the next.

Ana cringed at the quiet scrape of the knife on scales. “Why? Did he leave something behind?”

Aldo grinned, tossing her a sly look. “Apparently he left his heart at the inn, with the innkeeper's daughter.”

Ana's mouth dropped open. “He's courting someone?”

Aldo nodded. “Her name is Jesmina.”

Ana knew who he was talking about. They didn't have

much reason nor money to spend time at the inn, which doubled as a tavern, but they had been there on a few occasions, most recently to celebrate a villager's marriage. "The dark haired one, right?" If she remembered correctly, the innkeeper had three daughters, one with hair the color of a walnut, and the other two fair, like Aldo and Halia.

"Yep, that's her." Aldo let out a gasp, then a low curse. Ana jumped to her feet as blood welled from Aldo's hand due to a slip of the knife. Digging out a kerchief from her pocket, she handed it to Aldo as he dropped both fish and knife into the wooden bowl.

"Go let Mama tend to you," she urged. "I'll finish here." As much as she disliked it, the chore sounded better than being in the same room as her mother.

By the time Ana returned to the house with the fish to help cook them for supper, Aldo was settled on his pallet by the fireplace, drawing designs in charcoal on the stone hearth. It was awkward, as it was his dominant hand that was injured, but he persisted, probably viewing it as an interesting challenge. Halia and Luciano sat at the table, laughing together quietly.

Ana went about the task of fixing supper in silence, not wishing to draw attention and ruin the happy mood. She stoked the fire, then she shredded the fish into a pot before adding some chopped vegetables, rice, water, salt, and a couple fresh herbs from her foraging. After she hung the pot over the flames, she sat down next to Aldo.

"You okay?" She nudged him with her shoulder, shooting a pointed look at his wrapped hand.

"Yeah, fine. It wasn't that deep."

After supper, at dusk, her father accompanied her into the yard to put the goats away for the night.

Before they could round up the first nanny, her father caught her arm and turned her to face him before pulling her in close. Ana sank into the hug, breathing in the scent of dirt, hay, and male sweat.

"You and your mother got into it again," he murmured against her hair. "Why do you provoke her so?"

Ana pulled back, searching her father's face. "I didn't *do* anything, Papa, except race the boys home, and no one was watching. She overreacts."

He exhaled slowly, cupping her cheek in his palm. "I know she does. It's because she cares for you, and worries as well."

"She said I wasn't following the path of the Seven." Ana's chin trembled. She hadn't absorbed it at the time; now the meaning sank in. She wasn't devout like her mother, but what if? What if the Seven were real, and she displeased them? Her father was the only one she felt safe talking to about these matters. Everyone else she knew—the adults, anyway—held the same beliefs as Halia.

Luciano huffed a laugh. "I think you're following your own path, and I think that's what the Seven expect us to do. We have free will, after all."

She nodded slowly, staring into his gray eyes, so like her own. "You and Mama have always disagreed about the Seven. Doesn't it bother you?"

A soft, sad smile crossed his features. "It used to, sometimes. But my love for your mother is greater than any disagreements we have."

His voice was husky with emotion, and Ana's heart ached. "I hope I can find what you and Mama have someday." Just because she didn't wish to marry tomorrow didn't mean she had no desire for romance. It didn't help that none of the boys in the area caught her attention, other than when she was annoyed by their nonsense. And her experience with Gino had left her distrustful as well.

"I'm sure you will, my Ana. Don't settle for anything less."

Chapter Six

ANELA

Summer would soon come to a close; Anela could feel the change in the quality of the still-warm air as she and Henriella ambled through the gardens.

As they chatted about nothing especially important, Anela spotted a man approaching from the corner of her eye, foregoing the neatly kept paths as he strode across the grass. She recoiled inwardly when she recognized Lord Ruzo, one of Tirano's closest friends and advisors, and one of many at court whom she quietly considered an enemy. He walked with purpose straight toward them, the long legs of his reedy frame eating the distance quickly.

Hen followed her gaze and groaned. "Gods, that man is insufferable."

Anela nodded in agreement. "What does he want? That's always the question." She forced a smile and turned to face their visitor.

He stopped in front of them and bowed with a perfunctory, "Good day, Your Majesty. My lady." His shaggy, graying facial hair carried the remnants of his breakfast;

Anela cringed inwardly but managed to maintain a pleasant expression.

"Good day." Her smile remained pasted in place, vague and pleasant. Henriella dropped a small curtsy, saying nothing.

"May I have a private word, Your Majesty?"

She gave a gracious, queenly nod. "Shall we walk?"

He offered an arm and they set off. Henriella trailed about twenty feet behind, as was proper.

"It's a fine day," Lord Ruzo remarked, tilting his head of thick, silver threaded dark hair back to assess the sky.

"Indeed." Anela had no desire to waste her time in small talk with this man. He was clever, she'd give him that, but also devious and self-serving. "However, we need not have privacy to discuss the weather."

Taking her hint, he inclined his head in acknowledgement. "Yes, I suppose. I'll get to the point. I wish to marry again."

Anela frowned. His wife died a year past, so the proper mourning period was complete, thus this wasn't much of a surprise. Yet she'd no idea why he would talk about the matter with her. She hadn't noticed him making any efforts to pursue any of the ladies at court, but then, she tried not to notice him at all. His marital state was none of her business, and she preferred to keep it as such.

"I see. I offer my congratulations." Her voice was flat, indicating her lack of interest.

A small bit of egg flew from his face when he shook his head, before shooting a quick look over his shoulder. Voice lowered, he said, "I thank you for your kind sentiment, my queen. However, it is not a settled matter as of yet. That's the reason I asked to speak with you. I wish to ask Lady Henriella for her hand."

Anela's mouth dropped open, and she was glad he was looking at the flower-lined dirt path so he didn't see the shocked expression. Breathing deeply, she tried to settle herself.

Really, it shouldn't surprise her. Lord Ruzo had expressed interest in Henriella soon after she and Anela came to court, when Anela married Tirano. Henriella had turned down his advances repeatedly, and eventually he had moved on. But that was more than twenty years ago. Anela never knew that Lord Ruzo still harbored any feelings for her best friend.

At her silence, he pushed forward. "I understand you're surprised. I know she's a spinster and I could have my pick of the younger ladies, whether they be unmarried or widowed." He puffed out his thin chest in pride—for what, Anela wasn't sure. He had money and status, but his station hardly made up for his personality and his lack of care regarding bodily hygiene. "Yet I have always been fond of her, and she is my first choice."

"Sir," Anela said coldly. "You mistake the reason for my surprise. It is not because Henriella is a 'spinster' that I am taken aback. It is because I know she turned you down more than once all those years ago. Why would it be different now? Have you spoken with her? Has she expressed interest?" Anela knew Hen wouldn't have done so. Not only was Hen not interested in Lord Ruzo or marriage in general—Hen wasn't even romantically interested in *men*. She wasn't open about the fact, as Revas was much less accepting of same-sex pairings than their home country of Orakolas. But Anela was well aware thanks to … her *personal* experience of Hen's preferences.

A flush crawled up his tanned skin, and his voice grew sharp. "I know she rejected me. I was there. And no, I haven't spoken to her, thanks to that memory." He paused, inhaling deeply, seeming to remember to whom he spoke before he continued with less emotion. "Instead, I seek your assistance in convincing her, Your Majesty."

Anela barely suppressed a snort. "Why would I do that? She has no need to marry. She will always have a home and all of her needs met in my court. You are free to ask her whatever you wish, but I have no desire to influence my friend on your behalf."

"I thought you might say that. I have reason to believe you will change your mind and choose to help me in this matter." He held a familiar sly look in his washed-out blue eyes.

Anela scoffed but said nothing. This entire conversation was utterly ridiculous.

The odious man pushed on. "Because you see, if Tirano discovered your secret, he would be angry. Furious, even. I can't foresee what he might do, but the consequences would be severe."

Anela stopped in her tracks, yanking her arm away. She faced him, fists clenched. Henriella maintained her distance, pretending to examine a rose bush. Anela attempted to keep her voice from carrying, despite her indignation.

"How dare you try to blackmail me? I am your queen. Furthermore, I know nothing about this supposed secret," she hissed. She'd love to know where men like him found the audacity for such behavior. Alas, she had long given up on unraveling that mystery.

He shrugged and pushed a hand through his stringy, greasy hair. "I have served Tirano since our teens. My loyalty lies with him. I should have told him already, but my heart was soft with sympathy for your plight."

Anela barked a laugh at the idea of Ruzo having sympathy. Or a heart. "And what secret do you imagine you know about me? I am sure it is baseless rumor in any case." She had secrets, obviously. But she was quite meticulous in her efforts to ensure they remained just that.

His gaze narrowed shrewdly. "Must I really say it aloud?" When she simply stared at him and waited, he tilted his head, another sly smile creeping across his countenance. "I know of your *unnatural activities* with Lady Henriella."

Although determined to show no reaction, she couldn't stop the blood draining from her face. Her lips parted but no sound escaped. How? How could he know a secret so well kept that she and Hen had escaped notice for decades?

His tongue darted out to wet his bottom lip as his mouth widened into a victorious grin. "I've always wanted to know how she tastes. I've imagined the sweetness of her nectar. Tell me, how would you describe it?"

She was frozen. Years ago, she had promised herself never to react in this manner ever again, and she had kept that promise. Until now. All she could do was stare stupidly while wondering if it was possible for her heart to escape the confines of her chest in its frenzy. She pictured it breaking free, plopping onto the dirt between their feet, bloody and throbbing, as nausea bloomed in her center.

Lord Ruzo's grin transitioned into a knowing smirk as he bowed formally. "Your Majesty. I shall let you consider your options. Be ready with an answer when we next speak on the matter. You have one week. That should be enough time to convince Lady Henriella of her duty."

He waved at Henriella with a jolly, "Have a beautiful day, my lady!" before he turned and strolled toward the castle.

Anela's mind raced as she waited for Hen to rejoin her. She must tell her friend what Lord Ruzo planned, mustn't she? She bit her lip as sweat suddenly cascaded out of her body, pooling in the most uncomfortable places, one of the unpleasant episodes that happened more and more often now that she was well into her forties. She pulled her fan out of her pocket and flipped it open, waving it with a trembling limb. No, no, she must not say anything, because if she did, Hen would... Hen would do whatever she must to protect Anela. Hen would marry that snake of a man. Anela couldn't allow that to happen.

Nor could she allow Tirano to know about her and Hen. He would do something terrible. At the very least, he would banish Henriella, force her to return to Orakolas. Tirano was a jealous man. Hypocritical of course, as his unfaithfulness became evident in the first year of their marriage and never ceased. But still jealous, and vengeful. By the Seven, what should she do?

"Nel?" Hen's voice was tentative. "Are you all right? What did he want?"

"I..." Anela needed more time. Time to calm down and to think, alone. "I'm overheated. It's one of those episodes. It came on quite suddenly." Hen was a few years younger than Anela and had yet to experience the early marks of the change all women go through, but she knew of them—she had watched Anela struggle with all of the symptoms these past couple of years.

Hen's brow wrinkled. "Is that all? It seemed as though whatever he said upset you."

Anela nodded, then shook her head. "His very existence upsets me." Not a lie. Hen chuckled. "Right now, I need to rest."

They made their way back to Anela's quarters, where Anela stopped Hen at the door. "I'd like to be alone for a bit." At the hurt look on Hen's face, she rushed to amend, "I think I'll nap."

Once in her bedchamber, Anela crawled onto her neatly made bed, not even bothering to remove her shoes. She stared up at the swirling white and gold pattern on the ceiling, hardly noticing it.

How long did she have? What were his words? "You have one week." Only seven days.

How had he learned of their secret? Anela shook her head dazedly. She had no idea. That mystery would have to wait. What proof could he possibly have? She pushed that question aside as well; maybe he had none, but she couldn't take the risk.

As she calmed, Anela realized she had no option. She wouldn't let Hen be bullied into marrying, and she wouldn't allow Tirano to punish either or both of them for their shared love and intimacy. If he had been kind, had loved her as she thought she loved him, Hen may have never confessed her feelings in the first place and Anela may not have… Her lips pressed into a thin line as she pushed the thought away, redirecting herself to the current crisis.

She must contain Lord Ruzo and his schemes, one way or another, and quickly. Whether it meant attending his funeral service or simply discovering one of his own secrets to combat his blackmail, she needed to ruin his plans.

Anela detested violence. The threat of it, in various forms, had hung over her since her early days of marriage to Tirano. She had almost been assassinated at one point. Thus she shied away from the idea of it, initially.

She was not above blackmail, however; that is what saved her from Tirano's scheming and any future attempts he might have considered. She discovered information about his illegitimate heirs and used it to her advantage.

Was seven days enough time to dig up anything on Ruzo? What if she wasted her time trying, and then had no time left to enact a different plan? She could always flee and take Hen with her. They could return home.

But no. She couldn't abandon Milos, or her Revasian subjects. It would be cowardly and wrong to leave them all at Tirano's mercy, as he held little regard for the concept.

A hollowness settled in her belly as she concluded that Lord Ruzo may just have to die. Who would do the deed and how was what she must now determine.

Chapter Seven

VERANA

By the following evening after his injury, Aldo was unwell. He returned home from working for the neighboring farmer with their father and nearly collapsed onto his pallet, far paler than usual. As Halia cooked supper, Ana tended to him. His skin felt like a cauldron just removed from the fire, yet he shivered as though it was deep winter.

Kneeling next to him, Ana carefully unwrapped his bandaged hand. The cloth was filthy from working in the fields, and it had a strange odor to it. She gasped once she saw the injury, which looked far worse than the day before: red and swollen, secreting sticky pus.

Aldo glanced at it, then swiftly looked away, making a sound of disgust. "Ugh. It hurts, Ana."

"I know," she murmured, inspecting his hand more closely. "We need to clean it."

He groaned. "That'll hurt, too."

She wouldn't lie to him. "It will, but it must be done. It's festering, that's most likely what's making you ill. Mama, what should I use?"

Halia listed off several items and Ana rose to gather the supplies: clean cloth for a bandage, vinegar to clean the wound, a bowl to work over.

Her father returned from washing up—they used the small creek near the house in the warm months—and Leo arrived as well. Halia served the two of them supper before sitting down with Ana and Aldo.

As Ana prepared to rinse the cut with the vinegar, Halia took her son's uninjured hand in hers. "Squeeze as hard as you need to. It'll be over quickly."

Injuries weren't uncommon in their lives, as they all completed physical labor daily, sometimes utilizing heavy or sharp tools. But Ana had never seen a wound like this. The look of it combined with the smell made her stomach turn. She swallowed hard and proceeded to hold Aldo's wrist to keep his hand over the bowl, then poured the vinegar.

He squeezed his eyes shut and groaned, trembling harder, but didn't yank his hand away.

Once she had dried and wrapped the injury once more, Halia tried to persuade Aldo to eat. He refused.

"Just the thought makes my stomach turn inside out," he said, lying on his side on his pallet. "I could use some water, though."

Usually, Ana shared the bedroom in their two-room cabin with her parents, they in the larger bed and her in the small one. That night, Ana traded spots with Leo so she could tend to Aldo through the night from the neighboring pallet.

It was a miserable night. Her father rose first the following morning, and as soon as he came out of the bedroom, Ana scrambled to her feet.

"Papa, he's getting worse. I think we need to take him to the pastro." The men of the temples were the designated healers for most of the kingdom, outside of midwifery. They claimed being favored by the gods brought strength to their healing skills.

Ana had her doubts. She found it ironic that the royal family and much of the nobility did not seek out a temple-keeper during illness, instead preferring to pay for the services of one of the handful of physicians in the cities. However, her family and the other villagers had no other option.

Luciano frowned, rubbing the back of his neck. "Yes, all right." He ambled nearer to Aldo, squatting to speak with him. "Son?"

Aldo's blue eyes, hazed with fever, slowly opened. "Yes, Papa?"

"We need to take you to a healer. Can you stand?"

Ana dashed into the bedroom to dress. She woke her mother as well to let her know they were leaving. When Ana and Halia came out of the bedroom, Aldo was still prone on the floor, and Luciano wore a troubled expression.

As Halia hugged and kissed Aldo, Luciano murmured to Ana, "He can barely sit up on his own. I'll carry him."

Ana bit her bottom lip hard. "I'm coming with you."

Halia stayed back, as Leo would need to take his father's place in the fields for the day, and someone still needed to tend to the goats and garden and rest of the chores.

As they made their way through the village, folks stared and whispered, yet no one spoke to them or offered aid. Ana wasn't at all surprised; they had always held some measure of distrust for her family, due her father being a foreigner. He held no grudge against them for it and had explained to Ana that it wasn't their fault they were uneducated and ignorant. It's just how things were. Over time, she realized how much more educated her father was than anyone else she knew, her mother included. It was one more trait of his that made him “other” in the minds of the villagers, ironically.

When the three arrived at the door of the temple, a large, windowless stone structure situated halfway between their village and Sonos Harbor, it was still early and they saw no signs of life. Ana banged on the thick wooden door with a fist.

They waited several minutes, but no one came. Ana banged again, calling out, “We need the pastro for healing!”

Two minutes after, the door finally swung open. Pastro Emilio yawned and straightened his blue robes, his usually tidy, short hair still mussed from sleep. “Yes?”

“My son is ill,” Luciano stated, stepping out from behind Ana. “He needs a healer.”

The pastro’s gaze swept over the large man. “I suppose nothing else would motivate you to grace our temple with your presence, Luciano, eh?”

Ana bristled at his snarky tone. “Can you help us or not?” Aldo seemed barely aware of his surroundings, but he groaned, as though to emphasize his sister's question.

Pastro Emilio's dark eyes flashed as he turned his gaze to her. “Hello, Verana. Just as impertinent as ever, I see. Yes, come in.”

He finally stepped aside so they could enter, before leading them to a small, dark room off the main worshipping area. The light from the hallway sconces revealed an empty wooden table against one wall, while shelves and cabinets lined the others.

Luciano gently deposited his son onto the flat surface as Emilio lit two lanterns. Ana crossed her arms over her chest and pushed her back against the door to stay out of the way as the pastro gathered supplies. Their father hovered over Aldo, whispering reassurances.

Emilio examined Aldo's hand before he administered an oral medicine for the fever and then a different one for pain. "The cut festers," he said shortly. "I shall attempt a salve, but if it doesn't work, he will lose the hand."

Ana's hands flew to her mouth to contain her wordless cry. How would he draw? How would he work? To lose a limb was no small thing for anyone, let alone folks with their family's way of life. Not to mention the surgery itself was dangerous; if he lost too much blood, he would die.

Pastro Emilio shot her a stern look. "If you cannot abstain from hysterics, see yourself out."

Ana swiped away unbidden tears as she nodded, too shocked to be angry at the man's rudeness. She watched as he cleaned the wound once more, including a painful process of cutting away bits of flesh he deemed too damaged to be repaired. Aldo went limp during this, and Ana was grateful he lost consciousness. Hopefully he wouldn't remember any of this suffering. The pastro smeared a salve over the area, causing Aldo to whimper despite his sleepy state, then bandaged the hand.

He turned toward Luciano and Ana. "He should remain here for the day and night so I can observe him. Now all we can do is pray. I advise you to take the task seriously, as this boy's life is reliant on Sonos's mercy." The jab was pointed, another snarky comment about Luciano's lack of devotion to Sonos and the temple.

Her father's hands curled into fists, shoulders drawn back and jaw clenched. If he lost his temper with the templekeeper, it would help nothing. Ana touched his shoulder and whispered, "Papa. Should you go let Mama know how Aldo is? I'll stay with him."

Slowly, his fists uncurled as he turned to face her. "Yes, I'll do that. Thank you, Ana. Your mother or I will return in a few hours to check on him and relieve you."

Emilio wore a petulant expression now. "There is no need for any of you to hover over him. No harm will come to him here."

Ana raised her chin defiantly. "I don't want him to wake confused and alone. I'm staying."

The pastro gave an irritated shrug. "Suit yourself."

Luciano bid Ana goodbye, and Emilio left to tend to his other duties. Ana removed her apron and folded it before sliding it under her brother's head. Then she sat on the stool next to the bed and rested her hand on Aldo's arm. "You're going to be all right, Alleycat," she murmured. "I'm here." Then she closed her eyes, and for the first time in years, she prayed.

An hour later, Aldo woke. "Ana?" he whispered.

"I'm right here, little brother. Are you thirsty? Here, drink." Ana helped Aldo lift his head to drink the water Emilio had left.

He dutifully took a sip. "Ana, will you tell me a story?"

Ana blinked. He hadn't made that request of her since he was nine or ten years old.

"I'd love to, Alleycat. What story would you like?" Even when he wasn't sick, she had a difficult time denying him anything he asked.

He was quiet for a few moments, then said, "The one about the water sprite and the boy." This had been one of his favorites as a child. It originated from the times when the

Diona lived among the humans, along with a plethora of other magical creatures. Aldo used to pretend that the creek behind their yard was the water sprite's river home, and that he was the boy in the story.

Ana stroked his hair as she repeated the folktale.

Once, many years ago, there lived a young boy. His home was by a stream that fed into a huge lake. He and his brothers and sisters fished in the stream often but didn't go to the lake much. It was farther than they wanted to go just to fish, although sometimes they would go there to swim in warm weather.

One day, the boy's brothers and sisters were off playing a game, but he wanted to fish instead. If he could catch a string of fish all by himself, his mother and father would be so proud of him and they would have a nice supper.

As the boy sat on the stream bank, patiently tossing his line and bringing it back in, he heard someone singing. The song was unfamiliar, and it sounded sad. He set his line aside to seek out the voice. It sounded like it was coming from the other side of the flowing water, so he waded in a bit, to try to see better.

Suddenly, the water erupted in front of him, forming a figure, the song becoming much louder. He was amazed, because this creature in front of him could be nothing other than a water sprite. He thought they were only stories.

It stopped singing and looked at him. It seemed solid and not solid at once, made of flowing water, but with its body defined as if it had bones just as he did. The first thing he thought to ask was, "Why are you so sad?" For the song, although he couldn't understand the words, was heartbreaking. The sprite looked and looked at him, its eyes small whorls of water. Finally, it motioned for him to follow and disappeared back into the river, popping up every few feet to guide him.

"I can't swim in there like you can; it's rocky and moves too fast," the boy said. But he walked along in the shallows and along the bank, doing his best to keep up with the spirit.

The sprite led him all the way to the lake. The boy stood at the edge of where the stream flowed into the huge body of water, forming a small waterfall.

"This is just the lake," he pointed out. The sprite appeared in front of him again and nodded, as though in agreement.

"The lake is what makes you sad?" the boy asked.

Again, the creature nodded, gestured to the lake, and then began to sing its sad song again. The boy listened a while longer and then turned back toward home.

"I don't know why the lake makes you sad," he called to the sprite. "Maybe you should stay in the stream."

The river sprite visited the boy several more times in the following weeks, only ever when he was alone. He thought about it often, trying to figure out the mystery of why a lake should make the sprite sad. One day, while listening to its song, an answer came to him.

"I think I see," he said. "You are not only a water sprite, you are the caretaker of the stream. The lake is where the stream ends. The stream coming to an end makes you sad. It's almost as though the lake kills your stream."

The water sprite had stopped singing and looked at the boy. It nodded.

"But all things end. Not only the stream. Nothing is forever," the boy said.

The sprite started to sing its song once more, quietly.

"You want the water to keep moving. Sometimes it is better to be still, you know. Have you ever tried it?" The creature shook its head, still singing softly.

"No, I suppose not. It is not in your nature. Well, I'm sorry you're sad. The lake's nature is stillness, and I don't think it is sad that your nature is different. It needs your movement to stay full. You and your stream are very important to the lake, you know.

The sprite stopped singing very suddenly. It looked and looked at the boy. Then it turned and rushed toward the lake.

The boy followed as quickly as he could. He arrived just in time to see the sprite diving off the little waterfall into the lake. It went farther out into the water and then popped up and began a new song.

This song was one of love and joy.

The boy smiled. "That's better, isn't it?" He left the sprite to enjoy the lake, which needed the stream to exist, and walked home.

Chapter Eight

MILOS

While Milos didn't miss the dry air of the desert, he didn't particularly enjoy spending most of the travel time back soaked to the bone. He enjoyed the rain, as a general rule, but reflected that one *could* have too much of a good thing.

Most of the retinue remained at the border for the time being, as General Casio had requested the extra men. Milos and Bristio took no issue with it now that they were back in Revas.

The two reached a town a little after midday. Their intention had been to purchase some fresh food and continue, finding a spot to camp once darkness fell. The next portion of their journey primarily consisted of land cleared for crops, so they wouldn't be forced to spend the night in the woods. But they were both dripping and the horses were worn out from slogging through mud.

Bristio spotted the inn first. He pointed out the building, which appeared to be recently constructed, the wood still bright and unbowed. "I propose, if they have room, we stay the night. If not, we can keep on."

Milos nodded his silent agreement, shoulders sagging slightly in relief. His rebellious, indignant mood had been tempered upon further contemplation on his father's reaction. He didn't regret his actions, and he was still angry… Yet he had been on the receiving end of the king's wrath too many times to be eager for the prospect.

What would have happened if he had proceeded to the Kaosudan palace? At best, a forced and hurried marriage. At worst, he would be a prisoner, or even dead. No, he did not regret his decision.

It's not that he didn't wish to marry. But the idea of arranged marriage for political advantage chafed. A prince's duty, certainly, but not one he embraced. He wondered how the Kaosudan princess, Melliada, felt about it. He hadn't seen her in several years; younger than he, she had barely begun the transition to womanhood when they last met. He remembered her as quiet, shy, and entirely cowed by her parents—not that he could blame her. He was sure she would obey and wed their suitor of choice, when it came down to it, but he had no idea how she'd actually *feel* about it.

Marrying a stranger was one thing; marrying a stranger who didn't care for him, or worse, despised him, was unthinkable. After witnessing his parents' marriage all these years, he had no desire to be trapped in such a relationship.

Fortunately, the inn had space. Once the horses were stabled, Milos and Bristio retired to their shared room, which featured two simple, clean straw pallets, and dressed in dry clothing. Leaving the wet to hang in front of the hearth, they made their way to the main room, which had the feel of a typical tavern.

A woman, perhaps in her mid to late twenties, appeared by their table, looking harried. The weather had driven many of the townsfolk to seek company and shelter at the inn, so she had her hands full.

Her smile was strained, but her tone was friendly. “Good day. Will it be ale for you both?”

Bristio nodded. “Yes, thank you. And two servings of whatever hot food you have on hand.”

“Stew and bread today. I’ll be right back.”

Two minutes later, she delivered their tankards. “Just a few minutes for the food.”

Milos inclined his head. “Thank you, mistress.”

He and Bristio quietly sipped, letting the waves of conversation flow over them.

“Heard those damned Kaosudans started trouble at the border,” one nearby man said.

His companion answered, “That right? Well, the king’s soldiers will handle it. I can’t worry about that when my livestock keep going missing.”

“I told you the pen was too near the forest,” the first man chided. “The Seven only know what type of beasts are enjoying your sheep as their meal.”

The second huffed. “There was no better place for it. The only other area that’s big enough floods when the creek runs too high, you know that.”

The woman returned with generous servings of stew in large, shallow metal bowls and half a loaf of bread on a wood board, a dish of butter alongside. It smelled heavenly, and Milos said so.

The woman chuckled, pushing a loose strand of dark hair behind her ear. “Thank you, my lord. It is my own mother’s recipe, but I changed it up a bit, and now it’s even better, if you ask me.”

He smiled at her. “I believe you. Does the inn belong to your parents, then?”

Her expression clouded, yet she answered readily. "No, my lord. My father is dead and my mother recently relocated to Sonos City. My husband and I built this with my inheritance from my father."

"Ah, I see. I'm sorry for your loss. But you and your husband have done a fine job with the inn. You should be proud."

Her smile reached her deep brown eyes now, the corners crinkling. "That's very kind of you, my lord. Please, enjoy your meal. I'll bring more ale shortly."

Bristio shot him a pointed look as she walked away. Milos raised an eyebrow. "What?"

The older man swallowed his bite. "She said she's married. Behave yourself."

Milos rolled his eyes. "Stop being such a mother hen. I've never slept with a married woman. Well, not to my knowledge, in any case. I was just being polite."

Bristio lifted and dropped a shoulder. "Glad to hear it."

They devoted their attention to the food, which as Milos anticipated was simple yet excellent fare. He tuned out the conversation around him, thinking about his return home.

He pushed aside worries about his father's wrath, as there was nothing he could do about it. His mother and Hen would be excited to see him, and he them. He could return to his routine of training with the guards and soldiers most mornings, something he truly enjoyed—not only for the exercise, which cleared his mind, but also for the company. He was treated with respect, yet not like a *royal.* He was one of them during those hours, just a man determined to hone his skills to protect himself, his loved ones, his country.

It was so much simpler than the politics and intrigues of court. Straightforward and satisfying. Not to mention more stimulating than the hideously boring advisors' meetings, which he would also be expected to attend.

Once their meal was naught but crumbs, the two men agreed to remain in the common room. One traveler, an old man evidenced by his lined face and white beard, took out his instrument, and his skillful manipulation of the strings made the atmosphere even more merry. Soon folks were singing and clapping along, including Milos and Bristio.

Milos loved music. His mother had hired a piano instructor when he was young, but his father had deemed it a waste of time and effort for a prince and heir, and he fired the tutor. However, his father couldn't stop him from listening when others played or from learning popular song lyrics.

The elderly musician transitioned from several lively songs in a row to a slow song, a ballad about the Sundering Milos had heard countless times. Milos sang along to the final verse under his breath.

Departed from our lands, lives, and hearts,
Every fair Diona friend turned to foe.
We lost all knowledge of the magic arts—
The Sundering, our long and lasting woe.

Throughout the evening, Milos caught the attention of more than one woman. But he looked away from their inviting smiles and flirtatious glances. As much as he'd enjoy one more night of soft skin and sweet release before his return, he refrained, still stung by Bristio's comment.

He'd long ago given up on obtaining his father's approval. Bristio's opinion, however, he still cared about.

When they retired to their warm room and fell onto their pallets, sleep claimed Milos quickly. Despite his enjoyable, relaxing evening, some part of his mind clung to the knowledge that he traveled toward his father. He was young again in his dreams, small and defenseless. His father's dark gaze flashed with anger as Milos begged his pardon for some unknown offense or mistake, and then the king's fist flew.

The dream shifted. While he had never witnessed his father strike his mother, he always suspected, wondered, and in his dream, he was forced to watch it happen.

He woke just before dawn, his breath coming in gasps, sweat coating his brow. Nausea swirled in his center. Bristio snored peacefully a few feet away.

Milos didn't even consider attempting to fall back asleep. He threw the blanket aside, rose, and dressed quietly, letting the old guard sleep. Then he crept down to the stables, determined to find a treat for Bruna and give her a thorough grooming before they departed.

Alongside his weapons and combat training, Milos had always enjoyed spending time in the stables with the horses. Bruna knickered her welcome and accepted the carrot he had found in a basket near the entrance. He soon lost himself in the motions of her care, knocking dried mud from her hooves and brushing her broad back.

The stable hands had tended to her adequately, but he could admit this was more for him than for her, and she politely tolerated his attention. Light rain pattered on the roof, a soothing sound even if he hoped it would clear up before they left. An hour later, feeling much calmer, he returned to the inn to wake Bristio so they could be on their way to Sonos City.

It was time to go home.

Chapter Nine

VERANA

Two days passed before Pastro Emilio deemed it necessary to amputate Aldo's hand. "Otherwise, he will die."

Ana was devastated but resigned. She couldn't lose her little brother. Her parents struggled to accept the necessity.

"Is there no alternative? Nothing else we can do?" Halia almost begged as she fought back tears. Their family, minus Aldo, stood in the main room of the temple to the side of the rows of pews.

Emilio shrugged. "I am sad to say it, but perhaps if your *entire* family were more devout, the gods would have mercy." Leo and Halia shot frustrated glances at Ana and Luciano. "As it is... Well. One of the city physicians might have a Diona cure of some sort, I suppose. They have more access to Diona-made medicines than we humble templekeepers."

Ana barely stopped herself from rolling her eyes. By the Seven, if Emilio was humble, she was the water spirit from the folktale. Instead, she focused on what he said prior to that statement. Her emotions made a mad dash from resigned to hopeful.

"Papa, can't we take him to a physician in the city? Or send for one to come here?" She knew only the wealthy typically called on the physicians, but she had no idea how much it might actually cost to procure the services of one.

"Whatever you decide, we must act soon, or it will be too late," Emilio interrupted. "Time is not on his side. You may find me in my office when you've made your choice." With that, he hurried away, blue robes billowing behind him.

"Well, Papa?" Ana pressed. Leo focused on the ground, jaw clenched, but Halia turned a hopeful gaze to her husband.

Luciano released a breath, rubbing a hand over his face. "I don't know. It's very expensive."

"We must try," Halia said, tugging at the end of her blonde braid as was her nervous habit. "Ameleo, borrow a horse and ride to the capital. We will send a letter to explain, and everything we can afford to part with."

"I have some money," Ana blurted. She had forgotten all about her savings in the crisis of Aldo's illness. "I—I did some extra foraging this summer and saved some coin." If it was a question of Aldo losing his hand or putting off their travel dreams, the decision was easy.

"Whatever for? And you kept it a secret?" Halia glared at Ana, then waved a hand. "Never mind, it matters little right now. We need all the coin we can manage."

They informed Emilio of their decision. Leo left immediately to beg use of their neighbor's horse, and Ana to retrieve her money, while Luciano used Emilio's pen and parchment to write a note to the physician.

Soon, Ameleo was on the road to Sonos City. If the weather stayed fine, he should be able to return by nightfall. Halia wished to stay with Aldo, so Ana went home to take care of the goats and other chores. As much as she disliked leaving her brother, she was grateful for both the distraction of the work and to be away from Pastro Emilio.

Ana quietly fumed as she scrubbed the soup pot and remembered his full speech—not only calling himself humble but also blaming her father and herself for Aldo's condition. How would attending temple service every week make a difference in Aldo's healing? Did Sonos truly pay attention to every person, every prayer, every sick young boy? Ana seriously doubted it, and furthermore, Sonos was a horrible god if he would punish an innocent due to his family's religious choices.

Her father had spent most of the day helping the neighboring farm prepare for the imminent harvest. When he returned home, Ana prepared a simple supper of bread, goat cheese, and apples, and then they packed some of the food in her basket to take to Halia. Ana packed enough for Leo as well, just in case.

Ana took over the vigil at Aldo's bedside while her mother took a break to eat and talk with Luciano. When Aldo stirred, she said, "I'm here, Alleycat."

He opened his eyes and tried to speak, but his throat was too dry. Ana helped him take a few sips of water.

His gaze, still hazy with fever, met hers. "They're going to take my hand, aren't they?"

Her mouth opened and then shut. She couldn't promise him anything, nor would she lie to him. Finally, she said, "Maybe."

His head bobbed in a single nod. "Mama said no. I could tell she wasn't being honest."

Aldo did have an uncanny way of telling truth from lie. Ana had a similar instinct, but Aldo's was much sharper. Ana sighed. "We don't know anything for sure. Leo is trying to get a physician from the city to come heal you."

His mouth quirked up in an attempt at a smile, but he didn't reply. Ana thought he had fallen back asleep when he murmured, "I love you, Ana. Always."

Her eyes burned with tears. She patted his shoulder. "I love you too, Alleycat. Forever."

Leo arrived just after dark. Luciano and Halia were with Aldo, and the room was too small for more people, so Ana was outside sitting on the stoop of the temple as he came down the road and up to the church. Her heart sank, seeing that he was alone, and then observing the expression on his moonlit face.

She stood and met him in the yard as he dismounted. "It wasn't enough? The money?" she choked out.

He shook his head, lips pressed in a grim line. "We didn't even have half of the cost for a true cure. You know trade with the Diona is highly restricted, which makes everything we get from them that much more expensive." He pulled a small glass bottle out of his pocket. "But I bought this: a physician-made concoction. It's supposed to keep him asleep while Pastro Emilio..."

"Cuts off his hand," Ana finished bitterly. "Well, that's a mercy, I suppose." It was, yet she couldn't help the stab of anger in her chest. It simply wasn't fair that only the wealthy could obtain the best medical care. Aldo deserved it as much as any of the nobles.

"I'm sorry, Ana." Leo's voice trembled. "I tried."

"I know you did." She wrapped her arms around him for a rare hug. The two bickered often, but ultimately, family was family, and she needed some comfort from her big brother.

"He'll be all right," he whispered into her hair. "We'll take care of him. Always."

She nodded, tears dripping onto his shirt. "And forever."

Pastro Emilio brought in several additional lanterns for the surgery, muttering about how they could've done this earlier in the day as he had proposed so he'd have proper light. Then he cleared them all out, calling in a couple of temple novices to assist if needed. "If the medicine doesn't work as it should, my assistants can ensure he stays still. None of you need to watch this, however."

For once, Ana was grateful. She didn't especially want to watch the pastro saw off Aldo's hand, even though she felt guilty for leaving. Aldo had been so brave when they'd told him, offering *them* reassurances, trying to ease their worries. But Ana could tell by the look in his eyes he was terrified. She bit her lip, fighting back tears as she sat on a temple bench with the rest of her family while they waited.

The temple remained blissfully quiet. Ana had half expected to hear Aldo's screams at some point, and her relief that the medicine apparently worked was tangible. She had no idea how much time had passed when Pastro Emilio strode into the main room. She studied him closely. He must have washed and possibly changed his robes, because she saw no evidence of the completed task on his person.

"He is still asleep, but you may see him if you'd like. Call me when he wakes; he will likely be in a great deal of pain by then. Meanwhile, I need to prepare for service tomorrow." He turned abruptly and hurried away, heading down the hallway that led to his office.

The novices were departing with an armful of bloody

cloth and a mop as the family shuffled in. Ana cringed at the gruesome laundry. But the flagstone floor was fairly clean, as was the table where Aldo lay. Bare shoulders and collarbone peaked out from the blanket; they must be washing his tunic too. He was incredibly pale, but his chest rose and fell steadily.

Luciano gingerly lifted the blanket, revealing the bandaged stump of his son's right arm. Her father allowed the blanket to drop, bringing a hand up to cover his mouth and closing his eyes. His chest rose and fell twice before he opened them again.

Halia's tears slid silently down her wan cheeks as she approached, tentatively stroking the side of Aldo's face. "My sweet boy."

Leo wrapped a comforting arm around Ana's shoulders. "Thank the Seven the medicine worked." Ana met his gaze and he attempted a reassuring smile. "He's going to be okay."

Chapter Ten

ANELA

Hen stirred sugar into her tea as Anela pushed her food around her plate, her mind elsewhere. Of course, Hen noticed.

"You've been distracted these last two days." Hen set the spoon down on the saucer with a clink. "Is anything amiss?"

Anela forced a smile. "All the usual court nonsense, I suppose. And I'm still wondering about Tirano's power." None of this was a lie, even if it wasn't her primary concern.

"He's never said anything else since all those weeks ago, has he?" Hen sipped daintily, then set the cup down and picked up a bit of toast. She wrinkled her nose; it was much nearer to burnt than toasted.

Anela noted her own bread also appeared rather blackened, and she shook her head as she set it aside. "No. But I can't help wondering if it has anything to do with the prophecy." She closed her eyes as she recited the words from the dream that had plagued her for years.

"The One who will scatter the dream master's magic
will one day wake to a loss most tragic,
pushing her to seek the truth.

When three moons meet, the king will fall,
the deceived now able to hear the call
of the gods thanks to The One.

Warm upon the earth, her blood will flow,
lies washed away, the people will Know
a kingdom shaken with grief and joy."

They sat quietly, nibbling and pondering. Anela was one of few who knew not only the true nature of her husband's power, but also how he chose to use it. His magic gave him the ability to enter into the unconscious mind and deliver visions, messages, whatever he desired into the dreamer's mind. The dreams he created were vivid and cast a lingering influence in the person's subconscious. A spell, of sorts.

Fortunately, his power didn't work on her, likely due to the nature of her own ability. Tirano's grandfather and the rest who came before him had used this magic to influence their fellow monarchs ... or their enemies. It was supposed to be a defensive magic one could use to deter the actions of those who may seek to harm Revas.

But Tirano's father had taken a different path. He sent dreams to the templekeepers almost exclusively, influencing them to believe the dreams were sent from the god Sonos himself. That period of history was now referred to as the Awakening of the Dream God. Using this method, the former king—and the current one—directed the beliefs and values of those who ran the temples, which then were taught and spread throughout the kingdom.

In short, rather than using the power to defend the people, Tirano's father and then Tirano after him used their magic to control their own citizens—citizens who trusted the gods, the temples, and the pastros implicitly. Tirano also occasionally chose to influence the dreams of nobles at court, whether Revasian or visiting, but his focus remained on dispersing the message of utmost devotion and loyalty to himself and Sonos through the religious leaders.

It made Anela sick to her stomach, and there was little she could do to stop him. Thus she attempted to quietly counteract the effects of his rule in any way she could. But efforts such as selling all her jewels to feed the poor in the city weren't a long-term solution. Nothing she could do was ever enough to truly improve the lives of their citizens.

The prophecy the god Orix had sent her spoke of "The One" who would somehow destroy or incapacitate Tirano's magic. At least, she assumed it referred to Tirano, although it could refer to a future when her son would be king, or even his unborn son.

If Tirano's magic was slipping away from him, was it due to this mystery person? Who was it, and how could they do such a thing? Anela had no way to answer these questions.

Her mind wandered back to the higher priority for the moment: Lord Ruzo. She had less than five days left to figure out what to do about him. She had made no moves yet, the urgency of the task tempered by the need for utmost care and secrecy. If having him assassinated was the only solution, she needed to ensure it appeared to be an accident and could never be traced back to herself or Hen.

After all these years at court, Anela could count those

she trusted on one hand. She didn't wish to involve any of them in her scheme, however. Risking their safety would be poor thanks for their loyalty and friendship. Although, perhaps if Bristio was here, she could seek his aid. As a capable and experienced soldier, he at least could defend himself against any dangers. Alas, he was far away doing exactly what she had ordered him to years ago: protecting Milos. They wouldn't return for weeks yet.

Anela hadn't felt this alone since she first discovered her husband's true nature all those years before, simultaneously suffering the betrayal of an old childhood friend. At the time, at least she could confide in Hen. Now...

Hen interrupted her thoughts. "If there's anything I can do..." She trailed off, eyebrows raised in concern. She laid her hand on the table, palm up.

Anela covered it with her own. She wanted nothing more than to invite Hen to visit her rooms that night for one of their rare trysts, to revel in her lavender scent, soft skin, skilled touch, and comforting presence. But not knowing who had told Lord Ruzo about those trysts made her nervous. What if that person told someone else? If the rumor spread, the likelihood of them being caught increased exponentially.

Once she got rid of the threat of her husband's advisor, she would tell the head housekeeper, Mistress Danias, to assign new servants to her rooms. She couldn't imagine who else may have discovered their secrets other than one of the maids or messenger boys. She debated if she should have Mistress Danias dismiss her current servants entirely. Tirano would undoubtedly go much further; he'd imprison and potentially execute any servant he suspected of traitorous actions. Anela refused to punish potentially innocent people, though.

She inclined her head and responded to her friend's offer, giving her hand an affectionate squeeze. "Not at the moment, but thank you."

By supper time, Anela neared a state of panic, unable to determine how to enact her plan. She couldn't go into the city with a purse of coin and hire some disreputable tavern goer. She was too easily recognized; red hair wasn't common in Revas. And how could she trust a random stranger to do the job and succeed in making it appear to be an accident?

On top of all of this, she'd heard whispers of a standoff at the Kaosudan border, rumors that had made it to the city and thus into the gossip of the castle staff. Tirano refused to discuss it, even to confirm or deny—yet his refusal was confirmation enough. The one royal advisor who was sometimes willing to keep her abreast of such developments was away visiting his country estate and wouldn't return for weeks yet.

Worry for her son, who was visiting their southern neighbor, did not improve her state of mind. However, there was little she could do for the situation, and her powerlessness in these matters was an old wound. Long years of experience taught her that picking at it benefited no one. It niggled at the back of her mind, but she attempted to focus on the more immediate threat.

As she sat at the head table in the dining hall, ignoring the buzz of conversation, she spotted Lord Ruzo a few chairs away. He lazily swirled a goblet of wine as he chatted with another advisor. A faint smirk passed over his countenance when he met her gaze before turning his attention back to his conversation.

Anela pressed her lips together and looked away. But then her head whipped around, staring at him right as he brought the goblet to his mouth. A kernel of an idea planted itself in her mind.

Poison. She could get her hands on poison. Then all she would have to do was figure out how to sneak some into his food or drink.

A voice cried out over the din. "His Highness, Prince Milos of Revas, arrives!"

Quiet fell over the several dozen nobles, who paused their supper to acknowledge the prince with a brief bow of their heads. Anela's gaze snapped to the wide-open double doors as her son strolled through them.

What in the world was he doing home? Her brow wrinkled in confusion even as she smiled, relief brightening her usual happiness at seeing her son. She glanced at Tirano, who hadn't even acknowledged her when she sat next to him, and her smile faded. Brow furrowed and mouth set in a grim line, his jaw twitched as he clenched it. Why in the world did he look so angry at Milos's arrival?

Her tall, brawny, handsome son stopped before the head table and bowed. He looked so like his father, except for the color of his eyes and the shape of his mouth, which he inherited from Anela. His skin was a shade lighter than Tirano's, but nowhere near as pale as her own.

Straightening, he smiled warmly, nodding to her first. "Mother." His grin widened as he took in Tirano's expression. "Father."

Tirano said nothing, while Anela stood and bustled around the table, enveloping Milos in a hug. A thought occurred to her, and she blurted in a whisper, "Is Bristio with you?"

He raised an eyebrow, perplexed, but nodded. "Yes, we arrived only minutes ago. He chose to eat in the kitchens."

"Thank the Seven." At the question on his face, she shook her head. "Never mind that now. I will speak with him later. Come eat."

She returned to her place and Milos chose an empty seat directly across from his parents.

Tirano cleared his throat. "You should not be here." Anela shot him a look of rebuke, which he ignored. "What happened to the diplomatic task in Kaosuda? Did you visit the court as planned?" He kept his voice low, but his annoyance was apparent.

Milos shrugged as he piled food onto his plate and a servant filled his goblet. When the girl walked away, the prince's congenial expression hardened. He leaned forward, glaring daggers at his father. "No, Father, I did not. You see, there is an impending skirmish at the border. When we got wind of a possible battle, we were hard put to make it back into Revas before the fighting started, what with the Kaosudan army blocking our way."

Anela's mouth tightened at hearing the rumors confirmed, and she shot her husband a glare. He didn't notice.

Tirano's dark eyes flashed, but his voice was flat. "Who made the decision to return, in defiance of my orders? I don't care what was happening at the border. You had my instructions."

Milos didn't answer the king's question. Instead, he said, "I was hoping you'd enlighten me as to why you ordered this attack, knowing I was there on a *diplomatic* visit. To my knowledge, initiating a fight isn't exactly part of diplomacy. Quite the opposite, in fact."

"Hold on." Anela held a hand up and Tirano shot her an annoyed look. "*You* ordered an attack?" Her initial assumption was that Kaosuda initiated, not Revas. "While Milos was *there*? What were you thinking?"

"I don't need to explain myself to you, woman," Tirano growled. To Milos, he said, "Nor to you. A king's orders are to be *followed*, not to be questioned. I ask again, who made the decision to return? Guard Bristio?"

Milos took a gulp of wine before he answered. "No. It was my order." He set the goblet down, leaned back, and crossed his arms, his glare a challenge. "Being a royal hostage didn't sound appealing."

The king stood abruptly, prompting the rest seated at the table to do so as well. He looked at Lord Ruzo. "I want my advisors in the meeting room. Now." He pointed a finger at Milos. "This isn't over. I will deal with you later. Right now, I need to clean up your mess."

Once the king and his advisors were gone, Anela remained upright. Whatever was happening at the border, her son was home safe, and she had a different threat hanging over her head to address. "I'm happy to see you home, my heart, and we must talk soon. Will you break your fast with me in my quarters tomorrow?" He nodded. "Wonderful. Right now, though, I have some urgent business to address with Bristio. Please excuse me."

Ignoring the confused look on her son's face, Anela hurried toward the kitchens, hoping to catch the soldier before he left. Unfortunately, she didn't see him as she entered the biggest room of the kitchens, which held a table and benches for staff.

"Is Guard Bristio here?" she asked. Several servants

stumbled to a halt, fumbling to curtsy and bow, unused to seeing a member of the royal family in their workspace.

One of them spoke in a wavering voice. “He left only a moment ago, Your Majesty.” He pointed out the door that led to the kitchen gardens, and she hurried out into the night.

She spotted him heading in the direction of the guards' dormitory. “Bristio,” she called softly. He jerked to a stop and turned, peering at her through the moonlight.

As she approached him and he recognized her, he bowed low. “Your Majesty. To what do I owe the honor of your presence?”

She came to a stop in front of him. “I need to speak with you. It is a matter of utmost urgency—and we need to ensure it is a private conversation.”

He gave another bow. “As you say, Your Majesty.” He glanced around, as did she, at a loss as to the best place to have the conversation. “Maybe a stroll through the grounds?”

She nodded. It would seem odd to invite him to her rooms; someone might make note of it. Similarly, she couldn't enter his bedroom in the barracks. He offered his arm, and she took it as they turned left to head around the side of the castle.

They walked in silence until they were a decent distance from the castle, heading toward the woods. Unless there was a ball or some other event, castle residents rarely walked this area of the grounds at night, so Anela felt fairly certain they wouldn't be overheard. But she still kept her voice low as she drew to a stop near the edge of the forest.

Peering into the trees, Anela shuddered. Best not to get too close in the dark, given all the tales of terrible beasts that lurked within. Anela only ever rode or walked through the woods in the daylight, and even then, she swore she had felt eyes on her more than once.

"Thank you, Bristio. I know you must be worn out from travel, but this can't wait."

He inclined his head. "I am at your service, as always, Your Majesty."

She pulled her arm from his, wringing her hands. "I know, and I thank you for your loyalty. I need assistance with a very ... sensitive matter, and you are the only person I trust to help me."

"You honor me, my queen." He inclined his head in a small bow. Then he simply stared at her, waiting.

Anela's chest rose and fell in a deep breath as she steadied herself. "It is concerning Lord Ruzo. You're familiar with him?"

A grunt was his only reply to the rhetorical question. It sounded as though he didn't like the man any more than she did.

"I can't tell you everything, for the secret is not solely my own. Suffice it to say ... well, I need him gone."

Her heart fluttered as silence fell. The crickets chirped, and she held her breath until Bristio responded.

"I take it you mean permanently?"

She gave a single, sharp nod, turning pleading eyes on him in the dark. His countenance grew grim and she quaked, wondering if he was about to lecture her for impugning his honor. He was a soldier, not an assassin, after all.

His voice came out as a growl. "What did he do, Your Majesty? Did he hurt you?"

Her shoulders dropped in relief. He wasn't angry at her request; he was livid at the idea of whatever Ruzo must have done to prompt her to take this action.

She shook her head. “It isn't what he's done, but what he has threatened to do. If he follows through, it will hurt me and others I care about. Very much. You know I cannot go to the king. Lord Ruzo is his closest friend. He won't listen to me.” She hesitated. She was already asking so much. But... “If it's possible, it should look like an accident. So Tirano doesn't suspect anything is amiss.”

Bristio nodded his grizzled head slowly. “I understand. Is there anything else?”

She bit her lip and nodded. “It needs to happen in the next four days. That is the deadline he gave me before...” She trailed off, still reluctant to share the details. Yes, she trusted Bristio. But what she and Hen shared was theirs alone. It was no one else's business.

He cleared his throat. “I understand.” Taking her hand in his own, he dropped a light kiss on her knuckles. “You know I care for Milos like he was my own son. I will not let his mother down. Put yourself at ease. I will take care of it.”

Chapter Eleven

MILOS

Milos joined his mother in her quarters the following morning as requested. He wasn't at all surprised to see Henriella at the table as well. Auntie Hen, as he had always called her, spent most of her time by his mother's side. He kissed the cheeks of each woman in turn and took his seat, leaning back so the maid could pour his tea.

Once she did, Anela dismissed her so it was only the three of them.

"Did you find Bristio last night?" Milos slathered berry preserves onto a slice of toast, eyeing his mother with curiosity. While she had known Bristio for decades, as he had, it was odd for her to seek him out in such a rush. Bristio served Milos; he had never been part of the queen's guard.

A flush crept up his mother's neck as she cleared her throat and then took a sip of tea. "Yes, I did. I ... I just needed to ask him about some details of the border skirmish."

He frowned, unconvinced, but didn't press her; he had never known her to lie to him. If she wasn't being honest, she must have a reason. Still, he'd try to remember to see if Bristio would tell him anything.

"Ah, I see." He smiled and turned to Henriella. "How have you been in my absence, Auntie? Still breaking all the noblemen's hearts?" It was something he teased her about time to time. She was a beautiful woman who had caught the eye of many noblemen over the years, and she rebuffed them all. Honestly, it tickled Milos, and he respected her for it, even if he didn't know why she didn't wish to marry.

His mother coughed and sputtered before Henriella could answer.

"Nel, are you all right?" Henriella asked, pushing her chair back as though to stand.

Anela waved a hand as she coughed once more, then cleared her throat. "Yes, yes, quite. Something went down the wrong way. I'm fine now."

Henriella scooted back in and smiled at Milos. "I don't know if I'm breaking hearts at my ripe old age, but I remain unmarried and unpromised, if that's what you wondered."

He scoffed. "You're younger than my mother and still quite lovely. Any man would be lucky to have you."

Henriella chuckled. "Thank you, child. How did you enjoy Kaosuda? What exactly was this skirmish about?"

He explained the situation once more. Anger rolled off his mother, green eyes flashing and the corners of her mouth pinched, though she didn't say much. Henriella was flabbergasted.

"How could your father do that? He risked the life of his only son, and for what?" Then she glanced around quickly with a guilty look, as though worried about being overheard. To be sure, being overheard criticizing the king wasn't ... ideal.

He patted her hand to reassure her. "Don't worry, Auntie. It's only us. To answer your question, outside of possibly attempting to start a full-blown war, I had another thought." He absentmindedly stirred his tea, staring into the swirling depths of his cup. "Kaosuda has a princess of marriageable age. He has been hinting at arranging for a politically advantageous marriage for me for the last couple of years. Maybe he thought he could force my hand."

A sharp intake of breath made him look up at his mother. She nodded slowly. "I think that was likely his exact plan." Smiling weakly, she reached for him and cupped his cheek. "I'm so glad you made it home safely, even if your father is angry his plans were spoiled." She patted the scruff on his face before withdrawing her hand.

He grimaced. "I'm supposed to meet with him later today."

"In the throne room? Or the advisory meeting room?" Anela asked. He knew why she asked; she would be present if they met in the throne room. She wouldn't be invited into the meeting room, though.

He shook his head. "Neither. In his quarters."

A heavy silence fell. A meeting alone with the king in his quarters meant he wanted no one else present for the conversation—which meant it would be worse than unpleasant. Milos squirmed uncomfortably in his seat, remembering when being called to his father's quarters usually meant a beating. But Tirano had stopped doing that when Milos got big enough to fight back. He had probably wanted to execute Milos for striking him, yet he couldn't exactly murder his sole heir. Instead, his father had to get more creative with his punishments.

Milos changed the subject and they spoke on light topics as they finished their meal. Once he bid both women a goodbye, he went in search of Bristio to see if he could find out more about whatever his mother had wanted. But he couldn't find the man anywhere. Annoyed, he settled in the library with a book to pass the time until the meeting with his father.

The hours ticked by, and too soon, he placed the book back on its shelf and headed to the king's quarters. The guards announced him at the door and he strode in, back straight and chin high. He refused to cower like an abused dog.

His father sat at his desk, writing, and didn't look up. Milos sighed to himself and approached, stopping in front of the desk. He stared at the wall behind Tirano and waited.

His father finally set his writing aside. Barely looking at Milos, he barked, "Sit."

Milos complied, easing down onto the dark brown leather chair, which matched the one his father occupied. "Good day, Father."

Tirano leaned back, elbows resting on the chair arms. He steepled his fingers, the tips touching his chin, and said nothing for several beats. Then he straightened and pointed a finger at his son. "I've had enough of your disobedience and poor choices. This is what will happen. You will remain in the capital. You will marry. You will—"

A knock on the door cut him off, and Tirano's jaw clenched as a guard poked a head in. "I said no interruptions," he snarled.

The guard paled and bobbed his head. "My apologies, Your Majesty. One of your advisors told me to inform you at once. Something ... happened to Lord Ruzo."

Tirano waved a hand. "Go on."

The guard stepped all the way in, shutting the door behind him, and bowed. "Yes, Your Majesty." He hesitated, glancing behind him as though he wished to flee.

Tirano's voice rose in irritation. "Well? What is it?"

The guard swallowed visibly. "I am terribly sorry to inform Your Majesty that Lord Ruzo—that is—he... Well. He has died."

Milos's eyes grew wide and he looked back at his father. Tirano's jaw dropped open. Milos had never seen him at a loss for words.

The king finally spoke. "You're mistaken. I saw him at breakfast, alive and well."

The guard appeared truly miserable. Milos wondered how he got stuck being the bearer of this news. Perhaps all the guards on duty had drawn straws, or maybe he was the newest at the moment.

"Yes, Your Majesty, he was at breakfast. But the servant who brought his midday meal to his room found him, and..." The guard gestured helplessly.

"How?" Tirano's voice was sharp enough to cut glass. "How did he die?"

The guard shook his head. "I was not informed, Your Majesty. I think the royal physician is still determining the cause."

Tirano muttered a curse and waved a hand at the trembling man. "You're dismissed." He stood and looked to Milos. "You as well. Get out."

Milos didn't need to be told twice. Tirano was right on his heels, but they parted ways in the hall as the king headed toward the wing where the advisors lived. Milos had no particular destination and chose the opposite direction out of self-preservation. He recognized the signs leading to one of Tirano's infamous rages—his clenched jaw and icy calm, primarily—and Milos wanted nothing to do with the situation.

Lord Ruzo was not only Tirano's advisor. The two had been friends since their teens, growing up together at court. Milos honestly thought his father would be more upset at his friend's passing than he would have been if Milos himself died, or his mother.

Milos had never liked Lord Ruzo, and he wasn't the only one. In fact, Ruzo had probably made more enemies than friends over the years. If he had been killed, Milos wasn't surprised. But perhaps it was some natural cause. Milos remembered when, as a child, one of his favorite riding instructors dropped dead out of nowhere, apparently due to some problem with his heart. That was the first time he learned that a person need not appear to be terribly old or sickly before the gods took a life.

His feet finally found a direction, and he went in search of his mother to tell her the news, in case she hadn't been informed. Tirano would be very unpredictable in the days to come, and she should be forewarned.

After inquiring with a couple of guards and servants, he found his mother in one of her favorite summer pastimes: walking the gardens with Hen. A smile lit her face when she noticed his approach, then faltered when she observed his expression.

When he drew near enough, she grasped his forearm, searching his face. "What did he do? Are you all right?" She examined him from head to toe; she too remembered his childhood beatings, and he knew the guilt she harbored for not being able to stop them. But he also knew she had done her best and kept him out of his father's reach as much as she could.

"I'm fine, Mama." He used the old term of endearment and her shoulders slumped in relief. "He had barely started his lecture when a guard interrupted with an urgent message." He looked back and forth between his mother and Lady Henriella. "Lord Ruzo is dead."

Chapter Twelve

VERANA

While they were all relieved that Aldo survived and was recovering, albeit slowly, their new financial reality was far more precarious than it should have been headed into autumn. All their available coin had been spent on the medicine.

One evening after Aldo was safely tucked into Ana's bed, the rest of the family gathered around the kitchen table.

"We all need to do whatever we can at this point," Luciano said wearily. "I secured a position on a fishing boat—the one Leo has been working on—until the winter storms come." He much preferred to labor on neighboring farms in exchange for a crop share and a little coin. Ana knew he hated fishing. But it would be more consistent than the farm labor, especially once harvests wrapped up mid-autumn.

Halia patted his hand in sympathy. "It's temporary, my love." She sighed. "The innkeeper at Sonos Harbor agreed to take me on to help in the kitchens and cleaning rooms for the autumn and winter. Their business is busy until the winter storms, and once the season changes, one of their daughters plans to marry and move closer to the capital, so they will need the extra hands." Halia turned her blue-eyed gaze on Ana. "As for your part, I'm afraid foraging to sell at the market won't be enough, daughter."

Ana flinched internally. She knew what was coming, and now it would be more difficult than ever to argue her point.

"Let us help you find a husband, Verana. The only other option is to find work in the city." Halia's lips curled with distaste at the idea. She wasn't fond of the capital.

Halia wasn't wrong about it being the only other option; no fishing rig would hire a woman, and other consistent employment was difficult to come by in their tiny village or even Sonos Harbor.

However, she was wrong about which path Ana would prefer if it came down to a forced marriage versus leaving home to work in the city. Marrying might relieve her family of financial responsibility for her, but by the Seven, she refused to marry whatever stranger her mother found suitable.

"I am not ready to marry," Ana said firmly. "But I will do my part and find work in Sonos City."

The conversation didn't end there. Halia and Leo tried to convince Ana to choose otherwise. She held firm, and with her father's support, it was settled.

Her biggest regret was leaving Aldo, yet he was understanding. "Maybe you can save money again so we can go on our adventure. I'm sorry we had to spend it all."

"None of that. I'm not sorry at all. And I'll do my best," she promised. "You heal and get strong so you're ready when it's time."

When Luciano and Ana hitched a ride into the city on a trader's cart mere days after the family discussion, Cecil didn't try to follow her as she feared. Ever since Aldo fell sick, if Cecil wasn't with Ana, he was curled up next to Aldo. And that's where he remained as she bid her goodbyes to her mother.

Her father insisted on accompanying her, even if it meant missing work and therefore pay. "You cannot go to the city alone, Ana. It wouldn't be safe. Especially for a beautiful girl like you."

Ana had rolled her eyes. "It's not like you can stay there with me. I'll be on my own eventually."

He had sighed and pulled her to his chest for a hug. "I know. But I can make sure you find work and are safely settled somewhere. If you can get hired at an inn, they'll likely let you sleep there and look after you."

Ana had not visited the city in many years. The number of scraggly begging children in the streets saddened her. Their village might be poor, but no child went without food. Here in the cobblestone streets of the capital, most families couldn't keep huge gardens or forage in the woods.

Father and daughter approached several inns and taverns with no success. Frustrated, Ana insisted they take a break and eat. She pulled bread and goat cheese out of her basket, and they found a bench near a fountain in one of the city squares.

As she nibbled and watched a handful of children both playing in and drinking the water, a thought occurred to her. She let out an exasperated sigh, irritated she hadn't had the idea sooner. Her father raised his brows in a question, but she waved a hand and shook her head.

If she could apply her knack for finding hidden mushrooms and berry patches in the woods, this search for work might be much easier. She had never attempted to use her ability in a scenario like this, yet it couldn't hurt to try.

When they finished their food and began their search once more, she focused on what she needed to find. It only took a moment before she felt the tug deep inside.

"This way," she said, inventing a lie on the spot. "I heard someone talking about a popular place in that direction."

Her father narrowed his eyes but followed until they reached a tavern just outside the castle gates, aptly named *The Royal Gate*. Ana grinned as they walked inside.

It was much cleaner than other taverns she had seen, the floors well swept and the wood bar polished to gleaming. A faint hint of lemon and vinegar lingered in the air, as opposed to the smell of old food, spilled ale, and vomit that permeated many such establishments.

A few men in royal guard uniforms lounged in one corner playing cards, and a small scattering of other patrons dotted the room; a decent crowd for the time of day. Ana grew even more hopeful, as it appeared to be a successful business and, on first impression, one she wouldn't mind working in at all.

But when they approached the woman behind the bar to state their business, the barkeep shook her head. "I'm sorry, we have no need of more barmaids right now."

Ana couldn't hide her disappointment; they had walked across most of the city for nothing. Her skill had failed her, despite feeling like it was *working*.

The woman was kind. When she saw the crestfallen look on Ana's face, she said, "You're from the countryside, aren't you?" At Ana's nod, the woman continued. "I thought so. You have that overwhelmed look about you. Chin up, I'm sure you'll find something. Have an ale on the house."

Despite Luciano's protests, moments later she set two pints of ale in front of them. "I insist. Drink up." Then she bustled away to the other end of the bar to help another customer.

Ana was grateful for her father's patience; he sipped his ale and didn't pester her about where to look next or that they needed to be getting home. She distracted herself from her frustration by listening to the conversations around her. Two women and a man sat at a table nearby.

"I had to fire her," the first woman said. She was maybe in her late forties or early fifties, with light brown, silver-threaded hair, smile lines creasing her face, startling bright aqua-blue eyes, and a matronly figure. "What someone does with their personal time is one thing, but she brought her nonsense to work often enough that it couldn't be ignored anymore. Crying over a boy one day, kissing him in the pantry the next! Completely inappropriate, and it affected her work, too. His Majesty is very particular about his tea, and who do you think was yelled at for serving the wrong type? Me, of course, even though I had shown Elyse exactly which leaves to use."

Ana's eyes widened as she processed this anecdote. This woman must work in the castle … and maybe this was the conversation her innate ability intended her to hear.

"It's a shame; she seemed like a nice girl," the second woman, similar in age and build, offered.

"Well, she was then, perfectly nice. But nice doesn't get work done. Now we are more shorthanded than before, since Stella went to live with her new husband's people in their town right before I had to let Elyse go."

"You don't have anyone new lined up? The Seven know plenty of people are looking for work."

"No, not yet. It's difficult to find the time for hiring

when I am making up for the lack of two girls in the kitchens."

Ana decided to jump in before she lost her nerve. She stood and turned, angling herself toward them. "Excuse me, mistress?" The first woman turned to look at her. Luciano started, and then narrowed his gray eyes at Ana, frowning in silent reproval at her for interrupting a stranger's meal and conversation. He had his back to the other table, however, so they didn't see his reaction. Ana pretended not to notice.

"Yes, girl?" the woman responded. Ana approached their table, heart thrumming in her chest.

"Please excuse me for eavesdropping, I meant no harm by it. I think we can help each other. I'm in the city looking for work, and it sounds as though you have a need for someone like me. My name is Verana."

"Someone like you, eh? Well, I don't know anything about you, but I appreciate your eagerness. Who are you and what experience do you have?" Now both women focused intently on her, and the man had looked up from his food as well. Ana swallowed and pushed forward. After sharing her name and family background, she did her best to convince the women of her abilities.

"I am a hard worker, and I learn quickly. I need to find work to help support my family. That is my only purpose for being in the city today." The women looked at one another and then back at her during this speech. The man had lost interest and returned to his meal.

"Hmm. Well, Miss Verana, to be honest, and not meaning to insult you, but you're older than most kitchen maids that I hire. Are you not married?" Her gaze was both kind and shrewd as she looked Ana up and down.

"No, mistress, I'm not, and I have no plans to be any

time soon. Right now, I want to find a good job to help ease my parents' burden," she said. "And I've never been to the castle. I think it would be quite thrilling to work there." She looked down, affecting a hint of shyness and embarrassment. She could care less about the castle or its inhabitants, but she'd say anything at this point to succeed in her mission.

"I'm not sure about thrilling. It's hard work. But you seem to have a decent head on your shoulders, even if you are a bit forward. You'll have to know your place, working in the castle, you know," the blue-eyed woman warned.

"I completely understand. I am not usually so bold," Ana assured her. "Allow me to introduce my father."

Forcing a smile, Luciano turned to greet the strangers. The woman introduced herself as Mistress Danias, head housekeeper for the royal family and court of Revas. Within fifteen minutes, it was settled. Ana would go home with her father to gather clothes and other necessities, then would return two days hence.

The pay wasn't high, but all her meals were included, as well as a cot in a shared servant girls' bedroom. That meant most of her earnings could go to her family, while simultaneously relieving them of the burden of feeding her through the winter. She would have two days off per month to visit home.

Luciano, however, appeared less than thrilled as they left the tavern. Brow furrowed, he studied the cobblestones as they walked, brooding for no reason Ana could determine.

"Aren't you pleased, Father? I'm sure Mother will be."

"I'm not overly fond of the idea, but it'll have to do," he mumbled. "We have little choice."

Ana shrugged off his lack of enthusiasm; she was elated. Her mother may back off on the push for marriage now, but even if she didn't, Ana wouldn't be there most of the time.

Besides, upon reflection, she was rather curious about life at the castle. She was still bitter with the knowledge that only the royals and nobles could afford the highly skilled and trained physicians, and she couldn't help but wonder what else they had, and did, that everyone else did not. And ... why? Why were some living lavishly when children begged in the street on their doorstep?

These questions hadn't ever occurred to her; she had always accepted her life and kingdom as the way things were. After Aldo's illness, though, something inside of her rebelled against the idea that the status quo was the only option.

Not that she could make anything change ... but maybe she could at least understand.

Chapter Thirteen

VERANA

When Ana arrived at the castle, the guards at the gate let her pass at the mention of Mistress Danias. She stood completely still just inside the courtyard, overwhelmed by all of the activity. She gawked at the structure itself; she had never seen it up close. Stone towers and turrets loomed high in the lightly clouded sky. The double doors of the main entrance had to be at least twelve feet tall, with the kingdom's crest carved into them.

She swallowed and wished she had brought Cecil instead of leaving him to keep Aldo company. His warm, furry presence in her arms would have been a comfort. But Aldo needed him more, and she wasn't sure if her cat would be welcome at the castle.

When someone bumped into her with a muttered, "Get out of the way, girl," she turned to the man as he walked away.

"I'm sorry, can you tell me where the kitchens are? I'm new."

He glanced back at her and pointed. "Go around the east side of the castle, through the kitchen gardens."

"Thank you, sir," she called, but he was already hurrying in the opposite direction.

With a deep breath, she forced her feet to take her toward the east side, belatedly realizing she could use her own ability to guide her. There was more than one door leading inside, and the tug in her middle led her toward the correct one.

Her eyes widened when she saw the expanse of vegetables and herbs; it was the biggest garden she had ever seen, all laid out in neat rows with an occasional bench placed throughout. How many people actually lived at the castle? She had no idea, but it must be quite a few to require such a sizable garden.

She knocked at the door. No one answered. The clamoring of a great deal of activity filtered through the wood; they'd never hear a little knock. So she pushed the door open and poked her head in, followed by the rest of her body. She pulled the door closed behind her and leaned against it, watching cooks and servants rushing around.

An immense fireplace dominated one wall, with several large cuts of meat roasting on spits. Stone ovens flanked it, and the room was filled with pots and pans both iron and copper; the ones not in use on stove tops hung gleaming overhead. Through one doorway, a woman could be seen butchering a pig in the next room.

No one noticed Ana. But she spotted a familiar face.

"Mistress Danias!" she called over the din.

The older woman's gaze jerked to her, and Ana realized she had interrupted a conversation between the head housekeeper and someone else—a guard, it looked like.

The mistress held a finger to indicate she'd be with Ana

in a moment. Her brow creased with worry as she exchanged a few more words with the man. Then he nodded and left, heading down a dark hallway lit with wall sconces.

Mistress Danias hurried over to her. "Verana, was it? I admit I entirely forgot you were to start today. It is utter chaos here at the moment." The lines between her eyebrows continued to betray her state of mind.

Ana smiled. "That's quite all right. I'm sure you're very busy. And you can call me Ana." She hesitated before asking, "What is the reason for the 'chaos?' Is there anything I can do to help?" Maybe they were preparing for a banquet or party of some sort.

The woman shook her head. "There's nothing any of us can do. I may as well tell you, because you'll hear about it soon enough, and we all need to use caution in the coming days." She clasped Ana's elbow. "Come. I'll show you your bedroom; it's too loud in here to talk."

She pulled Ana down the same hallway the guard had gone down, and then another. The place was a maze; she realized she'd be using her secret ability more often, at least at first.

Something was strange about the lighting; the sconces appeared to hold lit candles, but they didn't flicker like a candle, and when she looked more closely, no wax dripped despite the steady flame. She asked the housekeeper about them.

"Oh, yes. Those are old Diona magic. You know, from when the Diona and humans lived together long ago. When they all decided to go live in the mountains, some of their enchantments lingered."

Ana knew about the Diona and their departure, as everyone did; folks called it the Sundering. She hadn't realized they had left magically imbued objects behind though. She had never seen one. Perhaps they were only in the castle. She was dying to ask what other Diona magic remained, but her employer was telling her about the castle and its inhabitants. She shouldn't interrupt.

Finally, they came to a door and Mistress Danias opened it. "The other girls are working. Come on in."

The room wasn't large, yet it was still bigger than the main room of Ana's cabin. It contained four cots and a four-drawer dresser, as well as a rickety wardrobe against one wall.

Mistress Danias pointed to a bed in the far-right corner. "That one is yours. Go ahead, put your things down. The third drawer down is yours as well, and there should be some space in the wardrobe."

Ana set her pack on the bed and turned to face her new employer. "I can unpack later. I don't want to keep you."

The housekeeper nodded once. "Very well. Anyway, the reason the entire place is in a tizzy is because one of the king's advisors died unexpectedly."

Ana bit her lip, taken aback. "Oh, that's terrible. I'm so sorry."

Mistress Danias waved a hand. "Thank you, dear, but it's not necessary. Most of us weren't overly fond of the man. However, that is neither here nor there. The point is, Lord Ruzo wasn't only an advisor to the king, he was one of His Majesty's oldest friends. King Tirano is quite distraught."

Ana nodded. That made sense, but there was something in the woman's tone, some underlying warning she didn't understand. "I see."

"You don't, but you will." She hesitated. "The king can be, shall we say ... unpredictable, when he is this upset.

Anything at all can make him fly into a temper, and—" She must have noticed the look on Ana's face. "Don't worry too much. You're not likely to have much contact with him. Those of us who do will be walking on eggshells for a bit. If folks seem less friendly than you'd expect, keep that in mind."

Ana nodded slowly, wondering what in the world she had walked into. "Yes, mistress. I understand."

"Very good. Come with me. You can unpack after supper. I'm going to have someone show you around, so you don't get lost."

They returned to the kitchens and the housekeeper paired Ana with one of her roommates, a teen girl not much older than Aldo, named Lisia.

When Mistress Danias left them, Lisia turned light blue eyes to Ana. "What do you think of the castle so far?"

Ana gave a small shrug. "It's ... a lot? Overwhelming, I mean."

Lisia smiled kindly, a gap in her front teeth only increasing her charm, alongside the sprinkle of freckles across her nose. "You'll get used to it. Come along. Let me show everything."

She led Ana to the dining hall, and then the laundry—which is when Ana realized the castle boasted pipes for running water, something she had only ever heard of—and then back to their shared room. As they went, the young servant gave Ana tips for finding her way around.

"See that painting?" Lisia pointed at a landscape of the forest and mountains. "You know if you see that, the dining hall is to the right, and the kitchens to the left."

Ana wrinkled her nose. "It looks like half the other

paintings we've seen." She wasn't truly concerned about it; her secret skill would keep her from getting lost. But the painting did look like several others they had passed.

Lisia chuckled. "Look more closely."

Ana stepped nearer, eyes sweeping over the art in the dim yet unwavering Diona-made light. She gasped when she realized the image was ... moving. Branches of trees swayed ever so slightly, as though in a breeze. A creek in the foreground seemed to trickle over rocks.

Lisia giggled at Ana's awe-struck expression. "It's Diona-made. The only other Diona-made paintings are in the royals' quarters. I guess no one wanted this one."

"Oh." Ana could think of no other response. Learning about the Diona in a historical sense was one thing; seeing proof of their magic and existence was another. Ana had never seen one, nor had anyone else she knew. Humans still acquired some Diona-made things, mostly medicines, but she had no idea how the arrangement worked.

Lisia also warned Ana about certain noblemen who frequented the castle. "If you serve in the dining hall, you'll need to know who to be careful of. Lord Cyrio—he's the one with the large nose and straggly black beard—he can get handsy if you linger near him too long. Same for Lord Kavio and Lord Folcon. And try not to *ever* be alone with Lord Vilos."

At Ana's questioning look, Lisia shook her head, a grim set to her mouth. "Just trust me. I'll point them all out so you know who's who."

Ana wanted to ask why these men apparently got away with such behavior, but she knew it was a silly question. They were men, and they had money. Still, it bothered her that grown adults weren't held accountable for their reprehensible actions.

As they made their way back to the kitchens, Mistress Danias came upon them in the hall. "Oh, there you are. Finished with the tour?" At Lisia's nod, the older woman continued. "Good, then. Lisia, please bring a tea tray for three to the queen's quarters. You may bring Ana along so she knows where it is, in the event that she must serve in that wing at some point."

The bottom dropped out of Ana's stomach. From their chat in the tavern, Ana knew she would do kitchen work and sometimes serve in the dining hall, as well as run errands in the city. But serving the queen?

She barely had time to imagine it, as Lisia pulled her the rest of the way to the kitchens and showed her how to prepare a tray of tea for the queen and two companions. *The queen.* By the Seven, her first day in the castle and she was about to see the queen.

Ana frowned in concentration as she watched Lisia arrange the tray, trying to memorize the placements. After Lisia finished by adding a small sprig of flowers from a basket in the corner of the room, she picked up the tray and gestured for Ana to follow with a jerk of her chin. Lisia kept up a constant chatter until they reached a set of double doors in a different wing, with guards standing outside.

One guard knocked and then called through the door, "Your Majesty, your tea has arrived."

A faint voice called back, "Yes, send her in."

The guard opened the door and the two young women walked past him. He looked Ana up and down as she passed, but she barely noticed. Her knees shook; she needed to focus on remaining upright.

Ana stayed near the door in the grand yet cozy room, seeing as she had nothing to deliver. She watched out of the corner of her eye as Lisia walked to the small dining table and placed the tray down before dropping a curtsy to the occupants. The queen, with her well known red hair, *and* the prince sat at the table, along with another woman around the queen's age.

"Your Majesty. May I do anything else for you?"

Ana's already rapid heartbeat doubled as her gaze landed on the back of the man's head, who Lisia next addressed.

"Or for you, Your Highness? My lady?"

Before either of the two could answer, the queen forced a smile. "No, thank you, Lisia." Then her green gaze landed on Ana. "Who is this?"

Lisia turned and gestured for Ana to come forward. "A new girl Mistress Danias just hired, Your Majesty. Her name is Ana."

Ana stopped beside Lisia and attempted a curtsy, which was far from perfect. "Your Majesty," she breathed, not daring to look into the monarch's face.

"Hello," Queen Anela said. "Welcome to the castle." She paused. "You're allowed to look at me, Ana."

At the prompt, Ana forced herself to meet the queen's vivid green eyes. "I'm s-sorry, Your Majesty. This is my first day, and I've never..." She trailed off, at a loss. She had never. Never been inside the castle, never interacted with the royal family, never been so nervous in her life.

The queen's smile was soft and kind. "I see. I'm sure it's overwhelming." She studied Ana quietly for a beat. "You look very familiar. Where are you from?"

"A small village near Sonos Harbor, Your Majesty. I'm the daughter of Halia of Revas and Luciano of Libeverro."

"Hmm." The queen waved a hand at the two people sitting with her. "This is my son, Prince Milos, and my friend, Lady Henriella."

Ana mumbled something to the effect of, “It's my pleasure, Your Highness, my lady,” and dropped another awkward curtsy. Lady Henriella gave her a polite smile, while Prince Milos's expression was more of a smirk. Perhaps because she was so obviously flustered? A flare of dislike rose in her at the thought that he was laughing at her, even as she noticed his handsome tan face, tousled dark hair, and green eyes. Ana had enough experience to know a handsome face didn’t mean a man was a gentleman.

Queen Anela turned to Lisia. “What duties will Ana have?”

Lisia gave her a blank look. “Um, I'm not sure what her main duties will be, Your Majesty. We recently lost two girls in the kitchens, so she'll probably be working there, either cooking or serving, if it pleases Your Majesty.”

The queen nodded. “Very well, thank you. Please ask Mistress Danias to attend me at her earliest convenience. You may go.”

Both girls curtsied once more, and Ana followed Lisia out into the hall.

When they were out of hearing range of the guards, Lisia gave Ana a curious look. “The queen took an unusual interest in you.”

Ana only shrugged. It had surprised her too, but she couldn't explain it. “I assume she doesn't usually take the time to get to know a brand new kitchen maid.”

Lisia chuckled. “Never, as far as I know. Don't get me wrong, Queen Anela is kind. But you know, she's also ... well, a queen. She's very busy.”

Ana nodded, unable to think of anything else to say. The queen had also said she looked familiar, yet Ana knew they had never laid eyes on each other. What a strange encounter.

Still, Lisia was right, the queen did seem kind. Which is better than Ana could expect from the king, apparently. She was much more concerned about encountering the enraged, grieving man than she was about his wife.

Working in the castle already proved to be an interesting experience—even more than she had anticipated.

Chapter Fourteen

ANELA

Anela didn't like the way Milos looked at the new maid. He was a far better man than his father ... but he was still a man. And Ana was a beautiful young woman, and appeared to be of age, unlike most of the maids. Once the two girls left, she gave him a pointed look.

"Don't even think about it," she warned.

He raised his hands in a gesture of innocence. "I don't know what you mean." One corner of his mouth twitched as he suppressed a smile.

She narrowed her eyes. "Yes, you do."

"Don't torment your mother, Milos," Hen chastised. "We both saw the way you looked at that girl."

He finally gave in and chuckled. "You can't expect me not to notice that kind of beauty, Auntie Hen. She's prettier than most of the princesses I've met." He held up his hand to ward off any more lectures. "But I'm a gentleman, as you raised me to be, Mama. Don't worry."

His reassurances didn't entirely hit the mark, but Anela dropped the topic. She was still shocked Bristio had done her bidding so quickly, and she was antsy to find out what gossip was going around. Had he made it look accidental or natural? She had no idea. Now that the threat was taken care of, she needed to plan for the inevitable aftermath, which she'd barely given a thought to in her desperation to protect Hen.

"The king will be very distraught," she said, sipping the tea Hen had poured for her. "We must speak with the council of advisors and ensure everything is being done to prepare for a proper burial and services." She paused, tapping a finger on the edge of the saucer. "No, proper won't be enough for your father. It needs to be quite grand, closer to a royal funeral." She thought back to Tirano's father's funeral, trying to remember all of the Revasian traditions for such an event.

"I agree." Hen reached for a pastry and set it on her plate. "If anything will mollify Tirano, it will be making it seem like the entire court grieves Lord Ruzo as he does."

Milos nodded, staring contemplatively at his tea. "What would you have me do?"

"First, you will arrange a meeting with the advisors for later this afternoon. I'll make sure Mistress Danias attends as well."

Milos drained his drink and stood. "Very well. That's only a couple hours away, so I'll go tend to it now." He bowed politely and then rounded the table to drop a kiss on her cheek. "It's good to be home."

Anela smiled up at him. "It's wonderful to have you back. I missed you."

Milos tossed a wave at Hen, and then he was gone, striding out the door with purpose in his step.

Anela looked at her friend to find Henriella studying her. "What is it?"

Hen gave a slight shrug. “I didn't want to say anything while Milos was here. Are you all right? When he told us the news, your reaction...” She pursed her lips. “I don't know. Something was off. I would expect you to look surprised, yes, but also perhaps relieved—not frightened.”

Anela scoffed and sipped her tea to buy herself a few moments. She wasn’t surprised Henriella had observed her in that moment, in an annoyingly detailed and precise manner.

She just hadn't expected it to happen that quickly, and the consequences of her actions—if Tirano ever discovered them—had flashed through her mind. If Bristio was caught, she would never forgive herself, nor would Milos if he discovered her part in it. Her husband... Well, she honestly wouldn't put it past Tirano to execute her and Hen alongside Bristio.

“You know what Tirano is like,” she replied. “Lord Ruzo was his closest friend. Of course I'm worried.”

Hen nodded slowly. “Yes, I suppose so.” She sighed. “You've just not been yourself recently.”

“I often don't feel like myself with these midlife changes.” It wasn't a lie, and her wan smile seemed to reassure Henriella, who gave her a sympathetic look. “And I’m still furious with Tirano for the nonsense with Kaosuda and Milos.” Again, a truth, but Anela’s stomach twisted with guilt for keeping secrets from her best friend and lover.

A knock sounded at the door and a guard announced Mistress Danias.

Anela first informed the housekeeper about the meeting later that day to plan the funeral services. “Please make sure one of the pastros attends as well.”

Mistress Danias nodded. “As you say, Your Majesty.”

Anela hesitated. “Can you tell me what people are

saying about his death? I need to be aware of any rumors that might upset the king."

The older woman tilted her head, considering. "I haven't heard much in the way of rumor or gossip yet. He seems to have died of natural causes. The physician assumes his heart gave out. There's no sign of injury or foul play. Obviously, His Majesty is upset."

Anela barely suppressed a huge sigh of relief. "I see. Thank you. Yes, it's to be expected that the king will grieve. As will we all." She tacked on the last bit, realizing she should at least appear to care that the man was dead.

"As you say, Your Majesty. Is there anything else I can do for you?"

"Oh! I almost forgot. I met your new hire earlier, Ana. I've been meaning to ask you to move around some of the maids. I think I'd prefer a more mature chambermaid. I'd appreciate it if you moved Bianca to the kitchens and replaced her with Ana." Someone brand new to the castle was perfect for her concerns about who may have spied on her previously.

Mistress Danias furrowed her brow. "Has Bianca done anything wrong, Your Majesty?"

Anela waved a hand. "No, no. Nothing of the sort. She's a nice girl. Lisia is as well, but I'd prefer to have Ana serve me whenever possible." The fewer servants entering her quarters, the better.

"She is still quite new and inexperienced," Mistress Danias hedged.

"I'm aware, and it is not a concern. She seems perfectly bright; I'm sure she'll learn quickly."

The older woman bobbed a curtsy. "Yes, Your Majesty. It will be as you wish."

If only life could be as she wished, Anela reflected, then chuckled at herself.

So many would wish to be queen. And here she was with a crown she would eagerly hand over if she had a choice.

Tirano didn't show up for the meeting with the advisors, for which Anela was grateful. The plans were set in motion for an elaborate funeral. Anela's jaw tightened, thinking of the cost of it all, but there was nothing to be done.

Supper-time came soon after the meeting and Anela braced herself to see Tirano for the first time that day. He would be expected to make some sort of official announcement, and she hoped he wasn't too emotional to complete the task properly. She hardly wanted to give a speech about the dead nobleman.

When he entered the dining hall, the king looked rather pale and haggard. He really did care about *some* people, she knew that. Just not many. Not her. She remembered when she had fancied herself in love with him and bit back a bitter laugh.

He stopped next to his chair but didn't sit. Everyone knew something of what had happened by now, so all eyes were on him already, and the room quieted quickly as he surveyed them.

"As many of you know by now," Tirano began, then stopped and cleared his throat. "As many know, Lord Ruzo, my old friend and advisor, was found dead earlier today. He appears to have died peacefully, if unexpectedly." He paused again, taking a deep breath. "Funeral arrangements are underway"—he shot Anela a questioning glance, and she nodded in reply—"And will be announced in the coming days. For now, let us raise our cups to my old dear friend, may he rest peacefully with the Seven."

The room echoed "May he rest peacefully with the Seven" with raised goblets. Anela's shoulders sagged in relief; that had gone better than she expected.

When he sat, she leaned toward him. "I'm sorry for your loss, my king."

He turned and eyed her, cocking his head to one side with a faint sneer. "Are you? You never liked him."

Touché. "But you did, and you will feel his absence. You have my condolences."

Tirano gave half a shrug and a nod, dismissing her by turning to speak with one of the other advisors.

Anela barely felt the snub. She was too grateful that he seemed relatively calm. For that moment, in any case. Forever volatile, she anticipated his raging temper would show itself in the coming days and weeks. She had weathered it before, and she would again.

Perhaps she should send Milos away once more, though, as Tirano was already unhappy with him. It made her heart ache to consider it, as he had only just returned. And if she did so, she would certainly risk Tirano's wrath over the matter.

By the Seven, she was so tired of tiptoeing around men who behaved like children. She pushed food around on her plate and then took a hearty gulp of wine, and another, before gesturing to a nearby servant to fill her goblet. Tonight, she would drink as a silent celebration, and try not to think about what was to come.

The following morning, Anela nursed a headache, but that wasn't the reason her hand shook. She reread the note in her trembling fingers. "Someone left this in your room?" she asked Henriella.

Hen nodded. Their breakfast remained untouched; as soon as Hen had arrived, she had handed a very short, yet disturbing, note to Anela. "They slipped it under the door."

"Tell the queen I know her secrets. She can't hide them forever."

Anela's thoughts reminded her of a time her horse was spooked by a snake; the beast had never run faster in her life, and Anela understood the impulse. She resisted, remaining in her plush dining chair. Question after question vied for attention.

What secrets? Her secret relationship with Hen? That might make sense as it was left where Henriella would find it. But then wouldn't the note hint at Hen being involved? Something like "The secret kept by you and the queen?" So was it about how Lord Ruzo died? Who could know that? She trusted Bristio with her own son's life and knew he would never tell a soul—not to mention if he did, it was his own life on the line. Did someone see him enter or leave Lord Ruzo's room, perhaps?

Her sharp intake of breath accompanied the realization that the note said "secrets," plural. Did someone know more than one damning truth about her? How?

Anela finally found her voice again. "Why would they leave this for you instead of me?"

Henriella shrugged with a frown. "I imagine because it's easier. No guards stand outside my doors."

"That makes sense. By the Seven, I can barely think straight." She set the scrap of parchment down as though it could burst into flames at any moment and rubbed her temples like that might help.

"It may be nothing," Hen said. "Just an empty threat to stir the pot."

Anela nodded slowly. That was possible, but she doubted it. "And if it's not?"

Hen finally reached for her tea, her own hand a bit shaky. "I don't know. That note doesn't give us much to go on. It doesn't ask you to do anything, or..." Hen drifted off and took a sip of tea, eyes fixed on the wall opposite as she thought. A Diona painting hung on that wall, with said magical beings dancing a circle around a fire in the woods, yet Anela could tell Hen wasn't seeing it.

Unfortunately, Hen was right. The message was a threat, but it didn't give her any way to respond. Whoever wrote it could have demanded ... something. Anything. But it was just a statement. Somehow, that made it worse.

Chapter Fifteen

VERANA

The first few weeks of Ana's employment at the castle flew by. As much as the assignment surprised her, serving the queen directly meant she didn't have to spend as much time in the dining hall or delivering meals to others' personal quarters. Therefore her exposure to the lecherous old men of the court was minimal—which she felt grateful for, but also guilty every time her roommates complained about them.

The castle inhabitants seemed to breathe a collective sigh of relief when the king decided to go on a hunting trip. The entire atmosphere of the castle was lighter once he left. Everyone was glad for a break from the king's moody outbursts, although Ana noted the queen wasn't pleased that the prince accompanied him.

Ana couldn't help but be very aware of the queen's moods and emotions. Being chosen to serve the queen directly so soon after joining the castle staff made her anxious and overly conscious of every facial expression and change of tone. For example, the queen smiled often, yet rarely did it reach her eyes—only when Prince Milos or Lady Henriella were around. Her small tells of worry or displeasure included a pinched quality to her mouth and an appearance of vertical lines on her brow.

Her Majesty did seem kind, as Lisia had claimed, but Ana didn't think she could be too careful when serving and interacting with members of the royal family.

Soon it was time for her first two days off. Mistress Danias gave her permission to take them consecutively, so she'd have a chance for a real visit with her family.

Leo met her at the edge of the city with a borrowed horse and let her ride while he walked most of the way. It was sweet, which was unusual, but Ana didn't complain.

"How's Aldo?" she asked as they meandered the road cleared through sparse forest. A breeze rattled through yellowing leaves that had yet to fall. Other than that, the only sound was the soft thud of the horse's hooves on the packed dirt. Ana relished the quiet, only now realizing how loud the castle and city always were.

Leo didn't answer right away, and she looked down to see a pained expression. "He's ... all right, I suppose. He's not gaining his strength back as quickly as we'd hoped."

Ana frowned but didn't press. She would see her little brother soon enough.

After a few beats, she said, "And you? How are you, big brother?"

He coughed, looking embarrassed. "I'm well enough. I proposed to Jesmina." A red flush crept up his neck.

Ana gasped. "By the Seven, Leo, why didn't you say something right away?"

He shrugged and gave her a small smile.

"I take it she accepted?"

He nodded and his smile grew wider. “We're to be married in a month's time.”

Ana's eyes burned with tears, but she blinked them away. Ameleo, engaged to be married. They really were all growing up. It was so strange to think of her brother as someone's husband. A pang of sadness bit into her chest; she wished she had been at home to hear the news when it happened. Sending messages between the village and the castle was too expensive unless it was essential.

“That's wonderful! I'm so happy for you.” She meant it.

He ducked his head sheepishly. “Thanks.”

Her visit went well, although it passed too quickly for Ana's liking. Halia was still prickly about Ana's pushback regarding marriage, yet she couldn't say much after Ana handed her a month's earnings from her job. Aldo was up and about, but he tired very easily. Ana could see why Leo had expressed concern.

Her younger brother hadn’t the energy for a walk to forage in the woods, so on the second day of her visit, the two found a spot near the creek behind the cabin and sat and talked for hours.

Ana told him all about the castle and the inhabitants, which entertained him a great deal. But when she mentioned that she hoped to save some coin for their travel plans once the family made it through the winter, his face fell.

“I ... I don't think I'm going to be able to go, Ana.” He held up his arm; his shirt sleeve covered the stump. “Everything is so much harder now, and I can't seem to get strong again. This is the farthest I've been from home since..." He trailed off. "I just don't think I can do it."

She leaned into him, bumping shoulders. "Nonsense. I'm sure by spring you'll be right as rain."

He gave her a weary smile. "Maybe. You should go anyway, even if I can't."

She frowned. "I'm not going without you. Hush. We only need to have some patience."

Leo escorted her back to the city that afternoon.

"Do you want me to see if you can sleep in the stables?" Ana offered. "I don't like you traveling that road after dark." The forest wasn't as dense for most of the journey, but everyone knew to avoid being in the woods at night. And there was some small part of her, though she'd never say it aloud to him, that didn't wish to watch him ride away.

She missed her family more than she cared to admit.

He smiled and shook his head. "I've done it before. I'll be fine."

"All right," she gave in reluctantly. "I'll do my best to make it to your wedding. Mistress Danias is quite kind; I'm sure she'll let me. I'll be due for my days off anyway."

That evening, Ana kept to her shared bedroom. She wasn't expected back at work until morning, and she wasn't ready to dive back into the hectic pace of castle life. She couldn't stop thinking about Aldo and wishing she was back home.

When her roommates returned, they had their usual hour of chatting and gossip before they went to sleep. Ana told them about her brother's engagement; Lisia and the other two girls, Fena and Cora, squealed with delight. And then, to Ana's dismay, they used it as an excuse to pounce on her own single status—not for the first time.

Ana had never had many girlfriends simply because most of the youth her age in her village were boys, and of course she didn't have sisters. However, she usually enjoyed the company of these girls, despite the fact that she was several years their elder. They could be a bit silly, but they were also hard working and kind, and she enjoyed listening to their chatter before bed.

However, this was the topic that pushed her patience to the edge. They often enjoyed a conversation of proposing and discussing the merits of various guards and stablemen to her, trying to play matchmaker.

"Ooh, what about John for our Ana?" Fena suggested as she brushed her long, dark hair. It fell to the tops of her thighs when loose; it was usually in a plait and then wound into a bun.

"John from the stables, or John from the armory?" Lisia asked, picking at a stray thread in her quilt.

"Oh the stables, to be sure. John from the armory is much too old," Fena stated, laughing, as her nimble fingers braided. "I could probably find a way to introduce you, Ana. To John from the stables. He spends time with my brothers sometimes. He's nice enough looking, and I don't think he's courting anyone."

Ana shook her head, trying not to clench her teeth. "I've told you, I'm not interested in courting."

"Well, you say that, yet we keep hoping you'll see reason and change your mind," Cora replied, winking one golden brown eye. "You will want a husband one of these days, but if you wait too long…"

"All the good ones will already be snatched up!" Lisia finished.

Ana rolled her eyes hard, but they weren't looking at her. "I suppose I'm just leaving you more options for husbands, then. Feel free to flirt with John from the stables, Fena, if you're so inclined. You're welcome."

But after they all fell asleep, their teasing made her wonder. Her mother wished for her to marry. Leo was getting married—in only a month! Was she being stubborn about the matter for no good reason?

As thrilled as she was for him, thinking about Leo's wedding made her sad. Sad that she missed it when he first told the family, and sad that she wouldn't be there to help with the preparation.

And Aldo. He was struggling, and while she knew the money she earned would help her whole family, she wished she could be there to help take care of him. And simply because she missed him. He was her best friend.

Soon, tears leaked down her cheeks as homesickness overwhelmed her. Restlessness snaked through her, and rather than trying to be still and quiet, she got out of bed. She borrowed Lisia's robe, as it was much thicker than her own, and snuck out. She saw no one as she made her way through the now familiar corridors. It was late.

Finally, she made it to the kitchen gardens. It was colder than she expected, and she wrapped the fabric more tightly around herself. She would regret her sleeplessness when she had to wake for work in the morning, and this thought pushed her silent tears toward louder, gasping breaths.

She sat on a bench, knees drawn to her chest so she could bury her face against them, muffling the sound of her sobs. After several minutes of believing herself completely alone and giving in to her despair, someone spoke.

"Excuse me, my lady? Are you unwell? Why are you out

here by yourself?" a voice inquired. Ana started and yelped. She looked up, but all she could see was his outline in the moonless night. She had been so startled it cut off her sobbing, and now she tried to catch her breath to answer him.

"I am well enough, thank you, my lord." She hiccupped and dropped her head again, embarrassed.

"It doesn't sound like it," he said, his tone friendly yet blunt. His voice sounded familiar, but she couldn't place it. There were so many noblemen at court—he did *sound* noble, his speech more refined than that of the men who labored around the castle. She knew it wasn't the king's voice, in any case.

"I am not ill; you need not worry yourself. Please go. I will be fine," she said miserably. Couldn't she even have one little breakdown in peace?

"Did ... did something happen? Did someone hurt you?" The concern in his voice was evident, and it softened her the tiniest bit.

"No, my lord. No one has hurt me."

"I'm glad. But it is late and dark, my lady," the man pointed out. "May I at least accompany you back inside?"

By the Seven, this man would not give up. "No, thank you. I know the way. My lord." She didn't quite hide the annoyance in her voice.

"Well, I can't just leave you alone here in this state," he said, also sounding annoyed. "May I sit?"

Ana blew out a breath, suddenly too weary to argue. "If you must." He sat on the opposite end of the bench, giving her plenty of space.

"May I ask your name, my lady?"

She hesitated before deciding to give her middle name. She didn't wish for her indecorous behavior to make it back to the queen or Mistress Danias. "My name is Elisa, and I am no lady, sir."

"Ah. Well, Miss Elisa, what makes you carry on in this fashion, in the middle of the night?"

"With respect, my lord, it is not your business. Nor would you understand." Unruly curls had escaped her plait, and she pushed them behind her ears.

"You're right, it's not my business, but I would still like to know," he said in a light tone. "And I am not generally lacking in understanding."

Who was this nosy man, to interrupt her much needed crying session and demand answers in this fashion? Her irritation transformed into anger. She wanted to scream and throw things, and her body trembled in her efforts to remain still and quiet.

But the emotion needed an outlet, and her only option was her words. In fact, it would be a relief. She felt so alone, and he thought he wanted to know. Let him have his own regrets for being so pushy. Everything poured out of her before she considered any potential consequences.

"If you *must* know what is wrong, my family and the rest of my village struggle to make it through the winter, while nobles in this castle have more than they could ever need. My brother was very ill and still hasn't recovered, and it's partly due to lack of food and medicine. There are starving children in the streets of the capital, right there." She pointed toward the city. "For no apparent reason, they starve. Can you give me a reason?" She didn't pause to give him a chance to answer, and couldn't keep her voice from rising. "Why is an entire kingdom, so many of whom suffer, so loyal to a king who cares nothing for them?!"

At his sudden intake of breath, she stopped, covering her face with her hands, instantly regretful. She knew nothing of this man, but obviously he belonged here, and he sounded like a noble. She had gone too far. Fear displaced her rage, a cold feeling slithering through her chest and belly. He was silent. By the Seven, what had she done?

"I am… Please excuse my words, my lord. I'm not well, as you said. I apologize." Her voice shook. Of all places to renounce the king, in the courtyard of his own castle! How could she have been so heedless?

"I can see that you aren't well." He spoke slowly. "What you say about the king... I would not repeat those words to others. Do you understand?"

"Y-yes, I understand. I don't know what came over me," she whispered.

"Good. And I'm sorry about your brother," he said more gently.

"Thank you, my lord. I'm ready to return to my room. Please, accept my apology for my … outburst. Excuse me." She said the last in a rush as she stood and fled.

Once back in her bed, she was mortified at her own lack of control and judgement. She was also thankful he seemed inclined to overlook it; at least, he hadn't called the guards to arrest her on the spot. *He.* She didn't even know his name! She had poured out her treasonous heart to a total stranger.

Her thoughts kept her awake for at least another hour. As she finally drifted off, all that remained was a determined declaration: she would not—could not—make such a mistake again.

Chapter Sixteen

MILOS

Milos meandered back to his quarters after an interesting encounter with one of the servants. The hunting party had returned after supper, but he chose to go straight from the stables into the city. After a couple weeks spent with his father, he had no desire to be in the same building as him. Fortunately for Milos, Lord Ruzo's death had distracted Tirano from whatever he had been planning for Milos. He had been lectured about his duty, yet the conversation started in his father's quarters wasn't picked back up, to his great relief.

Still, spending that much time with the king was a chore. So Milos went to The Royal Gate; he knew the owners, and they ensured he was left alone there, even if he was recognized. He always tipped generously, of course.

But then as he returned to the castle, he found Ana crying in the kitchen courtyard. He was almost completely sure it was the same girl his mother had requested as her new chamber maid, even though she called herself Elisa. The beautiful girl with the tawny skin that reminded him of the beach: the color of the smooth, damp sand at the water's edge. With thick, dark curls; soft, womanly curves; and striking gray eyes, she was exactly his type. It was too dark to confirm, but he thought her voice was the same, and she was the right height and size.

Obviously, she hadn't recognized him, which was for the better. He should have introduced himself; it was rude of him not to. But then she wouldn't have talked to him, and he wanted to know why she was crying in the courtyard late at night. He thought maybe someone had hurt her; if that had been the case, at least he could have done something about it.

Mainly, track down whoever the fool was and dish out a satisfying punishment. Outside of drinking, throwing a fist in someone's face was another appealing way to release his emotions after time spent with his father. All the better if they deserved it.

He never would have guessed what she would actually say. No one openly criticized his father. His mother and Hen dropped hints behind closed doors, and everyone in the castle was aware of the king's "moods." But no one said so aloud. And he had certainly never heard anyone accuse his father of ... whatever it was Ana accused him of. Not caring about the non-noble citizens of Revas, he supposed.

Were there so many children begging in Sonos City? He rarely spent any time in the city during the day. For one, he was away from home quite often. For two, he preferred to sneak into the capital in the cover of night, when he was less likely to be recognized.

He decided he'd visit the city the following morning to see if the young woman spoke the truth. Perhaps he should speak with his mother about it, too.

He took his time wandering the cold stone corridors to

reach his rooms. He enjoyed the castle most when it was like this—quiet, seemingly empty. That had always been the case; as a young boy, he sometimes snuck out of bed in the night just to walk the halls, look at the paintings, rifle through the books in the library, and maybe steal a snack from the kitchens.

When he finally made it into bed and closed his eyes, Ana's gray gaze edged into his mind. He grew hard picturing her full lips, and he scoffed at himself. He had never attempted to woo a castle inhabitant, whether noble, servant, or otherwise. He kept that kind of thing for his travels; he didn't want to deal with the inevitable gossip or rumors at court.

Not that anything would stop them from talking about him and making all sorts of wild assumptions. Yet at least he knew nothing they said had any basis in reality. His mother knew that, too, and that mattered to him. He never wanted to disappoint her by being too much like his father.

That thought was enough to help him ignore his aching cock, and to drift off to sleep.

The following morning, he invited himself to breakfast with his mother and Lady Hen. It wasn't because he wanted to see Ana—well, perhaps it was, but only to see if she seemed recovered after being so distraught the previous night.

Fortunately, she was still finishing up her tasks when he arrived, just before one of the other maids delivered their food. He caught a glimpse of her making the bed through the partially open doorway as he greeted his mother and Lady Henriella.

"I was hoping to see you last night," his mother chastised.

He shook his head ruefully. "Apologies, Mama. I needed to let off some steam, so I went into the city."

Ana came out just then and curtsied to the queen. "I have finished for this morning, unless there is anything else I can do for you, Your Majesty?"

Milos examined her closely. Her eyes were a bit puffy and tired-looking, but that was the only indication she might be unwell. Upon hearing her voice again, however, he knew with certainty it had been her in the courtyard.

"Thank you, Ana. I require nothing else, unless Lady Henriella or Milos have a request."

Lady Hen simply shook her head, smiling at Ana.

Milos said, "Actually, can I ask you to pour the tea before you go?"

Hen usually poured for them, and she shot him a suspicious look. Meanwhile, Ana's reaction solidified what he was already sure of. The color left her cheeks when he spoke. She recognized his voice too.

With a dazed nod, she said, "Of-of course, Your Highness."

As she poured tea for his mother first, as was proper, he said, "Are you quite well, Miss Ana? You look pale."

She pressed her lips together into a firm line before she answered. "Yes, thank you, Your Highness. I am well."

"Just a bit tired, perhaps?"

This time, pouring Hen's tea, she shot him a venomous look. "Perhaps, Your Highness."

He grinned. He couldn't resist poking at her, although he knew he wasn't ingratiating himself to her by doing so. She was too fun to tease, though.

"I hope you get better rest tonight."

She poured his tea, standing as far from him as she could manage. "Thank you, Your Highness." The words sounded forced.

She set the teapot down and looked at his mother, who nodded. "Thank you, Ana, that will be all."

The young woman hurried out of the room; he watched her go, admiring her figure. Once the door shut, his mother spoke.

"What was all that about? Didn't I tell you to leave the poor girl alone?"

He gave half a shrug as he stirred honey into his cup. "Surely asking her to pour isn't inappropriate?"

The queen pointed a finger at him. "Son, I know you better than anyone. Don't torment my maid, do you hear me?"

He ducked his head, mildly abashed. "Yes, Mama. I'm sorry."

Upon reflection while he ate, he realized his mother was right. He was only joking around and had no intention of revealing their conversation from the previous night, but Ana had no way of knowing that. She might even think she was at risk of being arrested for treason.

He would seek her out and try to have a quick, private word with her. He'd apologize and reassure her that she had nothing to fear from him. Hopefully that would put her at ease. Yes, that was the honorable path to take. The decision had nothing to do with wanting to see her and speak to her one on one again—nothing whatsoever.

The corner of his mouth curled in amusement at himself as his mother and Lady Hen chatted. He had never been a great liar, and apparently he wasn't any better at lying to himself than anyone else. He did want to see her again. Speak to her with no one else listening. Wipe away her angry, worried expression with his words of reassurance.

But that was all. Once he accomplished that task, he would leave her alone, as his mother ordered. As he should.

He didn't wish to examine why that sounded so entirely unappealing.

The following morning, Milos didn't join his mother for breakfast. Instead, he lurked in the corridors near her quarters and waited for Ana to leave once she finished with her morning duties.

When she came out, he let her move away from the guards and then caught up, falling into step beside her.

Her eyes widened when she realized who had joined her. She jerked to a stop and curtsied with a mumbled "Your Highness" and a wary look.

"Good morning, Ana. May I speak with you?"

She shot him a look of disbelief, glancing around. "To me? Here? Right now?"

He smiled. "Yes, you." He did want to speak with her right away, but now that she pointed it out... He didn't want any rumors spread around that might get her into trouble. As prince, he didn't make a habit of chatting up maids in the corridors, and it would certainly seem odd if anyone happened across them. "I wish we could have this conversation now, but I suppose that's not ideal." She stared at him, waiting, and he rubbed the back of his neck, suddenly embarrassed. "Can we meet in the kitchen gardens tonight? The same bench as last time?"

She pressed her lips together, narrowing her gaze.

Finally, she released a breath. "I can't exactly say no to the prince of Revas, can I, Your Highness?"

It was a challenge. He held up his hands, palms out. "You certainly can. I won't make you and you won't get in trouble." He hesitated. "But I'd really appreciate it if you'd give me just fifteen minutes of your time."

She sighed. "Fine. Tonight at midnight."

He grinned. "Thank you."

She nodded. "If that's all, Your Highness? I have other duties to tend to..." She glanced down the corridor, obviously wanting to be on her way.

"I'm sorry to interrupt your day. Please, don't let me keep you."

With another nod and a tight smile, she turned and hurried away.

Chapter Seventeen

VERANA

Ana's mind was in turmoil the rest of the day, wondering why the prince had approached her. Her distraction led to Mistress Danias chastising her more than once.

"What has gotten into you today? You've never been this clumsy!" The older woman gave her a reproving look after Ana almost dropped the queen's tray for her afternoon tea. She managed to keep hold of the tray, but the small dish of butter had slid to the floor.

Ana's cheeks burned. "I'm sorry, Mistress."

She was initially relieved when she and the other girls turned in for the night … until she realized she had to lay there and wait for more than an hour before she would meet Prince Milos. She just wanted to get it over with.

Was he going to threaten her? Blackmail her? Would she need to buy his silence? And if so, what could she possibly offer? He didn't need money, not that she had much anyway.

Ana frowned and turned over, restless. The only thing he might want was her body. A panicked, icy feeling washed through her. How would she respond if that was the case? One word from him could get her fired at best, imprisoned and executed at worst. Did she really have a choice?

He was much more handsome than any of the village boys who had chased her. Other than kissing and some fondling to satisfy physical want and curiosity, she had never given them much time or energy. Being handsome wasn't enough, though. It should be her choice, and she didn't know what she'd do if he tried to take that choice away.

She finally got out of bed. She didn't think it was quite midnight, but she couldn't see the small clock in the windowless room without lighting a candle, and she didn't want to wake the others. She took the risk of getting fully dressed, however. She'd be warmer and feel a little less vulnerable. Pulling a cloak out of the wardrobe, she tiptoed out of the bedroom.

As she passed through the kitchens, the wall clock read ten minutes to midnight. Close enough. She tossed the cloak over her shoulders; she had accidentally grabbed Lisia's instead of her own, so it was a few inches too short, but it hardly mattered.

It had been a warm autumn, yet the nights were brisk. She made her way to their last meeting spot and sat, glad for the layers of fabric protecting her from the chilled stone bench.

It wasn't as cloudy as the previous couple nights, and a small bit of moonlight from one of the three moons silhouetted the prince's figure as he made his way out of the kitchens. As he drew closer, she started to rise in order to curtsy, but he held out a hand. "Please, you don't need to get up."

She gave a single nod. "As you wish, Your Highness." And then she waited, wringing her fingers under her cloak.

He sat next to her, a little closer than the last time but still giving her plenty of space. "Thank you for meeting me, Ana. I'll try not to keep you up too late."

She gathered her courage and raised her head, meeting his gaze. "What did you need to speak to me about, Your Highness?"

He offered a soft smile. "It's only us. You can skip the formality." When she didn't reply, he sighed. "I wanted to apologize. I'm sorry for teasing you in my mother's quarters. And I wanted to let you know you're not in any trouble—regarding our last conversation, that is."

She blinked at him, brows drawing together. That was exactly the opposite of what she had anticipated, and she was at a loss for how to respond.

The prince just apologized to her. To *her*. Apologies didn't strike her as an especially royal-type thing to do in general. But for a prince to apologize to a lowly maid? Maybe she had fallen asleep before their meeting, and this was a dream.

His smile faded into an earnest look. "Will you accept my apology?"

Right. He expected her to say something. "I—I do. Yes, I accept it. Thank you." The last came out almost like a question. She was glad for the dark as a flush rose up her neck at her stammering.

"I appreciate it. Should I call you Ana, then, or Elisa?"

He sounded earnest rather than flippant. "Ana, if you please, Your Highness. Elisa is my middle name."

"Ana Elisa. That's a lovely name."

A smile tugged at the corner of her mouth. "Thank you. Ana is actually short for Verana."

"Even prettier. And I hope you won't worry about the

rest. My lips are sealed." He pretended to turn a lock over his mouth. "All right?"

Dazed, she nodded. "All right. Thank you." In her surprise, more words tumbled out of her. "This isn't what I expected at all. *You* aren't what I expected, Your Highness."

He chuckled. "What were you expecting?" The clouds had moved, and now the light of two moons shone brightly, illuminating the planes of his face. His extremely *handsome* face.

She cleared her throat. "Honestly?"

He inclined his head and a corner of his full mouth tilted up. "Please."

"Well, I ... I expected you might threaten to report what I said the other night. And require me to buy your silence." She ducked her head, not wanting to see his reaction. By the Seven, this entire conversation was so strange.

He sounded confused. "Buy your silence? I hardly need more money, and no offense intended, but I don't imagine you have much."

A soft snort escaped her. "No, Your Highness. However, most men would accept *other* forms of payment."

"...Oh." She risked a glance up to see the realization in his expression. Then he grimaced. "That's what you think of me?"

He sounded surprised, and offended, but not angry. "With respect, Your Highness, I don't *know* you. Noblemen at your court give maids unwanted attention all the time. Many men see women as objects, or treasure, to be conquered and owned."

He was silent for a few beats. "And you've known that type of man?"

She barked a laugh. "Not well, fortunately. My father and brothers are good people and kind to women. I've still met a few who are … not." She thought of Pastro Emilio, and the one older boy from her village who wouldn't leave her alone until Leo forced him to, and then all she had witnessed and heard about since coming to the castle.

"I see. These noblemen at my court… Have any of them—have you—I mean..." He floundered, but she understood what he was asking.

"No, Your Highness. Nothing worse than a pat on the rump, in any case."

His eyes bore into her as he clenched his jaw. "Who? Who touched you without your permission?"

Taken aback by the intensity of his tone, she paused. Was the prince angry on her behalf? It sounded like it, but she couldn't imagine why he would care that much.

"I don't know, Your Majesty. I don't know most of their names, and since I rarely serve in the dining hall, I don't have many chances to learn them." She studied him as her brain began to reorganize all her previous thoughts and assumptions. "The other maids have warned me against a handful of specific men, though. Lords, all."

He jerked his head in a stiff nod. "I understand. Will you promise to tell me if it happens again?"

She opened her mouth, but nothing came out. Why would he make such a request? Her mind spun from the unexpectedness of this entire encounter. When the silence lengthened, he continued.

"Believe me, I'd like to take all of them to task on behalf of any woman in the castle they've mistreated. Until I am king, my ability to do so is limited." His wavy, dark hair shifted, falling over his brow as he tilted his head. "But I can help *you*, if you'll let me."

He must have some ulterior motive. Mustn't he? Yet what could it possibly be? "That's very kind, Your Highness.

Surely you have more important things to do than worry about me. I'll be fine."

His eyes narrowed. "I just want you to tell me if anything like that happens again. Will you? Please?"

"You're quite stubborn, aren't you?" As sweet as his offer was, she didn't understand why he would make it. And she didn't fully trust him.

He threw his head back and laughed. The sound caused a strange feeling in her stomach, which she tried hard to ignore. "So I've been told. You don't seem lacking in the trait either."

That caught her by surprise, and she chuckled. "My mother and older brother would agree with you."

"Really? Why is that?"

He seemed genuinely interested, and it was refreshing to have someone to speak with outside of the younger maids, even if this situation was bewildering.

"If they had their way, I'd be married already, for one." She smiled ruefully.

He breathed a chuckle. "I know what that's like. Do you not wish to marry?"

She shrugged. "I would be open to it, if I found the right person. If I fell in love." She fell quiet for a beat. Would she ever fall in love? How would she know what it felt like? "My parents married for love. At least my father takes my side. I hate that my mother doesn't want the same for me. She wishes for me to make a match based on more material factors."

Prince Milos shifted and gazed around the moonlit gardens. "It seems we have more in common than expected. Except in my case, it's my father who is pushing marriage, and my mother who is patient."

She frowned. "To be fair, as a prince, your obligations

are different. My mother just wants me to find a husband for security. For financial support. She fears what will happen to me when she and my father grow old." Ana chewed the inside of her lip and shook her head. "I'd rather be poor and work myself to the bone than marry the wrong man. But you… Whoever you marry will be queen someday."

He leaned back, resting his head on the back of the bench to face the sky. The moons highlighted the stubble on his clenched jaw as he closed his eyes. "I'm well aware." Weariness blanketed his tone.

He said nothing else. She was curious about his reaction, but she didn't want to press. It couldn't be that difficult to find a suitable princess or noblewoman, surely, yet the subject was apparently a sensitive one.

The thought occurred to her that perhaps he, too, would rather marry for love, rather than for wealth or political gain. Being heir to the throne was such a privileged life, yet it came with its own burdens.

When he sat up straight again, he turned toward her. "I wanted to talk to you about something else you said. About the children in the city. But it's late and I know you'll be up early."

She nodded, glad he was giving her an out. She didn't want to talk to him any more about topics that might get her in trouble, no matter what promises he made to keep her opinions to himself. "Yes, I will." She stood, and he followed her lead and rose. However, now he stood much closer, facing her. Ana was average in height, yet she still had to tip her head to look at him. It was no wonder; both the king and queen were rather tall.

He looked like both of his parents. A rough shadow covered a strong chin and jawline, inherited from the king.

A half smile graced full lips and his green eyes shone: both traits from the queen. Standing so close, his scent washed over her, a combination of leather and sandalwood, maybe.

Some part of her wished to lean closer and try to better identify it, but instead she looked down, suddenly embarrassed. "Goodnight, Your Majesty." She curtsied.

"Goodnight, Ana. Thank you for coming to speak with me." His voice was low and husky—from the late hour and being tired, surely, she told herself—and tiny raised bumps spread down her arms.

She bobbed her head and turned to go. Then his hand brushed her arm, calling her attention back to him; even through the fabric, his touch made her skin tingle. "Can we talk again sometime?" he asked.

Part of her was eager to accept, but she shoved the impulse down. Yes, he was handsome, and yes, he seemed kinder than she had expected. But he, and this request, still made her far too nervous. Her indecision showed itself when she finally murmured, "Perhaps." She turned and hurried back inside, leaving him standing in the moonlight.

Chapter Eighteen

MILOS

Milos shouldn't have been as thrilled as he was that Ana was open to talking with him again. There was just something ... irresistible about her. And something about her guardedness made him want to earn her trust, to help her see he wasn't the same as the royals and nobles she—perhaps rightfully—despised. It didn't hurt that she was intelligent, quick-witted, and beautiful.

He still needed to be careful not to damage her reputation. His own would survive regardless, but a woman's reputation was much more fragile than any man's. He couldn't keep her late every night talking when she was up early to work, yet he wasn't sure how else to spend time with her that wouldn't garner attention.

His father demanded his presence in advisory meetings and other duties more than ever before. When he had a spare hour here and there, Milos found himself gravitating toward parts of the castle where he might find Ana. He didn't interrupt her work—he didn't even always show himself, which felt a little creepy, but he told himself it was to protect her more than anything. It took very little for rumors to develop and spread in the court.

He overheard a conversation between Ana and one of the other girls one afternoon—Livia? Lisa? Something like that. He listened intently from a shadowed spot in a hallway off the kitchens as the other girl helped Ana prepare a tea tray for his mother.

"How's your brother doing? Have you heard anything?" the other maid asked. Lisia! That was it.

"No. It's difficult for my family to send messages, so I won't really know until I can go back home."

"Your monthly leave is soon, right? Next week?"

"Yes, in five more days. Mistress Danias was kind enough to ensure it overlapped with my older brother's wedding. It will be in Sonos Harbor, so hopefully Aldo feels well enough for the trip."

"Oh, that's right! I forgot you told me he was engaged—to the innkeeper's daughter, right? A wedding! That will be fun! I wish I could go too." Lisia sounded wistful. She gave Ana no chance to reply, instead hurrying off to get back to work with a wave. "Ah well. I'll see you after supper."

Milos immediately moved out from the shadowy recess and made the quick decision to go into the kitchens to grab a snack, so it wouldn't seem as though he had been doing ... what he was doing. Ana passed him with a murmured, "Your Highness," and he nodded and smiled like a fool. Then mentally kicked himself for not at least saying, "Hello, Ana," in return.

He grabbed a fresh roll that was probably meant for someone's afternoon tea, but Mistress Danias was fond of him and wouldn't ever begrudge him anything from her kitchens. He munched as he headed outdoors for some fresh air before the next required meeting. A brisk autumn breeze ruffled his hair, but he was lost in thought and hardly noticed.

Ana would be gone next week, for at least two full days. What would he do with his spare moments? He scoffed at himself for being ridiculous when the thought entered his mind. He had plenty of things to occupy his time. Yet he would miss seeing her around.

At the thought of Ana not being there, an idea occurred to him. He wanted to spend more time with her, yet it was nearly impossible ... at the castle. But she'd be *out* of the castle next week. What if he could *also* be out of the castle? Maybe he could find an excuse his father would accept that would allow him to ride over to Sonos Harbor for a day.

The idea of seeing her away from their usual environment made his stomach flutter. What did she act like at home? With her family? He didn't understand why he wanted to know so badly, but he did. Would she be angry if he showed up? Hopefully not if he had some valid reason—a state reason—to be there. He'd have to work on that, but he had … what had she said? Five days. He could do that. He nodded decisively to himself and returned to the castle.

He was too busy the following couple of days to check in on Ana much. Finally, he was able to have breakfast with his mother and Henriella, which also meant getting a glimpse of the lovely maid. He wanted to ask his mother for ideas of a reason he needed to go to Sonos Harbor. He'd have to tell her he wanted a break from his father—which was true—and not mention Ana at all. He felt mildly guilty about that, yet not enough to change his plans.

Ana was leaving as he came down the hall. He straightened his back and smiled at her. "Good morning, Ana."

Her smile was small, but present. "Good morning, Your Highness."

And then she was off down the hallway and he was through the door. He repressed a sigh; a few meaningless words and hurried smiles exchanged with her every week was simply not enough.

His mother and Hen both seemed distracted, which was all the better for him; they didn't question him much about why he wanted to go to Sonos Harbor specifically. He mentioned wanting the calming presence of the ocean before winter storms made it too inhospitable. His mother was always sympathetic to the pull of the sea that ran in her family's line. She grew up on the coast of Orakolas; the origin story of her people claimed that their ancestors were sea-folk, tragically forced to seek safe haven on land by a vengeful sea goddess.

"I can't think of anything you'd need to do in Sonos Harbor, specifically. But Tirano won't know where you are once you leave..." She tapped a long, elegant finger on the table as she considered. Then her eyes lit up. "Maybe you could say you've found a noblewoman to court and you want to visit her family estate."

Henriella immediately shook her head. "No, Tirano will want to know details about that, and he'll follow up. He's too determined for Milos to marry as soon as possible."

Milos nodded in agreement.

Anela exhaled through her nose. "Yes, I suppose you're right."

They finally decided the most reasonable thing would be to say he was going to make sure all the fighting at the border was over and done with. They hadn't received a message from the general recently, nor was the army returned, so it was a logical action to take.

He would need more than two days for the task, though, and he'd need to come back with actual information. So he'd go to Sonos Harbor first, and then to the Kaosudan border before returning home. Now he needed to present the idea to his father. It was a solid excuse to leave, so he was hopeful.

Still, he had to make an effort to hide his relief when his father not only agreed but also seemed mildly pleased with Milos's "proactive consideration." Since he wasn't leaving Revas, Milos convinced Tirano that he didn't need a full retinue; Bristio would be sufficient. Satisfied, he informed his guard and prepared for their journey.

When the day arrived, they departed mid-morning. He knew Ana had left at least an hour prior, but she was on foot. He figured it was worth trying to catch up with her, feigning coincidence, and then maybe she'd allow one of them to offer her a ride. If she didn't want to ride with him, he'd happily offer his horse and walk alongside. He'd happily do just about anything to be in her presence outside of the castle and for more than a few minutes.

He shook his head at the thought as they rode through the city. "You ridiculous, pining pup," he muttered.

"What was that, Your Highness?" Bristio turned his sharp gaze on Milos.

"Nothing," Milos said.

He kept his cloak hood up, hoping no one would recognize him. His father had kept him too busy to come into the city during the day as he wanted, but now that he had made it, he couldn't help noticing Ana was right: there were far too many hungry looking urchins in the streets. He ordered Bristio to give them some coin. Bristio gave him a curious look but complied.

His plan worked—almost. They caught up with Ana. Unfortunately, she already had company. She was still well ahead when he recognized her; the hood of her cloak was down, and her dark curls, loose for once, shone in the sun. She was on a horse, with a man walking alongside, as well as one more unknown person on a second horse—a woman, it looked like. Perhaps her parents?

Damn.

He made Bristio leave the road to take a more circuitous route. As much as he wanted to know who accompanied her, it would be too awkward to run into her right now. It seemed odd that her parents would take the time to escort her, given how occupied they'd be with the wedding preparation.

Bristio looked askance at the detour, but Milos waved him off. "I want to avoid other travelers for now. You know I'm more likely to be recognized on the road, where there isn't a city full of busy people to blend in with."

When they arrived at Sonos Harbor, and then the inn, Milos saw no sign of Ana or her companions. Even taking a longer route, he had beat them there.

Bristio tried to obtain a room at the inn, but thanks to the impending wedding, there were no vacancies. The guard strode across the bustling innyard to tell Milos.

"Apparently there's a wedding here tonight. Do you want me to let them know who you are?" They both knew the innkeeper would clear out a room if he was aware.

Milos dismounted nimbly and shook his head. He didn't wish to displace any family of the bride or groom. "No. Ask if we can sleep in the stables."

They were granted permission, although the stables were fuller than usual as well. Still, there was an empty stall with fresh hay for the horses, and no one had claimed the loft, which would do well enough for the two men.

The stable hands were somewhat overwhelmed, but Milos and Bristio didn't mind tending to their own horses.

Once they finished, they went inside and found a table in the dining room.

When a serving girl came to take their orders, Bristio asked, "When will the wedding party start? We don't wish to intrude."

"Just after sunset," the girl said, smiling. "It's my older sister who is marrying. You're welcome to attend—as long as you have coin," she amended. "We have a couple of other guests who aren't here for the wedding either, and they'll be down here with us tonight. It will be a merry time." She eyed Milos with curiosity; his hood was still pulled over his head, but surely she could tell he was young and male. "Please do come, if you can."

"We just might." Bristio smiled at the girl, and then they ordered their ale.

After they enjoyed their refreshment, the two men walked down to the docks. A few fishing boats bobbed in the water; one big trade ship dominated the space. The closer to winter it was, the fewer traders they'd see.

Milos led them to the adjacent beach next. They sat on boulders at the edge of the sand, facing the ocean.

"This is why we're here, then?" Bristio asked, gesturing at the water.

Milos didn't look at him, only nodded.

"We're sleeping in the stables so you can spend an hour on the beach?" Bristio's tone was shrewd, but Milos still avoided eye contact with the old guard. "I'm not buying it."

The prince shrugged. "Does it really matter why I wanted to come?"

Bristio huffed a laugh. "I suppose not. I go where you go, regardless. However, I appreciate it when you're up front with me. It makes it easier to do my job."

Milos sighed and turned to meet the older man's serious

gaze. "Point taken. I suppose no one likes to be kept in the dark. Sometimes I just wish..." He wished no one cared what he did and why; he wished for privacy. But that didn't matter. He cleared his throat. "I happen to know someone who will attend this wedding. The sister of the groom."

"Ah, a girl. I should have known. And she invited you?"

Milos ducked his head, kicking his boot against the rock. "Not exactly."

Bristio blew out a breath. "All right. I appreciate you telling me, so I won't pry any further."

A corner of Milos's mouth quirked up. "Thanks."

Wishing to stay out of the way while the family prepared the inn for the wedding party, once they returned they obtained some bread and cheese, then kept to the stables. Bristio cleaned his weapons, and Milos fell asleep for a short while. He woke at sunset, and his heart immediately sped up. It was almost time.

They heard the hubbub when the newlyweds and their families arrived at the inn. Soon after, the prince and his guard made their way inside and managed to find a couple of seats. Simple decor involving pine boughs woven through with colorful ribbons added to the already festive atmosphere—quite a clever substitute for flowers, as it was too late to harvest summer blossoms. The clean, crisp scent helped to distract from the stuffiness of the crowded space.

Cloak hood still up, Milos scanned the crowd for Ana. He finally found her, across the room, sitting with her family—he assumed. A middle-aged couple leaned in close to each other, while Ana spoke with a pale, sickly looking boy. That must be the younger brother. Her older brother sat separately with his bride as friends and family members gave various speeches and food was served table by table.

Milos ate the stew mechanically, barely tasting it. When would he be able to talk to Ana? What should he say?

When most had finished eating, tables and chairs were pushed against the walls to make room for dancing. A fiddler started up, and Milos attempted to make his way over to Ana, looking down at the floor to escape notice as he bumped shoulders with the wedding guests.

But before he reached her, another man stopped at her table and spoke with her, offering his hand. She took it—worse, she accepted with a genuine and beautiful smile—and they joined the other dancing couples. Milos's stomach sank.

Chapter Nineteen

VERANA

Ana was happy the ceremony was over. It had gone smoothly, but Leo and Jesmina had chosen to hold it at the beach rather than the temple. She didn't blame them, as the temple was dark and depressing, and Pastro Emilio was cooperative enough about a different location. But the wind coming off the ocean at sunset had been icy.

As she listened to the speeches and toasts, her mind wandered back to her journey earlier in the day. She had come across a mother and son headed to Sonos Harbor to deliver a message and some goods to a trade ship, and they offered to accompany her, the young man even insisting she ride his horse.

His name was Benito, or Ben for short. The two were from the western region of Revas and had come to the city looking for work after Ben's father passed and his sister married.

"It just wasn't feasible to remain without my husband's income," Viv, Ben's mother, had explained.

"So you'll stay in the capital permanently?" Ana asked,

secretly hoping the answer was yes. Because the truth was, while she still didn't wish to rush into marriage, Ben was handsome and charming. She wouldn't mind spending more time with him. Not at all.

She told them about her position in the castle, among other things.

"You serve the queen in particular?" Viv asked. "That's quite impressive. Do you know a maid named Lisia? I met her one day while she was on an errand in the city. Lovely girl."

"Yes! Lisia is a good friend of mine."

Ana had insisted they stay for the celebration as thanks for accompanying her on the road, and to her delight, they agreed.

Her mind snapped back to the present when the music started. Only moments later, Ben stood before her. "May I have this dance, Miss Ana?" He smiled down at her, showcasing a dimple in one cheek. He really was pleasant to look at: tall and trim, with golden tan skin, wavy light brown hair, and hazel eyes. She even liked the scar which ran through one eyebrow over his forehead. It made him less perfect and more approachable. And, she admitted to herself, it gave him an exciting, rakish kind of air, even though he had been nothing but a perfect gentleman.

She accepted, heart pounding. She surreptitiously wiped her sweating palms on her skirt as they joined the other couples.

"You look beautiful." Ben leaned down to be heard over the noise. "I hope it isn't too presumptuous of me to say so."

A flush crawled up her neck as he led her through the steps. Her dress was nothing special, but she had taken time to arrange her hair in a pretty style, half up with curls framing her face. "I don't think it is. And thank you." She paused, unsure. She rarely made any efforts at flirting. "You look handsome too."

He smiled. "Why, thank you. I've been told I clean up rather well."

They soon eased back into the casual conversation they had on the journey. Halfway through their second dance, someone approached from behind Ben and tapped his shoulder. "May I cut in?"

Ben's brows drew together when he glanced back at the other man, but he released her and bowed politely. "I hope to spend more time with you this evening, Miss Ana. Thank you for the dance."

As he moved away, the stranger pulled the hood of his cloak back a touch—why wear a cloak, she wondered, as the room was overly warm from so many bodies—and Ana finally got a good look at him. Her eyes grew impossibly wide.

Milos. What was the prince of Revas doing at her brother's wedding? He smirked down at her.

She automatically allowed him to step in and take over the lead, one hand in hers and the other at her waist. Smirk still in place, he spoke as he gently guided their movement. "Hello, Ana. Congratulations to your family."

She blinked several times before she could find words. "What are you doing here? Your Highness." The formality was tacked on as an afterthought.

He winced. "None of that here. No one has recognized me, and I prefer for it to remain that way."

Hence the cloak, she supposed. She leaned closer and spoke low-voiced. "If I call you Milos, they'll still know."

"Fair enough. Call me Vincento. It's one of my middle names."

She nodded, her mind racing in its attempt to explain this strange situation. He led her in a spin, then pulled her back against him, closer this time, surprising her with his skill in dancing. His body was firm and warm against hers.

"Will that man be angry that I stole his lovely dance partner?" He smelled of leather and sandalwood still, and a tiny bit like mint.

She opened her mouth, then shut it and shook her head. "I doubt it. I barely know him."

His brow rose and his smile grew. "He's not courting you? I assumed..."

She tilted her head, studying him. Why would he care?

"No. I made his acquaintance only hours ago. And you still haven't told me what in the world you're doing here." She raised an eyebrow, expectant. "And why you're dancing with me, of all people."

His half-smile was impertinent. "Who else?"

The song ended, but the next started immediately and Milos didn't release her. All right then.

"What do you mean, who else? Shouldn't you be in a ballroom somewhere dancing with a princess?" she hissed, starting to lose patience.

His smirk faded. "Probably. But I don't want to dance with a princess. I want to dance with you."

She could only stare, speechless. Was he implying ... no. Impossible.

Movement in her peripheral vision distracted her. Her father approached them and gave Milos a hard look. "May I cut in?" The words were polite … the tone was less so.

Milos bowed formally. "Indeed, my good sir." He snuck a wink at Ana and strolled away. She stared after him, struggling to understand what was happening. He joined another vaguely familiar, older man—one of the royal guards, although she couldn't remember his name.

Her father stepped into her view to take Milos's place. He took her hand with a concerned expression. "You didn't look like you were enjoying yourself. Was he bothering you?"

"I—I wasn't—he wasn't," she stuttered. "I mean, no, not bothering me. He's a little irksome. In an endearing way, I suppose."

Luciano cocked his head. "I see. Has my little girl found someone worthy of courting her? Or perhaps ... more than one suitor?" He glanced to the side and she followed his gaze, seeing Ben dancing with his mother.

Her cheeks burned. "Papa, stop. No one is courting me."

He chuckled. "Not for lack of trying, it seems."

At the idea of the prince of Revas attempting to court her, she burst out laughing. The hilarity soon overwhelmed her, and her father led her off the dance floor. He handed her a mug of ale with a perplexed expression, the corners of his mouth twitching. They leaned against a wall, surveying the room.

"What was that about?" he asked once she had recovered.

She shook her head. "Nothing, Papa. Perhaps I've had a little too much ale."

"Was the idea of someone wishing to court you so funny? It shouldn't be. You're a smart, beautiful young woman, Ana."

She smiled at the love and pride in his eyes but couldn't help pointing out the obvious. "And poor as dirt."

He moved abruptly, pushing off the wall and standing to face her, hands gripping each of her shoulders. "The amount of money in your pocket does *not* dictate your worth, Verana Elisa. No matter what anyone says. Understand? *Any* man would be fortunate to wed you."

Surprised at the intensity of his response, she nodded. "Yes, Papa."

His grip loosened and his gaze grew fond. "I'm so proud of you, daughter. You deserve everything you desire."

He drew her into a hug, and she laid her cheek on his broad chest, warmth spreading through her as his words sank in. "Thank you, Papa."

Her father returned to her mother and Aldo, and Ana looked around, not even sure who she hoped to find. Ben? Milos? Both?

She found neither, and the sharp stab of disappointment surprised her. She shook it off as best she could; she was there to celebrate her brother and Jesmina, not to trail after a handsome man—or two—like a lost pup.

She danced one set with Leo, and then once more with her father. At that point, Aldo was barely able to keep his eyes open. She insisted to her parents she would take him home on her own. "Your oldest son only marries once. You should stay and enjoy this."

She said her goodbyes to Leo, Jesmina, and Jesmina's family, and they left to seek out their borrowed horse, as Aldo was unable to walk from the village to the harbor. Remembering their race home in the summertime, when he was whole and healthy, caused a sharp ache to bloom in her chest.

Luciano accompanied them to the stables. Once Ana mounted, he deposited Aldo in front of her so she could keep him steady. They draped an extra blanket over him, and then the two departed.

His clothes hid the devastating reality of how thin he

was, but she could feel it when she wrapped an arm around his waist, holding the reins with her other hand. She blinked back the sudden tingle of tears.

As the horse stepped away from the stables, someone said, "Ana, wait."

She turned to find the voice in the darkness. Milos stepped out of the shadows.

"Please, may I accompany you home?"

Her mouth dropped open. The prince hadn't left, after all—but why? What in the Seven's names was he doing?

She finally managed a response. "It's not necessary, Your—" She cut herself off. "Thank you, Vincento, but we will be fine. I know the way well."

"Please," he said again, green eyes pleading. "It's late and I want to make sure you're safe. It will only take me a moment to get my horse."

She inclined her head, too tired to argue. With as weak as Aldo was, she recognized it wasn't a terrible idea for someone else to come along. Why it would be the prince, however, she had no idea. Maybe he would satisfy her curiosity with some sort of logical explanation for his presence. "Fine, if you insist."

"I do. Thank you, Ana."

Milos headed into the stables and returned with his horse a few minutes later. She introduced him to Aldo as Vincento, and Aldo said, "It's a pleasure, Vincento. I'd shake your hand, but..." He waved his right arm, the sleeve wrapped and pinned around the stump of his wrist, and gave a weak grin. Ana and Milos both laughed with him, even though her stomach twisted at the joke.

They set off in silence, the late hour weighing more heavily on Ana now that she had stepped away from the excitement of the party. At least the clouds were thin, allowing two of the three moons to light their way.

As they drew nearer to the village, Milos's soft voice broke the quiet. "Are you both doing all right? Do you need a break?"

Ana shook her head and kept her voice soft. "I'm fine. He fell asleep, I think. Best to get him home and in bed."

Another few beats passed before Milos said, "May I ask what happened to his hand? I remember you saying he had been ill. We need not speak of it if you'd rather not."

She tightened her grip around her brother, as though she could protect him from something that had already happened. "I don't mind. He cut himself and the wound festered. If the pastro didn't take his hand, he would have died."

Milos inclined his head. His voice was so low, Ana barely heard it. "I'm sorry."

"Thank you. So am I." She hesitated, not sure why she wanted to tell him more, but gave in to the impulse. "He was an artist. He can't draw anymore. At least, not like before. And he barely has the energy anyway. He hasn't regained his strength."

Milos nodded, blowing out a breath, but said nothing. What was there to say? She appreciated that he didn't try to offer vague, unhelpful platitudes.

Changing the subject, she said, "You're a very good dancer, by the way. I suppose that's a required skill for a prince?"

He chuckled softly. "Thank you. And yes, to an extent. I quite enjoy music, so for me, the required dance lessons were a good excuse to partake."

Ana gave a nod. "I love music too. Do you play an instrument? My papa does."

It was silent for a beat. “I wanted to, but no. My father wouldn’t allow it. He said I had more important lessons to attend to.”

Sympathy washed over her at his tone. Being a prince brought more limitations than she realized. “I’m sorry. It’s not too late; maybe you can still learn someday.”

He inclined his head, saying nothing.

When they reached the moonlit cabin at the edge of the woods, Milos insisted on helping her get Aldo inside. She knew it would be difficult for her to accomplish without a few bumps and bruises, so she accepted, pushing aside her embarrassment at a member of the royal family seeing the inside of their humble home. To his credit, he gave nothing away, no hint of judgement in either his expression or his words.

Once Aldo was settled in her old bed, she found Milos sitting at her kitchen table in the lantern light. He looked so out of place that she stopped quite suddenly, honestly surprised he was still there.

“May I help you tend to the horse?” he asked.

She shook her head. “I need to walk him over the neighboring farm. We don't have a safe place to keep him overnight.” Especially near the forest, animals needed to be protected against roaming wild beasts, and the horse wouldn't fit inside the goat shed.

He stood. “I'll come with you.”

A tingling feeling spread in her chest at his concern for her safety. But she didn't show that reaction. Instead, she huffed and rolled her eyes. “It's not far. I've done it before.” Not strictly true. She had walked the horse back over in the daylight. If it was night, Luciano or Leo always did it.

“Lead the way.” He waved a hand toward the door. “I'll be right behind.”

"You are so stubborn," she grumbled.

He chuckled. "We already established that."

"Fine," she said as they stepped outside. "You may escort me, but only if you tell me what you were doing at the Sonos Harbor inn, of all places."

He pulled the door shut behind him. "It's a state matter, actually. All I can say is I'm on my way to the Kaosudan border, and we stopped for a night or two at the harbor."

She chewed the inside of her lip as she took the reins and tugged, encouraging the horse to walk. "Sonos Harbor is hardly on the way to the border."

He shrugged and said nothing at first, leading his own horse alongside. It was too late and she was too tired, so she let the matter drop. A few minutes later, he spoke. "What if I told you I came to see you?"

She stumbled over her own feet in surprise, but managed to catch herself, only yanking the reins a little. "Sorry, boy," she murmured, patting the beast. To Milos, she said, "Very funny. I wouldn't believe a word of that story."

"Why not? Is it so impossible to think I might want to spend time with you?"

His words echoed her father's from earlier in the evening and her heart tripped as her feet had, missing a beat. He couldn't be saying what she thought. "Do you have so few friends? Is that it?"

His response was measured, deliberate. "I'd be honored if you consider me a friend. However, it is not friendship I lack."

What in the Seven did that mean? But they had reached the neighbor's small stable, and she didn't answer, instead going about the task of tending to the horse. The neighbor's second horse knickered at the commotion, and she took a moment to offer some affectionate pats and rubs, not in a hurry to return to the mystifying man waiting right outside.

She didn't fight him when he offered his mount to ride. He walked alongside, and she wondered what he was thinking but didn't ask. They returned to her cabin without a word. She had no idea what to say or how to interpret what he had said, and she was exhausted.

When they stopped in front of her cabin, he wrapped large hands around her waist and helped her down, still wordless. His touch lingered a beat longer than necessary.

"Thank you," she said, stepping back. His hands dropped from her body, yet she could still feel their heat, or the absence of it. She wanted him to keep touching her, and the thought disturbed her enough that she took one more step away from him.

He inclined his head in acknowledgment with a soft, sweet smile that made her breath hitch.

He bowed. "Thank you for allowing me to escort you, Miss Ana." He turned and mounted his horse, then met her gaze again. "It was a pleasure to spend time with you this evening. I hope... Well. Thank you."

She nodded dazedly. He guided the horse back toward the road, so she stumbled to the door and let herself in. She leaned back against the wood, her head spinning.

The prince of Revas was *not* romantically interested in her. It was impossible. He must have something up his sleeve. And since she didn't know what it was, she must be cautious moving forward. It would be best to avoid him as much as possible. The conclusion made her chest constrict, but she breathed deeply and ignored her body's reaction.

She couldn't afford to care about Prince Milos of Revas.

Chapter Twenty

ANELA

Anela remained on edge after Henriella found the vaguely threatening message, but they hadn't received any others so far. She was glad they had come up with an excuse for Milos to travel, even if it wasn't far or for long. Whatever lurked in the shadows of the castle and court, Anela preferred to keep him far from the threat. Yes, he was an adult—but she was still a mother. The habit was deeply ingrained.

A week passed and Anela finally started to breathe a little easier. Then Tirano summoned her to his quarters.

He was sitting in front of the stone fireplace when she arrived, rather than at his desk. He stared into the flames and didn't acknowledge her until she sat down in the armchair across from him and spoke. "You wished to speak with me?"

Flames danced in his dark eyes when he flicked them to her. "Yes." He held up a scrap of parchment. "I found this folded into a freshly laundered shirt this morning."

Anela swallowed and managed to keep her voice even. "Indeed? What is it?"

Tirano held it up and read aloud, “Your friend did not die a natural death.”

Dread coiled in her belly. She feigned confusion, wrinkling her brow. “How odd. I assume by 'your friend' it references Lord Ruzo?”

Tirano nodded. “That's my assumption as well.”

Anela frowned. “It's a very cruel joke to play. What could be the purpose?”

He met her gaze again, his expression unreadable. “You believe it to be a joke?”

She lifted and dropped a shoulder. “The royal physician proclaimed Lord Ruzo passed of natural causes, correct?” Her heart pounded in her chest so violently she was surprised he didn't hear it.

He inclined his head in agreement. “Yes. Yet physicians are not all knowing. And as you say, if the note is false, what is the purpose of planting it?”

“To sow suspicion and doubt within your court, I suppose. May I see it?”

He handed the parchment to her. She wished she could compare it side by side to the note Henriella had received, but even without doing so, it looked like the same handwriting. “So strange,” she murmured, then handed it back.

They sat in silence, aside from the crackling and popping noises in the hearth. Anela desperately wished to be gone, but she didn't want to seem too eager to be dismissed, so she waited.

The king sat up straighter, and she mimicked him reflexively as he said, “You never liked him.” It was a statement, not a question.

One of her hands curled into a fist within the folds of her skirt, nails biting into her palm. “We learned how to get along over time. He wasn't all that popular in the court at large, as I'm sure you noticed."

He eyed her, and then stood, so she followed suit. "All of the servants who handle or have access to the laundry are currently being questioned. But I don't expect to discover the culprit so easily." The unspoken hung in the air: he *would* discover the culprit.

"As you say, my king." She hesitated. "Since you summoned me, is there something you require of me for your investigation into the matter?"

He shook his head, lips curled in a faint sneer. "No, I don't need your help. But I thought you should be aware."

Anela nodded. So really, he had wanted to see her reaction. "Thank you for keeping me informed, my king."

When he dismissed her, Anela hurried back to her quarters, fighting nausea. Who was behind these notes? What game were they playing? She broke out in a sudden sweat—another one of those damnable episodes.

When she reached her rooms, she instructed the guards she was not to be disturbed. Once in her bed chamber, she kicked off her shoes and wrestled off her outer gown, so she was only wearing her shift when she crawled onto the mattress. She tore pins out of her hair, tossing them aside, before flopping onto her back in a most unqueenlike fashion. Breathing deeply, she waited for the episode to pass, and she thought.

She may have no choice but to take Henriella and run. They would be welcomed back in Orakolas. Yet she'd also put her brother's kingdom at risk of war if they did so. What other options did she have?

She could go to Libeverro or maybe Kampatos. The monarchs there may not be willing to protect her, but perhaps she and Hen could simply go into hiding and try to build a normal life.

She snorted softly to herself. With what skills? The ones she had learned wouldn't be much use for earning a living, especially as she wasn't all that good at them—embroidery and the like. No, if they left, she'd need to be able to take a good amount of gold as well, which presented a different set of challenges.

Rolling from her back to her side, Anela stared at the large, elaborately carved wardrobe. As reluctant as she was to admit it, she needed to tell Henriella what was going on. She was involved in the whole mess, if unknowingly, and Anela felt it wrong to make any life-changing decisions on her own when it affected both of them.

She groaned at the conclusion. Henriella was going to be *so* angry with her.

Before she lost her nerve, she rose and went into the sitting room to call through the door to the guards. "Send a servant to fetch Lady Henriella for me, please."

"Yes, Your Majesty."

She didn't bother dressing again; the dress was too difficult to put on by herself, and Henriella had seen her in less.

When Henriella arrived, Anela was pacing across the plush carpet, anxiety getting the better of her in all respects. She halted in the middle of the room as Hen shut the door behind her.

When her friend looked her over, her eyebrows rose. "Whatever is wrong?" She walked over to Anela and took her hand, leading her to an armchair. "Sit. What happened?" Hen scooted the other armchair a bit closer and sat down as Anela tried to determine where to start.

"You know that note you found?" Hen nodded. Anela swallowed and continued. "Tirano found a similar one. I think it was the same handwriting. But his said that Lord Ruzo's death wasn't natural."

Hen's jaw dropped open. "It—he—what? That doesn't make any sense."

Anela shut her eyes briefly, then forced them back open. She should at least have the courage to look Hen in the face as she explained all she had kept from her.

"But it does. Unfortunately." She took a single deep breath. "There's something I need to tell you."

Hen's gaze narrowed. "And what is that?"

The story poured out of her, starting with Lord Ruzo approaching her in the gardens to blackmail her and ending with her earlier meeting with Tirano.

"Someone knows, Hen. Someone knows everything, or at least suspects. I don't know who it is, or how they discovered any of it. I don't know what they want and what I can do to stop them from exposing everything. And if Tirano finds out... Only the Seven can predict what he might do."

All of the color had drained from Hen's face, leaving her usually rosy skin looking sickly. Her smile was wan and barely there as she replied, "Oh, I don't think we need the Seven's help to know what he'll do."

Anela waved a hand with a bark of semihysterical laughter. "Yes, we're aware of the general idea, but he likes to get *creative*."

Henriella inclined her head in acknowledgment, then looked away, staring at the dying fire. "I can't believe you didn't tell me, Nel." Her voice was soft and full of hurt.

Anela rose and then dropped to her knees in front of Henriella, taking a hand in both of hers. "I was trying to protect you. I'm so sorry. I should have told you." She tried to blink away the tears that rose. "You have every right to be angry with me."

Henriella pressed her lips together into a hard line as she pulled her hand away, crossing both arms over her chest. "I am. 'Angry' isn't strong enough to describe how I feel, in fact. Livid. Betrayed. Those might be more accurate."

"I—I understand." Anela had nothing left she could say. Perhaps she had done permanent damage to their relationship, and the realization made her stomach twist. "If you want to leave…" She wasn't sure what she meant—leave the room? Leave Anela in the larger sense? She couldn't bring herself to finish the sentence.

The other woman shut her eyes for a breath. When she opened them, her blue gaze was sharp with resolve. Anela held her breath, waiting.

Henriella leaned down and cupped Anela's face with her free hand. "I am angry, and hurt. Yet it changes nothing—not how I feel about you, nor the situation. I'll move past it." She brushed her lips over Anela's trembling mouth. "I accept your apology. But you can't keep me in the dark anymore. We need to come up with a plan. Together. All right?"

Anela inhaled deeply, placing her hand over Hen's and giving it a squeeze. Then she rose, returning to her chair. She made an effort to control her emotions, including the wave of relief washing over her at Hen's forgiveness. She swallowed hard, then cleared her throat. "Yes, we do."

Chapter Twenty-One

MILOS

The journey to the Kaosudan border wasn't pleasant. The weather was turning cold, and Bristio was still angry that Milos had snuck off on his own the night of the wedding.

"You risk your life over some silly girl," he had snarled once Milos returned to the inn. "I have been patient with you. I keep your secrets. The least you could do is show me some respect and let me do my job instead of sneaking off like a damned..." He had held back whatever name he wanted to call Milos, but Milos got the gist. Bristio treated him more like a son than a prince much of the time—which Milos secretly appreciated—yet the guard still wouldn't allow himself to insult a royal.

Once Bristio regained a semblance of calm, he continued. "Your welfare is my primary concern, but you might consider keeping in mind that if something happens to you on my watch, my life is forfeit as well."

He hadn't outright called Milos selfish, although that was the implication, and Milos couldn't blame him. He recognized that he could be a bit heedless and impulsive, even if he thought the old man worried too much. He was able to defend himself, after all; hours upon hours of training for the last fifteen years ensured his capability.

He had apologized. Bristio had accepted, but he maintained a stony silence for most of their journey. Milos knew the old guard would get over it eventually.

Milos spent too many of the quiet hours remembering every word of his conversations with Ana, and contemplating his true feelings for her. Sadly, he reached few conclusions, aside from what he already knew: he liked her. A lot. And it wasn't only that he wanted to sleep with her, although the thought crossed his mind more than once. That urge would have been much more easily ignored, or redirected, than the knot of complicated feelings he experienced whenever he thought about her.

When Milos and Bristio reached the army camp, they found no active battle. Most of the Kaosudan army had dissipated, but the Revasian soldiers would remain in place to guard the border for the time being. The general had received intelligence that the Kaosudans weren't truly finished, and were instead attempting a ruse; only time would tell.

They remained at the camp for several days, but there wasn't any purpose in staying longer. Milos promised to send more supplies, and then they headed back to the capital.

Their travel was blessedly uneventful, aside from more rain than was enjoyable. They rode through the castle gates midafternoon, just under two weeks after they had departed.

Milos knew he should seek out one or both of his parents first, but instead he wanted to find Ana. On their way back, he had almost convinced himself it was likely only a passing infatuation. He wanted to test his theory by gauging how he felt when he saw her again.

He found her as she returned to the kitchens with the remains of his mother's tea. She didn't see him at first, and he watched her as she deposited the tray and went about taking care of the dishes. As he observed, he realized the feeling in his stomach and the tightness in his chest indicated he had not gotten over his "infatuation."

When she entered the hallway, he stepped out from the shadowed recess. She ground to a halt, startled.

He offered a gentle smile. "I'm sorry. I didn't mean to frighten you."

Already regaining her composure, she curtsied. "Welcome home, Your Highness." The words were polite, but her tone was flat and formal. "If you'll excuse me."

She took a deliberate step to the right and moved around him, and he nearly tripped over himself in his attempt to follow her. Stumbling, he righted himself, falling into step beside her. "Are you well, Ana?"

She gave a curt nod. "Quite, Your Highness."

He frowned. Something was different about her. "I'm glad to hear it." Against his better judgement, he lowered his voice to ask, "Will you meet me tonight in the courtyard, so we can talk?"

She shook her head. "I really shouldn't, Your Highness. You must realize that."

In fact, he did. But he didn't care. He tilted his head. "Why not? It harms no one."

She stopped and faced him, hands on her hips. "Are you giving me an order, master to servant, to meet you tonight? Or are you inviting me as a friend?"

"The latter. As a friend." His heart sped up, waiting for her answer.

She sighed. "Thank you for clarifying. I must decline your invitation. Good day, Your Highness." She turned on a heel and hurried away.

That hadn't gone as he'd hoped. Was she angry with him? If so, for what possible reason? Because he escorted her home like a gentleman and spoke with her as a man does with a woman, rather than as a prince to a servant? By the Seven, why would she be mad about that?

Maybe she wasn't. Maybe she understood what he'd been trying to tell her ... and she wasn't interested. The possibility felt like a knee in the groin, but for his ego. He reluctantly admitted to himself that he wasn't accustomed to women turning him down, whether they knew he was royal or not. He was good looking and charming, but more than that, unlike some men, he truly enjoyed the company of women. And they could usually tell.

He rubbed a hand over his face, releasing a breath. He'd worry about it later. For now, he shouldn't put off his duty any longer. He would find his father first to give his report, then check in with his mother to let her know he was back.

An hour later, both tasks were completed. His parents seemed on edge, but neither gave him any pertinent news, so he dismissed it. If they wouldn't tell him, he didn't need to worry about it.

His father required nothing of him for the remainder of the day, so Milos returned to his quarters to clean himself up and change into fresh clothes. He had a couple of hours until supper. After Ana's tepid reception and his parents' jitteriness, he felt restless.

He considered finding Bristio and dragging him into the

city. Maybe he could purchase a gift for Ana to apologize for whatever he might have done wrong.

But when he walked out of the castle to find his travel guard, it started to rain. The wind picked up, and he took pity on Bristio, as they had already ridden through the miserable autumn rain for days.

Still, he didn't want to be indoors. He drew his hood up and meandered the grounds.

The sting of Ana's rejection lingered. He thought he had been making progress toward earning her trust, but apparently not. He shouldn't care. He should leave her alone and move on. Yet something in his core desperately fought against that reasonable conclusion. He wouldn't give up quite yet.

After half an hour, thoroughly wet and chilled, he turned toward the kitchen gardens. The rain came down harder, so his gaze was on the ground when he bumped into someone.

When he looked up, Ana's startled gray eyes met his gaze from under her hood. "I'm so sorry, Your Highness. Please excuse me."

She attempted to step around him, but he moved to block her. "Why are you out in this miserable weather?"

She grimaced. "Mistress Danias needs me to fetch something in the city."

His eyebrows rose. "In this? It can't wait?"

She scowled at him. "If it could wait, she wouldn't have sent me."

"What is it? I can fetch it for you."

Her head tilted in confusion. "Why would you do that? You're not an errand boy."

He shrugged and smiled. "To save you the trouble."

"I don't know." She looked uneasy. "I don't think

Mistress Danias would like it. It's my task, and you're..." She trailed off, waving a hand. "What might she say if she realized you, of all people, did it for me?"

He saw her point. He hadn't thought it through when he offered, but he had tried to be careful thus far to not give any reason for rumors to spread about his interest in Ana.

"You have a point." He turned to stand next to her, facing the same direction, and offered an arm. "Then the least I can do is accompany you." His earnest expression pleaded with her to accept. "What are we fetching?"

She eyed him and gave a sharp nod, though she didn't take his arm. "Do what you will. I need to be on my way. Apparently, we have run out of the king's favorite tea and he isn't pleased. The shop should have Mistress Danias's order ready."

He fell into step beside her. "Ah, I see now. My father certainly wouldn't care that he's sending someone out in this mess."

"As you say, Your Highness."

The guard at the gate recognized him. "Your Highness. Is Bristio not accompanying you?"

Milos flinched inwardly. "No need. We aren't going far." Under his breath, he said, "Hurry, let's go."

"Wouldn't you prefer a carriage, Your Highness?" the guard's voice carried after him, fading as they moved farther down the cobblestone street. He would, in fact, prefer a carriage in this downpour. But then everyone would recognize him and speculate as to why Ana was with him.

"You're not supposed to leave without a guard, then?" Ana asked.

"Not exactly," he admitted. "But it's unnecessary. I'm perfectly capable of defending myself for half an hour in the city." He gestured to the dagger on his belt.

They hurried along toward the tea shop, dodging citizens and puddles. The children who were usually out and about with their hands open had taken cover, it seemed. At least, Milos hoped they had somewhere to go to stay dry and warm.

The door to the shop creaked as he pushed it open, and a bell dangling from the top clanged.

"I'll wait here," he murmured and she nodded, leaving him by the door as she approached the counter and took her place in line, lowering the hood of her cloak to reveal her slim neck and her hair twisted into a low bun, with curls escaping every which way. An impulse to move closer and nuzzle the exposed soft skin struck Milos, but he pressed his lips together and stayed put.

The shop was busy, which wasn't surprising given the season. The space smelled earthy and tangy both, with a dozen other lighter notes from the various tea leaves.

The door opened again, admitting a middle-aged burly bear of a man. He quickly selected a canister from one of the shelves and took his place in the line behind Ana, then leaned in and said something to her. Milos couldn't hear the words, but he didn't like the stranger speaking to her. He frowned and inched closer, hoping to listen in on their conversation.

Ana had turned partly, her expression surprised and also wary. "...quite the storm," was all Milos heard, and he breathed a sigh of relief. They were only speaking about the weather.

"You look cold," the man rumbled. "Need a little help warming up?" He reached for her, his hand pushing her cloak aside to grasp her waist as Ana stepped away, bumping into the woman in front of her.

"Watch yourself," the woman hissed. Milos was already

moving toward Ana and the bastard who dared to touch her uninvited.

"No, I don't," Ana replied through gritted teeth, using both of her hands to try to peel the larger one off her body. "Let go of me!"

Milos reached them; the man hadn't even noticed him. He kept one hand on his dagger and used the other to shove the man's shoulder. "She said 'let go,'" he snarled. "Get away from her."

The man's hand dropped out of surprise as he turned toward Milos. Squinty black eyes set in a ruddy face looked him up and down. The two men were about the same height, but the older man was wider, stockier. "Who'll make me? You? You're just a pup. Mind your business." He sneered and turned back toward Ana, who was inching away from him, fists clenched.

The man reached for her again. Milos drew his dagger and placed the tip against the man's ribs in a blink, slicing into the fabric of his dirty tunic. "I said, don't. Fucking. Touch her," he growled.

The man's hand dropped as he gaped at Milos. Other customers turned to stare at the ruckus, and the woman behind the counter said, "Oy! None of that in my shop! Sir, put your blade away this instant, or leave."

Milos slowly lowered the knife, but he didn't take his gaze off the oaf. "Apologues, mistress. We can take this outside if we need to."

The stranger smirked, holding up his hands, one of which still held a canister of tea. "Yeah, yeah, fine. It was just a little joke. Wasn't it, sweetheart?" He flashed a cruel grin at Ana as she edged back to her spot.

She didn't deign to reply, standing straight and stiff in

front of him. She pulled her hood back over her head and wrapped the cloak around her, holding it closed in the front.

Milos spoke quietly to the older man, steel laced into his words. "This is sharp enough to take your hand if you put it on her again." He pointedly looked down at his dagger, which was indeed very fine … and very sharp. The man rolled his eyes, and Milos smiled a slow, predatory smile that had the man leaning away from him.

Satisfied, Milos slipped the knife back into its sheath and remained nearby until it was Ana's turn. The woman gave her the total, and Ana hesitated. "Mistress Danias said it was already paid for."

The shopkeeper checked the ledger in front of her and shook her head. "I don't believe so, dear."

Ana's shoulders fell in defeat. "I shall have to come back then." She turned to go, but Milos had reached the counter. He dug out coins from the pocket at his belt and set them on the wood before grabbing the parcel. "That should cover it."

The woman nodded, making a mark in her records. "Yes, very good. Next!" She waved the older man forward as Milos offered his arm to Ana once again. She hesitated only a brief moment before she took it and he led her out of the shop.

Chapter Twenty-Two

VERANA

Ana shivered as they stepped out of the cozy warmth into the wind and rain. It was markedly darker than twenty minutes prior, but the streetlamps were lit. Ana had only visited the city in daylight, and she was surprised to recognize the same unwavering light cast over the wet roads as the Diona-made sconces in the castle. In those dark halls, the lights never faded. Here in the city, perhaps they were designed to magically detect the darkness, lighting up only after sundown. The Diona must simply ooze with magic.

Milos pulled her a bit closer to his side, and she hated to admit to herself that his presence and his warmth was comforting. She insisted on taking the parcel of tea, so he handed it over.

They walked quietly for a block before she said, "Thank you, Your Highness."

His voice was low. "You're welcome. I only behaved as any gentleman should."

He wasn't wrong, but still... "You're not just 'any gentleman,' are you? Why are you doing this? Why is the royal prince and heir to the throne escorting me on kitchen errands?" Her voice started to rise and he glanced around.

"Shh, let's not announce my presence."

She nodded jerkily and spoke more quietly. "I apologize. But I still want to know *why*." She couldn't make any sense of his behavior. Was he simply bored? Or did he want something from her?

He looked around, then pulled her toward the overhang of a darkened storefront. Even with the shelter, the wind ensured they weren't going to avoid the rain entirely, but it was better than out in the open.

"We can stay here for a bit and see if it lets up." He smiled down at her. She only raised an eyebrow and cocked her head to one side, waiting.

Green eyes flecked with gold and brown pierced her with their stare. She held her breath, only releasing it when he started to speak. "I tried to tell you the night of your brother's wedding. I *like* you, Ana. It's as simple as that."

"Except it's not simple. At all." Her reply was barely a whisper, but he heard. How she wished it *was* that simple. She allowed herself to imagine it: what if Milos was a part of the castle staff, instead of being royal? Would she allow his courtship? She silently admitted to herself that she would not only allow it, she would desire it. Encourage it.

He blew out a breath. "Ana, I don't know what it is about you. There are all the obvious reasons: you're beautiful, intelligent, kindhearted. Yet I've known other women who could also be described as such, and I didn't feel like this for them." Pulling his arms from hers, he moved to face her. He took her free hand in both of his, and she thought she might forget how to breathe entirely as his hooded eyes bore into her.

"I wish to be near you all the time. To see your stunning

face and hear your voice and know that you're safe. To talk with you about anything and everything. To laugh with you and hold you when you cry. And I want to *destroy* any cause of your tears. I wished to kill that man for touching you, for frightening you. I've never felt like this."

She opened her mouth to reply, not even knowing what to say, but he held up a finger. "Let me finish. I'm not asking anything of you that you don't wish to give. And I understand if you don't feel the same way. But if you—" He stopped and shook his head. "I'd like to get to know you better, if you'll let me. I desperately want a chance to earn your trust."

The rain pattered down, yet not as loudly; it was slowing, as he predicted. She swallowed hard against the odd sensation of her heart being in her throat as her brain tried to process his inconceivable confession.

The prince of Revas called her beautiful, stunning even, as well as intelligent and kind. He wished to spend time with her and get to know her. It was all so overwhelmingly sweet ... and ridiculous. Utterly and completely ridiculous and impossible.

"Are you saying you wish to court me?" That's what it sounded like, but she wanted to be very clear.

He ducked his head. "I suppose I am."

"Openly?"

He flinched, meeting her gaze again. "I'm not sure if ... I don't know how it would work."

She pulled her hand back into the folds of her cloak. It felt cold without his warmth. "Exactly. You can't. We can't. Even if I wanted to, this doesn't make any sense. It's not possible. You can't court a maid. A commoner."

His shoulders fell. "Even if you wanted to. Are you saying you don't?"

That was the one part he singled out of her statement? She rolled her eyes in exasperation. "I'm saying it doesn't matter either way!"

He stepped closer, crowding her against the wall of the building. "It matters to me. I want to know how you feel." He placed a hand on the wall above her shoulder, leaning even closer. "Forget everything else. Pretend I'm not royal for the next few moments. Tell me how you feel about me."

It was as though he had read her mind. His warm breath washed over her face as they shared the same air, inches away from each other.

She bit her lip and tried to look down, but he gripped her chin between thumb and forefinger and tilted her face back up. "Don't hide. Just tell me. *Please*, Ana." His palm moved to cup her cheek, and he ran his thumb over her mouth, gently pulling her lip out from between her teeth.

The shake of her head was barely perceptible. "I—I like you. More than I should. And I *want* to trust you, but…" She trailed off with a small shrug.

With a slow, encouraging nod, he said, "That's a start. You can trust me, Ana. I'll prove it to you in time, if you let me."

He sounded so earnest it squeezed her heart. Seemingly of their own volition, her lips moved closer to his, drawn like moths to moonlight. His gaze darkened as he met her partway, barely brushing his mouth against hers, seeking permission. The mere featherlight touch was unlike any kiss she'd ever shared with one of the village boys. It sent a warm, buzzing feeling straight to her stomach, and between her legs. Against her better judgement, she found herself leaning into it.

His hand slid from her face to grasp the back of her

neck. He slid his tongue along the seam of her lips, and she opened for him with a soft moan as her eyes fell shut.

He tasted like mint and rain. His stubble scraped against her as he deepened the kiss, and she shivered, reveling in the sensations. She explored his mouth, and it wasn't until he emitted a low, rumbling groan from deep in his chest that she came to her senses.

She gently pushed him away, feeling breathless. Rather than point out the impossibility of their pairing, she stuck with an excuse he couldn't argue against. "We need to get back. Mistress Danias is waiting for this. I don't want to get in trouble." She held up the parcel.

Panting slightly, he grimaced. "You're right." His voice was like gravel, and the sound rekindled the slowly dying flame in her core. It was all she could do to resist throwing herself at him.

She took his arm and they went. Regret settled in her stomach like sour milk by the time they reached the gates. She shouldn't have kissed him. Caught up in the moment, and his flattery, she had given in to something they wouldn't ever be able to pursue.

Maybe he thought he could have her in secret, but that wasn't going to happen. No way would she give herself to him, physically or emotionally, and then watch him eventually wed a princess or noblewoman. She was well aware that many wedded men at court kept mistresses; the servants always knew, and they talked. But she had no interest in filling the position—not even for the prince of Revas. Despite her station in life, she clung to her father's words: she deserved more.

Several days passed, and fortunately, Milos was kept busy with advisors' meetings, weapons practice, and everything else his duties entailed. She hardly even saw him roaming the castle, but she still regularly used her ability to sense if he was nearby—and when he was, she headed in the opposite direction.

She missed their little daily encounters. She missed the way his eyes softened when he saw her, and she missed the smirk that pulled at his mouth more often than not when they interacted. She missed *him*. But it was for the best.

He would never be hers. It was impossible. And she shouldn't waste her time or energy wishing for the impossible.

One afternoon, one of the young messenger boys found her in the kitchens preparing the queen's tea tray.

"This came for you, Miss Ana," he said, handing her a small, folded piece of parchment.

Her heart sped up as she took the note from him. "Th-thank you," she managed.

No one sent her notes. Her family couldn't afford to send regular messages, but if something was wrong...

She tore it open with shaking hands and immediately recognized Leo's handwriting. Most of the children in their village never learned to read or write, but her father had insisted on teaching all three of them.

"Ana,

Aldo is seriously ill and we fear he may not make it.

Please come. He asks for you.

-Ameleo"

One hand covered her mouth to dampen the cry that escaped her. "Oh no," she whispered. "No, no, no." She stuffed the note in her apron pocket and went to find Mistress Danias.

The head housekeeper gave her permission to go home. "But you should wait for morning, honey. You don't want to travel alone in the dark. Sunset isn't far off."

Ana clenched her fists, frustrated that the older woman was right. But maybe she didn't have to go alone. "I might have someone with a horse who can escort me. A friend in the city. May I go ask?"

Mistress Danias blew out a breath. "Yes, I suppose. Has the queen had her tea?"

Ana, already walking away, stopped in her tracks. "Ugh, by the Seven... No, I was preparing it when I got the message."

The housekeeper nodded. "Go. Lisia or I will take it to Her Majesty."

"Thank you, Mistress," Ana called back over her shoulder.

She made it outside before realizing it was far too cold to leave her cloak behind. Cursing under breath, she rushed back in to retrieve it, then hurried through the courtyard.

As she approached the gates, nearly running, someone called her name. Her head swiveled and found Milos jogging away from the training yard toward her. His shirt was plastered to his body with sweat despite the autumn chill; if she hadn't been in a panic, she might have admired how the fabric clung to the muscles in his arms, shoulders, and chest. As it was, she shoved the observation away, annoyed at the delay.

She slowed but didn't stop. As he reached her, he looked her up and down, taking in her expression.

"I saw you running and I was worried. What's wrong?"

"Nothing you need concern yourself with, Your Highness. I am needed at home." The people milling about the courtyard would notice that she didn't stop for the prince, let alone curtsy. She couldn't bring herself to care.

He grabbed the edge of her cloak, forcing her to halt. "And you're leaving now? By yourself? It's not safe. Let me take you. We can ride."

She stamped her foot in frustration. People were definitely watching now; the Seven could damn them all. She needed to get to her brother. "I didn't ask for your help! I'm not planning to go alone. I have friends in the city. I'm going to ask if one of them can lend me a horse and escort me."

"Friends? Who?" One thick eyebrow raised, skeptical, which irritated her. Just because she wasn't from the city didn't mean she couldn't have friends there.

"Yes, friends. If you must know, they're the ones who traveled with me to Leo's wedding. They were at the party." She yanked her cloak out of his grip. "I need to go!"

His expression morphed into a scowl at her explanation, but she didn't care. She ran full out now despite the wet cobblestones.

She found the shop where Ben's mother had said she worked, and fortunately, Viv was there. She couldn't leave, but she called for Ben. Soon Ana and Ben were riding toward Ana's village.

When they arrived at her cabin, it was full dark.

She dismounted, handing over the reins. "Thank you, Ben."

He cupped her face from the saddle. "Any time, Ana. I mean that."

She gave him a tremulous smile before he led the horses back the way they had come; he would stay the night at the inn in Sonos Harbor. She made her way to the front door and let herself in, taking care to do so quietly.

Her father looked up when she entered. He sat at the

table, picking at a piece of bread, but he discarded it and rose immediately. He looked exhausted.

"Oh, my Ana. I'm so glad you could come." He embraced her and she sank into him, his scent and the feel of him familiar and comforting.

"Is he...?" She couldn't say the word.

"He's still with us," her father reassured. "He's in the bedroom with your mother and the pastro."

She removed her cloak, brow wrinkling at the information. "The pastro? Did he bring medicine?" She still didn't know what ailment Aldo suffered from.

A pained look crossed Luciano's face. "None of the medicine he tried has helped much. He's here to pray." His throat bobbed as he swallowed.

Ana knew what her father meant. The pastros had a specific ritual and prayer for the dead and dying. Fear stabbed at her chest, sharper than the knife that had sliced into her brother's hand all those weeks ago.

"Where's Leo?"

"He had to go back to the inn for a bit, but he'll return soon."

A horrible, hacking cough came from the bedroom. She left her father standing by the table to seek her brother.

Halia sat next to the bed in one of the kitchen chairs. Pastro Emilio stood at the foot of the bed, murmuring what Ana assumed was a prayer. Cecil lay against Aldo's legs, curled into a ball.

Halia rose when she noticed Ana and walked the few steps to embrace her. "Thank you for coming. He's been asking for you." Her face was pale and drawn.

"You know I couldn't stay away, Mama."

Halia nodded and gave her a watery smile. "I'll leave you with him. But call me if anything changes."

Ana swallowed hard. "I will."

Pastro Emilio stepped away from his spot. "I have done all I can. I will wait with your parents."

She took her mother's place in the chair and gripped Aldo's limp hand, which was far too warm. Even with the sheet and blanket drawn over his body, he seemed to have shrunk. He shook with another devastating cough, which left him wheezing.

"Hey, Alleycat," she whispered. "I'm here."

His eyes cracked open. "Ana?"

"Yes, it's me."

"You came. Where ... were you? I ... I looked for you." The words were a struggle, escaping through labored breathing.

She bit her lip hard. He was delirious. "I was in the city. But I came home to see you."

One corner of his mouth lifted in an attempt at a smile. "I'm glad. Missed you."

She swiped away the tears running down her cheeks. "I missed you too. I love you, Alleycat. Always."

"And ... forever?" His eyes drifted shut.

"Yes. Always and forever."

"Tell me ... a story?"

"Which one? The boy and the river spirit?"

"One ... one I don't know." He coughed again, and Ana thought the sound might break her heart. She wracked her brain for a new story and recalled one Lisia had shared. That would do.

"This story is about how the castle in the capital came to be.

When Sonos City was built generations ago, they chopped down many trees for building, as well as for fires to stay warm through the winter.

The king, a young general of the conquering army, sought a wife. One day while out hunting, he met a beautiful maiden in the woods and fell in love with her instantly. But she was a forest spirit in disguise. When she revealed herself to him, he wasn't deterred and begged for her hand in marriage. She promised to be his wife if he ordered his people to cut down fewer trees, which would allow the forest to renew itself as nature intended.

He agreed. They married and he ordered their castle to be built out of stone.

It was quiet for several beats. Ana thought Aldo had fallen asleep. But then he spoke, barely a whisper. She leaned in close to hear him. "Did ... did the forest spirit miss her true home?"

Ana smiled. "I imagine she did. But she made the sacrifice willingly, as nobly as any true queen."

"Hmm," was Aldo's sleepy answer.

Ana sat, watching him breathe, willing his body to keep fighting. Eventually, she heard the front door open and shut, and then murmuring voices. Leo appeared in the doorway and came to her. He knelt and lightly brushed Aldo's hair off his forehead.

"How is he?"

Ana shook her head. "He struggles to breathe. He can barely speak."

Leo ran a hand over his face. "Not any worse than earlier today, then."

"How long has he been sick?" She had been so eager to get to Aldo, she hadn't gotten many details from her parents.

"Since shortly after the wedding. It wasn't so bad, at first. But the last few days..." He shook his head, mouth pressed into a thin line. "He can't eat, he barely drinks, his breathing is much worse."

Leo met her gaze, and she couldn't identify the emotion on his face until he spoke. "If I hadn't married—or if he hadn't attended the wedding, then maybe—" He stopped and swallowed hard. "It was too much for him. Jesmina and I could have waited until spring, and maybe he would have been stronger. I fear this is my fault." A tear escaped, sliding down his cheek, and he brushed it away absentmindedly. "I'm sorry, Ana. I should have taken better care of him. I was too wrapped up in my own concerns."

"No, brother. Don't do this to yourself." Tears flowed freely down her face as she laid a reassuring hand on Leo's broad shoulder. "He wouldn't blame you. We don't blame you. It's no one's fault. Do you hear me?"

Leo exhaled heavily. "Nothing I can do now anyway. I can't change the past."

The truth hung heavy in the stifled air of the sickroom. She knew the feeling. If she had only volunteered to clean the damned fish that day…

What Ana wouldn't give to be able to change the past.

Chapter Twenty-Three

MILOS

Milos waited for Ana to return for two days before he couldn't stand it anymore. On day three, he rose early, had a stable hand ready his horse, and left. He didn't even bother seeking his father's permission. He'd deal with the king later. He sent a message to his mother with a servant; it was vague, but enough that she wouldn't worry about his disappearance.

He arrived at Ana's cabin around midday, bringing the horse to halt at the edge of the yard, unsure how to proceed. It suddenly felt awkward to simply show up unannounced at her door. As he debated, the front door opened and a truly haggard-looking woman emerged. It took him a moment to recognize Ana's mother, she was so changed since her son's wedding. Her hair, usually a vibrant golden blonde, hung limp and dull; her creamy skin was pale, marked by dark half-moons of tiredness.

She stood on the porch, shading haunted blue eyes from the sun with one hand. "Can I help you, sir?"

She must have seen him through the window. He cursed silently to himself.

"Good day, Mistress. I'm a, uh, a friend of Ana's. From the city. I heard she had a family emergency, and I was in the area and wanted to check on her..." He trailed off, afraid she would see through the weak lie.

But the woman didn't question him. She considered him for a moment, then nodded. "My youngest s-son passed away last night." His heart dropped into his stomach hearing the news. She pressed her lips together, a visible attempt to control her emotions. "I don't know if she'll want to see anyone, but I'll ask."

The woman was back inside before he could find the words to offer his condolences to her. Dismounting, he shook out his trembling hands and waited.

Damn the Seven. He knew how much Ana loved her brother. She spoke so fondly of him, and he had seen their bond with his own eyes. Envied it, even, as an only child. She would be devastated. And he couldn't fix this for her.

He hadn't asked what called her home. If he had known, he could have offered money, medicine, anything to help her brother. Why didn't he insist she explain? But then, would she have accepted his help? She was proud. Yet maybe she would have for her brother's sake.

The boy had seemed weak, but not as though he was dying. He must have fallen ill, and now ... now Milos was too late to help. He should have come days ago, he should have followed her out of the city as soon as she left, then maybe—

His thoughts came to an abrupt halt as Ana emerged from the cabin. Her hair was down, dark curls loose and wild, falling past her shoulders. Her face was drawn, smooth light brown skin far too pale.

He moved toward her as she stepped off the porch, his words stuck in his throat. She didn't say anything either. She didn't look surprised at his presence. When he met her sorrowful gray gaze, he opened his arms without thinking. She walked into them, wrapping her own around his middle. He held her close as she laid a cheek on his chest.

"Ana," he finally managed, murmuring into her hair. "I'm so sorry, love." The endearment escaped without thought.

She looked up at him with glassy eyes. "He's gone. My Alleycat is gone." She angled her face down again, squeezing him more tightly as her shoulders began to shake with sobs.

"I know," he whispered. "I'm sorry. I'm here." It was all he could offer, although he was woefully aware it wasn't enough.

As her crying eased, a throat cleared nearby. Milos whipped his head toward the noise; he hadn't heard anyone approach.

It was the man Ana had mentioned, the one from the wedding. Ben. He stood next to his mount, arms crossed, looking mildly irritated. Milos tensed, jaw tightening, although he wasn't sure what it was about the other man that put him on edge.

Ana must have felt his reaction, because she drew her head back and then followed his gaze.

"Oh, Ben. It's you." She pulled away from Milos and he immediately felt the loss. She folded her arms over her stomach and looked at the ground. "Did you hear?"

Ben eyed Milos as he stepped closer, stopping in front of her. He placed his hands on her shoulders and Milos's hands fisted on their own accord, but they paid him no attention.

"Yes, Leo told me. I'm so sorry, Ana."

She nodded jerkily. "Thank you. Um, Ben this is..." She looked toward Milos and her face went blank—probably struggling to remember the false name he had used at the wedding.

Ben stepped back and gave a slight bow. "Prince Milos of Revas. Please excuse me, Your Highness. I knew you looked familiar, but it took me a moment to place you." He paused, looking back and forth between them. "I admit, this is the last place I'd expect to see you."

Milos cleared his throat. He wasn't going to explain himself to this man. "Yes, that's understandable. Don't worry yourself; it is of no consequence. Pleasure to make your acquaintance." It wasn't, yet he didn't wish for Ana to think him abominably rude.

The awkward silence stretched. Milos broke it by asking, "Ana, is there anything you need? Anything I can do to aid your family?"

She shrugged helplessly, looking around the yard like the answer might pop up from behind a tree. "We need to dig his grave, but I can't ask that of you. There's really nothing else."

"I'd be happy to help," Milos said.

At the same time, Ben answered, "I can do that for you, Ana."

Ben gave Milos a tight smile. "Please don't trouble yourself, Your Highness. The ground is already hard from the cold, so it will be a rough task. Such labor is beneath a prince, is it not?"

Milos bristled at the implication that he wasn't strong enough to do the job. He didn't bother to answer, focusing on Ana instead. "Where do you keep the spade? And where do you wish to lay him to rest?"

Her chin trembled again, but she maintained a steady voice. "The spade is out back, by the goat pen. We picked a spot near the creek behind the cabin."

Milos nodded and strode toward the side of the house to go around the back. He heard Ben say, "Four hands will be better than two, I suppose. Does your neighbor have another spade we can borrow?"

Milos didn't pause to hear more. He found the tool leaning against the small goat shed and made his way to the creek, where he waited for someone to instruct him on the exact spot. The water still flowed, but it wouldn't be long before it froze over.

Ana found him a few minutes later. "You really don't need to do this. Ben is fetching another spade, and Leo will be back in a while to help too."

"I *want* to. Please, let me do this for you, Ana. It would mean the world to me." It couldn't begin to make up for how he had failed her, but he had to do *something.*

She gave half a shrug. "If you insist. It's over there." She led him toward a section of ground under an old tree. Most of its orange and yellow leaves had fallen, yet he imagined in the summer it was a lovely spot of shade right next to the water.

"This is a beautiful place for his final rest," he said gently. She inclined her head in agreement; tears welled in her eyes once more, but she blinked them back. He removed his cloak and hung it on a low branch, then the gold-threaded vest, leaving him in his shirt. He left his riding gloves in his pocket; the wood on the spade handle was smooth from use, not a potential splinter to be seen.

He kicked aside most of the leaves and dug the metal into the dirt. The ground had some frost, as Ben said, but it wasn't that bad yet. Ana went back inside, and Ben joined him some twenty minutes later.

They worked in silence for a long while, which suited Milos just fine. Eventually, Halia brought out a bucket and ladle. "The creek water is clean." She set the ladle inside the bucket and left it on the bank, returning to the cabin.

The two men took a break to drink. Ben filled the bucket and they sipped the ice-cold water. Milos caught Ben examining him and raised an eyebrow in challenge. "Yes?"

Ben dropped his gaze, glancing toward the flowing water. "You look more like your mother than your father, despite your coloring. I suppose the same could be said for me."

Milos narrowed his eyes at this odd statement, unsure how to reply. It was true, but why would this stranger notice, or care, which parent he favored?

Ben blew out a breath, still not looking at him. "I don't mean to be impertinent, Your Highness, but why are you here? Your presence is baffling."

"It isn't your concern," Milos replied, picking up the shovel again. "And I could ask the same of you. You aren't part of their family, and you barely know Ana." He thought that was true—all right, maybe it was more of a hope.

"Why do you assume that?" Ben grunted as they dug, each at opposite ends of the hole. "I could be courting her, for all you know."

Milos jammed the spade into the ground with a vicious thrust, thoroughly irritated. "Are you?"

"It isn't your concern," Ben mimicked him. "Y*our Highness*."

Milos's teeth ground together as he resisted the urge to find out how Ben's face felt against his fist. The last thing Ana and her family needed was men brawling over Aldo's grave. When he spoke, his voice was tight, controlled. “Let's just get this done.”

“Fine with me.”

They finished as the sun started to sink behind the trees and hills. Folks had gathered from the village and harbor to see Aldo laid to rest, including the local pastro.

The burial was simple yet heartfelt. Aldo had been well liked in his community, and his youth made it all the more tragic.

Milos remained off to the side, huddled in his cloak with the hood drawn against the wind, which turned bitter as dark fell. The sweat lingering on his skin from the physical work didn’t help, but the chill and discomfort wasn’t hard to ignore given the circumstances.

He hoped Ben didn't point out his presence or identity; he knew Ana would not. He didn't want to take any of the attention that should go to the dead or the family. He'd rather be by Ana's side, but he didn't want to risk it. At least her family surrounded her—which meant Ben couldn't be at her side either.

After the initial short prayer, Ana's father fetched Aldo from the cabin, wrapped in the traditional shroud. The tall, broad man with Ana’s gray eyes and dark curls walked slowly, his steps measured, deliberate. The light of a neighbor’s torch highlighted a single tear escaping to slide down his bearded, drawn face.

He laid the body down so gently just beside the grave, as though the boy could still feel … anything. Then he climbed down into the earthen hole and gathered his youngest son in his arms once more, tenderly placing him onto the dirt at his feet. He remained kneeling for several beats, shoulders shaking with silent sobs.

Tears streamed down Milos's face as he watched.

No one should have to bury a child.

Afterward, as folks trickled back to their respective homes, Ana's parents and older brother thanked Ben and "Vincento" for their assistance, and then left Ana with a lantern to say goodbye to the two men out front.

Cue the return of awkward silence. Ben spoke first. "Would you like me to pass along any messages to the castle staff? Mistress Danias?"

Milos glanced at the other man, confused. Why would he have reason to speak with anyone at the castle?

"Only if it's not an inconvenience. When do you start at the stables?"

"In a few days. But I don't mind making an extra trip."

Milos interrupted. "Wait, what do you mean, 'start at the stables?'"

Ben's smirk was faint, yet definitely there. "I was hired as a stable hand at your humble home."

Snarky son of a bitch. "I see." Milos turned to Ana. "I'm happy to pass any message to Mistress Danias on your behalf. No extra trip involved for me, after all." He hesitated. "I can let her know when you're coming back ... if you're coming back?" He held his breath waiting for her answer. He wouldn't be surprised if she decided to stay home and help her parents.

Ana nodded slowly. "I do plan to return to my job there, yes. The extra coin will still help my family, and honestly..." She swallowed visibly. "It's really hard to be here, without him. I'd like to take one more day, though. I'll return the day after tomorrow."

Ben jumped in. "In that case, I can stay at the inn and escort you back."

She smiled as she shook her head. "It isn't necessary. Leo can use the inn's cart. I'll see you both when I return. Thank you again for everything." She nodded at Ben, then did a small curtsy as she focused on Milos. "Your Highness."

Milos took her hand, dwarfing it in his own, and raised it to his lips. "I'm sorry for your loss. I'll see you soon, Ana." He brushed his mouth across her knuckles before he forced himself to let go. He walked toward his mount, then turned, waiting for Ben to leave as well. He'd be damned if he'd leave them alone together.

Ben leaned in to murmur something to Ana, and she nodded. Then the bastard leaned in and pressed his lips to her forehead before turning to gather his own horse. Milos glared at him, as useless as the gesture was in the dark.

The two men mounted as Ana walked back into the cabin, giving them one small, final wave.

Without a word, Milos turned his mount toward the creek. After Bruna drank, he headed back to the road. Ben was nowhere in sight. Good. They were both headed to the same place, but Milos had no desire to travel with the other man.

The man who so obviously wished to court Ana. His chest rumbled in a low growl at the thought. It wasn't only that Ben was competition; something about him was off. Milos would have to keep a close eye on him until he figured out what it was.

Chapter Twenty-Four

ANELA

Although Anela hadn't wished to burden Hen, knowing she didn't have to figure out their predicament alone was comforting. Henriella had stewed, and contemplated, and asked questions in their various discussions. While Anela assumed their only option was to flee, Henriella came at the problem from a different angle.

"What if we publicly call out whoever is writing these notes?" she had asked. "You could summon the court to the throne room for an announcement. Then tell everyone about the notes, denying the truth of them. Accuse the anonymous sender of stirring up trouble unprovoked, for whatever their own treasonous plans must be. Demand them to turn themselves in, or tell the nobles if they know anything or suspect anyone, they should come forward."

The idea had merit. By sharing the notes, Anela would make a compelling case for her own innocence. By involving all of the nobles, she would muddy the waters. She knew what the nobles at court were like—backstabbing hypocrites, for the most part. They would fight among themselves and accuse each other for the sake of long-held family grudges.

Whoever sent the messages played a dangerous game, and maybe it was time for Anela to make her own move. All she had to do now was convince Tirano.

He typically took his midday meal in his quarters, a quiet break between official business in the throne room and various meetings.

Note in her pocket, she took a deep breath as a guard announced her.

Tirano sat at the small dining table with a tray of food. He had a scroll laid out next to the tray, weighed down so he could read while he ate. He glanced up as she entered. "I assume this is important, or you wouldn't disturb me."

She stopped in front of the table but didn't sit. Instead, she said, "Your assumption is correct." She drew the note out of her pocket and handed it to him. "Someone left this in Lady Henriella's room. Does it not look like the same handwriting?"

His eyebrows rose as he read. "It does." His sharp gaze darted to her. "Secrets, hm? Any idea what they could be referring to?"

She shook her head decidedly. "Indeed not. I am convinced someone is playing games with us, and I won't accept it. This is treasonous behavior."

He set the note down on top of the flattened scroll. "It's possible. I haven't discovered anything about the identity of the messenger, nor determined my next steps."

"If I may make a suggestion?" she asked, then held her breath while she waited for him to answer.

He waved a hand. "I suppose."

"What if you formally invited the court to the throne room for an announcement? And then we make the notes public and demand that anyone who knows or suspects anything about the matter come forward."

He tilted his head, considering. "But then we're admitting that the notes worked, that whoever sent them succeeded in causing all that theater."

She inclined her head. His damned pride *would* be the obstacle. "Perhaps. But we're also sending two important messages. First, that cowardly anonymous notes cannot divide us or be used to bully the monarchy. Second, that we know the notes to be untrue, so we're not afraid of them."

He nodded slowly. "All right. I will consider it. Is that all?"

"Yes, my king. I apologize for the interruption. I'll leave you to your meal."

Without a word, he slid the note aside to focus on the scroll again, and she left.

She had done her best. Now she must wait. She hoped he made his decision quickly, before the note-sender made their next move—whatever that might be.

A day passed, then two. Anela attempted to stay busy to distract herself, but she still felt on edge during every waking hour.

But at supper on the second day, Tirano rose from his seat to address the dining hall. When the room quieted, he said, "Tomorrow morning, I will make an important announcement. Noble members of the court are expected to be present. You will join me in the throne room directly after breakfast."

Anela breathed a sigh of relief as he sat down. She

didn't dare say anything to him; he was likely irritated that she had the idea before he did.

When she finished eating and excused herself, he caught her arm before she could stand. "Directly after breakfast tomorrow. Do not be late."

"I understand, my king. It will be as you wish."

He nodded once, satisfied, and released her.

The following day, the throne room was stuffed wall to wall with a quiet murmuring buzz of anticipation. They probably thought this was an announcement of Milos being engaged or something similar, as Milos had returned just in time for this gathering. Everyone had been dying for years to see who he might marry.

Tirano sat on his elaborate throne, carved and gold gilded, while Anela sat behind him in a more modest but still elegant seat, Milos in a similar chair on Tirano's other side.

When Tirano stood and held up a hand, the room rapidly fell silent. The king wasted no time with pleasantries. "I'm sure you're all wondering why I've called you here today, so I shall tell you. There is a traitor in our midst, and I will not stand for such subterfuge in my kingdom."

Anela half expected an outcry of some sort, but it was so silent they could have heard a pin drop.

"Someone in this castle is leaving notes for your queen and myself. Perhaps I should call them written threats." He reached into his pocket and held up the two scraps of parchment. "They speak of secrets. And murder."

A collective gasp swept through the room this time. The word "murder" never failed to catch people's attention.

Tirano continued. "Perhaps this is a joke of some sort, but I assure you, if that's the case, I am *not* amused. I demand that anyone with any information about the sender of these notes come forward. It's very possible that there is more than one culprit—likely, even, that the traitor has at least one accomplice. If you fear retribution, you may request a private audience. I want answers, and you *will* give them to me."

Murmuring broke out around the room, nobles eyeing each other suspiciously. Tirano sat down and waved a hand. "Unless someone wishes to come forward this moment, we are finished here."

Guards opened the large double doors and the audience poured out of the throne room. Tirano spoke low-voiced to Anela. "That should be sufficient."

She nodded. "Yes, my king."

He rose and left without a backward glance. Anela and Milos followed suit more slowly. Her son offered her his arm.

"Will you return to your quarters? I will walk with you."

Anela nodded.

Once they turned a few corners and distanced themselves from the throngs of people, Milos said, "You never mentioned any notes to me."

She could hear the hurt in his voice. "I didn't take it seriously at first, and I didn't wish to worry you. Your father is handling it."

He nodded and let the topic drop, which surprised her. They walked quietly for the length of one corridor before making the final turn toward her rooms. "What is on your mind, my son?"

He glanced at her, and she noticed a flush crawling up his neck. "Nothing, Mama."

She shot him a suspicious glance as they approached the doors, which the guards swung open. He tried to extricate his arm, but she held firm. "Come in and talk to me."

So he shuffled along, and when the door shut behind them, she pointed to an armchair. "Sit. Talk. I've hardly seen you." He rolled his eyes but obeyed, and she sat across from him. "If it's not those silly notes bothering you, what is it?"

He smiled. "I'm not *bothered* so much, only ... distracted." The earlier flush spread into his face, and Anela raised an eyebrow.

She had a good guess now about the nature of his thoughts. "It's a young lady, isn't it?"

His gaze jerked from the carpet to her, and she smiled, triumphant. "I thought so."

His smile was weak. "It's complicated."

"How so?" Anela settled back into the chair, happy to have a normal, mother-son conversation. It was a much-needed break from all of the recent stress.

He shrugged. "Too many ways to list, really."

Anela chose another tack. "All right. Can you tell me about her? What is she like?"

A small smile lifted the corners of his mouth. "Yes, I can tell you about her, I suppose. Are all mothers this nosy, or only queens?"

She chuckled. "Pretty certain it's all mothers. Go on."

He huffed a laugh and leaned back in his chair as well, a dreamy look overtaking his features. "She's... She's smart, and witty. She has a kind heart." He swallowed. "She's beautiful."

Anela smiled. "Sounds like she's perfect."

He huffed a laugh. "No one's perfect. She's also

distrusting and stubborn, and although I know she likes me ... I think she'd prefer if she didn't." His face fell.

Anela nodded slowly. "The whole prince thing is a lot, is that it? Not all women are clamoring to be queen." This fact might surprise some, but not her. Not at all. If anything, it gave her an even better opinion of this mystery woman.

He inclined his head. "Something to that effect, yes."

"I see." Her heart ached for him, and she hoped the young lady would come around, yet she didn't say so. "I suppose if the Seven will it, then it shall work out for you both." Anela wasn't even sure if she believed this, but she said it almost unthinking; it was a standard reply to comfort someone.

His brows drew together in a scowl. "Damn the Seven," he growled. "They don't control my life."

She tilted her head, surprised at his vehemence. "She's important to you, isn't she?" She eyed him critically. "You're in love with her."

He groaned and scrubbed his hands over his face. "It hardly matters if she won't give me a chance."

Anela had no response to that. Instead, she said, "I hope you will be able to introduce me eventually."

One of his shoulders lifted and dropped. "Maybe. We'll see." He didn't sound confident.

Chapter Twenty-Five

VERANA

When Ana returned to the castle, she immediately knew something was different, despite her numbed state. Folks rushed around, avoiding eye contact, or they whispered and darted suspicious glances at those around them.

Mistress Danias was nowhere to be found, so Ana headed to her room. Traversing the corridors only confirmed her assessment that something was amiss.

She found Lisia in her bed, taking a break between meal services due to pain from her cycle. Ana could tell because she held a heated, wrapped brick to her belly. Lisia rose to hug Ana, the question written across her face.

"He's gone," Ana managed. "I don't want to talk about it."

Lisia gave her a sympathetic look but didn't push. "I understand. I'm sorry, Ana."

She lay back down, curled on her side around the warm bundle of brick and cloth.

As Ana hung up her cloak, she said, "What's going on here though? Everyone is behaving strangely."

"Oh, that." Lisia grimaced. "You missed His Majesty's announcement."

Ana sat on the edge of her bed across from Lisia. "What announcement?"

"Apparently someone has been sending threatening notes to both the king and the queen. But they don't know who it is. They asked for anyone who might know anything to come forward, and since the offense is treason, anyone who is reported..." Lisia trailed off with a grimace.

Anyone suspected of treason could be executed. "I see." Ana's stomach hollowed at the idea; she'd had enough of death.

Lisia nodded. "Yes, exactly."

"And has anyone come forward?"

"No official accusations." Lisia looked paler, maybe a little green now.

"Ah. I'm sorry to bother you, I can see you're not feeling well. I'll leave you to rest."

Lisia didn't object. Ana remembered Ben should start in the stables either that day or the next, so she grabbed her cloak once more and went to look for a friendly face. She was happy—as happy as she could be about anything right now—that he would be working at the castle. She'd be able to see more of him, assuming he wanted to.

She was fairly certain he wanted to. She was grieving, but not blind. And the more she considered it, the more appealing it sounded. A good distraction.

A pang of guilt hit her as she crossed the courtyard. Did she *only* want him as a distraction? It would be unkind to use him in such a manner. She pushed the thought away, unwilling to examine it. They enjoyed each other's company; surely that was reason enough for her to seek him out.

Unfortunately, he wasn't there. The stable master responded to her inquiry with, "The new lad? He should be here in the morning for his first day."

"Thank you," she murmured.

"He's a handsome young fellow, is he?" the stable master teased.

Ana mustered a smile and replied with a simple wave goodbye. So much for that idea.

It was the first sunny day in at least a week and she didn't want to be inside. She followed the path around the side of the castle that led to the fields and gardens in the back. Everything was dead and gray, waiting to be hidden for the winter with fresh white snow. But it was more peaceful than a walk in the city.

She went all the way to the edge of the grounds near the tree line of the woods. Most didn't come out so far, which suited her fine.

When she heard voices, she stopped, unsure which way to go to avoid them. She'd rather not run into any nobles. Calling upon her secret skill, the tug in her abdomen led her to a large tree. She darted behind it and waited for whoever it was to pass.

As they came closer, she recognized the voices. She heard them most mornings while going about her duties: the queen and Lady Henriella.

"...relieved that your idea worked," Queen Anela said. "The entire court is in a tizzy. Hopefully whoever sent the notes has lost their credibility."

"But? You say you're relieved, yet I can tell there's something on your mind."

"You know me too well, my Hen." Queen Anela's chuckle sounded rueful. "I keep coming back to the prophecy, and it's driving me a little crazy that I still can't figure it out. It feels ... relevant. Imminent. I didn't have the dream for years after the first time, and now I'm having it almost every night. I still don't know what it means, what it predicts. I've filled my journal with notes and speculation, but..." She trailed off.

Hen released a breath. "Yes, it's quite frustrating. If it really does predict the king losing his crown, it would be lovely to know what we need to do to ensure it happens."

As the two women continued, their voices grew more faint, and Ana couldn't understand the queen's reply.

She stayed where she was for several more minutes, heart racing as she considered what she had heard. The queen received prophecies, which made sense, as she was from Orakolas. That would be a gift from the god of prophecy (and ignorance), Orix. But a prophecy about the king losing power? And Lady Henriella implied both she and the queen would like to see it come true?

Wasn't that treason?

And yet, knowing the little she did about King Tirano ... Ana wasn't so surprised when she considered it. He seemed vengeful, and he didn't care much about his non-noble subjects. The royal couple rarely displayed any sort of affection; indeed, they seemed to hardly see each other.

Supposedly, King Tirano ran his kingdom according to the will of Sonos, but Ana had her doubts. Everyone in her family and village believed that the will of the king was the will of their god, and the pastros were the king's mouthpieces—everyone she knew, except for her and her father.

And if the people stopped believing? What then? They might look around and see the inequity that tried to swallow them all whole daily. The disparate realities of the royals and nobility versus the rest of the population, who benefited and who suffered. Her lack of belief combined with her experience at court had solidified the truth of this for her.

But the people *did* believe. When they expressed doubt, the pastros shamed them for it, and they risked outcast status.

Someday, Milos would be king. Would he be any better than his father? She wanted to think so. And what if that day came sooner than later, like the queen hinted?

Maybe there was some way she could help.

She shook her head at the idea as she walked back toward the castle. How could she, one lowly servant, possibly help bring King Tirano to his knees?

And yet, if she could, it would be justice of a sort for Aldo. For all the families who lost loved ones due to the greed of the few at the top.

A journal. Her Majesty mentioned a journal that held her thoughts about the prophecy. And Ana spent time in her chambers every single day.

A sudden knowing overcame her: she needed to read those pages. Fortunately, no matter how well hidden that journal might be—she had never noticed one going about her chores—Ana had the ability to find it.

The following morning was back to work as usual, and Ana was allowed into the queen's quarters first thing to start the fire, make her bed, and generally tidy up. She helped the queen dress as well, but only with the final parts of lacing and tying.

As she moved about, Ana focused on her goal: to find that prophecy journal. The inner tug led her toward a chest next to the wardrobe. She waited until the queen and Lady

Henriella were busy breaking their fast and chatting in the other room before she lifted the latch. The hinges squeaked and she cringed, freezing in place, but the two women carried on with their conversation.

Lifting the lid a few more inches, she spied a small leather-bound tome right on top of a pile of folded fabric—maybe spare blankets, or old dresses, she couldn't tell. She hadn't ever had a reason to look inside. She snatched up the journal and stuck it in her apron pocket. Hopefully the queen wouldn't notice it was gone before Ana could bring it back the following morning.

After finishing her tasks, she checked in with the queen, managing to maintain a semblance of calm, and then she was dismissed until teatime.

She checked in with Mistress Danias to get a list of her other chores for the day, as usual. But then she went to find Lisia, who was helping with the laundry that day.

The laundry room was always warm and humid, which was pleasant enough this time of year. Ana only hoped she'd never be assigned there in the warm months. She found Lisia hanging a pillowcase on a wood rack near the large hearth. The weather was too questionable to dry anything outside.

"Lis, can I ask a favor?"

Lisia jumped, almost dropping the fabric. "Oh, Ana! I didn't see you. What do you need?"

"Is there any way you can cover a few of my chores today?" Ana had helped Lisia and the other girls in this way before, for various reasons.

"Probably. How much time do you need?"

Ana appreciated that Lisia didn't ask why, or what Ana needed to do. "An hour? Two, if you can?"

"Sure, I'll be finished here soon."

Ana relayed her list of tasks and Lisia chose a few to take over.

"Thanks, Lis. I owe you." Now she just needed to finish the rest of her work and find a quiet place to read where she wouldn't be disturbed. She knew of a couple less used supply closets, but that would be too dark unless she could manage to sneak a lantern in as well, which would look odd if anyone noticed.

She ended up checking her bedroom first, and she breathed a sigh of relief when it was empty. It usually was during the day, but sometimes one of the girls was ill or injured, or on their day off without anywhere to go.

Removing her shoes, she sat on the bed with her legs crossed in front of her and her back against the wall before she pulled the journal out of her pocket with trembling hands.

Chapter Twenty-Six

VERANA

Ana committed as much of the journal to memory as she could before returning it the following morning, the queen none the wiser. Unfortunately, she didn't feel like she had found any answers, only more questions.

She rolled the words of the prophecy around in her head as she went about her chores. It spoke of "The One," who was apparently female, and the fall of a king with dream magic. That part must refer to either King Tirano or possibly Milos. Aside from that, the wording was annoyingly vague and perplexing. Anela's speculations about it were just that—wonderings, guesses, nothing concrete. What was the point in receiving prophecies no one could understand?

Around midday, Mistress Danias sent Ana on an errand into the capital. As she passed the stables on her way to the gates, someone called her name. She turned to see Ben emerge from the poorly lit depths of the tack shed, and a smile broke over her face.

"Oh, Ben! You're here!"

He walked over to her, grinning. "I am, and so are you.

Such luck." He winked. Despite the cold, his sleeves were rolled up, and the shirt pulled tight over his chest, hinting at solid muscle underneath. His light brown waves were tousled, messy with bits of straw peeking out but somehow appealing anyway.

She forced herself to stop ogling him and laughed. "Why is that?"

He gave a small bow. "Because I was hoping to ask you to go into the city with me this evening after supper." She blinked in surprise and he rushed to continue. "A few of the other stable hands and maids are going as well. If it's too soon, after your brother, I understand."

His hazel eyes looked so hopeful. Ana bit her lip. She knew some of the staff went into the city to blow off steam at a tavern occasionally. She'd been invited and had always declined; her family needed the coin more than she needed the social time.

"It sounds fun," she said honestly. "But I send all my pay to my family. I can't spare any for things like that." She was a little embarrassed but shook it off; he had met her family, seen their home. He knew they didn't have much.

Granted, there was one less mouth to feed now. Her hand fisted at the thought as she swallowed hard, willing away the tears that threatened to flow. She refused to fall apart in the middle of the castle courtyard.

Ben chuckled, seemingly oblivious to her struggle. "Do you really think I'd invite you and expect you to pay for anything? It's my treat. Meet you at the gates after supper?"

Ana hesitated. Should she? What could it hurt? And was this Ben's way of initiating a courtship? If it was ... how did she feel about that?

She was overthinking. They'd be with other staff, so it wasn't inappropriate—more proper, in truth, than when

Milos escorted her to the tea shop—and it would be a good distraction. The less time she was left alone with her thoughts, the better. The hardest hours of the day since Aldo passed were the ones where she lay in bed at night, trying to fall asleep, and then when she woke up, the moment she remembered he was gone.

She gave him the best smile she could muster. "I'd really like that. Thank you for inviting me."

His eyes lit up. "Oh good. Honestly, I wouldn't wish to invite anyone else."

Ana felt a flush spreading over her chest at his confession. "I'll see you this evening, then. I must be going. Mistress Danias sent me on an errand."

"Of course. I'll see you tonight." He brought two fingertips to his lips and then brushed them against her cheek. Tossing another charming smile her way, he turned, striding toward the main stables. She stared after him for a beat, her skin tingling from his touch.

The rest of Ana's day went by in a blur. Between the prophecy nonsense and the looming outing with Ben, as well as her work, she had more than enough to occupy her mind.

Ana felt even better about the evening plan when she discovered Cora, the oldest of her roommates, would also be there, as well as the infamous John from the stables, and a handful of others. Once supper was over and their work completed, the two young women cleaned up and traded in their aprons for their cloaks.

They met their escorts at the gate as planned. John and Cora walked together, and Ben offered Ana his arm, which she accepted. The other four bunched into an informal group, chatting and laughing as they tripped over icy cobblestones.

The only tavern Ana had visited in the city was The Royal Gate, but their group headed to another one farther away. "Less likely to run into the housekeeper or the stable master this way," Ben explained. Ana had recently discovered Mistress Danias was the wife of the stable master, and she knew they frequented The Royal Gate from the first time she met Mistress Danias.

"I suppose it'll be more fun without them watching our every move," she agreed.

Their group split up upon arrival at the tavern; the establishment was busy, and none of the remaining tables would fit everyone. Ben and Ana drank their first two tankards of ale with Cora and John, until the couple announced they "needed some air."

When Ben offered her a third round, Ana politely declined. "I get up really early," she explained. She already felt the effects of the first two.

"So do I." Ben grinned. "But we're only young once, right? How about we split a third?"

She relented. "I suppose that would be fine."

It felt strangely intimate to share a cup with Ben. Ana was overly aware of where his lips touched the rim as compared to hers.

"What do you think about the notes everyone's talking about? The ones someone sent to the king." Ben raised a curious eyebrow.

Ana shrugged. "It caused a lot of gossip and rumors. Everyone seems more on edge. It's ... uncomfortable sometimes."

He studied her, intent and unwavering. "Discomfort is often the price of change, even if it's for the good."

She tilted her head to one side, frowning. "But nothing has changed."

"Maybe that's the purpose of those notes, though. Someone trying to initiate a change."

"You think so? I figured they were a prank."

He leaned in and spoke in a lower voice. "I know it seems like everyone is happy with their lot. But there are some in Revas who desire change. Some even in this city. Probably more than we realize, as many don't have the courage to admit it yet."

It took a moment for his words to land. She kept her voice low too. "Change in the monarchy, you mean?"

He nodded. "It could do a lot of good. Don't you think?"

She did, in fact, agree with him. That was the primary reason she was obsessing over the prophecy. But the entire conversation was treasonous, despite his nonchalant tone. "Do you think people would really do it? Rebel against the king?"

He grew more serious and leaned even closer to whisper in her ear. "I *know* they would."

It was all too much. His closeness, the loud tavern, her head swimming from ale, and this dangerous topic. "Um, I think I need some air too."

"All right, that sounds good." Ben drained the rest of the ale and then stood, offering her a hand to help her up.

When they walked outside, Ana spotted Cora and John in a shadow off to the side of the entrance, deep in an embrace and kissing. She averted her eyes and went the opposite direction, moving to the closed shop next door.

Pulling the hood of her cloak up, she leaned against the wall, taking deep breaths. It was cold enough to see fog in the air when she exhaled, but it felt good after the crowded tavern.

Ben touched her shoulder. "Hey. Are you all right?"

She nodded. "I'm fine. It was just a little stuffy in there."

He moved closer, his hand sliding down her arm to cup her elbow. "I hope our conversation didn't upset you."

She huffed a laugh. "It ... surprised me, was all. I'm not upset."

"Good." The corners of his mouth turned up. His other hand came to her waist, and suddenly he was so close as she stared into his hooded eyes. "I'd never want to upset you, Ana. I like you too much."

Heart hammering in her chest, she laid a tentative hand on his arm. "I like you, too."

Angling his head down, he pulled her even closer and brushed his lips over hers. His wide mouth was soft and warm; he smelled of ale and horses. A memory of mint and rain tried to get her attention, and she shoved it down.

He pulled back, barely, and studied her face in the light from the streetlamps. She worried her bottom lip between her teeth, nervous but not wanting to stop this. Whatever this was.

Apparently, he could read that in her features, because he kissed her again, more firmly this time. Her arms automatically came around his neck, and now both of his hands gripped her waist.

She tried not to, but she couldn't stop her mind from comparing this to when Milos had kissed her. Or when she had kissed Milos, she wasn't sure which it had been. Both felt nice, but also different. Milos had seemed so earnest and unsure of himself, at least at first, whereas Ben exuded confidence and self-assurance. She thought it odd that the stable hand would be more confident than the prince.

She opened to allow him in, and one hand slid up her body until it rested under her breast as he thoroughly explored her mouth.

When his warm, calloused hand cupped her breast, she gasped into his mouth. Her mind spun, not only from the sensations but also all the drink. He squeezed, just enough for her to feel the pressure. The combined sensations of his tongue, his body pressed against hers, and his hand cupping her started to feel overwhelming.

It didn't help that she couldn't keep a pair of sultry green eyes out of her mind.

Her hands slid down to his chest, trying to get a little distance as she broke the kiss and turned her head to the side.

He didn't give her any space; his breath came heavy, and his voice was raspy. "What's wrong, sweetheart?"

She attempted a smile, also catching her breath. "I need a moment." She pushed the smallest bit, and he finally got the hint.

He dropped his hands as he stepped back, giving her space. "I'm sorry, was that too much? It seemed like you were enjoying it..."

"I was. I did. It was just intense." She placed a hand over her still-racing heart, willing it to slow.

He pushed his cloak hood back and grinned, running a hand through his hair. "Intense is good, right?"

She nodded. "Yes. But I think ... I think I'm ready to go back now." Her stomach roiled uneasily; perhaps it was the ale.

He didn't quite mask the disappointment that flashed across his face. But he held out his arm, forcing a smile. "Whatever the lady desires."

She chuckled as she took her place at his side. "I'm no lady."

He gave half a shrug. "Maybe not, but your beauty surpasses all the ladies I've seen at court so far."

She silently scoffed at the exaggeration, even as her cheeks warmed. "If you say so. Thank you."

"I do, and you're welcome."

They chatted about nothing important on their walk back. He dropped one last chaste kiss on her lips at the gates before heading back into the city to the small flat he and his mother currently shared. "Thanks for coming out with me. I'll see you soon, Ana. Sweet dreams."

"Goodnight, Ben."

She entered the castle through the kitchens, since they should be empty at that time of night. To her surprise, she heard a voice as she shut the door behind her.

"Ana, is that you?"

She whirled around and Milos stepped out of the shadows, a bottle of wine in one hand.

"Your Highness. I didn't see you there." She braced herself with a hand on the door, willing her heart to slow.

He held up the bottle. "Decided I wanted this, but I didn't want to wake anyone to get it for me."

"I see. That's thoughtful of you. Well, goodnight, Your Highness." She took a step toward the hallway, ready to flee from his presence. Embarrassment flooded her, although he had no way of knowing how thoughts of him had pushed themselves to the forefront even as she kissed another man.

"Were you in the city tonight?"

She stopped, holding back her sigh, and nodded. "Yes. A group of us went out."

"Where's the rest of the group, then?" He studied her closely, unnerving her. Why did he care? Her eyes darted to his lips, then she forced herself to look away.

Staring at the floor, she said, "Most of them are still at the tavern."

"You walked back to the castle alone, this late at night?" His tone was incredulous. "Ana, that's dangerous."

She bristled, shooting him a glare. "No, I wasn't alone. One of the stable hands escorted me to the gates."

"Who?"

She raised an eyebrow. "I don't think it's your concern, Your Highness."

"Was it Ben?"

She was almost glad he was being so irritating; it helped her evade the desire to feel his mouth on hers. She pressed her lips together. "G*oodnight*, Your Highness." She pushed past him, but he caught her arm.

"Be careful. With Ben, I mean. I don't trust him."

She scowled at him, yanked her arm back, and fled down the hall.

Who did he think he was? The thought made her snort. "The heir to the crown, obviously," she muttered to herself. He was accustomed to people listening to him and obeying his demands. He claimed to want her friendship—more even—but treated her like a … like a child. Or a lowly servant.

Chapter Twenty-Seven

MILOS

Milos strode swiftly back to his quarters, muttering to himself. Fucking Ben. Of course it was Ben. The fact that she hadn't denied it made him certain.

He must have looked truly angry, because the guard outside his door said, "Your Highness, is everything all right?"

"Yes, fine," was his gruff reply. Once inside, he opened the bottle and filled a large goblet.

He thought there was something off about Ben, but maybe it was nothing. Maybe it was only jealousy on his part.

He pictured Ana, rosy cheeked and lovely, walking arm in arm with the handsome stable hand and drained his cup. Then he pictured her kissing Ben like she had kissed him, and instead of throwing the goblet across the room like he wanted to, he refilled it to the brim.

It didn't take him long to finish the entire bottle.

When he woke the following morning, regret churned in his belly, in the form of nausea. An entire bottle was perhaps overkill. But he had duties to attend to, and his father would have no sympathy for his plight.

Not that Milos could blame him in this particular instance.

So he rose, washed, and dressed. Standing and walking made his head pound and seemed to amplify the roiling in his stomach, and he inwardly cursed himself for being a stupid, jealous ass.

Food. He needed food. He absolutely did not want to sit in the loud dining hall, however, nor did he have time to order someone to bring a tray. His father expected him for a meeting with a foreign diplomat from Bonsanco within the hour. Straight to the kitchens it was.

Every step down the stone corridors seemed to make the vibration in his skull more intense. He focused on the floor, trying to keep his stomach under control. Just as he turned the corner into the kitchens, he ran into something. Someone, rather: a maid carrying a tray of food for the dining hall, which crashed to the floor. Sausages when flying and the maid squealed as she lost her balance and fell, ending up on her hands and knees.

"Oh, Your Highness, I'm so sorry, that was so clumsy of me," she babbled. He recalled her name more quickly this time: Lisia.

"No, I apologize. I wasn't watching where I was going."

Mistress Danias appeared. "Oh goodness. Well, let's get this cleaned up. Are you all right, Your Highness?"

He stood there stupidly, completely unharmed, while the maid knelt on the flagstone. "I'm fine. She may have hurt herself, though."

Lisia looked up at him with a shaky smile. “No, I'm fine, Your Highness. Might have bruised my knees a little is all.”

She was placing the sausages back on the tray with Mistress Danias's help. He considered joining them to assist, but his stomach wavered skeptically.

“I, uh, just need to grab some bread or something,” he said, inching around the two women. “Sorry again.” He spotted something on the floor that was not sausage—a slip of folded parchment. He picked it up, offering it to Lisia. “I think you might have dropped this.”

Her face flushed rosy red. “Oh—I—yes, it must have fallen from my pocket. Thank you, Your Highness.” She practically snatched it from him.

What an odd reaction. Perhaps it was a love letter or something equally private. He dismissed it and went to grab a plate, piling bread, cheese, and dried apple onto it, then took it out into the kitchen gardens.

It was cold and he didn't have his cloak, but the temperature felt infinitely better than inside. It seemed to help his head. He sat on a bench and munched.

Mistress Danias found him a few minutes later, bringing him a steaming cup of tea. “You looked a bit peaky, Your Highness.” He could smell the mint as he took it from her. His favorite, even when his stomach wasn't upset.

He smiled. “Thank you.”

She nodded and turned to go back inside when a thought occurred to him.

“Mistress?”

She looked back at him. “Yes? Can I get you anything else?”

“No, I'm fine. I wanted to ask you about one of the stable hands.”

She faced him again, one hand on her hip. "Which one?"

"The new one. His name is Ben. Has your husband mentioned him?"

Her brow wrinkled for a moment, then her face lightened. "Oh yes, he did. What about him?"

"I'm curious what Master Danias thinks of him."

She studied him, obviously wondering his reasoning for these questions. "So far, he hasn't had any complaints." She pursed her lips. "Oh, except he did get into an argument with one of the other stable hands. My husband didn't know what it was about. He just told them to get back to work."

Milos inclined his head. "Thank you. I won't keep you any longer."

"I hope you feel better soon, Your Highness." She hurried back inside.

The food and tea helped him substantially, and by the second meeting of the day, he felt back to normal. He made it through several meetings as well as the midday meal before he had a break.

Wanting to find out more about Ben, he made his way to the stables that afternoon. He wasn't sure what excuse to use for his inquiries. Not that he'd have to answer to anyone, but he didn't need folks commenting on his odd behavior, either. It would be best to speak with Ben directly; if nothing else, he could cement his dislike for the man, or maybe he'd get a different impression.

When he arrived, Master Danias had a horse in the pen, expertly guiding the animal through groundwork exercises. Milos missed his younger days when he could spend more time at the stables. He watched, not wishing to interrupt, until the older man noticed him.

The stable master released the horse, who wandered toward the trough. Brushing weathered hands on his faded britches, he met Milos at the fence. "How can I help you, Your Highness?"

Unfortunately, Master Danias said Ben had asked to leave early that day, something about helping his mother in the city. "Would you like me to give him a message?"

Unable to think of anything he could pass along that wouldn't come off as strange, Milos just smiled and shook his head. "No, that's all right. I'll let you get back to work."

He didn't wish to go back inside, so he wandered around one side of the castle to stroll the grounds. It was gray and cold, but not raining at least. It likely wouldn't be long before the first snow.

He spotted a couple walking together and frowned, considering if he should turn around. He wasn't in the mood for small talk. He squinted, trying to figure out who it was, and recognized the head of blonde hair from earlier: Lisia.

And ... was that Ben with her? Yes, it seemed so.

He pulled his hood forward and sat down on a bench to watch them from a distance. So, Ben had begged off work to "help his mother" and instead was meeting with one of the maids. Milos scowled; he didn't know how old Lisia was, but he'd guess no older than fifteen, whereas Ben had to be close to Milos's age, in his mid-to-late twenties. Not unheard of, yet still distasteful in Milos's opinion.

Also, Ben had just taken Ana for a night out in the city, and now he was here with Lisia? Milos knew there was something off about him, the bastard.

As the two walked back toward the castle, they separated, Lisia heading inside, while Ben made his way toward Milos.

Milos stood and waited for him to get closer. As the other man approached, looking contemplative with his hands in his pockets, Milos pushed his hood back. "Hello, Ben. I'd like to speak with you."

Ben started, eyes wide, before he recovered and gave a small bow. "Your Highness. I am at your service."

Milos doubted that. "The stable master said you were in the city."

Ben shrugged. "I'm headed there now."

"What were you doing with Lisia?"

Ben blanched. "What do you mean, Your Highness?"

"Lisia? The maid you were just walking with?"

The other man blinked. "You know her name?"

Milos grunted. "Answer my question."

"We were ... walking. And talking." Ben's gaze darted around; Milos noted the nervous gesture.

"And last night, with Ana? Were you also 'walking and talking' with her?"

Ben's cheeks grew red. "You take an uncommon amount of interest in the castle maids, Your Highness."

"They work in my home and are subjects of the kingdom I am heir to," Milos said calmly. "You're avoiding the question."

Ben threw his hands up. "Look, I don't know what you're implying, but I wasn't doing anything bad."

"With Lisia? Or with Ana?"

"Neither. Er, both." He was still flustered. "I'm not doing anything wrong, all right?"

"We'll see in time, I suppose," Milos said coldly. Then he took a page from his father's book. "You're dismissed."

Ben bowed again with a mumbled, "Your Highness," before practically running away.

No, nothing suspicious about him at all.

Milos meandered the grounds for another hour, deep in thought, before heading back inside. He hadn't seen Ana at all that day, so it was time to remedy that. Maybe he'd be in time for his mother's afternoon tea, which Ana would deliver.

Chapter Twenty-Eight

VERANA

Ana brought the queen her afternoon tea as usual. Upon leaving the queen's quarters, she slowed, taking her time getting back to the kitchens. She was so very tired. Partly it was all the ale she drank the night before, and the other reason was the strange dreams she had afterward—maybe also due to the ale?

Ben was in most of them, and she flushed as one of the more vivid dreams came back to her. In it, she didn't step away from Ben's kiss and have him escort her back to the castle. Instead, she dreamt that they returned to his home, and his bed, where he proceeded to worship her entire body.

It felt so real; she remembered the warmth of his mouth and his hands on her skin—her breasts, her stomach, between her legs. Just remembering it caused a tightening feeling in her core. She almost regretted her insistence on ending their night out.

"Ana?" A voice pulled her from her thoughts, and she jerked her head up to see Milos approaching.

She stopped and gave him a small curtsy, avoiding his eyes. "Your Highness." His behavior the night before was still fresh in her mind … and so was the damned kiss in the rain. She didn't know how to feel, and she was too tired to figure it out right then.

As she continued down the corridor, he fell into step beside her. "Ana, I'm sorry." His voice was soft. "About last night. I was worried, but that doesn't excuse how I acted. I had no right to interrogate you."

She gave a single curt nod. "Thank you. I accept your apology." She hadn't much of a choice of saying otherwise; he was the prince, after all. The apology sounded genuine, at least … yet she didn't understand him, his motives.

"Do you really, or are you just saying that?"

She tilted her head to one side, considering her answer. "If you really mean it, so do I, I suppose." Staying angry felt like work, in any case; she didn't have the energy. She glanced up at him to see his beautiful eyes searching her face. He looked like he wanted to say something more, but he held back. "What is it?"

He pressed his lips together and shook his head. "I don't want to meddle." He paused. "I think you need to be careful with who you give your trust. And your heart. Maybe—maybe ask more questions. I say this as a friend. I don't wish to see you get hurt."

His smooth, deep voice was so genuine, so earnest. It was impossible not to believe him. "I appreciate your concern, Your Highness. I'll consider your words." She still thought his bias and jealousy were to blame, but it was evident his intentions were good.

A relieved smile tugged at the corner of his mouth. "Good. Thank you."

His remorse seemed sincere, and she couldn't resist asking him, "So you were worried, not jealous?"

He ducked his head sheepishly. "Both, I suppose," he mumbled, confirming her suspicion. "But mostly worried."

As they reached the kitchens, she had a thought. She hesitated, unsure if it was a wise idea. Yet he still hadn't turned her over to the guards for her treasonous speech the first night they met. Maybe she could trust him … and maybe the guilt and regret he obviously felt could benefit her in some way, if he wanted to make it up to her.

The idea of being so manipulative brought an uneasy feeling, which she stubbornly ignored. "Can we talk tonight? In our usual spot?"

His face lit up. "It would be my pleasure."

Guilt crept through her, as he obviously hoped she wanted a romantic encounter, when in actuality she wanted to ask him about his mother's prophecy.

She mustered a smile. "See you then. Good day, Your Highness."

When it was time to sneak out to the cold courtyard, Ana wished she had asked to meet Milos the next night instead. She was still tired from going out with Ben, followed by interrupted sleep due to the odd dreams. But she kept her word and crept out to the kitchen gardens, clutching her cloak around her. It would likely snow any day now.

He was already waiting on the bench, and he stood when she approached. Even that simple movement displayed his strength and grace, and she couldn't help but admire his broad shoulders and trim waist. Her sleepiness faded as she took him in—this handsome prince who made time for her, a lowly servant, in the middle of the night.

Despite her exhaustion, she enjoyed the feeling of being with him when there was no one else around.

When they settled on the bench, he placed himself closer than usual, with their thighs almost brushing. She imagined she could feel his warmth through the layers of fabric; she should move, put some space between them, but she didn't.

"How are you this evening, Ana?"

"Fine, I suppose. Tired. And you?"

He smiled. "About the same. And curious what you wish to talk about."

"Right." She took a deep breath. "It's cold and we both want to go to bed, so I'll get right to the point." He gave an encouraging nod. "Do you know about your mother's prophecy? The one referring to a king with dream magic?"

His jaw dropped. He finally managed, "Yes, I do. How do you know about it? It… It isn't something we discuss openly."

She focused on her tightly clasped hands resting in her lap. "I overheard the queen and Lady Henriella discussing it. It was quite on accident." She hesitated. She wanted to tell him she had also read his mother's journal, but she couldn't bring herself to confess it. She was mildly ashamed, and also wasn't sure if he would run and tell the queen immediately. The two were close. "And then I was curious, I suppose. I wanted to hear your thoughts about it. I didn't really understand it." She risked a glance at him and her shoulders relaxed; he didn't look outraged, only surprised.

"I see." He spoke slowly, deliberately as he raised a brow. "Why do you want to understand it?"

Heat crept into her face and she was glad for the dark. "I ... I guess I'm simply intrigued, in part. But also..." She trailed off, looking down again, nervous to say the words aloud. Then his fingers gripped her chin, tilting her head to look at him.

"Tell me. You can trust me."

He let her go, and she forced herself to meet his gaze. She took a deep, shuddering breath, but couldn't bring herself to tell him she would love to see his father dethroned. She assumed the king wouldn't have to die for it to happen; still, it would be a dangerous admission on her part. She needed to be careful.

She spoke quickly, the pace of the words matching her racing heart. "I have my reasons, but I can't share them. I'm sorry." She blew out a breath, leaning her head back to look at the dark clouds above as she willed herself to be calm. The clouds seemed to glow, as though the moons they covered lit them from within.

Silence stretched between them. Ana chewed on the inside of her mouth, waiting for Milos to reply. Was he angry?

"So you want me to help you understand a prophecy that might predict my father's downfall, and you won't tell me why." It was a statement, not a question. He cleared his throat. "I have to say, Ana, you have courage in spades."

She huffed a laugh. "Is that a compliment?"

He chuckled. "An observation, at the least. But yes. I admire you for it." He took her cold hand in his warm one—how were his hands warm? It was freezing—and squeezed it. "And I'm glad you trust me enough to ask me about this. The problem is, I don't know that I have anything useful to offer as far as the prophecy. My parents have puzzled over it for decades now. My father becomes quite angry about it on occasion. I think the fear of that prophecy is what drives a lot of his choices as king, honestly."

A feathery touch of cold landed on Ana's nose, and she looked up to see snowflakes dancing down from the sky. She smiled despite her disappointment in Milos's answer. She loved the first snow of the season. It was magical.

"I understand," she finally said, focusing on Milos again. "I figured it couldn't hurt to ask. As you said, most don't know about it, so my options were limited."

He nodded. "I'm sorry I don't have any answers for you."

She lifted and dropped a shoulder, then waved a hand toward the clouds. "I adore watching the first snowfall."

He scooted closer, their thighs now touching from hip to knee, heat emanating from him alongside his irresistible scent. She didn't dare look at him, even though she wanted… What did she want? Part of her wanted to climb into his lap, to feel his hands explore her. The other part wanted to run, to escape back to her room. Before he could make her want him even more than she already did. Her indecision froze her into stillness.

He gripped her chin again, drawing her attention. "I adore watching you," he said in a husky voice, and then he kissed her.

Her body chose her reaction without consulting her. She melted into him. By the Seven, he was gloriously warm. His heat seeped into her lips first, soon traveling throughout her body. She moaned as his hand cupped her cheek, then slid to the back of her neck, holding her in place while he took his time exploring her mouth. Her eyes slid shut as she gave in to her want for him, reveling in the sensations his mouth and tongue evoked.

A few moments later, the tiny, icy sting of a snowflake on her eyelid brought her back to herself. She remembered where they were: a public courtyard. It was late, yet it was still possible for someone to see them.

She pulled away, and he let out a small groan but didn't stop her. She rested her forehead against his and breathed deeply as she tried to slow her racing heart.

"Ana," Milos murmured. "I wish I could taste you all night. I want you so badly, love."

Love. He had called her that once before. How could he say such a thing? She sat up straight, shaking her head. "You can't say that."

His brows drew together. "Why not?"

A laugh bubbled out of her. He couldn't be that stupid, so he was being purposely obtuse. "You know why." She stood. "This needs to stop. We can't do this."

He rose as well. "Please, Ana, don't—"

"No! I *can't* do this." Stinging tears surfaced. She didn't need him to see her cry. She turned and fled, hurrying back to her bedroom. She half expected him to follow, but no footfalls sounded behind her. She stamped down the twinge of disappointment.

All was quiet. Once undressed, she settled on the cot, quilt pulled up to her chin. Only then did she allow the tears to come.

Why did he insist on behaving this way? He knew she liked him, but he also knew they couldn't be together, so why torture them both? Infuriating man!

Now she had two memories of his lips against hers and she wished she didn't. It was impossible not to compare them to the one she shared with Ben, and she had to admit to herself she enjoyed kissing Milos more. She couldn't pinpoint why, but it hardly mattered. It would never happen again.

Damn him. Her pillow grew damp as she stifled her sobs, not wanting to wake her roommates.

Eventually, she was spent. With a shuddering breath, she said a silent goodnight to Aldo, as she always did, and had started to drift off to sleep when the door banged open.

She whipped her head around. It was men—guards, one of whom held a lantern. By the Seven, they must be here for her. Someone had seen her with Milos, or maybe the queen somehow discovered that Ana had read her journal.

"What's happening?" one groggy voice asked. Cora, Ana thought.

"Which one of you is Lisia, daughter of Samuel?" a gruff voice demanded, sweeping the lantern around.

Unthinking, all of the girls glanced at Lisia, and the guard had his answer. "You, girl. You're under arrest. Get up."

Ana's mouth dropped open. Lisia, under arrest? What in the Seven was happening?

Lisia stood, her eyes wide with fear. "W-why, sir?"

The guard snorted. "Treason. Let's go."

Lisia cowered as he stomped forward and took her by the upper arm. "M-may I dress?"

"No."

Ana finally found her voice. "Wait, sir! I think there must be some mistake. Lisia would never—"

"Shut your mouth unless you want to come with her," one of them snapped. Then they were gone, the door slamming shut behind them, leaving the remaining girls in the dark as Lisia's sobs echoed off the walls in the stone corridor.

Chapter Twenty-Nine

ANELA

Anela and Henriella chatted about nothing in particular while they waited for Ana to bring a tray to break their fast.

Finally, Hen said, "Should I go check in the kitchens? She's much later than usual."

"I suppose," Anela started, but then a knock sounded at the door, and Ana was admitted.

She hurried forward and Anela could immediately tell something was wrong. "Good morning, Your Majesty, Lady Henriella," she said. "I'm very sorry for the delay. Mistress Danias sends her apology as well."

Her hands trembled as she set the tray down and distributed plates and cutlery on the dining table. Dark circles shadowed her eyes. She looked almost ill.

"That's all right," Anela said. "You look unwell, Ana. Are you all right?"

Ana pressed her lips together. "Yes, Your Majesty. I'm well." Everything about her appearance and demeanor said otherwise.

"I can tell something is wrong. Is it to do with why

breakfast is late? Please tell me what's going on." Anela phrased the request politely, but the command in her tone couldn't be missed.

"Yes, Your Majesty." She took a deep breath. "It's only that we, um, lost one of the kitchen maids quite unexpectedly. Everyone—the other servants, that is—are upset about it, and now we're shorthanded."

"Indeed? Which maid was it?"

Ana's gaze grew glassy. "Lisia, Your Majesty."

"And when you say 'lost'...? Did the girl run away, or die? What happened?" Lisia was a sweet girl; Anela was sad to hear anything bad had befallen her.

Ana shifted from one foot to the other, wringing her hands. "No, she did not run away, and thankfully, she isn't dead. She … she was arrested last night. I understand she is being kept in the castle dungeons."

Anela's mouth dropped open. "Arrested? Whatever for?"

A tear escaped down Ana's cheek and she hastily swiped it away. "T-treason, Your Majesty." She shrugged helplessly. "I don't really know anything else."

"I see. Thank you for the information. You may go."

Ana dropped a curtsy and rushed from the room.

Anela turned to Henriella. "Treason? I can't imagine it, can you?"

Henriella shook her head, frowning. "It is difficult to believe."

"I shall speak to Tirano directly after breakfast," Anela decided. He would have to know; whether he ordered the arrest or only approved it, he'd be aware of any accusations of treason.

Anela ate quickly and was soon outside the door of Tirano's quarters. But he wasn't there.

"Advisors' meeting," the guard explained.

Anela nodded and turned on her heel to head to the meeting room. When she arrived, the door was still open, so the meeting hadn't started. She found Tirano inside, reading over some scroll while they waited for everyone to arrive.

"May I have a word before your meeting starts, my king?" she asked, stopping before him.

He glanced up at her and sighed. "What is it?"

"I heard a servant was arrested for treason. What is she accused of doing? I know the girl, I can't imagine..." She trailed off, an expectant expression on her face.

"Ah, yes, the maid." He gave her a tight smile. "It seems your idea worked. An informant came forward and told us she was involved in those ridiculous notes. The guards arrested her last night, and when they searched her belongings this morning, they found another one." He pulled a piece of parchment out of his pocket and offered it to her. "I'm not sure if it was intended for me or for you, but the handwriting matches the other two."

Anela scanned it, and the writing did seem to match. "*It's almost time. Are you ready for a new king and queen?*" She frowned and handed it back to him. "Who turned her in? Has she been questioned yet?"

Tirano shrugged. "Anonymous tip to one of the guards, and no, I want to be present during the interrogation and there hasn't been time yet. Now, if that's all, we must get to work." He gestured around the room, where all the advisors had found their seats.

"Of course," she said. With a polite smile directed toward the rest of the room, she left swiftly.

As soon as she was out of the room, the smile fell from her face. Stomach twisting, she leaned against a wall, feeling one of the episodes coming on. Ice and heat swept over her body as she shivered and started to sweat all at once.

Of all people, she never would have expected Henriella's solution to deflect the problem of those notes to come down to *Lisia* being arrested. That's what her actions had caused: a fifteen-year-old maid being imprisoned. She had no idea if Lisia was actually guilty of the charge; someone could have framed her by planting that note in her belongings. But regardless, Anela felt awful about it. If Lisia was involved, she was no doubt being manipulated and used by others. She was barely more than a child.

And now the poor girl was at the mercy of the king, his guards, and their interrogation methods.

Anela shook her head hard. No, she had to try to get ahead of that nightmare. If she could get Lisia to tell her who was actually behind all of this, then perhaps she could convince Tirano to be lenient with the maid.

She waited ten minutes until the episode passed. Determined to get to Lisia before the king, she forced her shaky legs to carry her toward the dungeons.

Unfortunately, Lisia wouldn't tell her much.

"Lisia, honey, please. Tell me who gave you those notes. I know you didn't write them."

Lisia sniffed and shook her head. "I can write my name, but that's about all."

"So you don't even know what they said." It was unsurprising.

"N-not exactly," the girl sniffled. "And I can't tell you who gave them to me."

"Why not, my dear? The king would certainly be much more lenient on you if you did. And trust me, he's going to try to get answers too, and he won't be as nice about it as I am."

Lisia shuddered. “I can't! Th-they said they'd hurt my family. I have little sisters. I can't do that to them.”

“So you didn’t want to help them? But they bullied you into it.”

Silence. Then, “I did want to, at first. But then I changed my mind and tried to tell hi—them that I didn't want to be involved. And they threatened my family.”

“What if I made sure your family was protected?”

Lisia gave half a shrug. “I don't know. Maybe, if I knew for sure...”

Chapter Thirty

MILOS

As soon as Milos entered the library, he spotted his father sitting at one of the heavy wood tables with a pile of scrolls and tomes in front of him. He stopped next to the table and cleared his throat. "Father. You sent for me?"

Tirano glanced up, then returned his gaze to the book open in front of him. "Yes. Sit down."

Milos suppressed a sigh and sat across from the king.

Tirano finally closed the book and met Milos's gaze. "The Kaosudan princess and her retinue will arrive soon, sometime in the next few days most likely. In a few weeks, we will hold a ball to announce your engagement."

Milos's jaw dropped.

His father smirked. "Any questions? I'm quite busy."

Milos snapped his jaw shut. "Yes, I have questions," he said through clenched teeth. "What in the Seven are you talking about?"

Tirano's voice grew tight with impatience. "You heard me. The princess will arrive soon and we'll announce your engagement at a ball. I wanted you to be prepared." Tirano reached for a scroll and unrolled it as Milos fought to keep his temper controlled.

"Why?" he bit out.

Tirano's gaze sharpened. "I would think it obvious. You need to marry and produce an heir. The Kaosudan king will cease hostile engagement if you take his daughter as your wife." Tirano paused, considering. "So he says, anyway. I think he'll follow through, as he won't want anything ... unfortunate to happen to his daughter. A new trade arrangement will be put in place after the wedding. It's the perfect solution."

Milos thought his teeth might crack from how tightly he clenched his jaw. He wanted desperately to argue. To refuse. Yet he was too aware how little good it would do. Better to go along for now. Maybe his mother could find some way to get him out of this arrangement.

"I see." He stood. "I'll let you get back to your task." He walked away, not waiting to be dismissed. He thought he heard a soft chuckle behind him. He ignored it and kept going, letting his feet carry him to his mother's quarters.

He felt powerless, impotent; a grown man shouldn't need to run to his mother to fix his problems. But he had no idea how he would be able to get out of this. If he even could.

Unfortunately, Anela wasn't there.

He obtained his cloak and stormed out of the castle with no plan. Once outside, he decided to seek out Bristio. The old guard wouldn't have the power to change the king's plans, but he would at least be sympathetic. Besides, he had been missing Bristio. When they were at the castle, he was assigned to a regular guard rotation and Milos didn't see him as much, especially now that Tirano kept Milos so busy.

He found Bristio in the barracks, fortunately off duty, and convinced him to take a walk around the grounds.

"Aye, I can see you're not about to sit still," Bristio observed. "Let's go then."

By the time they reached the frozen gardens behind the castle, Milos had told Bristio all about the arranged marriage.

Bristio tsked. "I see why you're upset. But you knew it would likely come to this, no? You *are* heir to the throne. An advantageous marriage is expected."

Milos groaned. "I guess I thought I'd have *some* choice in the matter."

Bristio hummed. "You don't know the young woman, correct?"

Milos shook his head. "We've met before, years ago. I was barely grown, and she was still a child."

"It wouldn't hurt to give her a chance, then, would it?"

Milos pressed his lips together and said nothing. Bristio wasn't wrong. The issue was that another woman already possessed Milos's heart. She wasn't a princess, or even a noble, but he wanted her regardless.

Bristio eyed him. "Well? What's the problem?"

Milos blew out a breath. "The problem is I've already met someone."

"Ah. Who is she? One of the ladies at court?"

Milos shook his head miserably. "No. She's not a member of the nobility, and she's not royal."

Bristio's eyebrows crept closer to his hairline. "A commoner?" He pursed his lips, then his face lit with understanding. "That girl from the wedding in Sonos Harbor. Tell me you didn't fall for her?"

Milos's silence answered the question.

Bristio gave a low whistle. "I assumed she was one of your many single-night conquests."

Milos jerked his head in a negative. "No. I haven't—we haven't even..."

Bristio chuckled. "Oh, you have it bad, then."

Milos sighed wearily. "You could say that. What am I supposed to do?"

Bristio clapped a hand on his shoulder, voice full of sympathy. "I don't think the king is giving you a choice. I'm sorry, son."

When Milos returned to the castle, he entered through the kitchens. It wasn't even supper time, but he needed an ale, or wine, something to take the edge off his mild panic. The servants were rushing around, all abuzz. He spotted Mistress Danias.

"What's going on?" He gestured vaguely at everyone.

"Oh, as if you don't know!" Mistress Danias trilled. "We have orders to prepare for the arrival of the Kaosudan princess, as well as the ball in a few weeks. How exciting for you!"

He tried to smile but wasn't sure how successful the effort was. Mistress Danias didn't notice, already bustling away to direct the preparations.

Fantastic. Now the entire castle knew. He exhaled through his nose as he ducked into the wine closet and snagged a bottle. He piled some random bits of food on a tray as well, turning down several offers of help, and took it all to his quarters. He just wanted to be left alone.

He didn't go down to supper.

Chapter Thirty-One

VERANA

Ana felt terribly guilty going home on her next days off as though everything was normal, leaving Lisia in the castle dungeon. But what could she do for Lisia? Absolutely nothing.

Hearing the gossip about the Kaosudan princess, how everyone thought she would likely end up engaged to Milos, didn't improve Ana's mood. She chastised herself for being silly; this was exactly what she knew would happen. This was the reason she had tried not to let him get too close.

The fact that she dreamed about the taste and feel of his lips made her irrationally angry about the whole situation. Equally frustrating was when that dream was followed by another steamy one about Ben. Why was her brain torturing her, lusting after not just one man, but two?

Out of her would-be suitors, Ben was most accessible. Ana begged him to accompany her on the journey. She felt obligated to go home, yet at the same time was dreading it: her first time back since Aldo's funeral. If Ben came along, she would have the pleasant distraction of someone to talk to. He agreed, although he couldn't stay. He'd escort her and return to the capital, as he was needed at the stables.

They took Ben's horse and Ana borrowed his mother's. On the road to her village, Ben was much quieter than usual. Ana didn't wish to be left alone to her thoughts; that was her entire reason for asking him to come along. It didn't help that the weather was miserable, drizzly and gray.

"Is anything the matter?" she asked after half an hour of silent riding. "You're so quiet."

He glanced at her, then shook his head with a small smile. "My apologies. I have a lot on my mind."

"If you wish to talk about it, I'm happy to listen."

This time, when his hazel eyes slid to hers, they remained focused on her, considering. "Can you keep a secret, Ana?"

Her heart sped up. "Yes. We're friends, aren't we?"

He gave her a knowing look. "Maybe more than friends."

She blushed and looked away. "Maybe."

He cleared his throat. "All right. I trust you. Do you remember that night at the tavern, when I told you there were folks who'd be eager to see the king overthrown?"

She swallowed, suddenly nervous. Too late to back out now. "Yes, I remember."

He pressed his lips together, then blew out a breath. "I know that's the case because I know a lot of those people. I'm one of them."

Ana stilled at his admission, although it wasn't all that surprising. "I see."

He chuckled dryly. "You don't, but you will. Everyone will. There are a lot of us, and we're making plans." He paused. "I planned to tell you eventually, because I don't want you to be in any danger."

"Oh. Well, thank you." She stared at the road ahead, processing his words. "What plans?"

He grimaced. "I'm afraid I can't tell you that part... Unless you'll join us. I really wish you would."

"Will—will there be fighting? Bloodshed?"

He gave half a shrug. "It's pretty much inevitable, unfortunately. But you wouldn't be part of that." He sounded so determined, and she wasn't sure if he was trying to convince her or himself. "I'd never let anything happen to you."

She gave him a weak smile. "I know you wouldn't. Is that why you went to work at the stables, then? To spy for this rebellion?"

He cleared his throat, swiveling his gaze to the road ahead. "Yes. We could use someone inside the castle as well."

She gasped at a realization. "Lisia. Lisia was part of this?"

He nodded with a frown. "Yes, she was. She is. She knew the risks. We all do. When the time comes, she'll be set free again. She is more fortunate than our other ally in court; poor man ended up dead, although I have reason to believe he may have become greedy and brought it on himself. But that means I'm the only one on the inside. I'm sure Lisia would appreciate it if you could be her replacement."

He stared at her expectantly, and she tried to think of what to say. She didn't love that the rebels had allowed a fifteen-year-old girl to risk her life for them. Yet, fifteen-year-olds were notoriously headstrong with poor judgement; maybe Lisia would have involved herself regardless. As to this other man he referenced, she searched her mind for who he might mean. Perhaps the king's close friend, the lord who died just before she started working there? Would the king's own best friend betray him? She had heard of no other recent deaths at court.

"Thank you for telling me. As far as joining you, I need some time to think about it."

He inclined his head in acknowledgement. "That's fair."

They rode quietly for a few minutes before he spoke again. "So, what do you think about this visit from the Kaosudan princess? It seems everyone expects her to marry Prince Milos."

She pressed her lips together as her stomach lurched. "I don't think anything of it. It's none of my business."

He raised a brow. "It seems like you two are friends. Is that not right? Most people would have an opinion about a friend's potential marriage."

She huffed a laugh. "We are on friendly terms, at best. That hardly makes us true friends. Come now, Ben, do you really expect a prince to befriend a maid?" Bitterness tinged her words.

"I admit, it seemed odd. I must have misunderstood."

She gave a single sharp nod but said nothing, the dishonesty heavy in her chest. Even if she and Milos had been friends—or more—that would be over soon. Her eyes burned with tears, which she hastily blinked away.

The drizzle soon turned into hail, and they took cover in the woods for the sake of the horses. The pines didn't offer full protection, but they at least slowed the hail stones.

"It probably won't last long," Ben said dubiously. "We just need to wait it out."

Ana nodded as she dismounted. She stood shivering, looking out at the road.

Ben noticed and moved closer to her. He held his cloak in one hand so he could wrap it around her along with his arm, holding it in place. "You're cold," he murmured.

"I am." She snuggled into his side. "Thank you." She tilted her head to look up at him. One corner of his mouth quirked up as he stared at her. Then he bent his head, brushing his lips over hers.

All of her recent—nearly nightly—dreams about him rushed to the forefront of her mind, in startlingly vivid detail. Warmth pooled between her legs. She leaned into the kiss hungrily, and he responded in kind. His tongue demanded entrance and she welcomed him into her mouth. It wasn't the same as kissing Milos, but as soon as that thought came, she shoved it away. She refused to think about him.

He turned her, pulling her in until her chest was flush against his. His hands came to her face, her neck, caressing and exploring. She wrapped her arms around his waist, urging him closer until she could feel his length hard against her belly. She groaned at the sensation, and a growl rumbled in his chest. The tingling in her core grew stronger and she squeezed her thighs together.

Suddenly he broke away, his arm coming down under her knees while the other wrapped around her shoulders. She let out a quiet yelp of surprise as he lifted her and carried her farther into the trees, laying her down on a patch of leaves and needles free of snow.

His upper body hovered over hers, his legs and groin pressing against her as he captured her mouth again. She moaned against his lips as she let him in.

His skilled tongue, his firm touch, his male scent—he was all encompassing. Every other thought flew from her mind. She noticed it long enough to feel grateful for the reprieve, and then she was lost in the sensations again. She never wanted this to end.

Then his mouth was on her neck, sucking and nipping, moving down her chest. He nuzzled her breasts as she panted. "You're so beautiful," he murmured against her skin. "And you taste so good. Gods, Ana, I want you."

His words only stoked the fire deep in her belly. She gasped at the intensity of the sensation between her legs. "You have me," she breathed. "Please, Ben." Another thought of Milos flitted through her consciousness—when he warned her to be careful of who she trusted—but she pushed it aside. He wouldn't want her to be doing this, yet he'd be doing the same with the Kaosudan princess soon enough.

That realization hurt, and she sought comfort in Ben's ministrations to her body, focusing only on the physical sensations.

He groaned, moving up again for a searing kiss. "Since you asked so nicely." He smirked at her as he nudged her legs apart before kneeling between them. He pushed her skirts and her shift up to her waist, exposing her to the frigid air. It didn't matter; she was fairly certain her skin was on fire.

His hands came to her hips, stroking up and down. "So soft," he murmured. Then he looked up to her. "Have you ever...?"

She shook her head. "No. But I want to. *Please.*"

He nodded. "I'm going to make you feel so good, sweetheart." He palmed her thighs and pushed them apart farther, then lay on his belly. "Gods, Ana, you're so wet for me. I can't wait to taste this little cunt."

Even as he was face to face with her most private parts, she blushed at the coarse language and almost recoiled ...

but she could feel his hot breath on her center, and then he kissed her there. She thought her heart might stop. "Oh... Oh, gods, Ben..."

He chuckled against her. "You'll be screaming my name soon, honey." He flattened his tongue and licked her, bottom to top. Her back bowed and he placed one palm on her belly, pushing her down. "Be good and stay still now," he rumbled.

She tried, but it was very difficult not to move as his tongue explored all of her. It dipped inside of her, then moved up and circled the spot that had only ever been touched with her fingers, and once or twice by the clumsy fumbling fingers of teen boys. Ben was a man, not a boy, and everything he was doing to her was evidence of his experience.

All she could do was moan as her hands came down to rest on his head, her fingers curling into the soft waves. "Please don't stop," she whimpered.

She felt the vibration of his laugh against her. "As the lady commands."

His hand moved from her stomach, and he slid a finger inside her wet heat, once again circling her clit with his tongue. He went deeper inside her and she felt a small pinch, barely noticeable among all the other sensations. Then he withdrew, and when he entered her again, he used two fingers.

She gasped as he stretched her. He hummed. "Just making sure you're ready for me, honey. I don't want to hurt you."

His touch drove her mad, and she rolled her hips over and over as he pumped in and out, always circling her most sensitive spot. Something in her core grew tighter, and hotter, climbing higher. It felt like when she touched herself, but about a thousand times more intense.

"Ben, I—I..." She couldn't complete a sentence.

"I know, sweetheart. Come for me now." His lips wrapped around the small, sensitive bundle of nerves and sucked as his fingers plunged into her.

Her breath caught as she shook, falling apart, the sensation spreading through her entire body, and then again, waves of ecstasy washing over her. She cried out his name, more than once, as he had promised. He kept licking and moving his hand, carrying her through the sensations.

When she came back to herself, she looked down at his grinning face. "I think you're ready for me." He raised his eyebrows in a question.

She nodded eagerly, still wanting to feel closer to him, to capture how she felt when he was with her in her dreams. Because something was missing… The physical pleasure, as intense as it was, didn't mimic the connection she felt with him in those dreams. But maybe that was because they hadn't done *everything* yet.

He rose to his knees again and undid his britches, exposing his throbbing cock. Her breath caught.

He moved over her once more, bracing himself on his forearms on either side of her. She felt him against her core, his tip resting at her entrance.

As he started to push inside, a worry passed through her mind. "I'm not ready for a baby, Ben."

He nodded, biting his lip as he forced himself to move slowly. "I know, honey. I won't leave my seed in you."

She smiled, reassured, and then gasped as he pressed deeper, stretching her much more than his two fingers had.

He blew out a breath, pausing. "Fuck. You're so tight. You feel amazing."

It did feel amazing. She lifted her hips, wordlessly urging him to keep going. He groaned, withdrew, then thrust all the way inside.

"All right?" he asked, panting as he looked down at her.

"Yes," she breathed. "I want more. Keep going."

He obliged, withdrawing once more and then sliding back in. She met him thrust for thrust, feeling that sensation building in her core all over again. Her hands wandered under his shirt, running over his stomach and chest, wanting to be even closer to him and wishing it wasn't too cold to get completely naked.

"Ben..." She wriggled underneath him as she got closer and closer to the precipice. But she needed something...

"Touch yourself," he rasped. "Come for me again."

Sliding her hand between their bodies, she did as he said, and the coiling in her belly tightened. She contracted around him once and his pace grew frantic.

Another moment and she fell off the edge, crying out. He thrust hard once more and then stilled, letting out a long, low groan. That's when she felt heat flood her insides and hazily questioned the strange sensation.

When she came back down, she realized. Still panting, she said, "Ben, you said you wouldn't—"

"I know, sweetheart, I'm sorry. You just felt too good. You're not likely to get pregnant your very first time, though."

The words didn't sit quite right in her mind. She frowned. Her mother had explained all the basics of sex, and she never said anything about the first time being different in any significant way, other than it might be uncomfortable.

But looking up into his hazel eyes, she *wanted* to trust him. He had no reason to lie to her.

He peppered kisses over her face before he pulled out of her. He stood and did his pants up. "Stay there," he said as he walked back to the horses. He pulled a spare handkerchief out of his small bag and returned, handing it to her.

She thanked him and cleaned herself up. He offered a hand to help her stand, then pulled her into an embrace.

"Thank you, Ana," he murmured into her hair. "For giving me something you've never given anyone."

She released a soft exhale. "Thank you for taking care of me. For making it feel good."

He drew back and gave her an indignant look. "Good? That's it?"

She threw her head back and laughed. "Fantastic. Amazing. Better?"

He winked at her. "Much." Dropping a kiss on her forehead, he continued, "I suppose this means you've given your official permission for me to court you?"

Her breath caught in her chest, almost painful, as Milos's face appeared in her mind, with his soul-piercing green eyes and infuriating smirk. She bit the inside of her lip until it hurt, willing the image to fade. Forcing a smile, she said, "I suppose so."

Chapter Thirty-Two

VERANA

Ana's homecoming was subdued, as expected. Her parents were happy to see her, but it had only been a month since Aldo passed. Everyone was still deep in their grief, and being back home made Ana feel it more intensely.

Her sadness didn't override the unease she felt after Ben spilled inside of her, however. She surreptitiously made a cup of her mother's contraceptive tea after Halia went to bed. It couldn't hurt.

The following day, when her father invited her to go fishing with him, she happily accepted despite the cold. Their cabin felt so empty without Aldo's cheerful presence, and everything reminded her of him.

Her thoughts returned to her conversation with Ben as they ambled to the water. Should she join a rebellion against the king?

Once they settled on the bank of the creek, Luciano cast his line into the water beyond the frozen edge. "I can tell you have something on your mind. Do you want to talk about it?"

She smiled at his perceptiveness. "I *shouldn't* talk about it. I promised to keep it a secret."

Luciano frowned, staring at the water. "Who asked you to keep a secret from your family? That's odd behavior."

She bit her lip. "Do you remember Ben?"

He wrinkled his brow, just barely visible in the shadow of the hood of his cloak. "The nice boy from the wedding? He helped when Aldo—" He cut himself off with a grimace. "He helped dig the grave, along with the Vincento fellow."

She nodded. "He works at the royal stables, and he rode most of the way here with me." She paused, unsure how to continue. The topic was bound to shock him, and she didn't want to betray Ben. "He wants me to do something, and I'm not sure if I should."

A scowl formed on Luciano's face. "No real man would pressure you into something you're not ready for, daughter."

She huffed a laugh. "No, it's not like that. I'm not talking about sex, Papa."

"Ah." A stray curl peeked out near his lightly bearded jaw; he scratched the spot, then pushed the tendril behind his ear. "What is it he wants you to do?"

She took a deep breath, looking down at the ice, and made her decision. She trusted her father more than anyone else. "Join the rebel group he's a part of and spy for them in the castle." She risked a glance at him, but he didn't appear shocked. He rubbed a gloved hand over his face and the crease between his eyebrows deepened

"I see. And you're considering it?"

She stared at him. "Papa, you aren't even surprised. Did you already know there's a rebellion brewing?"

He lifted and dropped a shoulder. "I've heard a few

whispers. Considering the rule of King Tirano, it's not surprising."

Ana blew out a breath. "Oh. Well ... yes, I'm considering it. I don't blame the rebels for wanting change. It will probably be violent, though, and I don't like that." She frowned. "I serve the queen, so they'll want me to spy on her. And Papa, she's truly kind. She's not like the king at all."

For a few minutes, the only sounds were the drips of melted ice and the breeze whistling through the trees.

"What else?" Luciano said abruptly. "That's not everything, is it?"

Ana chuckled, blowing on her hands. "How do you always know?"

He smiled thinly but said nothing.

"I—I've already done a little spying. Not for the rebels, though. It was an accident. I overheard a conversation and it made me curious." She was babbling. She took a deep breath. "The queen is from Orakolas, as you know. So her gift is from Orix. And she received a prophecy, many years ago, about the fall of a king. She thinks it refers to King Tirano. I've been trying to figure out what the prophecy means. Maybe if I understand it, I can help it come about. It might be a better approach than a bloody rebellion. It refers to someone—a woman—seeking truth."

This time when she looked up at her father, his gray eyes were wide, his body utterly still. "Papa?"

He shook himself and focused on her, speaking carefully, as though not to allow any emotion to escape. "What does the prophecy say? Do you remember?"

"I memorized it." Ana recited it for him, watching him closely. His brown skin, usually several shades darker than her own, took on a sickly, paler hue as his jaw clenched.

Silence fell when she finished. Luciano was still, almost frozen in place. “Papa, what is it? Are you all right?”

He pressed his lips into a firm line, shaking his head slowly. Finally, he said, “I think I have to tell you something, Ana. It ... it will come as a shock. And I want you to know the only reason I never told you was to keep you safe, but if you're angry, I understand.”

Her heart skipped a beat. “What is it, Papa? Please, tell me.” It was something serious, that much she could see. She couldn’t imagine what would have him so upset.

He pulled the line out of the water, coiling it as he went, and set it aside. Then he turned to her and enveloped her hands in his own, his expression deadly serious.

“First, a question for you. Do you have any ... any odd skills? A special ability no one knows about?”

The blood drained from her face. “How did you know?”

He didn't answer her question. “I thought so. Do you remember how I could always tell when you children were little and lied about something? And Aldo ... he was good at that too, telling truth from lies.”

She nodded, biting her lip. “Yes. I remember when I knocked over a bucket of goat’s milk and tried to blame the goats. But you knew.” She had a bit of that instinct as well.

A soft, fleeting smile crossed over his face as the memory. “I remember that too.” He took a deep breath. “You already know the Seven gods and goddesses gifted the seven royal families with special abilities. Magic of various sorts.” He swallowed, gaze drifting to stare into the woods. “You’re most familiar with Sonos. And you mentioned Orix. Do you remember the patron goddess of Libeverro?”

She searched her memory; the pastros taught all children certain facts about the seven kingdoms, and the Seven themselves. “Is it Veyra?”

He gave a single sharp nod. "Yes. The goddess of truth and lies."

Her mind raced, trying to put it all together. "I don't understand. You're from Libeverro, but..." She trailed off, not stating the obvious: her father was a poor farmer and fisher, not a royal or even a noble.

He grimaced, then sat up straighter, looking her in the eye. "I was born Prince Armando Luciano Vertitio, second son of King Vertitio and Queen Alanna, younger brother to the current king, Aluzio."

Ana's mouth dropped open as she gasped. "You—what—"

He held up a hand. "It's a very long story, and for this moment, you only need the short version. You and your brothers—brother—are descended from the Libeverran royal line. You and Aldo, at least, inherited the gift of Veyra. I'm not sure about Leo." He waved a hand, dismissive. "So when I heard this prophecy about a woman, this 'One' who seeks truth and washes away lies, and there you are, working in the castle... Well. It gave me a shock."

Ana couldn't even process his statement about the prophecy. She was still stuck on the first piece of information. "What is a Libeverran prince doing *here*?" She looked around at the woods pointedly. She had so many questions—did her mother know?—yet this was the most pressing.

"Essentially, my brother, the heir to the throne, was born without Veyra's gift. He tried to hide it, but obviously, he couldn't get away with lying about it." He chuckled softly. "And I had the gift in spades. Everyone whispered and gossiped, saying the goddess must have chosen me as heir, even though I'm not the eldest." He sighed. "I didn't wish to be king. My brother did, and he saw me as a threat. I told him over and over that I didn't want the throne. That I would support his rule, lend my abilities for the good of the kingdom. He didn't have the ability to know I told the truth." His laugh was bitter. "The irony doesn't escape me. I had two choices: stay at court where he would find a way to do away with me eventually, or leave. I chose exile."

"Oh, Papa," Ana breathed. She didn't know what to say. How awful, to lose his home, family, and friends purely because of a jealous sibling.

He squeezed her hands once before letting them go. "It was a very long time ago. I was allowed to take nothing except the clothes on my back and a few coins, enough to buy passage on a ship and a few basics to start a new life. I came to Revas. I didn't intend to stay here… Then I met your mother." He saw the question in her gaze. "No, she doesn't know—not the whole truth. I told her I was a disgraced Libeverran nobleman's son." He winced. "I didn't want to lie, but I also didn't know her well at that point, and I didn't want any word to get out about where I was. I wouldn't have put it past my brother to seek me out and kill me anyway."

Sorrow squeezed her chest. "You gave up everything. It's not fair."

He smiled and patted her leg. "I gave up material wealth and status in exchange for keeping my life and having a beautiful family with a home full of love. I have no regrets." His eyes turned glassy. "Well, I didn't. Until your brother got sick, and we couldn't..." He shook his head, swiping his forearm across his face.

A tear trickled down Ana's cheek and she wiped it away. He stood and pulled her up into his embrace. "I'm sorry I never told you. I thought you and your brothers would be better off not knowing."

Fishing forgotten, they gathered the supplies and started

back toward the cabin. Ana's mind spun at a dizzying pace as she tried to absorb everything her father had confessed.

She was *royal.* Her secret skill was actual magic gifted from Veyra. Her father, a prince. Memories surfaced as she pieced the truth together.

Luciano was far more educated than anyone else she had met in their village—even the pastro. He was well-spoken and well-mannered. How had she never seen it before? He behaved more like nobility than any other poor farmer or fisher she had ever met.

Yet, having this knowledge changed nothing, as far as she could tell. Her father was in exile. Their life was their life. So she had a touch of Veyra's gift. What did it matter?

She wasn't sure how she felt about the fact that he had kept it all a secret. However, that was neither here nor there; it certainly wasn't the most urgent issue.

"So you think I'm 'The One' in the prophecy?" she asked as they trudged through the snow and ice.

"I can't know for sure. But it's quite the coincidence, isn't it? For you, with Veyra's gift, to hear about the prophecy, and have reason to want it to come true. Seems possible that it's the gods meddling."

When she returned to the castle, the Kaosudan retinue had arrived. She wanted to seek out Ben, but all of the servants were even busier than usual, and she didn't get the chance.

She caught glimpses of the princess despite trying to avoid her. The young woman was lovely to look upon, and everyone said she was sweet and demure, perhaps a little shy. Ana had no doubt all of that was true, yet every time she saw the princess, she couldn't help picturing her with

Milos—Milos kissing her, for example. The images Ana's brain conjured tied her up in knots of sadness and jealousy.

To her dismay, Mistress Danias ordered her to check on Princess Melliada one afternoon. "See if she desires a tea tray—sometimes she does, other times not. If she's not in the guest quarters, you'll most likely find her in the library."

That was where Ana tracked her down ten minutes later. The princess sat in a large armchair, feet curled under her, a huge tome open in her lap.

Ana took a deep breath and curtsied. "Good afternoon, Your Highness. Mistress Danias sent me to ask if you'd like tea today."

Melliada looked up from the pages, blinking owlishly. "Oh, hello. What was that? Tea? No, not right now. I can't risk ruining the texts with food or drink, but I also desperately want to finish this section." She smiled sheepishly. "Thank you for checking."

"You're welcome. I'll let you get back to your reading, Your Highness."

She turned to go. Melliada said, "Wait! Do you have a few minutes to spare? There is something I'd ask of you."

Ana turned, doing her best to maintain a neutral expression. The woman *was* sweet and demure, and beautiful on top of it—everything a princess should be. Ana did her best not to picture the princess with Milos. Every time she did, her guts twisted unpleasantly. When they married, she wasn't sure if she'd be able to stay on at the castle. Then again, with the rebellion, she had no idea what might happen.

"It would be my pleasure," Ana gritted out. "What can I do for you, princess?"

Melliada straightened, setting her feet on the floor. "You're from Revas, are you not?"

"I am."

"I was wondering if you could tell me what types of tales your people tell about the Diona."

Ana blinked at the unexpected request. "The Diona?" she asked stupidly. Melliada gave an encouraging nod. Ana swallowed. Every single thing she had ever heard about the magical folk flew from her mind. "The usual types of tales, I suppose."

Melliada chuckled. "What I mean is, the 'usual' tales can differ from kingdom to kingdom. I'm curious what the average citizen of Revas believes about them."

"Oh." Ana took a deep breath, searching for an answer. "Um, well, they have magic, obviously. After the Sundering, they left some of it behind, imbued into objects like lanterns and paintings. I didn't realize that until I came to work at the castle, though." She chewed on her lip. "As a child, I heard all sorts of things. Some folks claim they're dangerous, that they used to kidnap infants and children. Others say they were kind to our people long ago, lending their magic to help us with things like healing. I suppose I always assumed it was probably a mix of both."

Melliada gave a slow nod, pursing her lips. "That is the most likely scenario, I agree." She exhaled a long breath before the corners of her mouth rose in a polite smile. "I'll let you return to your duties. Thank you for humoring me."

By the Seven, this woman was … sweet. Earnest. "Good day, Your Highness." Ana turned and made her way back toward the kitchens, furiously blinking away unwanted tears.

What was there to cry over? She should be happy Milos would have a beautiful, intelligent, kind wife. She should want *him* to be happy, if she cared for him.

And she did wish that … while also being devastated he wouldn't find that happiness with *her*.

The day before the highly anticipated ball, Ana finally managed to sneak away for a short while to seek out Ben. She wouldn't be needed for an hour at least. He would likely be at the stables, but she didn't want to waste any time, so to be sure, she focused on that pull inside of her and followed its guidance.

He was indeed working. She waited as he finished his grooming task, feet shifting in impatience until he finally came out to join her.

"To what do I owe the pleasure of your presence?" he asked with a smile as he kissed the back of her hand.

She felt her cheeks warm. "I want to talk with you, if you can get away for a little while?"

He called out to another groom. "Cover me for a few?"

The other man looked Ana up and down with a smirk. "It would take me more than a few minutes, personally, but all right."

Ben chuckled as Ana's mouth dropped open in indignation. "Ignore him," Ben advised. "Come, let's walk." He offered his arm.

With one last glare at the rude stable hand, she allowed Ben to lead her away.

They walked all the way to the edge of the woods. "I assume you'd like privacy?" he said with a wink.

She nodded, and he led her into the trees, stopping a few minutes later. He turned to her and brought his hands to cradle her face, dropping a light kiss on her lips.

She smiled against him. "As much as I'd like to continue,

I don't have much time, and I really do need to speak with you."

He pulled back. "Will you be joining us, then?"

She stared at him, momentarily lost. "Oh. The rebels, you mean?"

He frowned. "I assumed that's what you wanted to talk about. You told me before that you wanted time to think."

She pressed her lips together, leaning against a tree trunk. "I did. But that's not exactly what I wanted to tell you. I suppose it's somewhat related..."

He quirked an eyebrow, crossing his arms over his chest. "What is it then?"

Was she really about to tell the secret her father had kept for over two decades? Surely it would help to have someone at the castle on her side, someone who could help her make the prophecy come to pass.

She took a deep breath. "There might be a different way to make a change in the monarchy. You see, the queen herself was given a prophecy about the fall of the king."

He listened, eyes growing wide, as she recited the prophecy and then explained why her father thought it might involve her.

When she finished, he stared at her, jaw working. "By the Seven, Ana. This is..."

She shrugged, chuckling. "A lot."

"You're a royal." He still sounded stunned. "Really?"

"Apparently. I can't see why my father would lie."

He inclined his head. "Fair point. And this prophecy…" He trailed off, staring into the distance. "It makes sense. You had a tragic loss. You have Veyra's magic." He paused. "How does that work, exactly? Your ability? The same way as your father?"

She shook her head. "Not exactly. I have a little intuition

about when someone is lying, but not like Papa and Aldo. When I need to find something, I can just ... do it. When I explained to Papa, he said it sounded like being able to seek the truth in a physical form. That's how I found the queen's journal." She paused, considering. "Maybe if I practiced with it more, I could learn how to detect lies better."

He heaved a sigh that almost sounded … relieved? "Perhaps." Then he shook himself, looking around. "We better get back. We'll be missed."

"Yes, I suppose so." As they turned back toward the castle, she asked, "So, would you be willing to help me figure it out? See if we can determine what to do to ensure it comes true?"

He glanced down at her, expression unreadable. "Aren't you worried about the 'her blood will flow' bit?"

She bit her lip. "I've barely thought about it. A little, I suppose. Papa said it might not mean real physical blood. It might be what he called a metaphor." She stood straighter. "But if I can help the whole kingdom, I'm going to try, regardless of any consequence to myself. I won't be selfish." More softly, she added, "I need to do it. For Aldo."

His smile was soft, yet strained. "That's brave of you." He blew out a breath. "I need some time to think as well before I give you an answer."

"Right. I understand," she said, although she couldn't help the sharp stab of disappointment.

Chaos reigned the following day, preceding the ball. The last of the food had to be prepped, the entire castle scrubbed to gleaming, plus they had all of the regular tasks to complete and small problems to solve.

Ana hurriedly ate a bit of bread and cheese after helping with the midday meal, as she walked to her bedroom to switch out her apron. Her current one had gotten berry preserves all over it when one of the other maids fumbled the jar. When she arrived, several castle guards stood outside her door.

One of them pointed in her direction. "I think that's her."

She froze, a bite of bread halfway to her mouth.

"Verana, daughter of Luciano and Halia?" One of the guards approached her.

She nodded, lowering her hand and squeezing the bread in her fist, reducing it to crumbs.

"Come with us." He grasped her upper arm and pulled her past her room.

"Wait!" She pulled back, which had no effect on his strong grip. "Why? What's happening?"

The man looked back at her, face set in hard lines. "You're under arrest by order of His Majesty."

She hardly heard them over the blood pounding in her ears, but she managed to make sense of the words.

"For what? I've done nothing!"

No one answered. The man yanked on her arm again. Recognizing she couldn't possibly fight off or escape several armed guards, she forced her feet to cooperate. She glanced around desperately for help, but no one else was around.

Several corridors and two flights of stairs later, she was in the bowels of the castle, facing a hall of barred cells. Marching her down toward the opposite end of the hall, one guard pulled out a key and gestured to an open cell. They shoved her in, and by the time she turned around, the door clanged shut and the guard flipped the key in the lock.

They left without another word. Back against the cold

stone wall, she slid down to the floor, wrapping her arms around her, already shivering. As their footsteps faded, she swallowed back a sob. Then she heard a tremulous voice.

"Who's there?"

She sat bolt upright. She knew that voice. "Lisia? Is that you?"

"Yes..." Her voice held a question.

"It's me, Ana."

A sharp intake of breath preceded the reply. "Ana! By the Seven, what are you doing here?"

Ana choked back a hysterical laugh. "I don't know. They didn't tell me the charge." She stood and moved to the bars, where she could see Lisia's pale face peering out at her from the opposite cell. "Are you all right?" The hall was dark and gloomy despite the handful of sconces lining the walls.

Lisia's laugh was bitter. "I'm still alive. For now."

"What exactly did they accuse you of?"

"Remember the notes that caused such an uproar? The ones left for the king and queen?"

Ana gasped. "That was you?"

Lisia's voice held tears. "Y-yes. I also spied on several members of the court, even Her Majesty, and reported anything I found out to one of the lords, but he's … he's dead now." Her voice held a note of fear. "I don't think they know about that part, though."

Ana's mind raced, thinking back to Ben mentioning a man on their side who had passed. It must be one and the same—what was his name? Lord Ruzo. She dismissed this revelation. "But they know about the notes. You sent those?"

"Kind of. I didn't write them. I don't even know how to read or write, other than my name. I only delivered them."

"For who? Who gave them to you?"

Lisia hesitated, answering in a low whisper. "Ben. I think you know him? He works in the stables."

All of the air left Ana's lungs. Ben. Why hadn't he told her when they spoke of Lisia? An uneasy feeling settled in her stomach.

"I do know him," she finally managed, voice faint. "Did he write them? Or was he only passing them along?"

"Since he's the leader of the rebellion, I'm pretty certain he wrote them."

"The—the leader? Are you sure?" Lisia must be incorrect. Surely Ben would have told her.

"Yes. He claims to be a bastard son of the king. And he's older than Prince Milos, so he plans to take the throne for himself."

Chapter Thirty-Three

MILOS

As the hours ticked away, getting closer and closer to the ball, Milos became more and more determined. He needed to speak with Ana. He would tell her exactly what he felt for her, and if she would agree to be his, he simply wouldn't show up that night. They could hardly announce his engagement if he wasn't present. He wasn't sure what would come after that. Maybe he'd have to run away, but he was willing to if Ana came with him. He would figure all of that out after he spoke with her.

He had been trapped in his quarters all day for final fittings and other such nonsense. When he finally emerged only a couple of hours before the feast would begin prior to the ball, he wandered the castle looking for Ana.

He couldn't find her anywhere. She had been working that morning, but she had disappeared shortly after lunch time.

"If you find her," Mistress Danias said, "tell her she needs to get back to work! Of all days to wander off..."

Milos walked away as the older woman continued to grumble.

The stables was his last resort. Ana was friends with Ben; maybe he had seen her.

He found the man shoveling fresh hay into the stalls and cleared his throat to get his attention.

Ben stood up, panting. “Your Highness. Do you need your horse readied?”

Milos shook his head. “I'm wondering if you've seen Ana today.”

Ben wrinkled his brow. “I haven't, Your Highness.” He paused. “Last I saw her was yesterday. She came and found me for some *private time*, if you know what I mean.” He winked suggestively, and Milos's heart thudded hard in his chest as his meaning sank in.

“You—you mean you and Ana...” He couldn't bring himself to say the words aloud.

Ben smiled smugly, taking a step toward Milos. “Yes, me and Ana. We made our courtship quite *official* on her last trip home a couple weeks past.”

Milos swallowed hard, his hands fisted at his sides, forcing himself to breathe and trying to convince himself to walk away.

“I'm sorry, Your Highness, does that bother you? She claimed the two of you weren’t friends. I'm still confused as to why you take such interest in your female servants. In any case, I know without a doubt that it was her first time with a man, so you never claimed her. I must say, that was your mistake. She tastes divine.”

Milos pulled back his arm, then sank his fist into Ben's stomach.

The other man doubled over with a gasp, obviously taken off guard. Milos's next punch landed on Ben's jaw, and he lost his balance, falling to his knees and catching himself on the doorway with one arm.

"Fuck you," Milos spit, then turned and stomped out of the stables.

He wandered the grounds aimlessly, his thoughts in turmoil, torturing him with every step.

Ana and Ben had sex. They were officially courting.

Ana *chose* Ben. Not Milos. Ben. And she told him Milos wasn't her friend, if Ben could be believed.

Milos trembled with anger when he replayed the conversation. Not only had she chosen Ben, she had allowed him to...

A growl rumbled in his chest; he shook his head violently, as though he could shake the images away.

He was an idiot. She had told him more than once that they couldn't be together. Yet somehow he still thought she was falling for him as hard as he was falling for her. He thought he might have a chance, even though she said otherwise over and over.

Such a fucking idiot.

Eventually he made his way back to his room. He was expected at the feast and the ball, and he resigned himself to his fate. If Ana didn't want him, he may as well please his parents by agreeing to marry Princess Melliada. Bristio had been right, anyway; his father wasn't going to give him much choice. Short of running away, it was unavoidable. But he wouldn't run. Not without Ana. What was the point?

Mellia, as she had asked him to call her, seemed like a nice enough girl. She was young—younger than Ana, barely nineteen. Quite old enough to wed, though. And she was pretty, with long, straight, dark hair and caramel skin. She didn't talk much, and he barely knew her. Still, it could be worse. She often hid in the library; assuming she liked to read, that counted in her favor.

He washed and dressed in a daze, sending the servants away so he could have a bit more time alone. Checking his appearance in the mirror, he barely recognized the face that stared back at him. His entire world had shifted, knowing he couldn't have Ana; nothing looked the same, not even his own visage.

He arrived at the feast on time, waited patiently to be formally announced, and sat at his place next to his mother, across from Princess Mellia.

He attempted to make small talk with her, but she was obviously nervous, replying only with a word or two. Until, that is, he came up with the correct question.

"I've noticed you're in the library often. What is it you've been reading? I enjoy books as well, although I don't have much time to read."

Her face lit from within, a sparkle shining in her deep brown eyes as she sat up straighter. "Oh yes, I love to read! I've been scouring your collection for histories about the Diona and the Sundering. It's kind of a special interest of mine, and I was hoping your library would have different texts than ours."

He smiled at her excitement. She really was lovely, with smooth, glowing skin and plump lips, but his heart wasn't moved. She wasn't Ana. "And does it?"

She nodded eagerly. "I've found at least half a dozen scrolls and tomes on the topic I've never seen before. One of them…"

She started to go into detail about her findings, and he attempted to listen as he picked at his food and drank too much wine, occasionally giving a nod or a vague comment such as, "Oh? How interesting."

In the background, his father spoke to one of the advisors, something about how the trade agreements with Kaosuda would alter after Milos married. Milos didn't pay close attention until the king turned to the queen and lowered his voice. If Tirano didn't wish to be overheard, Milos certainly wished to know what he had to say. He watched out of the corner of his eye, listening intently.

"The day has been so chaotic, I hadn't a chance to tell you the news."

The queen arched an eyebrow. "What news is that, my king?"

"It might concern that prophecy of yours. Even if not, I ousted a potential spy from our midst. I discovered that one of the maids might be a Libeverran royal in disguise. And the informant had reason to believe she could be 'The One' your prophecy refers to. I had her arrested, although I haven't had the time to verify the suspicions yet."

Milos set down his fork when his father mentioned the prophecy, straining to hear every word. His mother drew a sharp intake of breath.

"A royal? Who do you speak of?"

"Her name is Verana, daughter of Luciano—or apparently, daughter of Prince Armando Luciano Vertitio. I believe she is known as Ana here at the castle."

Milos had stopped breathing. His chest ached from the harsh thrum of his heart.

He barely heard his mother's reply. It was obvious she was surprised. Ana had served her directly, after all.

She was the daughter of a prince? And she had kept it from him? To what end? She kept harping on a royal not being allowed to court a common maid. But if she was royal as well, there was no issue, was there?

Something wasn't adding up. Why would a Libeverran

royal be sent to spy in a foreign court? If her father was indeed a prince, why did they live as they did? He could think of no reason that made sense.

His mind spun. He had to talk to Ana; that was what it came down to. Maybe this “informant" had lied. Maybe she was being set up. He needed to hear her side of the story, Ben be damned. No matter how much his heart ached knowing about their courtship, he couldn't allow her to rot in a dungeon without even trying to learn the truth.

Mellia's voice broke through his panic. “Are you quite all right, Your Highness? You look…” She trailed off, brow wrinkled in concern.

He stood abruptly, startling the princess, who almost dropped her goblet. “Please excuse me,” he muttered, forcing a polite smile.

As he walked away, his mother said, “Milos? Son, the feast isn't over.”

He glanced back at her. “I have to go. I can't do this right now.” He waved a hand. “Just—cancel the ball. Or don't. I'm leaving.”

His father's sharp voice reached him as he took another step. “*Milos*. You will return to your seat. Now.”

Milos ignored him. He made it out of the dining hall and halfway down one corridor before several guards caught up to him.

“Your Highness, His Majesty requires your presence in the dining hall.”

Milos set his jaw. “No.”

The man made a resigned sound. “In that case...” His hand shot out, gripping one of Milos's arms, as another guard grabbed his other arm.

Milos tried to pull away and got one of his arms loose

before the other two guards stepped in. Between the four of them, they wrestled him down the hall.

"Your Highness, it would be better if you'd cooperate." The guard grunted as Milos managed to elbow his side. "His Majesty said if you don't come willingly to the dining hall, you will be confined to your quarters."

He only thrashed more, and two of the guards released his arms in order to pick him up by the ankles.

Thus he was unceremoniously carried back to his rooms, where they dropped him into an armchair.

One of the guards caught his breath enough to say, "You will remain here until His Majesty says otherwise. We'll be outside your door to ensure it."

Milos's chest heaved. He knew the guards had no choice but to obey the king, yet he couldn't rein in his anger. "Fuck. Off."

The four men left without another word, shutting the door behind them.

Chapter Thirty-Four

ANELA

Tirano was livid. Anela did her best to calm him, with marginal success.

After a fraught, whispered conversation, they decided to proceed with the ball, sans engagement announcement. Anela announced that Milos had taken ill but encouraged all of the guests to enjoy themselves.

The hours of the ball passed by in a blur, Anela counting down the minutes until she could reasonably retire. When she was finally able to leave, she went straight to the dungeons to speak with Ana directly.

The dungeon guards were surprised to see her; she provided no explanation, however, despite the questioning looks. As queen, she didn't have to. They directed her to the cells where the two young women were being held.

"Thank you. I do not need an escort; please remain at your station." She swept through the dimly lit hall, her fine satin dress whispering over the dank, dirty flagstones.

It seemed as though every cell was occupied, which was unusual; most were sleeping, however. When she reached the correct location, she slowed and called out softly, "Ana? Are you here?" A figure was slumped over in the back corner of the cell, but she couldn't tell if it was her chamber maid in the poor lighting.

The person quickly lifted her head. "Yes. Your—Your Majesty?" The young woman rose on shaky legs and moved closer to the bars, allowing the sconces to illuminate a surprised and wary expression.

"I must speak with you, Ana. And I need the truth."

Ana nodded slowly. "I'll do my best, Your Majesty. You've always been kind to me. I trust you."

"Are you the daughter of a Libeverran prince?"

Ana bit her lip, looking down. "Yes. I didn't know until a few days ago. My father never told us. He's in exile."

Anela vaguely remembered that the youngest son of the previous Libeverran monarch had disappeared all those years ago. Rumors and speculation had circulated when the news reached the court of Revas, but no one had been all that concerned, as it didn't affect them.

Now she knew why Ana had looked familiar. Her uncle and grandfather had the same gray eyes and dark curls, and she had met them many times. "You weren't trying to trick anyone? Or spy?"

Ana shook her head once. "No, Your Majesty. I wasn't. Is that why I was arrested? They wouldn't tell me anything."

Anela inclined her head. "Yes, in part. My husband was also told you might be relevant to a prophecy I had years ago. Do you know anything about that?"

Ana barked a bitter laugh. "I do. And I think I made the mistake of telling the wrong person about it. That's really why I'm here. Did His Majesty say who told him about me?"

"No, he didn't." Anela blew out a breath, leaning against the bars. "How do you know about the prophecy?"

Ana hesitated. The silence grew. Anela tried to hide her impatience. "If you trust me, as you say, and wish for me to trust you, I need answers, Ana."

Ana's voice was small. "I know. I still think you'll be angry."

"I can't promise I won't be. However, I can promise you won't be punished for anything you tell me. How's that?"

Ana inclined her head. "Thank you. The prophecy... I overheard you and Lady Henriella discussing it one day. Quite on accident," she rushed to clarify. "But I was curious. It's a long story, but my brother died, and..." She shrugged. "If the prophecy referred to His Majesty, I had my own reasons for wanting it to come true."

Anela gave her an encouraging nod. "I understand."

"So I—" Ana winced and cleared her throat. "I found the journal where you write all of your thoughts about the prophecy. I borrowed it and read it, then put it back. I'm sorry." She hung her head.

That explained why the girl was nervous about making Anela angry. It was a breach of privacy, yet it hardly mattered now. "I see. Thank you for telling me. Is there anything else I should know?"

Another voice whispered behind Anela; she whirled at the sound. "Ana, you need to tell her about Ben."

It was the other maid, Lisia. She ducked her head and backed up. "I apologize for interrupting, Your Majesty."

Anela turned to Ana. "Who is this Ben?"

Ana's eyes welled with tears. "I—I thought he was a friend. It turns out he's the leader of a rebel group. And he's the reason I'm here." She shook her head violently. "By the Seven, I'm so stupid!" Tears streamed down her face as she continued. “He was working in the stables here at the castle. I didn’t know this, but Lisia said he claims to be a bastard son of the king's. And he's older than Milos. He wants to claim the throne. I don’t know why he would turn me in, but he’s the only person I told.”

All the air left Anela's lungs. “B-Ben? Is this Benito, son of Vivianna?”

Ana nodded miserably.

Anela wrapped her arms around herself, trembling. So Tirano's indiscretions were finally coming back to bite him. It was during their courtship that he impregnated a daughter of one of the lesser noblemen, and she gave birth to twins, a boy and a girl. Anela didn't discover this secret until she and Tirano were already married and she was pregnant with Milos. Not that it would have changed anything.

She felt for her husband's bastard son and his sister. She truly did. But that didn't mean she'd sit back and allow him to take the throne from Milos, age be damned.

“What is he going to do?” she whispered.

Ana wiped her face with her apron. “I don't know exactly. He didn't tell me, I swear. He wanted me to join them, and I said I’d think about it. Then I told him about my father and the prophecy, and...” She waved a hand around her with a choked laugh. “The very next day, the guards came for me.”

Anela could certainly sympathize with the consequences of trusting the wrong man. “It wasn't your fault, dear. I'm sure you meant well.” She shivered. “It's quite chilly down here. Do you have a blanket?”

Ana shook her head mutely. Anela pressed her lips together. “I will send someone with a blanket and your cloak as soon as I can.”

"Th-thank you, Your Majesty," Ana stuttered. "Can Lisia have something as well?"

Anela smiled. "Indeed." She leaned closer to the bars, lowering her voice. "And I do intend to get both of you out of here once I determine the best way to go about it. You'll have to be patient for a little longer, all right?"

"Yes, Your Majesty. Thank you again."

Anela hurried from the dungeons, pondering everything she had learned. Ana could have been lying, but Anela didn't think so. Her intuition told her the young woman wasn't a threat, so she would give her the benefit of the doubt and act accordingly.

Instead of retiring to her quarters, she went directly to see Milos.

Six guards manned the double doors to his rooms. She raised a brow as she approached, stopping directly in front of them. "Open the door. I will see my son."

Several of the men exchanged looks. "Your Majesty, we're under orders to keep him confined until His Majesty tells us otherwise."

Anela drew herself up, glaring at them. One of the younger ones flinched. "I didn't ask you to release him. I asked to see him. He will still be 'confined' even if I'm visiting him, will he not?" At their confused looks, she instilled steel into her voice. "Open the Seven's-damned door, or you will face the consequences of disobeying your queen."

One of the older men heaved a sigh. "Yes, Your Majesty. Our apologies." He reached for the handle and pulled the door open. She swept past him without a backward glance and the door shut swiftly behind her.

Milos, slumped in a chair, looked up as she entered. "Mama? What are you doing here?"

She sat in the armchair opposite of him. "You really don't wish to marry Princess Melliada, do you?"

His gaze shuttered. "No."

"Do you dislike her?"

He shook his head. "No. I don't feel any particular way about her.

"So this is concerning the other woman you told me about?"

He grimaced. "Kind of. She's made up her mind, though. She chose someone else. But I can't be rid of my own feelings so easily."

"You love her?"

He sat up straighter, meeting her gaze. "Does it matter? I told you, she doesn't want me." His jaw clenched; she heard the pain in his voice.

"Is it Ana? Verana, daughter of Luciano?"

His mouth dropped open. He blinked. "I—how do you—"

She raised a hand. "You ran from the feast right after your father told me she had been arrested. That was ill-advised, Milos; you're fortunate he didn't put it together as well." He shifted uncomfortably under her reprimanding gaze. "I went to speak with her."

His hands gripped the arms of the chair, knuckles white. "You did? What did she say? Is she really..."

Anela nodded. "She is of royal descent. But it's not like your father said. She wasn't hiding anything. Her father is in exile, and he didn't tell her who he really was until a couple days ago."

He blew out a breath. "I see. What else did she say?"

Anela braced herself. "I think we worked out that the person behind her arrest, and Lisia's, is a man named Ben."

"What?" Milos shot out of the chair to pace in front of

the fireplace. "But she—they—" He rubbed his hands over his face. "He's courting her. She chose Ben. Why would he do that?"

"There's no easy way to say this. It seems he was using these poor girls for the sake of a rebellion he claims to lead. You see, he is the bastard son of your father. Your half-brother. And he's a couple years older than you, with delusions about claiming the throne."

Milos faced her, utterly still. Then he moved abruptly toward the door. "I'm going to kill him."

Anela jumped up and caught his arm. "There are six guards in the hall, son. You're not leaving, at least not this moment. Come sit and help me figure out what we need to do."

Chapter Thirty-Five

VERANA

The night passed slowly. Eventually, Lady Henriella brought cloaks and blankets for Ana and Lisia, as the queen promised. Ana was grateful. She laid the blanket on the dirty straw pallet and covered herself with her cloak, and she managed to doze off and on.

A guard brought her a bowl of cold porridge in the morning. "Eat quickly," he ordered. "The king is expecting you shortly; he wishes to interrogate you himself."

She blanched and could only manage a few bites. Soon the guard dragged her down the hall, up one flight of stairs, and shoved her into a mostly empty room. It held two chairs and one table. "Sit," the man ordered.

She obeyed, easing down onto rickety wood. The guard stationed himself in a corner, and they waited.

She had no idea how much time passed before the door opened again. King Tirano entered, followed by another. Ana gasped when she realized the second person was none other than Ben.

The king sat in one fluid, graceful movement, while Ben

stood beside him. His face was bruised and swollen on one side, but otherwise he looked like his usual handsome, charming self.

"You may go," the king directed the guard.

"Yes, Your Majesty. I'll be in the hall if you need me."

Tirano gave a single nod and waited until the door shut behind the man before he spoke again. "So, you are Verana, daughter of Prince Armando."

Ana wrapped her arms around her middle, heart pounding. "Yes, Your Majesty."

"I remember his parents, and I've met his brother many times. You resemble the family." He glanced up at Ben. "You know my son, Benito."

She couldn't help the scowl that formed on her face. She gave a sharp nod. "I do, Your Majesty. I'm surprised to see him here, though. Seeing as he's been planning a rebellion against you."

The king chuckled, smoothing a lock of dark hair back from his forehead. "I see he was very convincing. Especially impressive given your potential gift from Veyra."

Ben smirked. Ana frowned. "I don't understand."

King Tirano waved a hand. "It hardly matters. I'm pleased he earned your trust, however; otherwise, I may never have known of your lineage, and your possible role in the prophecy."

Ana's mouth dropped open, but nothing came out.

"You see, when I realized Milos may never meet my expectations as heir, I ordered Ben to travel to Sonos City. It was a test of sorts. I had him use his true identity to stir up a 'rebellion,' which would help me identify enemies in the city and even in the castle. We have quietly arrested at least two dozen traitors these last two days thanks to his efforts. But you, my dear, are surely the prize. His discovery of your lineage in relation to the prophecy cemented his position as heir."

Ben grinned widely; she continued to glare. "What about Prince Milos?" she asked.

Tirano shrugged. "He had ample opportunity to prove himself to me. Yet he is soft, and weak. It's my own fault, leaving so much of the raising of him to his mother." The king sneered. "But we're here to talk about you, aren't we, dear?"

She pressed her lips together as he studied her.

"Tell me your understanding of that cursed prophecy my useless wife received."

She only stared stonily. She didn't understand it better than anyone else, but she didn't want to admit that.

Tirano exhaled. "Ben, if you'd help her find her tongue..."

Ben stepped forward and reached across the table in one smooth movement, slapping her across the face before she could register what was happening. She cried out, bringing a trembling hand to her cheek, staring at him in horror. Her teeth had cut into the inside of her mouth, leaving the metallic taste of blood on her tongue.

How could this be Ben? Her sweet, kind Ben? The man she gave her virginity to, for the Seven's sake? It felt like a nightmare. How could she have been so stupid?

Milos had tried to warn her, and she had dismissed it as jealousy on his part. She recalled other warning signs as well. Yet she had ignored them, flattered by his attention. And after her brother died and she realized Milos would marry Melliada, she had been over-eager for a distraction.

"Thank you, Ben. Now, Verana, you will tell me what I wish to know, won't you?"

Her eyes watered, but she refused to cry. "I don't understand the prophecy any better than the rest of you. I don't know for sure it has anything to do with me."

The king's mouth thinned. He turned to Ben once more. "Do you believe her?"

Ben shrugged. "I admit she didn't seem to be terribly knowledgeable about any of it when she told me."

Tirano rubbed one side of his jaw. "I suppose it's safest to be rid of her, just in case. We need to determine the best method. Given the words of the prophecy, I'd prefer not to spill any of her blood."

"A hanging is simple enough, Father."

This calm, cold statement about how to kill her made Ana want to leap over the table and slap him across the face. How could he do this? Fear and anger made her tremble, and she clenched her fists.

Tirano nodded thoughtfully. "It's too quick, too kind really, for a traitor's death. But you're right; it is the simplest solution."

"If you want her to pay for her transgressions with pain beforehand, I'm sure I can manage without drawing blood." Ben's easy smile as he said the words turned Ana's anger into nausea. She tried not to imagine what he might do to her.

The king chuckled. "The apple doesn't fall far from the tree." He waved a hand. "Yes, perhaps. But we have much to do; for now, she can rot in the dungeon until I have time to deal with her. We need to announce you as heir, as well as your engagement to the Kaosudan girl. Perhaps we can execute all of the traitors at once, after the wedding."

Ben nodded, nonchalant. "As you say, Father. I am yours to command."

Ana looked back and forth between them, knowing her horror, terror, and anger must show plainly on her face.

Not that they cared.

Tirano stood. "Very well. Let's get to work, then."

Ben nodded. "May I have just a moment alone with the girl?"

Tirano gave half a shrug. "Keep it short." He turned and left. Ben walked around the table, and Ana shot up from her seat, placing it between them.

"Don't you dare come near me," she bit out.

He pouted. "Oh Ana. I wanted to let you know I am terribly sorry it turned out like this. The truth is, I'd prefer you to the Kaosudan wench. You and I—we're the same, aren't we? Royals raised away from this life." He waved a hand to indicate the castle. She pressed her lips together, refusing to agree with him even though he wasn't wrong. "I could have convinced Tirano, I think, given your lineage. But that damned prophecy." He shook his head. "You dug your own grave there, sweetheart."

"Don't call me that." Her fingers clenched the back of the chair. "You should go. I have nothing to say to you."

He kicked the chair out of the way and she stumbled backward. Crowding her against the wall, he took her face in one hand and squeezed until she yelped from the pain. "I only want a goodbye kiss." He crushed her mouth with his as she grabbed for his arm, trying to pull his hand away.

He was too strong. Another wave of nausea swept through her, leaving her feeling cold and weak. She was about to bite down on his tongue, his lip, whatever she could manage, when he pulled away. He shoved her, knocking her head against the stone before he let her go. "I'll miss you, sweetheart."

He strode out of the room, and within minutes, she was back in her cell.

Chapter Thirty-Six

MILOS

Milos hadn't climbed out of his bedroom window since he was a boy. He forced himself not to look down and prayed to the Seven that the trellis was sturdy enough to hold his weight, and for no one to see him. It was pitch dark, which made his climb all the more nerve wracking, but it also reassured him that he was unlikely to be spotted. He had dressed in dark clothing, hood drawn up over his face.

It was his mother's idea for him to sneak away. She didn't think Tirano would allow him out of his quarters quickly enough for them to do anything for Ana. Not to mention, her intuition blared a warning. She didn't know specifics, yet she felt in her bones that something else was afoot. Something more, some plan of the king's that they couldn't possibly predict. His mother's intuition was part of her gift from Orix and not to be ignored.

He had waited for a day, as directed. If he wasn't allowed out and she didn't return with new instructions, he'd leave. He thought he had heard her raised voice in the hall around midday, but she hadn't come in. He had no way to know if the guards hadn't allowed it, or if she hadn't intended to in the first place.

He heaved a deep breath when he finally reached the ground safely. He didn't dare get his horse from the royal stables, but he needed to be quick, so he had brought enough gold to rent or buy a horse in the city.

First, he would go to Ana's parents. They needed to know what happened to her. He thought they should consider leaving, or hiding at least temporarily, because he wouldn't put it past his father to arrest them as well. She would never forgive him if something happened to her family when he could have prevented it.

Despite the danger, he couldn't help the tingle of hope in his chest. From what his mother said, Ben had betrayed Ana, and she knew it. While it still hurt that she had picked Ben over him, now that she saw what Ben was, maybe Milos would have a chance. She couldn't argue any more tha it was impossible due to their stations; she was of royal blood.

His thoughts returned to Ben. He shook his head as he walked, keeping to the shadows. He had known there was something off about the man. Perhaps he had inherited a drop of his mother's gift in addition to his father's. As soon as he had a chance, he would ensure Ben suffered for everything he had done—especially to Ana.

He hesitated as he passed the guards' dorm. He hadn't discussed it with his mother, but he felt an urge to find Bristio and convince the man to come with him. Once Tirano discovered Milos was gone, Bristio would probably be questioned. Besides, Bristio wouldn't want Milos to leave the city without him, and the guard would be able to get horses from the stables without raising too much suspicion.

And honestly, he could use a friend. He saw a guard heading into the building and hurried to catch up with him.

The man agreed to fetch Bristio; Milos waited in the entryway.

Ten minutes later, a sleepy, grouchy-looking Bristio appeared. "What's all this?" he rasped.

"It's a long story. I have to leave the city. We'll need horses, but I can't risk going into the stables. Can you come?"

Half an hour later, they rode through the quiet, dark streets of the capital, toward the southbound road.

"Where have you been hiding?" Bristio grumbled. "I expected I'd see you yesterday, after the king's announcement."

Milos frowned. "I was confined to my quarters after I refused to attend the ball the night before. What announcement?" Other than guards bringing in meals, he hadn't spoken with or seen anyone the entire day.

The moonlight showed the surprise on Bristio's face. "No one told you anything?"

Milos gave a sharp shake of his head.

"Ah. Well, I hate to be the bearer of this news, but you need to know. Your father announced his bastard son, Benito, as heir in your place. And he is engaged to the Kaosudan princess."

Milos inadvertently jerked the reins as he tensed, causing his mount to stumble. He loosened his grip, patting the mare on the neck automatically. "I'm sorry, did you just say my father announced a *new heir* to the throne?"

Bristio nodded. "Everyone was shocked. Benito worked in the stables, so folks knew him. Although we didn't know he is a son of the king." Bristio grimaced.

"Fuck," Milos muttered. This was worse than he and his mother thought. She must have tried to come tell him, but the guards didn't allow her in. Now what was he supposed to do?

They weren't far out of the city when Bristio held up a hand, pulling his horse to a stop. Milos, lost in his own thoughts, glanced around and strained to hear or see whatever Bristio had. Then he saw it: faint flickering lights in the distance. A lot of them. They could be torches coming near, or campfires farther away.

Bristio motioned for Milos to leave the road, and they both made their way into the woods. Milos shivered, but not at the temperature; he had always avoided the woods at night. Everyone knew it wasn't safe. Fortunately, he saw no beasts or monsters lurking as they crept nearer to the lights.

It was campfires. Specifically, campfires surrounded by Kaosudan soldiers.

Milos gave Bristio a horrified look and they silently retreated.

"What is this?" Milos hissed. "Are they invading? What in the Seven is happening?"

Bristio shook his head. "I don't know. But we can't risk trying to get to that village. We have to go back and report this."

Milos agreed. Ana's parents should be safe enough, in any case; if he couldn't reach the cabin, neither could his father's soldiers.

Ana. He needed to get her out of those dungeons before his father... He didn't let himself complete the thought.

"I need your help with something else, Bristio," he murmured. He explained who Ana was, her possible role in the prophecy, and the rest. "I need to get her out and as far away from my father and Ben as I can manage."

Bristio whistled low. "This is quite the mess. How do you propose we manage that?"

Milos jerked his head in frustration. "I don't know. I doubt the guards will even let me see her, let alone walk away with her."

Bristio grunted. "Aye, all right. Let me think." A few minutes passed before he spoke again. "I have a few guards loyal to me, and to you. Above the king, even, I would wager."

Milos nodded. "What are you thinking?"

Bristio shrugged. "I'll arrange for two of them to take a shift in the dungeon. They let Ana go with me. Simple. The distraction of the Kaosudan soldiers outside the city should make it even easier."

Milos rolled his lips between his teeth, then blew out a breath. "Your men will be in trouble if anyone figures it out."

Bristio nodded solemnly. "Aye. They'd likely have to leave the city for good. It's a sacrifice some of them might make ... but can you ask it of them?"

Milos considered. "The thing is, I don't intend to let my scheming half-brother take my crown. If Ana is key to the prophecy, we need her with us. If my father is dethroned, it won't be difficult to take care of Ben."

"True. If you succeed, the guards who help you can keep their positions."

"Exactly."

They continued to discuss the plan as they wove through the city.

"I don't think you should return to the castle yet," Bristio said. "We don't know what your father plans to do with you, and he'll be angry when he discovers you escaped."

Bristio made a point that Milos couldn't disagree with, even if he hated it. "So you'll fetch Ana by yourself?"

Bristio nodded. Milos wanted to be the one to rescue her—desperately—yet he recognized his ego wasn't the priority. "All right. I detest the idea of hiding while you do all the work, but I trust your judgement."

Bristio chuckled softly. "I appreciate it, son." They were almost to the gates. "Dawn is near. Gather some supplies in the city first, and then I want you to go to the forest north of the castle. Bring enough to tide you over for at least a few days. I don't intend for it to take that long, but we'll play it safe. Once I have Ana, I'll bring her to you and we'll go from there."

Milos nodded. "Where shall we meet?"

Bristio specified a clearing where he used to take Milos for hunting lessons. Milos shuddered at the idea of spending the night—maybe more than one—in the woods. But if Ana could survive the castle dungeons, he could survive the wilderness for her sake.

He parted from Bristio, heading to a street lined with shops so he could purchase everything he needed as soon as they opened.

Chapter Thirty-Seven

VERANA

Ana struggled to keep track of time. Was it morning or evening? Had she been there for two days? Three? She hadn't slept much, the timing of guards bringing food seemed erratic at best, and she was losing her bearings.

When she heard footsteps approaching only an hour after being fed, she shuffled over to the bars, curious. Perhaps the queen was back. She tried not to get her hopes up as she waited. When she could make out the silhouette, her shoulders dropped. Definitely a guard, not Her Majesty. She huddled back into a corner, afraid she might be taken to meet with the king again.

The man stopped outside her cell. "Ana?" His voice was soft.

She answered reluctantly. "Yes?"

Keys jingled in his hand as he found the correct one. The door opened and he stepped in. His whisper was so quiet, she strained to make out the words. "Ana, come. My name is Bristio. Milos sent me."

She gave a small gasp and scrambled to her feet, hurrying to him. She stopped abruptly a foot away, suddenly suspicious. He might be trying to trick her. After Ben, and even Lisia, she hesitated to trust. "What do you want?"

He held out a hand. "Come. Quickly now. I'm getting you out of here and taking you to the prince." He tilted his head to glance down the hall, and the low light of the nearest sconce revealed his face. She recognized him; she had seen him with Milos several times, including at her brother's wedding.

Making a hasty decision, she nodded and placed her freezing hand in his large, warm one. They stepped out, and she hesitated. "Wait. We need to bring Lisia too." She pointed to the cell across the way. She could see the vague shape of the young maid asleep on her pallet.

Bristio jerked his head in a negative. "It's too risky. I'm sorry. She'll be all right for now."

"But—"

He gripped her hand tightly and started to walk, pulling her along. "We must hurry, Ana. Do as I say and I will get you safely away."

Ana's chin trembled, guilt gnawing in her belly. She took a deep breath and quickened her steps to keep up with him. She was in no position to argue. The king planned to execute her, and if he did, she could do nothing for Lisia or anyone else.

"What about the guards?" she whispered. He only shook his head, holding a finger to his mouth.

When they passed the two men at the guard station next to the staircase, Bristio simply nodded. They both inclined their heads. "Go carefully, sir," one said.

"You as well," he muttered as they passed.

"Won't they be in trouble?" Ana panted as they hurried up the stairs.

Bristio shook his head. "When the next shift comes to relieve them, they will disappear. Hide in the city until all of this blows over. Those were my orders." He sounded certain that they would obey, so she nodded and saved her breath for the climb.

When they reached the top of the second flight, Bristio cracked the door open, peering out and pausing to listen. After a moment, he nodded. "Hood up," he ordered, and she drew her cloak over her head.

He led her down the corridor. No one was about; it must be very late, or very early. Her heart pounded as though it wanted to escape her chest as badly as she wanted to escape the castle. She tried to step lightly and keep up as he led her through lesser-used halls in the guest wing.

They finally reached a servant's entrance, one Ana had never had cause to use. Again, he peeked out, listened, waited. Then they were out in the frigid air and snow. It wasn't falling fast, but it was steady.

"Excellent," Bristio muttered. "Our tracks will be covered within the hour."

She followed him along the edge of the grounds, darting to one dark shadow after another. A patrolling guard rounded a corner. Ana froze, and Bristio tugged, pulling her along.

"Who goes?" The man sounded almost bored.

"It's Bristio. That you, Sergio?"

"Aye, sir. What's brought you out so late?" As he got closer, he shot a curious glance at Ana. She immediately looked down at the ground, letting the hood obscure her face entirely. "Or should I say, who?" He smirked.

Bristio chuckled. "You mind your business, Serg, and I'll mind mine, aye?"

The man laughed. "Keep your secrets, then, old man. Cold night for it, though."

He continued past them, humming as he went. Ana released the breath she was holding as they continued. Soon they reached the edge of the woods. He jerked his head toward the trees. "Milos is waiting for us."

She swallowed hard. "In—in the forest?" As badly as she wanted to see Milos, to hear his comforting voice, going into the forest at night was a questionable decision. Yet what choice did she have?

He nodded. "Quickly, now, before the snow grows too thick to see."

She blanched at the idea of wandering in a snowstorm in the eerie woods, and she increased her pace. Perhaps her ability would keep her from getting lost; however, she had no wish to put it to such a test. Bristio pulled a dagger from his belt, which made her both nervous and reassured.

The snow muffled the sounds of the night; all she heard was their footfalls. They walked and walked. Between the cold, the exercise, and her mostly empty stomach, she grew tired quickly, but she pressed on, deeper and deeper into the trees.

Eventually, she smelled woodsmoke, though she couldn't see it through the snowfall. They entered a clearing with a lean-to built of fallen branches against one of the larger trunks, a blanket hanging over the opening.

Bristio gave a sharp whistle.

The blanket whipped away and the prince clambered out of the shelter, fighting his way toward them through the deepening snow. "Ana!"

A sob escaped her as she met him partway, throwing

herself into his arms. He held her tightly, stroking her back in firm, soothing movements. "Shh," he whispered. "You're all right. I've got you."

Bristio cleared his throat. "I need to get back while I still can."

Milos glanced at him. "Is it worth the risk?"

Bristio nodded. "I'll manage. One of us needs to be there, to know what's happening. It seems the Kaosudans have surrounded the city on all sides, except here." He gestured.

"What?" Ana gasped.

"I'll explain," Milos muttered. To Bristio he said, "That makes sense; these woods lead into the mountains, and they're coming from the south. All the better for us, I suppose."

Bristio gave a wave. "Stay here at least for another day. If I can't make it back with news, I'll leave a message with the owner at The Royal Gate."

"Thank you, Bristio. For everything." Milos turned his attention back to her as the older man strode back the way they had come. "Let's get you inside, love."

She followed him, ducking down to crawl in. He arranged the blanket again, tying it to keep out the falling snow. A small fire burned on the opposite side near a smaller opening. She collapsed next to it, holding out her hands to warm them. He settled next to her, reaching to push back her hood. "Let me see you. Are you all right?"

He gripped her chin, turning her head to look at him directly. His brows drew together and his jaw tightened as he traced her cheek bone. She winced; as light as his touch was, the spot was tender. She didn't know how it looked, but Ben's strike had surely left a bruise.

"Who?" he gritted out.

"I'm fine," she tried to assure him.

"Who. Did. This?" he demanded.

She ducked her head, ashamed. Ashamed at how naive she was, how stupid she had been to trust Ben, despite Milos's warning.

He cupped her other cheek, tilting her head up. "Ana, I'm sorry. I'm not angry with *you*, only on your behalf. All right?"

She nodded, biting her lip. He *should* be angry at her. She owed him the truth, at least.

"It was Ben," she whispered.

He swore under his breath and gathered her into his arms, pulling her onto his lap. "Oh, my Ana. I'm so sorry."

She choked on the tears she struggled to suppress. "Y-you're sorry? What for? I should be the one who's sorry. I *am* sorry."

She broke down completely then, sobbing into his chest. He rocked her, whispered soothing words, smoothed her hair. His kindness only made her cry harder. She would have to tell him everything. How could he forgive her?

When her tears were spent, he continued rocking her, stroking her back, warming her hands in his. When she gathered the courage, she looked up at him. "Thank you. For sending Bristio to rescue me."

His half-smile was sad. "You don't know how badly I wanted to come myself. But the old man's arguments were too sensible." He chuckled and she gave him a tentative smile.

His gaze dropped to her lips and he leaned in, brushing her mouth with his. Although she wanted nothing more than to kiss him back, she forced herself to pull away. "I need to tell you something, before we..." She trailed off and gave a helpless shrug. "I understand if you're angry. But I owe you the truth, if nothing else."

His mouth tightened. "Is this about Ben?"

"Yes." She forced herself to maintain eye contact despite the cowardly part of her that wanted to hide. "He escorted me on my last visit home. We took shelter in the forest from a hailstorm." She paused, taking a deep breath. "And we—"

He cut her off, placing two fingers over her mouth. "You were intimate with him. I know. He told me."

Her mouth dropped open. "He what?"

"He was trying to get under my skin. It worked, I'll give him that; I lost my temper and hit him. Repeatedly." He hesitated. "I hoped that maybe he had lied."

She shook her head mournfully. "I was so stupid. I can't believe I trusted him. I had been..." She blushed at the memory, unsure if she could admit it.

"You had been what, love?"

She pushed on, determined to tell him everything. "I was having a lot of, um, dreams about him. For weeks, before..." She shook her head. "And I had heard about your engagement to the princess. I was sad and angry, but I also—those dreams, they made me *want* him so." Tears formed again; she blinked them away.

"Dreams?" Milos's voice held a dangerous edge. "Dreams about being intimate with him? Sex?"

She nodded, staring down at her hands, shame washing over her. "That's never happened before, not like that. It was almost every night, and they were so vivid. I don't know what got into me."

"His magic did." His tone was grim. "He gave you those dreams. He's my father's son, remember? He must have the gift of Sonos, or my father would never consider making him heir."

She gasped, a hand flying up over her mouth. "By the Seven. It didn't even occur to me." She closed her eyes. "Gods, I really am *stupid.*"

"Hush," he murmured, pressing a kiss against her forehead. "You're not remotely stupid." He paused, tightening his arms around her. "I admit, I hate that he—that you—it was your first time, wasn't it?"

She nodded miserably.

A growl rumbled in his chest, and she flinched. He patted her gently. "No, love, I'm not angry with you. You did nothing wrong. I have more reasons than I can count to want *him* dead, though." He took a deep breath, as though bracing himself. "You don't need to tell me details, but was he at least kind? He didn't hurt you?"

"No," she breathed, biting the corner of her lip hard. She didn't want to think about it, didn't want to remember. It had felt special, and real, and it was neither. She felt disgusting, somehow unclean. Worse, she felt like a total fool. "He didn't hurt me. He was kind."

"Good," he rumbled. "I can kill him outright then. No need for a long, slow, torturous death." He sounded completely serious.

A slightly hysterical giggle bubbled out of her, and he chuckled. "You think I'm joking, but I'm not. Enough about him, though. I have you here with me, and you're safe."

She dropped her head against his chest once more, and they sat quietly for a while. Eventually, he gently scooted her off his lap, settling her on top of a pile of pine needles so he could add a few more sticks to the fire. When he sat next to her again, he offered her a genuine smile.

"At least one good thing has come of all this."

She blinked. "What's that?"

His smile grew. "I hear you're a princess?"

She shrugged. "Kind of? If my father is in exile and he's not the heir, am I still a princess? It hardly makes a difference."

"You're wrong about that. Your bloodline is royal, regardless. Which means you can't argue with me anymore about us not being allowed to be together."

Her mouth dropped open in shock. In all of the chaos and terror, it hadn't occurred to her, not once. "By the Seven. You're right."

Her heart leapt, and the truth she had shoved into a deep, dark corner of herself now shone bright as the flames in front of her: it had always been Milos who had her heart. She had been too stubborn to give in due to their hopeless circumstances, but even during her moments with Ben, she couldn't get Milos out of her head.

He laughed. "Now, if you simply don't like me, that's a different—"

She leaned over to silence him with her mouth.

Chapter Thirty-Eight

MILOS

He pulled her back onto his lap, pushing the fabric of her skirts out of the way as she straddled him. Her kiss was hungry and seeking, and he returned in kind, exploring her with his tongue, nipping her bottom lip then gently sucking on it. She moaned into his mouth and his britches grew uncomfortably tight.

He unclasped her cloak with one hand and tossed it, fanning it out so it covered most of the space inside the shelter. Between the fire and the insulation of the needled branches and snow, she should be warm enough … especially since he intended to share his own body heat as well. She unclasped his cloak next and it slid off, pooling around him.

Then his hand was in her hair, which was a mess—half plaited, half loose and tangled—but he didn't care. She was beautiful always, and he had been wanting this for so long. He cupped the back of her head and brought his other hand to her waist, slowly sliding it up her side until his thumb rested under her breast. She moaned and he cupped her soft warmth, massaging through the fabric, feeling her nipple growing hard.

She moved her hips, grinding against his length, and he gasped. Pulling away, his lips trailed down along her neck, nuzzling under her jaw. He tasted her there, then continued down, nipping at her collar bone, dropping kisses onto her heaving chest.

Placing both hands at her waist, he lifted her, setting her down on her cloak. He lay on his side and pulled her down next to him for another searing kiss. Yanking her skirts up farther, he caressed her thigh up to her hip and then back down. She whimpered, pressing herself closer to him.

He wanted to spread her legs and lay between them to feast, but the lean-to wasn't large enough. Instead, he stretched out on his back, knees bent. "Sit up," he rasped.

She complied, breathing heavily. Her eyes wandered up and down his form, pausing on the bulge in his pants. She licked her bottom lip, and he chuckled.

"You'll get your turn, if you want it. First, I need you to do something for me." She looked at him expectantly, a small smile playing on her swollen mouth. "Kneel with my head between your legs."

She hesitated. "I haven't been able to wash in days..."

"Couldn't care less. I need to taste you. Come here."

"Yes, Your Highness," she sassed, then got on her knees and flipped her skirts over one shoulder before straddling his face. "Like this?" she whispered.

He stared at her swollen, gorgeous, shining wet center and groaned. Then he grasped her hips. "Sit."

She hesitated again, and he yanked her down. She inhaled sharply but stayed put.

"I'll suffocate you," she protested, sounding breathless.

"Then I'll die a happy man," he muttered before dragging his tongue through her folds. Her body jerked at the sensation as a small gasp escaped her. He held her firmly in place and licked her again, slowly, loving her little mewling sounds.

"Fuck, love, you taste so good," he growled against her. He planted an open-mouthed kiss before moving his tongue to circle lazily around her clit.

"Oh gods, Milos, please," she begged.

"Take what you need," he urged. "Use my mouth to find your pleasure."

Thus encouraged, her hips rolled, then again, finding a rhythm. He licked, sucked, and nipped as she rode him.

When her movements grew more frantic and erratic, he knew she was close. He stilled her hips. "Come for me, Ana," he rasped, then he took her clit between his lips and sucked.

She trembled, crying out as she tipped over the edge. His grasp remained firm and his tongue flicked against her as she fell apart. The sounds escaping her were more beautiful than any music he'd ever heard.

Eventually, she pulled away, moving to sit next to him. He turned on his side and grinned at her. "You did so well, love."

She laughed, still panting, and reached to rest her hand on his length. He hissed as she gave a gentle squeeze.

"May I?" Her voice was soft, unsure.

"By the Seven, I might die if you don't," he groaned with a chuckle.

"We can't have that," she murmured as she undid his pants, pulling them open so his cock was on full display. She stared, as though in awe, then wrapped her small hand around the base. Leaning over, her pink tongue darted out to lick the droplet off his tip. His hips jerked.

She looked at him, earnest and shy. "I don't really know what I'm doing. Will you teach me?"

He huffed a laugh. "It will be my pleasure. Quite literally."

She giggled, still gripping him. "What do I do first?"

"You're off to a good start," he ground out. "Honestly, men aren't that difficult to please. Use your mouth, your tongue, and it'll feel good if you suck ... hard. Careful with your teeth. That's all, really."

She nodded seriously. "I can do that." Her head lowered and she licked around his tip, then took it in her mouth, slowly enveloping him. Her hand still fisted his base as he met the back of her throat. She made a small choking sound but recovered quickly, moving her tongue against him.

He shuddered, overwhelmed by the visual and the feel of her. She drew her head back. "Are you all right? Did I do something wrong?"

He shook his head frantically. "Fine. I'm fine. I'm amazing. You're amazing. Keep going."

She breathed a laugh and did as he said.

Her enthusiasm more than made up for her inexperience. The next time she let him pop out of her plump mouth, she said, "I love how you taste."

"It's mutual," he assured her. He wasn't going to last much longer if she continued, but he didn't want this to end. "Lay down now, love. On your back."

They switched places, and he pushed her skirts up before settling his legs between them. "I'd rather take off all our clothes, but it's a little cold for that. Next time." He leaned down, kissing her deeply, adjusting his hips until his cock rested against her center. "Are you ready? It's all right if you don't want…" He trailed off, captivated as he watched her pull her bottom lip between her teeth, her gray eyes piercing him.

She nodded, letting her lip free itself. By the Seven, that *mouth*. "Yes. Please."

Slowly, he pushed inside her wet heat. Gods, she was so incredibly tight. Despite their joining, he wanted to be closer to her still. He would never tire of this—of her, under his body, or in his arms.

He would never let her go.

She moaned, reaching to place her hands on his shoulders. He paused halfway in, letting her adjust. His chest heaved as he fought to maintain control; part of him wanted nothing more than to fuck her hard and fast, while the other part wanted this to last as long as possible.

"More," she whispered. "Please, Milos, I need..."

"Oh gods," he gasped as he thrust the rest of the way. "You can't beg me like that. I'll lose all control, love."

"I want you to." She met his gaze, and the firelight reflected in her blown pupils. "Please, Milos."

He loved hearing his true name fall from her lips. Not "Your Highness," or Vincento. "Fuck," he grunted as he withdrew before slamming back in to the hilt. "Gods, my love. You feel so good."

"Yes," she whimpered. "More. I want more."

He lost all capacity for speech as he set a punishing rhythm. It didn't take long for him to get close to the precipice. He sat back on his heels without withdrawing, pulling her with him, and found her clit with his fingers while she held her skirts up out of the way. He pressed down on the sensitive spot as he continued to plunge into her, and she cried out, pulsing and squeezing around him.

He slipped out of her at the last moment, as was his habit, spilling himself over both of their stomachs. Spots edged his vision with his release. "Ana, oh gods ... love ... *fuck*..." Words he didn't consciously choose fell from his lips.

When they had regained their senses, he melted snow and helped her to wash as much as she could without getting fully undressed. She yawned as they finished. "I'm so tired. I didn't sleep much in that cell."

Milos scowled, but not at her; she wasn't looking at him anyway. "I'm sorry, love. We'll rest soon." He sat behind her, legs spread so he could be close. "Let me fix this for you first." He untied the string at the bottom of her plait and carefully undid what was left of it. Then he painstakingly untangled her curls with his fingers bit by bit. He plaited it once more, tying off the end. It wasn't perfect, but it was an improvement.

"There, that's better," he said, dropping a kiss on the back of her neck. "Are you hungry? I have some food."

"Not really." She reached back and felt the braid. "How'd you learn how to do that?" She sounded mildly suspicious, and he chuckled.

"Horses. My riding instructor insisted I learn the care of them, not only how to stay in the saddle. Come, let's sleep for a bit."

He tugged her down. They lay on her cloak and covered themselves with his, while he curled around her, pressing his chest to her back. He rested his palm on her belly and sighed deeply. Everything was still a mess—the Kaosudans, his father choosing Ben as heir, and gods knew what else—but at that moment, he didn't care about any of it. All that mattered was Ana, and she was tucked safely in his arms, right where she should be.

He woke in the middle of the night when he heard noise outside the lean-to. He cursed silently; he had been lucky thus far, not encountering anything in the woods outside of a deer and a few owls. The sound of sniffing and a low growl assured him this was less benign.

He woke Ana, urging her to stay quiet with a finger laid over her lips. "There's an animal in the clearing. Maybe a bear. Stay here."

She nodded with wide, fearful eyes and sat up, watching him. He pulled on his boots and cloak, cinched his belt with his dagger, and grabbed his sword, unsheathed. Then he carefully peeked through a crack between the branches of their shelter. He sucked in a breath when he found the source of the noise.

Not a bear. If he had to guess, based on books of folklore and history he had read, the beast was a lupa bonega, commonly called the Great Wolf. The name deceived, however, because the creature only vaguely resembled a wolf. The lupa bonega weighed the same as a man, with wickedly sharp antlers and razor-sharp teeth dripping with venom, and it could also stand upright like a man. The wolf comparison came from the thick pelt of fur and the shape of the snout, Milos assumed.

The creature sniffed around the clearing, pawing at the ground with disturbingly long claws, moving closer and closer to the lean-to. "Stay near the fire," Milos breathed. "I think they're afraid of it."

Ana moved toward the flames, grabbing a makeshift torch he had devised in his hours of waiting. "Then take some with you," she whispered, holding it in the fire until it caught.

He took it from her and quickly shoved the blanket aside

with his sword arm, bursting into the clearing with a shout, blade and torch held up in front of him.

The beast stilled, considering him, before it continued toward him. "Fuck," Milos muttered as his heart rate picked up. "Go away!" He used a deep commanding voice, then took a deep breath, watching the creature's every move.

The beast stopped once more, cocking its antlered head, and bared its teeth.

When it pounced, Milos was ready. Sharp teeth met sword, and the beast wrenched its head, trying to rip the weapon out of Milos's hand. But when Milos swung the torch toward its face, it leapt backward, giving another menacing growl. Blood dripped from its jaw; the sword had done some damage.

Fast as lighting, it swiped its claws at him, ripping into his forearm. Somehow, he managed to keep hold of the torch, and he swung his sword with a roar of pain and anger. A chunk of antler fell into the snow.

The beast snarled and seemed to consider for a moment, debating if Milos was worth the trouble. Then it turned and loped into the trees.

Milos remained where he was for several more moments, blood dripping onto the snow, turning in a slow circle to make sure it wasn't a trick. He had no idea how intelligent the thing was. Finally, feeling confident it was gone, he dropped the torch into the snow—the flame was uncomfortably close to his hand now—and crawled back into the lean-to, cradling the injured arm against his stomach.

He set his sword down and Ana was on him. "Oh my gods! What was that thing? Are you all right?"

"A Great Wolf, I believe. Yes, I'm fine. Just a scratch. It's gone." He reassured her before capturing her mouth.

Adrenaline still coursed through him, and he suddenly wanted her, badly.

She pulled away. "Let me see that 'scratch.'"

Giving in, he offered up his arm, and she gasped. It did look a little worse than it felt; three distinct claw marks had shredded his skin just below the elbow. She rinsed it off with more melted snow, making him hiss, then used his knife to cut strips from her cloak to fashion a bandage.

The minute she finished neatly tying it off, he pulled her against him, still ravenous for her. He couldn't stop kissing her, even as he pushed her gently down, spreading her legs with his knee. He used his good hand to undo his pants. The small noises escaping her drove him absolutely wild. When she grasped his backside and pulled him closer, he couldn't wait any longer.

She was wet and ready for him as he pushed inside. "Gods, Ana," he panted. "I've wanted this for so long. Wanted you. And now I never want to let you go."

She gave a breathless chuckle. "Never? That's a long time."

He slid out of her and eased back in slowly. "Not long enough, love. But it'll have to do."

It didn't take long for both of them to reach their peak, and she fell back asleep wrapped in his arms. He dozed a bit, trying to stay aware in case danger found them again.

It was daylight when they woke, and the fire was down to coals. It had stopped snowing. After taking care of their personal needs, including a small meal, they waited to see if Bristio would return with news.

Huddled in the shelter near the rekindled flames, Milos

and Ana had time to talk. Just to sit and talk with no interruptions. Despite the circumstances, Milos was grateful for it. He delighted in feeling her near him and couldn't resist wrapping an arm around her shoulders.

She talked about her family, including Aldo. "We wanted to travel together. Go on an adventure. I wish we could have."

Milos dropped a kiss on her forehead. "So do I. But I'll take you wherever you want to go, when all of this is settled. I know I can't replace him, but I think he'd want you to live out that dream."

Eventually, she asked about his magic. "Is it like Ben's? You can put dreams into someone's mind? Or like your father's? Or is it both for all three of you?"

"Our abilities are the same," he murmured. "We can send dreams of all sorts into sleeping minds. I was trained in the ability, but I haven't had reason to use it much. I never intended to use it the way my father does. That's probably part of the reason he decided to renounce me as heir." His lips pressed into a thin line.

"Doesn't the king receive dreams from Sonos that help him rule? And through him, Sonos sends messages to the pastros as well, right? Does that part only happen after you're crowned king?"

He barked a bitter laugh. "He doesn't receive dreams from Sonos. He uses that lie to increase his influence and power."

Ana quirked a brow. "He doesn't?" She looked genuinely confused. "But the templekeepers, they say—"

"I know what they say. It's probably what they believe. But it isn't the truth. He sends dreams to the pastros and tells them he's passing on messages from Sonos. It's all self-serving manipulation."

"Oh." Silence fell for several beats, then she breathed a chuckle. "I never did believe, you know. Not really. My family wasn't favored by the local pastro, because my father and I aren't devoted to Sonos and the king the way they expect us to be."

He laughed. "That sounds about right. You're so smart, I'm not surprised. I'm sure plenty of people only pretend in order to get by. But you're not a pretender."

"I'm not." She shook her head. "He—the pastro—he implied that Aldo died because Sonos didn't favor us due to our lack of worship." Bitterness laced her voice.

Milos wasn't surprised, yet it still angered him. "Fuck him. Nothing about what happened to Aldo was your family's fault."

She nodded, leaning her head against his shoulder. "I know that the way your father and brother use their gods-gifted magic is wrong. But I can't fathom how such a magic could be used for good. What will you do with yours?"

Milos rubbed a hand over his bristly jaw. "According to the historical texts, my ancestors used it in many ways. It was a quick and efficient method to send out communications around the kingdom—not in the way my father does, but to spread important news or information. Previous kings have also used the power against their enemies, like sending nightmares to their enemy's military the eve before a battle to frighten and destabilize them. There are many ways a ruler can use the ability to benefit their people, rather than take advantage of them."

Ana absorbed this in silence, looking deep in thought. In the quiet, they both heard someone approaching, snow crunching under feet.

Milos stiffened. "Stay put." He moved to peek outside. "Oh good. It's Bristio."

They left the shelter to meet him partway, eager to know what news he brought.

"Glad to see you made it safely through that storm." The old man smiled.

Milos clapped him on the shoulder. "You taught me well. Tell us what's happening."

Bristio nodded, taking a breath. "The Kaosudan army demands that your father step down and allow an heir to take the throne."

Chapter Thirty-Nine

ANELA

The entire castle was in chaos. Tirano's announcement of Benito replacing Milos as heir had everyone beside themselves with excitement, concern, and confusion. When Anela realized that Ben and Tirano had been working together the whole time, and that Ben had written those notes, she was livid at the deception. As expected, her husband brushed her off. She was almost sure Lord Ruzo had been in on the king's schemes as well, but at least she need not worry about him anymore.

Tensions only grew when the Kaosudan army surrounded the city, except for the northern mountain side. Given the current season, however, the mountains could hardly be considered a potential refuge.

And the army's demand?

Tirano had shared the contents of the message in an emergency advisors' meeting, which she had insisted on attending. "Princess Melliada must marry the heir to the throne—Ben or Milos, they didn't care—and they said I must pass the crown to said heir immediately." He had stood and placed both hands on the dark, polished table, leaning forward and glaring at each advisor in turn … as though daring them to suggest he comply.

Apparently the Kaosudans were completely done with his nonsense. Anela could hardly blame them, although the situation was less than ideal. Tirano had no intention of giving up the throne that night.

Milos was gone. Somehow, after he left, Ana also disappeared. No one could find the guards who were on duty when she mysteriously escaped. Anela and Henriella secretly celebrated that both of the youngsters were out of harm's way, while Tirano was beyond livid.

Battle was imminent. The snow and ice were to no one's advantage, but Tirano wasn't going to give in so easily. The citizens in Sonos City were on house arrest to minimize civilian casualties.

Mid-afternoon, she was paid a visit by Bristio. He found her as she made her way back to her quarters.

"May I have a private word, Your Majesty?"

"Yes, of course."

They entered her sitting room shortly after. Having a man visit her alone wasn't entirely appropriate, but everyone was too distracted by the army at their doorsteps to comment.

They sat down in front of the fire in the opposite armchairs.

Bristio cleared his throat. "I have spoken with Milos and told him what's happening."

Her eyebrows shot up. "Oh? You know where he is then?"

He nodded. "Yes, and Ana as well. They're safe."

Her shoulders dropped in relief. "Thank you. I admit, I'm not sure where to go from here. What did Milos say?"

"He has a plan. He needs a public audience with the king. Audience being the key word; we need witnesses, members of the court. He is relying on your husband's pride to ensure his idea works."

She frowned. "What does he intend to do?"

"Challenge his father." Bristio shifted, rubbing a hand over his stubbled jaw. "I wanted to talk him out of it, but I don't have any better ideas."

Anela nodded thoughtfully. "What about Benito? He has been openly named as heir, so if Tirano is forced to step down, it would be he who takes the throne."

"That would be one of the conditions. If Milos wins, he is heir, and Tirano steps down. Another condition is that Milos will not marry the princess. But he will alter the trade agreements to Kaosuda's benefit."

The fire crackled as Anela considered the plan. "I suppose it's preferable to open battle." Her chest tightened at the idea of the duel. "My husband is skilled with a sword. Do *you* think Milos can beat Tirano?"

Bristio smiled. "Aye. I do. Can you arrange some way for Milos to publicly challenge the king?"

"When?"

"The sooner the better. Milos is waiting nearby. He's ready."

Anela waved a hand. "Easy enough. Tirano intends to give a speech at supper to the court about the impending conflict, so we know he'll be there this evening. Have Milos come then."

Shortly after Bristio departed, Henriella arrived. Anela still sat before the hearth, deep in thought, but she smiled when Hen sat down across from her.

"Catch me up?" Hen asked, her blue eyes intent, mouth turned down in concern.

"Of course." Anela recounted the advisors' meeting and Bristio's visit. She leaned back as she finished, staring up at the ceiling. "No matter what happens, everything is about to change."

Hen hummed her agreement. "Yes, that's true. It may change for the better, though." She rose and padded to Anela, holding out her hand. Anela took it and stood, and Hen enveloped her in a comforting embrace. "I'll be here, no matter what."

Anela buried her face in the soft skin of Hen's neck as she blinked away her tears. "Thank the Seven for that."

Hen chuckled softly and drew back enough to meet Anela's gaze. "Not even the Seven could keep me from your side, Nel."

"I know," Anela breathed. Unable to resist, she let her lips brush against Hen's. A guard could open the door and see them, but she couldn't bring herself to care.

Hen took the invitation and kissed her back, soft yet eager. It had been far too long since they had been willing to risk this type of intimacy. With an army almost at their door, it could be their last chance.

Their tongues met, caressing and exploring, and both women let out a soft moan.

A knock sounded, and the two sprang apart, wide eyed. "Yes?" Anela called.

"Your afternoon tea, Your Majesty," a guard called.

Anela cursed quietly and straightened her shoulders. "Yes, bring it in."

She and Hen made their way to the table as Mistress Danias bustled in with the laden tray. She would be short-handed, Anela reflected, having lost both Lisia and Ana. She forced herself to smile and thank the kindly woman.

The housekeeper left and Hen poured for them both.

"Someday," Hen murmured. "Someday, Nel, we *will* get to be together."

In the afterlife, if not before. Anela didn't voice the thought. "I hope so."

At supper, Anela barely touched her food, being far too anxious as she waited for Milos to arrive. Henriella sat across from her and managed to eat some of her meal, at least, although she was tense as well. To be fair, no one was at ease with the Kaosudan soldiers surrounding the city.

Milos had impeccable timing. As Tirano stood to gain the room's attention, their son stalked into the dining hall.

Anela spotted him first and glanced at the king. He opened his mouth to speak, then snapped it shut as he noticed Milos. His brown eyes flashed as his jaw tightened.

The crowd fell silent, watching as Milos approached the head table, where Tirano and Ben both now stood.

"Mother," Milos nodded at her first, and she returned the gesture. "Father. Brother." The last was said with a faint sneer.

"What is this?" Tirano ground out. "Give me one reason why I shouldn't order the guards to remove you from my hall."

"Gladly," Milos replied, the picture of calm and strength. He turned slightly so he could address both the king and the rest of the room. Raising his voice, he got straight to the point. "I am here to challenge you, Father."

A collective gasp told Anela this wasn't what anyone had expected.

Nor had Tirano. "You—what?" he stuttered as his face flushed with rage.

"The Kaosudan army wishes for you to step down.

Have you told the court? They will leave peacefully if your heir takes your place."

Unsurprisingly, Tirano and his advisors had kept that part of the message under wraps. A buzz of murmurs grew.

Milos continued. "I think it best to avoid unnecessary bloodshed."

"Because you're weak," Tirano accused, finally recovering.

Milos smiled and shook his head. "No, Father. It takes strength to sacrifice for the good of your people." He paused, his gaze resting on one table, then the next, before turning to face his father directly. "If you're not strong enough to do what's right for your kingdom, to make the sacrifice that would save many lives, are you at least brave enough to accept my challenge?"

Ben interrupted. "Little brother, you're not heir anymore. Has no one told you? This conversation is pointless."

Anela's jaw tightened at his reminder of their birth order. However, it didn't matter: the challenge had been given and as predicted, Tirano could not reject it in front of the court. He held up a hand to quiet Ben. "We hardly have time for this, but if you insist that I best you with a sword, I shall indulge the whim. It will be your last, in any case. You will be exiled, if you survive."

Anela sucked in a sharp breath. A duel should end at first blood drawn… Although, that could happen with a sword through the gut. Would Tirano truly do such a thing?

She swallowed hard, not wanting to admit the answer to herself.

Milos nodded once. "If I lose, I willingly give up my position as heir to my brother and leave Revas. However, if I win, I take the throne. Immediately."

Ben grunted. "And if I wish to challenge you? I am the eldest, after all."

A slow grin spread over Milos's face. "If you really think you can best me, I welcome you to try."

Ben said nothing, only pressed his lips together and looked away. Good. He must realize Milos had received excellent instruction in weaponry; hopefully he wouldn't take the risk.

Milos focused on the king. "If we don't deliver on the Kaosudans' demands by dawn tomorrow, they will attack. So now is the time, Father. Choose the location and I will meet you there in one hour."

"The training arena," Tirano gritted out. "One hour."

Anela flinched. The grounds were covered with snow and ice, and a duel could happen just easily in the dining hall or the throne room. She wasn't sure of Tirano's reasoning, but she didn't dare ask.

Milos gave a single sharp nod and strode from the room.

The whispers and murmurs increased as folks abandoned their meals, no doubt to prepare to witness the event in the bitter cold. The crowd bunched together as they all tried to exit at once, and soon, the space emptied, meals left half eaten. Steam still rose from trays of meat. The wine from overturned goblets dripped onto the stone floor, loud in the silence.

Tirano turned to Anela, and she attempted to maintain a neutral expression. "Your son is a fool."

She gave half a shrug. "Perhaps. But he's also brave."

A growl rumbled in her husband's chest though he said nothing in reply. Instead, he hurried out of the room, barking at Ben, "Come."

Ben hesitated, looking at Anela, a flicker of worry evident in his eyes. She raised a brow and waited. He opened his mouth, then shut it with a shake of his head and followed the king.

Anela and Henriella were left alone. Hen blew out a breath. "Well. That was ... interesting."

Anela barked a laugh. "Let's fetch our cloaks and gloves. It's freezing."

Forty-five minutes later, the court stood huddled in small groups around the training arena. Someone had taken it upon themselves to clear away some of the snow, and frozen dirt peeked out underneath. Guards held lanterns and torches at intervals around the arena, but the night was clear, and the moons were so bright they were hardly needed.

Two of the three moons overlapped slightly, while the third moved slowly and steadily to join them. A rare three moon eclipse. *When three moons meet, the king will fall.* Did Tirano even notice the three celestial sisters joining? Was the prophecy coming true?

Tirano arrived first, stalking into the arena with arrogant confidence. Anela linked elbows with Hen, who patted her arm with a whispered, "I'm here, Nel."

Murmurs of the crowd signaled Milos's arrival before she saw him.

Anela held her breath.

Chapter Forty

MILOS

Milos had insisted Ana stay away; they would have noticed her escape by now, and he didn't want her to risk being recaptured. But he couldn't help wishing she was there. Her presence bolstered him in ways he couldn't explain.

The arena was lit up with torches and lanterns. As he strode through the audience, unnoticed at first, he heard their speculations.

"Who do you think will win?" one woman asked.

"The king, without a doubt," one of the noblemen replied. "He's far more experienced."

"I rarely see him train anymore, though," another man argued. "The prince is in the training yard quite often."

As he drew nearer to the fenced square yard, folks noticed him, and the mutters and murmurs increased. His father stood in the center, cloakless, sword already drawn, his entire being radiating irritation and impatience. So eager to hurt his own son.

Then again, that was nothing new.

Milos tried to ignore the buzz of conversation as he

entered the open space and removed his cloak. When he turned around from laying it over the fence, Milos took a single deep breath before he unsheathed his own weapon and met his father in the center of the space. Their gazes locked as they stood a few paces apart.

Milos wasn't surprised that all their years of clashing had led to this, yet it was also disconcerting to know the man who stood before him might very well be willing to end his life ... even though that man was his father.

He swallowed hard. Was he willing to kill the king? His own sire? He hoped it wouldn't come to that, but Tirano was unpredictable. If the older man didn't stop at first blood drawn, Milos didn't intend to surrender.

"This is selfish of you," his father said abruptly. "You've always been selfish, self-absorbed. Yet after neglecting your duties all these years, your pride won't allow you to bow to your older, and more capable, brother."

Milos blinked, ignoring the sting of the comparison. "Me? I'm the selfish one? You're willing to sacrifice countless soldiers, good men, because you can't fathom losing control of this kingdom. You're the one who made an enemy of our southern neighbor, not me."

The king's jaw tightened. "Let's get this over with. I have more important matters to attend to."

Milos gave a single nod and raised his sword. "At the ready."

Tirano lunged, and time slowed, as it always seemed to when Milos fought. He blocked the attack easily as he allowed his years of training to take over. All that mattered was the flow of the fight, his grip on his sword, the placement of his feet.

Flames and shadows from the torches danced around

them as Milos attempted to maintain full control of his movement despite the invisible icy patches.

They were evenly matched, which Milos had anticipated. Tirano might not train as often, but he had decades more experience. Similar in height and reach, it was as fair a fight as one might hope for. Endurance might be the deciding factor, fortunately for Milos. Despite his injured arm, he felt confident that his consistent training would ensure his stamina as compared to the king.

Thrust. Parry. Slide to the left, step forward, swing. Sword play had its own rhythm, a tempo coursing through his body with every breath. Sweat soon trickled down his back despite the cold. All he could hear was his own heartbeat and the clash of metal when their weapons met.

As the ball of his foot came down, a slick bit of ice tested his balance. He wavered and withdrew from his planned attack, stepping back to gain stability.

His father sneered, chest heaving. "Tired already? So weak. Let me know when you wish to surrender."

Chapter Forty-One

VERANA

Ana couldn't bear to stay away, no matter what Milos demanded. How could she hide in a back room of The Royal Gate while he challenged his own father?

She kept her hood pulled forward, and the guards at the gate barely gave her a glance. The air buzzed with tension and excitement; the challenge must have been issued, so no wonder the guards were distracted.

She saw the torches and heard the grating sound of metal on metal—the duel had already begun. She stood on tiptoes to see over the noblemen in front of her and saw Milos slip on a patch of ice. She barely held in her gasp. Fortunately, he recovered quickly.

Fists clenched, she tracked every lunge, every block. Riveted, heart racing, she had no attention for anything but the scene unfolding in front of her.

Suddenly, arms wrapped around her, one around her middle and the other covering her mouth, and she was dragged backward. No one seemed to notice, as the duel held their full attention.

"Look who I found," Ben breathed into her ear. "Our little prisoner." He spun her around and pressed a knife to her throat before she could scream. "I wouldn't, sweetheart."

He clasped the back of her neck and pulled her closer, kissing her roughly, the tip of the knife still under her chin. She bit his lip, hard, and felt the blade break her skin, but he drew back. "So feisty all of a sudden. We can have our fun later. For now, you're my insurance if my brother actually wins this."

As though on cue, a gasp rose from the crowd. Ben looked over her shoulder and scowled. She couldn't see anything, but her guess was that Milos was winning, or had won already.

"So glad you decided to come," Ben breathed. "Turns out I do have a use for you, and not only for your cunt."

He spun her again and pushed her forward through the crowd, who hardly seemed to notice; all eyes remained on the two men in the training yard.

Chapter Forty-Two

MILOS

Lips pressed together in a grim line, Milos didn't bother replying to his father's taunts. The king's cruelty over the years benefited him now; his jabs and insults had little effect at this point. He spun to one side and lunged, knees bent to sweep the weapon low.

The tip cut through the fabric of Tirano's pants just above the knee, causing him to stumble. A thin red line appeared where the fabric gaped.

Milos hesitated, waiting to see if the king would allow this to be over, as it should be. First blood.

He shouldn't have paused. He knew his father too well, chastising himself as he belatedly moved to block the next attack. He avoided the brunt of it, but the tip of the blade sliced through skin on the bicep of his already injured arm. He gritted his teeth, grateful it wasn't his sword arm.

And so they continued the dance. Tirano limped, panting heavily. A corner of Milos's mouth rose in satisfaction as the clang of metal reverberated around the snowy courtyard.

Tirano held out for longer than Milos anticipated … until the blood flowing down his leg ran free of the cloth of his pants to join forces with a patch of ice, and he slipped. His arms flew out to his sides in a desperate but failed attempt to keep his feet. He fell hard, landing on his sword arm.

Milos stood above him in an instant, sword tip inches from Tirano's neck. "Drop your blade."

Tirano's chest heaved and his face wore a glare of pure hatred as he released the sword. Milos kicked it away. A voice rang out from the crowd.

"Very impressive, brother."

Milos scanned the audience, stopping on a movement as folks were pushed aside. The first face he saw was Ana's, and her expression was a mixture of terror and outrage.

Ben's arm was wrapped around her waist as he held her from behind, a knife to her throat. He forced her to move forward, through an opening in the fence.

Tirano attempted to rise while Milos was distracted. Milos pressed his sword even closer to his father's jugular. "Stay. There," he gritted out, then gave him a kick in the stomach for good measure, ignoring his grunt of pain.

"What exactly do you think you're doing?" Milos demanded of Ben.

Ben, peering over Ana's shoulder, grinned. "I should think it obvious, but our father always did say you're not the brightest. I happen to know you're attached to this woman —this maid." A collective gasp rose from the crowd.

Milos smiled, predatory, showing all his teeth. "Hadn't you heard? She's actually the daughter of a prince. And she's your future queen, if she's willing." He finally released his father, moving quickly to take hold of Tirano's sword. "So, you need to take." He punctuated each word with a step toward Ben and Ana. "Your. Fucking. Hands. Off of her."

Ben chuckled and pressed the dagger harder against the delicate, soft skin of Ana's neck. She gave a sharp inhale.

"So you do care for her. I thought so. I will release her ... in exchange for the crown you just won."

Chapter Forty-Three

VERANA

Her ears buzzed and pounded with the beat of her heart, making it difficult to process the words the two men exchanged. She gathered it amounted to Milos demanding her release, and Ben stating that he would only do so if Milos gave up being heir.

Milos approached them slowly, step by step, drawing to an abrupt halt when Ben stated his terms. Ana noticed movement behind Milos—Tirano was on his feet, and the torch flames flickered off the dagger in his hand. Milos hadn't disarmed him entirely, being distracted by his brother.

Ana opened her mouth to warn him, but Ben growled, "*No.*" He pressed the knife into the previous cut; blood trickled down her neck. She remained silent, trying to communicate to Milos with her eyes despite the poor light.

Milos must have understood, or heard his father, because he whirled, raising his sword … not quite quickly enough. Tirano lunged, his dagger aiming at Milos's chest.

Milos managed to sidestep, so the blade slid across his ribs rather than plunging into his heart.

Now his sword stretched between the two men, forcing Tirano to halt, a frustrated scowl on his face. Ana bit her lip when she saw the blood seeping through Milos's tunic.

“Guards!" Milos bellowed. “You all heard our agreement, made in good faith in front of the entire court. If I win, he steps down. I am your king now, and I demand you take my father into your custody.”

A beat of silence passed as the crowd waited to see if the guards would obey. Bristio strode forward first, then several others joined him. They wordlessly surrounded the defeated king, grasping both of his arms and dragging him out of the arena.

Milos turned back to Ben and Ana, who hadn't moved.

“Ana,” Milos said. “Are you hurt?”

She tried to shake her head, then flinched as she felt the sharp metal. A warm trickle of fluid dripped down her neck, yet she didn't feel any pain. “No,” she rasped. “I—I'm all right.”

That obviously wasn't true, but at least she wasn't badly injured.

Thoughts raced through her mind as swiftly as icy wind through leafless winter trees. Would he sacrifice the throne for her? *Should* he? Could he, in good conscience, leave the care of the kingdom and all its citizens in his brother's greedy, deceitful hands? Should she even want him to?

Of course she wanted to live. However, she refused to be so selfish.

“What will it be?” Ben taunted. “Your crown, or your woman?”

“Milos,” Ana said. “Don't let him steal your future.” To

Ben, she whispered, "You may as well cut my throat now. He won't give in." Ben hissed but said nothing.

Milos pointed his sword toward the ground. He smirked, though it was forced. "I take it you don't think you can beat me in a fight? Else you'd challenge me and leave an innocent woman out of it." He raised his voice to ensure their captive audience could hear every word. "Is that the kind of king you'll be? Threatening innocents to satisfy your hunger for power? Pick up a sword and fight me for the right to sit on the throne of Revas, if you're not a coward, *brother*."

Ben tensed behind her. His breath came hot and ragged in her ear. Was Ben's pride as excessive as Tirano's? She didn't even know what to hope for at this point. Ben might be a better fighter than Milos; at the least, he would go in fresh, whereas Milos had already fought hard. Yet she didn't want Milos to simply hand over his inheritance, especially not to a man such as Ben.

Their standoff stretched on with the avid audience muttering and whispering around them.

Ben finally spoke. "It is not cowardly to know your strengths and limits. I wasn't trained at court by the finest Revasian warriors as you were, so it's hardly a fair fight." Ana flinched. Not so proud as Tirano, then. "This is your last chance. Do you surrender the crown?"

Ana's stare beseeched Milos to do what was right. To serve his people and protect his kingdom.

An agonized expression overtook Milos's face. "Let us talk further. We can—"

Ben interrupted. "No. I am the eldest son of the king. You will pay for denying me what I am owed. Or rather, she will, with a slow and painful death. If I can't have the crown, you can't have her."

Milos lunged toward them, but not before Ben whipped his hand down and plunged the knife into her belly. Searing pain spread through her body like cracks in an frozen lake.

Chapter Forty-Four

MILOS

Milos gaped in horror as Ben released Ana and she fell, knife still in her stomach. She lay on her back, gasping.

"Guards!" Milos bellowed as he ran to her, slipping on ice and finally collapsing next to her. "Put him in a cell! Get the physician!" He knew the castle physician was nearby, as was protocol for a duel. As badly as he wanted to run Ben through, it could wait. Ana could not.

"Ana, love, I'm here." He wanted to gather her into his arms, but he was afraid to move her. He took her hand, leaning over so she could see him. Blood flowed around the sharp metal, dripping from her body onto the freezing ground. "Hold on. You'll be all right. Just hold on for me."

"I'm—I'm so cold," she murmured. "Gods, it hurts." She moaned and shut her eyes.

"I know, love, I know. I'm so sorry. Stay awake, Ana."

The physician knelt on her other side. His mother and Lady Henriella stood nearby as well, but Milos couldn't concern himself with them. He felt a strange, strong pulse of energy in the air and flinched. Some of the onlookers cried out, and he heard a couple of screams. He ignored it all. No time to investigate whatever in the Seven that was.

The physician looked dazed. "What was that? I—"

"It doesn't matter!" Milos barked. "Tend to her!"

The man shook himself. "What of your own wound, Your Highness?"

Milos wasn't surprised the royal physician would try to prioritize him as prince—no, king—but he had no patience for it. "Only scratches. Help her. Now!"

The physician pressed his lips into a thin line. "When I remove the blade, you must put immediate pressure on the wound or she may bleed out in seconds."

Someone dropped his cloak next to him, and he grabbed it. "I'm ready."

The other man gripped the hilt. "It will hurt," he warned, and Ana gave a nod. Then he swiftly yanked the blade out and tossed it aside. Ana grunted in pain.

Before the weapon hit the ground, Milos was pressing down on her stomach with his bunched-up cloak.

"We need to get her inside." The physician barked orders Milos only half-listened to. His gaze locked on Ana. As her eyelids fluttered, he willed her to stay alive. A minute later, a guard laid a rectangular wooden board on the ground, one usually used for target practice.

Two guards lifted her as the physician led them back inside, Milos still right beside her, pressing on the wound. Fortunately, the surgery chamber was nearby in order to be easily accessible from the training grounds.

They didn't bother sliding her off the board, instead laying it on top of the table. The physician rushed about, gathering what he needed from cupboards and shelves.

"So m-much for the prophecy." Ana's constant shivers

blurred her speech. "It wa-wasn't about me. Nothing changed."

Milos remembered the mysterious pulse of energy and frowned. "I'm not so sure about that. I think something happened. Don't worry about it right now, though, love."

His mother appeared in the doorway. "Milos."

He didn't look at her. "Not right now, Mother."

The physician said, "No, go with her. You'll only be in the way while I work. If you want me to save her, get out." He gave Milos a small shove as an assistant took over applying pressure to Ana's abdomen.

Milos glared at the man. "I'll be right outside, Ana," he said as he stalked over to join his mother. He shut the door gently.

"I'm sorry, son. It's important." Anela placed a hand on his forearm. "Something has happened."

Could she be any more vague? "I'm not going anywhere until I know Ana is all right."

Anela sighed impatiently. "You are king now, even without a coronation. You are responsible for the safety of our people. We just received reports of the Kaosudans marching on the city."

"What?" Milos almost ran a hand over his face before he saw that it was covered in Ana's blood. Clenching both jaw and fist, he said, "They gave us until dawn!"

She shrugged helplessly. "Yes. But they're coming now."

He cursed, low and with feeling. "I need to stop them before they're at the castle. I'll take a unit so we can intercept them, and I'll demand to speak with their general." He took a step, then turned. "Can you stay here? With Ana?"

Anela nodded, so he strode away.

As he expected, he found the Revasian soldiers readying

themselves for battle. After a quick word with his own army general about his plan, he went to find Bristio.

The old guard insisted on tending to Milos's wounds, but he did so with haste. Once the arm and abdomen wounds were bandaged, the older man clapped a hand on his shoulder. "Good to go." His eyes shone as some emotion crossed his face. "Proud of you, Milos."

Milos ducked his head, warmth spreading in his chest. "Thank you, old friend."

They retrieved their horses and met a group of soldiers at the gates. Milos addressed them all. "My hope is, once I explain that we've met at least one of their requests—the most important one, I imagine—we will avoid a battle." He paused, then pointed at one of the younger soldiers. "If that isn't the case and they engage us in a fight, it's your job to return to the castle to inform the other units." He briefly wondered where General Casio was. Had the Kaosudans fought the Revasian soldiers at the border to get across? Or had General Casio left the border unguarded, thinking the threat was over? If the latter, the general and his troops would be marching back to Sonos City. Milos desperately hoped that was the case.

"Yes, Your High—I mean, Your Majesty."

Milos suppressed a shudder. That was the first time anyone had addressed him as such. He hadn't imagined taking the throne for years, yet here they were.

Despite the late hour and the cold, folks came out of their homes to see what was happening. It seemed everyone had felt the great pulse of energy, and they cared more about getting answers than obeying the curfew.

"What was that magic? What is happening, Your Highness?"

They shouted other questions at him—about his father,

about Sonos and the pastros—and none of it made sense. He couldn't stop to listen, to try to understand; he had to reach the Kaosudan force before they marched on the city.

He tried telling the people to stay inside where it was safe but gave up the effort as more and more appeared. Hopefully they had the sense to run and lock their doors if the Kaosudans attacked.

He could hear the other army marching, although he didn't see them until they reached the central square. The Kaosudans flooded the space, coming from the main road. A handful rode, while most were on foot. This wasn't all of them; others were surely approaching from different directions.

Milos and Bristio halted their soldiers and rode forward. "I am Milos, son of Tirano, and now king of Revas. I demand to speak to your highest-ranking officer."

Within a few moments, a mountain of a man emerged on horseback. He halted about six feet from them and gave a small bow from the saddle. "Your Majesty. My name is Lieutenant Jarvo."

Milos wasted no words or breath. All he wanted was to resolve this as quickly as possible and return to Ana. "Why are you here? Dawn was the agreed upon deadline."

Jarvo studied him for a beat, then nodded. "It was. But we won't allow you to attack us with magic without repercussion."

Milos blinked. They had felt that strange surge all the way in their camps outside of the city? "You speak of the … the pulse of power a short while ago?"

Jarvo inclined his head in affirmation.

"We felt it too. I assure you it was not an attack of any sort. We don't know what it was, and we intend to investigate. No one was hurt, correct?"

The burly man considered him in the moonlight. "You're right, no one was hurt by it. I can't be sure you're telling the truth, but I will believe you for now, if only because it seems your monarchy decided to comply with our demands." A grin spread across his features. "I wish I could have seen Tirano's face when he finally lost his crown. And what happened with the brother? We were told he would ascend, as he is the eldest."

Milos pressed his lips together to keep from snarling at the man. He was too distressed about Ana to have patience for this conversation. Once he had his temper under control, he said, "It's a long story, and inconsequential for the time being. My father abdicated. We have not met all of your demands. However, I hope this step is enough for us to move forward peacefully. I will be happy to negotiate further terms in the near future."

Jarvo frowned. "Are you not engaged to Princess Melliada, then?"

Milos shook his head. "No. I am not going to marry her." Might as well get it all out in the open. "I will provide a generous trade offer to benefit your people, as a compromise."

Jarvo pursed his mouth, considering. "I see. It's not my place to make those sorts of agreements. For now, I will order our men to stand down and return to camp … if you can provide surety of your intentions."

"Surety?" Milos glanced at Bristio, not understanding.

The old guard grunted, studying Jarvo. "A hostage, then?"

Jarvo shrugged his massive shoulders. "That would work."

Bristio gave a sharp nod. "I'll come with you."

Milos's jaw dropped as understanding dawned. "Bristio, you can't—"

Bristio held up a gloved hand. "I'll be fine. I believe you will negotiate successfully." He stared at Milos, determined. "Trust me."

Jarvo interrupted. "If it's to be soldiers as hostages, one is not sufficient."

"I am the king's personal guard. I've looked after him since he was a boy. But if you insist…" Bristio waved a hand toward the soldiers waiting behind them. "We will all come."

Everything in Milos wanted to object. Yet Bristio asked for his trust. He bit his tongue.

Jarvo nodded. "Fine. Turn over your weapons and come with us." To Milos, he said, "We will expect a messenger to bring your negotiation proposal by sunset tomorrow. Bring our princess as well and we will make the exchange. Otherwise, your hostages are forfeit, and we will march on the city."

Milos gave a single sharp nod. "If any harm comes to them before that, I will hold you personally responsible."

He met Bristio's gaze a final time, a wordless exchange of love and trust even as his stomach felt hollow with worry. Then he turned his horse back toward the castle, and Ana.

Chapter Forty-Five

VERANA

Ana could barely make out their words of the physician and his assistant through the haze of pain. And she was so, so sleepy. Someone palmed the back of her head, raising it up as they put a small glass bottle to her lips.

"Drink," they urged.

So she did, although the potent taste made her cough and sputter, pain spiking with every involuntary movement. Was this what they had given Aldo? Would it take the pain away? She hoped so.

Soon a tingling numbness spread through her body, and the sleepiness intensified. She drifted off.

When she opened her eyes, she knew she was dreaming. She stood in the snowy woods in a flimsy but clean dress, yet she couldn't feel the cold, nor was she injured. Glancing around, she marveled at the beauty of the forest in a state of ice and silence.

A deep, smooth voice reached her through the trees. "Verana, daughter of Armando and Halia." A man stepped out from behind a cluster of pines. Ana couldn't help staring; he was taller than any human man, with skin the color of the night sky and odd white eyes that shone from within like distant stars. He wore little, only a piece of dark, shiny cloth wrapped around his hips.

"Sonos?" she hazarded a guess. She had never dreamed about Sonos before, but this must be him—because who else could it be?—even though he didn't look anything like the temple depictions.

He stopped in front of her, only a few feet away. He smiled as he towered over her. "Indeed."

"What's happening? I don't understand." His eyes both captivated her and terrified her; she focused on his chin instead.

"Did you not know the god of dreams and nightmares can manifest in whatever dreams he wishes?"

She bit her lip, embarrassed. "I mean, I suppose. Is this real? Are you really here, speaking to me?"

He chuckled. "I am. You have done well with Veyra's gift. The Seven are pleased." His mouth twisted in annoyance. "Most of us, anyway."

"You're talking about the prophecy?"

He inclined his head. "Yes. Orix is being quite insufferable about it, as always." He waved a hand, dismissing the topic. "You have served your intended purpose. And now, as a reward, we offer you a choice."

Ana's brow wrinkled in confusion. "Which is?"

"Where you go from here. Your injury is serious, and you are only still alive because I will it to be so. You must decide if you want to cross over, or if you wish to continue life in your mortal form."

Ana blinked. "By 'cross over' you mean dying, right? Why would I choose to die?"

He considered her with those unnerving, glowing eyes.

"To be with loved ones whom you grieve. Such as your brother."

Ana gasped. "Aldo? I can see Aldo again?"

Sonos nodded. "If you choose to release your mortal existence, yes, you can spend eternity with him."

How she wanted to be with Aldo. She still missed him dreadfully. Her answer was on the tip of her tongue, but she hesitated.

Being with Aldo meant leaving everyone else behind. Her parents. Her friends.

Milos.

It meant never traveling the world, as her prince had promised. She was so young and had so many plans for her future. Could she give all of that up for her brother?

Sonos hummed. "Not an easy decision, I suppose. Shall I give you some time to think?"

Her throat was thick with tears. "Yes, please."

"Very well. I will return, and when I do, the choice must be made. You cannot remain in the dream realm forever."

His body blurred, dissolving into a mist of darkness as it floated up toward the night sky. And then she was alone.

Collapsing into the snow with her back against a tree, she briefly marveled at how she could somehow smell the crisp piney air yet not feel the cold. If only winter was always this comfortable.

Then her mind turned to her choice. To be with her best friend and baby brother for eternity, or to return to her life. Her complicated, messy, beautiful life.

What would her death do to her parents? They didn't see her often anymore, but that didn't mean they wouldn't be devastated. She would be, if she lost one of them. And if she didn't go back, she would lose both of them, even though they still lived.

And Milos. He was young and had only known her a few months. Surely, he would heal and fall in love with someone else. The idea of him being with another woman made her stomach twist.

She scowled up at the clear, starry sky, hoping Sonos was watching. If he had the audacity to give her the choice and pretend it was a reward, she didn't owe him gratitude, god or not.

Her thoughts continued to run in circles. She kept returning to the concept of eternity. Sonos had said she could be with Aldo for eternity. If she chose to go back, she would miss him every second of every day for the rest of her life. But really, what was a mortal life compared to eternity? For him, it would pass by in a blink, wouldn't it? And when she eventually died, she assumed he would still be waiting for her, and then they'd never be parted again. He would understand why she hadn't come to him sooner.

Not only would he understand, Aldo would tell her to live her life. He might even be angry if she sacrificed it for him. Eventually, certainty settled over her like a warm blanket.

She stood, once more looking to the sky. "Sonos? Are you there?"

And she waited.

Chapter Forty-Six

MILOS

Milos felt torn in half. He didn't want to leave Ana's side, yet he had to negotiate with the Kaosudans and bring Bristio and his other soldiers home safely.

His compromise was to force everyone to come to him as he sat by Ana's side in the bedroom they had transferred her to. He had wanted her placed in his quarters, but his mother convinced him that it wasn't proper. So he delegated and made decisions in low voices and whispers as she slept in a room in the guest quarters.

Once his mother and a few others helped him devise his proposal and the messenger departed to deliver it, he sent for Ana's parents.

Then, all he could do was wait. Wait for an answer from the army, wait for Bristio to return, wait for Ana's parents to arrive … and wait for her to wake up.

She would wake. She had to.

Fortunately, the Koasudans accepted his proposal, which he had been very generous with, knowing the stakes. Bristio found him immediately upon his return to the castle.

Milos stood from the chair next to Ana's bed when Bristio walked through the door. "Thank the Seven. Is everything all right?"

Bristio nodded as they met in the middle of the room. The old man embraced him and Milos leaned into the hug, needing some comfort.

"You did well," Bristio rasped as he released Milos and stepped back. "I always knew you'd be an excellent king." He glanced at the bed. "How is she?"

Milos's mouth tightened. "Still alive. She hasn't woken."

A frown crossed the older man's face. "Well, alive is better than not, eh?" He looked Milos up and down, seeming to notice his state of disarray. Someone had brought him clean clothes, but he hadn't fully washed; between sweat, blood, and exhaustion, he surely looked haggard.

"Want me to stay with her so you can clean up? Get some rest?"

Milos shook his head. "I don't want to leave her." He hesitated. "But I wouldn't mind some company, if you're not too worn out." The guard looked tired yet not unwell, for which Milos was grateful.

"I'm happy to stay, as long as I can eat something. They fed us, but their supplies were low, so it wasn't much."

Milos ordered food for both of them. Mistress Danias brought it herself. She gave Bristio a fond pat on the shoulder on her way out. "Glad to see you home safe."

"Thanks, Mistress. Glad to be here."

Milos had sent a carriage for Ana's parents, and they arrived around noon the following day. Only once they were there did he give in. After a quick greeting, he left briefly to take a full bath and sleep in his own bed for an hour or two. Then he went right back to Ana's room.

Luciano tracked him as he strode in and stopped by the bed to see if anything had changed. It hadn't. At least she looked peaceful.

Her father spoke first. "I knew you wanted to court my daughter." He huffed a laugh.

The corner of Milos's lips quirked up. "I did. I do. That is… I hope to marry her. Do we have your blessing?" He hadn't meant to ask so suddenly, abruptly; too late now. "I love her more than anything. I promise to take care of her, always."

Ana's mother's mouth fell open. She said nothing, instead looking at Luciano.

The man's gray gaze focused on his daughter, so still; her only movement being the rise and fall of her chest. "If that is what she wants, you have our blessing. Assuming she…" A pained expression crossed his face and he shook his head.

"She'll wake. She *will* live." Milos's voice was gruff but determined. He took one of her hands in his, squeezing lightly. "She's too stubborn not to."

A laugh escaped Halia. "You know her well, then."

Milos smiled. "Yes, I do."

Chapter Forty-Seven

VERANA

"Hello, Ana."

She jumped; the god had materialized behind her. She turned and straightened her shoulders. Her body shook despite her confidence in her choice. "I want to ask you a question before I tell you my decision."

"Go ahead."

"This is all more complicated than it needs to be. Aren't the Seven omnipotent? Why play around with people's lives with prophecies? If you didn't wish Tirano to rule, couldn't you have simply stopped him?"

He tsked. "That is more than one question, but I understand what you're curious about. How to explain this..." He looked up at the sky for a few beats, then directed his glowing gaze back to her. "We are not omnipotent in the way that you mean, no. We have the power to create entire worlds, yes. However, with that power comes limitations. We can only interfere so much with beings whom we gave free will. Yet free will is what makes the game interesting, wouldn't you agree? In any case, it's nearly impossible to create life that has no free will."

"Our lives are a game to you?" she sputtered.

He continued as though she hadn't spoken. "Think of it like this. Your parents chose to create children. Each child is its own world in a sense; it's all about scale. But after your parents created you, were they able to control your every thought and action? Not at all. The creation is too powerful for that. The child becomes a creator in her own right. They can *influence* you, yet they cannot *control* you. Do you see?"

Ana wrinkled her nose. "Kind of, I guess." She was still irritated about his reference to "the game," but there was little point in arguing with a god. "I've decided to go back. I want to live out whatever is left of my mortal life."

"Very well. I should tell you that the world will be different when you return. When you fulfilled the prophecy, the gift of truth seeped into the earth with your blood, you see. All of the people of Revas received the revelation."

Her mouth hung open. "Revelation?"

He nodded. "They know how the kings in recent history manipulated them, and that the messages spread by the so-called templekeepers were not sent by me." He paused. "Some are confused, and many are angry. It is to be expected. I'm afraid the new king will have quite a lot to manage in the near future."

Ana blew out a breath. "All the more reason for me to return. Milos will need help."

Sonos bowed his head. "I'd wish you luck, but that isn't my area of expertise. Must not step on any godly toes." Ana snorted softly; would Tavros take offense if Sonos wished her good fortune? How petty were these gods? "In any case, goodbye, Ana."

He disappeared, as did the woods. She was nowhere, and nothing, enveloped by darkness. Then she heard voices murmuring, and she could feel her body once again. Warm tingling in her center spread through her in a soft wave. She forced her eyes open, blinking in the light filtering through the window. She wasn't in the surgery chamber anymore, but she was definitely still in the castle.

Something warm and furry butted up against the side of her head, and she recognized a familiar purr. “Cecil?” she croaked. The cat purred louder.

“Oh, she's awake!" someone cried. “Go tell the king.” Footsteps sounded; a door opened and shut. “Ana, thank the Seven. How do you feel, sweetheart?”

It was her father. He leaned over her, curls falling over his forehead. The streaks of silver running through them looked more prominent than a month past. Worry and relief warred on his features as he took her hand.

“Papa,” she rasped. “How did you get here?” Did someone fetch him in the middle of the night? Maybe, if they thought she was dying.

Halia appeared on her other side. “Oh, my daughter.” Tears flowed down her face. “I'm so glad you're still with us. And I'm s-s-sorry for—” A sob cut her off.

“I'm here,” Ana whispered. “All is well, Mama.” Cecil languidly stretched and then moved to curl up on her chest, as though to remind her who her most important visitor was. She huffed a laugh and stroked his back.

Her father squeezed her hand, and she turned to meet his gaze. “The physician didn't think you'd...” He shook his head and attempted a smile. “You've been unconscious for nearly a week.”

She blinked and her mouth dropped open. “A—a week?” It had felt like an hour, or maybe two. Damn Sonos and his creepy eyes. He could have warned her. No wonder she was so thirsty. She looked around and spotted a cup on a small table next to the bed.

Her father nodded as he fetched the cup and helped her drink the watered-down wine. "Yes. King Milos has barely left your side, but today he was forced to attend to some of his duties." He set the cup aside and took her hand again.

The door to the bedroom burst open, startling her when it cracked against the stone wall. "Ana?"

It was Milos. Her mother stepped away to wipe her face with a handkerchief, and Milos took her place, laying a hand on Ana's arm. "Oh, love, thank the Seven. You gave us quite a scare. How do you feel?"

She wasn't sure how she felt. She stretched her legs, assessing, and placed a hand over the spot where Ben had stabbed her. It was a little tender, not terrible. "I feel fine?"

Milos's laugh turned into a choked sob. "I thought..." He trailed off, wiping his cheeks viciously with his forearm.

Her father squeezed her hand once more. "Maybe we should give you two some privacy." He wrapped an arm around Halia's shoulders and guided her out of the room, shutting the door gently behind him.

Milos took several deep breaths before he could speak again. "I thought I'd lost you before I could tell you how I feel. Gods, Ana, I love you. So much."

Her chin trembled, and her heart pounded hard in her chest. "I love you too," she said softly.

He climbed onto the bed with her, boots and all, and Cecil relocated near her feet as Milos gathered her into his arms. "You're mine, love. I'm never going to let you go."

She savored his warmth and his scent, laying her cheek against his chest. "Promise?"

"I promise. I am yours, and you are mine, for as long as you'll have me."

Chapter Forty-Eight

VERANA

In an odd turn of events, Ana and Melliada took a liking to each other. The Kaosudan princess had returned to the castle once both sides were satisfied with their negotiations, at Melliada's request, as her belongings and retinue remained there. They prepared to travel back to her home. Ana asked her to tea before she left. As they sipped, the princess confessed she was in no hurry to return home, even though she seemed just as relieved as Milos to be free of their engagement.

"My parents may be pleased with the trade agreements and having King Milos on the throne, but they won't be happy I'm not getting married after all." She frowned, looking down into her cup.

Ana's smile was kind. "You're so intelligent, and beautiful too. I'm sure you'll find a good match."

Mellia had only shrugged, appearing unconvinced.

"Besides, you can come visit us any time. I'd love for you to be at our wedding. Please," Ana begged. "I don't have many girlfriends, and I would love to see you again."

Melliada promised she would try, although she could make no guarantees without her parents' blessing. And she delayed her departure until the day after Milos's coronation.

Planning the coronation had been a challenge. Traditionally, a pastro would preside over the ceremony, but the aftermath of Tirano's downfall had left Revasians of all statuses highly suspicious of the templekeepers. It was still unclear how many of the religious leaders knew of the corruption versus how many were victims of it just as everybody else was. Ana's father, with his ability to tell truth from lies, had initiated the slow process of interviewing each individual templekeeper to determine which should be allowed to continue in their calling in the official sense.

While Milos had decided to maintain a handful of temples for worship of Sonos and the rest of the Seven, he couldn't assign pastros to them until Luciano finished with the interviews. And with the general simmering of anger toward the pastros among the population, they decided it would be better to avoid involving them in the coronation.

Another tradition was to involve the previous king, in the cases when he still lived as opposed to a crown being passed down upon his death. Tirano did indeed still live, but for obvious reasons that wasn't a path they desired to take either.

In the end, Ana watched in satisfaction as they broke every tradition by choosing Anela to lead the ceremony. The expression of joy and pride on the beautiful queen mother's face as she gently placed a crown on her only son's head was an image Ana would never forget.

Once the coronation was over, Milos finalized his advisor choices, breaking yet another tradition when he invited Mistress Danias to the advisory council, which had only been comprised of men in the past. He also appointed Bristio and Luciano.

And then it was time to deal with Tirano and Benito.

They had tried to track down Ben's mother Viv, with no luck. She had disappeared from the shop where she worked without a word or a trace. Their conclusion was she likely knew exactly what her son had been up to, and she didn't wish to be punished alongside him.

Ben was brought to the advisors' meeting room, where Ana, Milos, and the seven advisors waited. Anela and Henriella had declined the invitation to be present for either of the two men's sentencing.

Milos got straight to point once Ben was seated, his hands restrained in front of him, surrounded by two guards. "The penalty for insurrection and treason is death. Exile is the only other potential option. Plead your case."

Ben, dirty and pale, straightened his shoulders and cleared his throat. "As your only brother, I would beg mercy of you."

Ana couldn't repress her sneer. Ben had in no way treated Milos as family should, yet he invoked their sibling status in hopes of mercy.

Ben continued. "My mother's bitterness and jealousy affected me from a young age. I believed myself to be cheated for not inheriting the throne despite my eldest son status. My mother poisoned my mind, but I understand now that she was wrong."

Ana's fists clenched under the table; now it was his mother's fault. So much for personal accountability. Luciano grunted, shooting Milos a warning look. Ben wasn't being honest.

Milos glanced at Ana's father in acknowledgement.

"Somehow, I doubt that. Do you have anything else to say for yourself?"

Ben's shoulders slumped in defeat. "Only that if you choose exile rather than execution, I swear I will never return to Revas."

Ana and Milos glanced at Luciano, who gave a single nod. The truth this time, then.

Milos asked his final question. "And what of your gods-gifted ability?"

Ben winced. "It's—it's gone. I can sense no power. I can't reach into anyone's dreams."

Milos and Ana glanced to Luciano, who inclined his head in affirmation.

Milos ordered the guards to take Ben to the hallway. The brief discussion with the advisors confirmed their decision. Milos wanted nothing more than to kill Ben with his own hands. But he had chosen his advisors because he trusted them, and they urged him to consider otherwise. Executing his own sibling would be a vengeful and bloody start to his reign, which isn't what Milos wanted to convey.

When Ben returned, Milos ordered the guards to keep him standing. Again mincing no words, Milos said, "Benito, son of Tirano and Vivianna, you are hereby exiled from the kingdom of Revas for life as punishment for your treasonous actions." Then Milos stood and stalked over to his brother, stopping in front of him. He drew back his arm, and although Ben could see what was coming and tried to flinch away, the guards held him in place.

Ana opened her mouth to object, but she was too slow. Milos's fist smashed into Ben's jaw, immediately followed by a punch in the stomach. Then he stepped back and calmly stated, "And that is punishment for hurting Ana. I wanted to kill you for that alone, so know that if you ever show your face in these lands, you will not survive the trespass."

With the wind knocked out of him, Ben could only nod as he wheezed.

Milos spoke to the guards. "Arrange for a unit to escort him to the border of Kaosuda." It was the only option, as no ships sailed from the harbor this time of year.

Ana sighed in relief when the meeting was over, then flinched inwardly as she remembered the next hearing would likely be far more difficult.

Milos still hadn't decided what to do about his father, and the advisors weren't in agreement with each other on the matter either. But the decision needed to be made, and ultimately it was up to him. All she could do was remain by his side, no matter what.

Chapter Forty-Nine

ANELA

Anela couldn't be more relieved. The prophecy was fulfilled, Ana had survived, and Tirano was down in the dungeon where he belonged.

Weeks had passed since Ana woke, and they would be announcing the engagement at supper that evening. Anela had offered to throw another ball, as was traditional. The happy couple declined.

"We need those resources elsewhere," Ana had said, and she wasn't wrong. All these years, Anela had wished to do more for the citizens of Revas, and now they could. And Ana would.

Ana promised that Anela could help with the wedding. They still wished to keep it modest, but there would be a ball for that celebration.

Anela smiled to herself as she sat down to breakfast in her quarters with Henriella, already so pleased with her soon-to-be daughter.

As she stirred sugar into her tea, Henriella asked, "Have

you given any thought to what you want to do once everything is settled?"

Being free from Tirano meant Anela had options. She could stay at the castle to guide and assist Milos and Ana, yet she wasn't required to. She was, in fact, entirely free of obligations now, and it was a bit overwhelming and daunting.

"I'm not really sure. As much as I always hoped for this, planning for it seemed ... presumptuous, somehow." She breathed a chuckle, smiling at Hen. "I'm not going to make any decisions without your input, either. What are your thoughts?"

Henriella lifted and dropped a shoulder as she sipped her tea. "You know me. I just want to be where you are."

Tears prickled Anela's eyes and her chest tightened at the overt reminder of Hen's devotion to her. "I know. But you can have opinions and preferences. We both can, now." She smiled ruefully, pausing to think. "Do you miss home at all?"

Henriella nodded. "Every day. Don't you?"

"Yes. I'm thinking we should go on an extended visit after the wedding. Then we can see how we feel and what we want to do." She knew her brother, the current king of Orakolas, would always welcome them back to the seaside palace where she grew up.

Later that day, Anela made her way toward the dungeons. She had been debating whether to visit Tirano or not, and she finally decided she would, at least once. She didn't plan to gloat, but maybe it would provide some closure.

The cells were mostly empty, as Milos had pardoned all of the supposed rebels, and it was eerily quiet.

Halting in front of Tirano's cell, she could see the shape of his body in the dim light, sitting on the cot against the far wall. She cleared her throat and his head jerked up.

"What do you want?" His voice was devoid of emotion; he didn't even sound curious, despite the question.

"A conversation. Nothing more." She gripped her elbows with opposite hands. "Are you well?"

He snorted. "You always did ask stupid questions."

Her jaw tightened. "Physically, I mean. Do you need anything?"

He said nothing.

"I..." Now that she was here, she wasn't sure what she really needed to say. But she had spent nearly thirty years with this man; it felt strange to pretend as though he no longer existed. "I suppose I came to say goodbye. Once Milos and Ana are married, Hen and I plan to go back to Orakolas for a while. Maybe permanently."

He sniffed, his tone bored. "I care not where you go, Anela."

A bitter laugh escaped her. "No, I suppose not. You never cared about me at all, even if it seemed like you did in the beginning." She swallowed hard. "I did love you once, you know."

He barked a laugh. "I'm aware. You were a fool."

She stared at him for a few beats. "I was never enough for you, was I?"

He sighed wearily, his shoulders slumping. "Anela, this *life* was never enough for me. Or maybe I'm the one who wasn't enough, if my father was right. You know I didn't wish to be king."

It was true. When they met, he had been charming, but also moody and petulant, resentful of the weight and responsibility of his crown. Of the care and work it entailed. She had assumed he would mature and grow into his role, or at least resign himself to it. Instead, his resentment grew into spite and vindictiveness, and a desire to be worshipped like the gods themselves.

She decided to accept his statement as a gift. It hadn't been about *her.* It wasn't personal. She was only one small piece in a game he never wanted to play. Deep down she knew that, even if she had never quite recovered from his early betrayals.

"You haven't asked me what's going to happen to you."

"Does it matter? I have nothing left. No power of any sort, political or magical. No ties to family or friends. No real future. In a way, even though I'm locked up here, it's ... freeing." He almost sounded surprised.

So, his dream magic was gone entirely. She had guessed that was the case, but she hadn't known for sure.

"It's as well, since I don't have an answer. Milos and Ana haven't decided."

He shifted, then lay down on his back, moving slowly. Once settled, he said, "Goodbye, Anela." A dismissal, as usual.

"Goodbye, Tirano," she whispered before turning and hurrying back the way she had come.

Back to the sunlight, Henriella, and her new life.

Epilogue

"We can't just leave him in the dungeons forever," Ana chided, throwing up her hands. She referred to his father.

Milos sat in the armchair across from her. He remained in his old rooms, at least until they could be rid of everything that reminded him too much of Tirano in the king's quarters.

A corner of his mouth tilted up. "Why can't we?" He was happy to have Tirano out of his hair.

One corner of her mouth twitched, but she repressed the smile. "Be serious. Ben was sentenced; it's time to do the same for your father."

"We've been busy. Waiting won't kill him."

Once Ana had woken, he turned his attention fully to the chaos in the kingdom. Letters poured in from noble families all over Revas, full of questions, accusations, and demands. Many folks in Sonos City, and likely other places, had been desperately furious at the betrayal of their previous king.

Since they couldn't reach Tirano, they attempted to take

out their wrath on the templekeepers and the temples themselves. Milos understood their reasoning, but he couldn't allow such lawlessness. Besides, he had plans to turn those temples into schools, so burning them all down wasn't helpful.

He had handled most everything on his own or with his mother's help thus far, as Ana had been weak and needed time to recover.

Ana huffed. "I suppose."

"Why are you so worried about him?" he asked, tilting his head to one side to study her. "He was hardly kind to you."

She closed her eyes briefly before meeting his gaze. "I know. But he is your family. And I think people will settle down once news of a sentencing gets out."

Milos blew out a breath. "That's probably true. What do you think his punishment should be?"

He had no idea what to do about his father. His corrupt ways had betrayed every citizen of his kingdom and caused many to suffer needlessly. Objectively, Milos knew most kingdoms would sentence a man to death for what his father had done.

Yet, it was his father. Could he execute his own blood? Could he become a king-killer?

Ana shook her head. "I really don't know." She bit her lower lip, leaving it pink and swollen when she released it.

Suddenly he wanted nothing more than to taste her lips. He could never get enough of her, and his need had only been amplified by almost losing her.

"We don't need to decide tonight," he said softly, holding out a hand. "Come here, love."

He loved the little noises she made when his mouth was on her. He loved her scent and her soft skin. More than anything, he was still acutely aware that he almost lost her, and he always felt reassured when he was physically touching her. She was still alive, still with him.

Soon he cradled her in his arms and stood up, taking her to his bed. Setting her on her feet, he rasped, "Turn around."

Cheeks flushed, she bit her bottom lip and slowly moved to put her back to him. He unlaced the back of her gown and then moved it off her shoulders, down her arms, allowing the fabric to fall and pool on the floor at her feet.

He dropped a light kiss on the back of her neck as he reached around to untie the string of her shift, which ended up on the floor as well.

Her breast was full and warm in his hand, and she moaned when he gave her nipple a light pinch. "On the bed now, love."

She turned in his arms and nipped at his bottom lip, then traced it with her tongue, eyes sparking with mischief. He smiled against her mouth and brought his hand down on her ass, just hard enough for a little sting. She jumped and giggled. He tilted his head toward the mattress. "I said now."

"Yes, Your Majesty," she sassed as she turned and crawled onto the center of the blanket. Sitting back on her heels, she cocked an eyebrow, waiting.

He left his pants on for the moment. Savoring how her hungry gaze roamed his body, he joined her, guiding her to lay on her back.

He explored her body with his lips, tongue, and teeth, starting at her neck. He lavished her breasts with his attentions before continuing down, stopping just above her hot, wet center. Then he crawled between her legs and continued teasing her, starting inside her knees and moving up, again halting just short of the apex of her thighs.

"Milos," she breathed. "Please."

He huffed a laugh. "Patience, my queen." He loved calling her that, even if it wasn't official yet.

She made a wordless whining sound, and he chuckled again before using two fingers to spread her lower lips open, allowing him to see her gleaming, soaked core.

"So wet and needy, aren't you?" he murmured, then dropped a light, barely-there kiss directly on her center. Her hips jerked, so he placed a hand on her lower belly and pushed down. "Stay still."

A strangled noise escaped her as he dragged his tongue up her center, pausing to swirl it once around her clit. Then he did it again. Lick, swirl, never quite touching the most sensitive part. And again.

Panting, she buried her hands in his hair, gripping and tugging. "By the Seven, will you just..."

He didn't reply, but he slid two long fingers inside of her, curling them to stroke the spot that always drove her mad as he circled her clit once more. She cried out as she rolled her hips.

He loved seeing her like this: raw and undone, begging him with both words and body to pleasure her.

He pulled his hand back, then added another finger as he thrust inside her while dragging his flattened tongue over her core. She whimpered, and he took her sensitive pearl between his lips and flicked with his tongue as he sucked.

A crescendo of pleasure made her body jerk and tremble as she shattered under his mouth. "Yes ... oh gods, Milos..."

"You're doing so well, love," he murmured as her walls fluttered and squeezed around his fingers.

Once he had wrung every last drop of pleasure from her, he rose, standing next to the bed, and gestured. "Come here."

Still panting, a corner of her mouth quirked up. As she moved toward him, he finished undressing. Sitting in front of him, she wrapped her hand around his base and bent to lick the shining drop of liquid from his tip. He hissed, grabbing her hair to pull her head back up. He wouldn't last if she used her mouth.

She pouted but let him maneuver her into position, bent over the side of the bed. Her toes barely touched the rug; she was at the perfect height for him to take her from behind.

He positioned his cock at her entrance, then took hold of her hips and plunged into her in one motion. Her gasp turned into a groan, and he gritted his teeth, forcing himself back from the precipice.

He gave her a couple moments to adjust to him before he withdrew and thrust again, and again.

"Gods, love. So tight and wet for me. Fuck."

She whimpered. "Harder, Milos. Fuck me harder."

A feral growl rumbled in his chest hearing the obscene language in her soft, sweet voice. His grasp on her hips would probably leave bruises, but he did as she asked, lifting her ass just enough to improve the angle as he slammed even deeper into her hot, soaking center.

So close to the edge, his voice was guttural when he said, "Touch yourself, love. Come with me."

She pried her fingers loose from their death grip on the linens and did as he said. When she fell apart only a breath later, the feeling of her climax strangling his cock made him come undone. "*Fuck*, Ana. Oh gods..."

He rested his forehead on her back for a breath before

gently withdrawing and helping her on to the bed and fetching a towel to clean up.

After, they lay naked in each other's arms, sleepy and satiated.

"What if I hadn't been royal?" Ana murmured. "Would you still have chosen me?"

His arms tightened around her. "I would have done anything to be with you, love. Anything. You're mine."

They had Tirano brought to the throne room a few days later, as many members of the court had requested to bear witness to the sentencing. A good number of servants turned up too and were given permission to stay. The space was packed when guards escorted Tirano up the aisle between the rows of benches, stopping in front of the dais.

Milos and Ana sat on their thrones—Milos had insisted, despite Ana not being an official queen yet. Chairs had been brought for all of the advisors as well, distributed to either side of the royal couple.

Tirano surveyed all of them, his look of distaste deepening when he spotted Mistress Danias among the advisors. Then he looked directly at Ana and openly sneered. Ana smiled demurely, and Tirano's expression settled into a scowl.

It took several minutes to get the crowd to quiet down. When they did, Milos opened with, "Tirano Damian Rafaelo, son of Kinos and Avellia, you are accused of using your gods-gifted abilities to deceive and manipulate the citizens of Revas, to the detriment of many. The gods have already seen fit to punish you by taking away your magic, correct?" Anela had reported that was the case, but they needed to make sure.

Tight-lipped, Tirano gave one sharp nod.

"Speak your answers aloud," Milos ordered.

"Yes," Tirano bit out. "My powers are gone."

Ana glanced at Luciano, who nodded.

"Good." Milos studied the older man. "Is there anything you wish to say?"

This was Tirano's chance to at least try to make amends. He could offer an apology, or at least a believable explanation as to why he made the choices he did.

Tirano's hostile gaze bore into Milos. "I would rather be dead than watch you try to rule. If you view me as a traitor, the law says you should execute me. But you are weak. You always have been, and always will be. Undoubtedly too weak to kill me, even as I ask you to."

Gasps and murmurs trickled through the crowd like melting snow, quickly heightening to avalanche proportions.

"He deserves to die!"

"Execute the traitor!"

Milos glanced at Ana as the uproar continued.

"It's up to you," she said. "I support your decision no matter what."

The grim lines of his face softened a touch. He stood and walked deliberately toward his father. The audience grew quiet with anticipation as he came to a stop right in front of the older man.

"Compassion is not weakness. That aside, I will serve the people of my kingdom to the best of my ability. If they demand your death, in accordance with your own wishes, who am I to deny them? Because you are my father, I will show mercy and make it swift." In one quick motion, he drew his dagger and slashed it across Tirano's throat.

Blood sprayed, and then gushed. Tirano's eyes opened wide, his mouth opening and shutting soundlessly. His knees buckled, and the guards lowered him to the floor, where the pool of blood continued to expand.

Ana rose, determined to maintain her composure. She walked to Milos's side and handed him a handkerchief from her pocket. Looking dazed, he took it and used it to wipe the red spatter from his face.

He looked down at her, his expression sorrowful. "Thank you, love," he murmured.

She mustered a smile, then directed her gaze toward the shocked audience. "There is nothing more to see here. This sentencing is over. Please leave us."

As nobles and servants alike filed out of the throne room, Ana took Milos's hand. "We're finished for today. Come, let me take care of you."

They returned to his quarters, where she threw his blood-stained shirt and coat into the fire and painstakingly washed away all the traces of it from his skin. Then she had him sit in one of the armchairs before the fire, and she settled herself on his lap, where he wrapped his arms around her. Cradling his head and stroking his hair, she held him as he wept.

Eventually, emotions spent, he cupped the back of her head, tangling his fingers in her hair, and pulled her to him to claim her lips.

When they broke apart, chests heaving, he rested his head on her shoulder. "Now our new life truly begins. I love you, Ana."

"Always?" She stroked his hair, running her fingers through its length.

He gathered her in his arms and stood, carrying her

toward the bed, and dropped a kiss on her forehead. “And forever.”

More by Cara Blaine

vinci-books.com/LuxeInBetween

She was never meant to exist—now three fae would burn worlds for her.

When Luxe's hidden magic awakens, she's thrust into a deadly fae prophecy—and into the arms of three powerful males who would die to protect her. Between danger, desire, and destiny, Luxe must decide if love can survive the fire it ignites.

Turn the page for a free preview…

Luxe in Between: Chapter One

CONDOLENCES

Luxe couldn't remember how many times in the last six months her aunt jokingly said, "It shouldn't be this expensive to die!"

The advantage of a drawn out, painful disease like cancer is that it gives the person it ravages time to make plans and say goodbye. So when Luxe's Aunt Rhea passed, over a year after her initial diagnosis, Luxe didn't have the burden of figuring out what came after. Days after the doctor muttered the word "terminal," Rhea was getting organized. She made arrangements, wrote down explicit instructions, and left enough money in her savings account to pay for everything, if only barely.

Thus, four days after her passing, Luxe was accepting condolences from her aunt's friends and neighbors, and even some loyal customers of her shop. It was a simple memorial service, held in the community room of their apartment complex. A small table held an altar with an urn containing Rhea's ashes. More tables lined a different wall, covered with food. Several people gave short speeches—

again, details arranged ahead of time. No one seemed to mind that Luxe couldn't bring herself to speak in front of the crowd aside from a very brief, "Thank you so much for coming to honor my aunt."

The first person who spoke was an old friend of her aunt's named Liz who came to the service from out of town. Luxe had only ever met her a couple of times, but she knew the two women stayed in close touch via phone calls and emails. It was Luxe's understanding that they were friends before Rhea and Luxe moved to their current town; she didn't remember, since she was only four or five when that happened.

"Rhea was the most down-to-earth person I've ever met," Liz said. "I tend to get myself worked up over things I shouldn't, but I always knew I could call her, and she'd talk me down and have me laughing by the end of the conversation. That woman was hilarious."

Luxe smiled, tears stinging her eyes. It was true; her aunt could have done stand-up comedy, especially after a glass of wine or two.

A long-time customer of Rhea's occult supply shop, Hecate's Boutique, was the next to speak. His name was Charlie. "I remember the first time I met Rhea, had to be around twenty years ago now," he said. "Her shop had just opened a week or two before, and curiosity got the better of me. I didn't know anything about anything back then, but I sure was searching for something." He smiled sadly. "At first I thought I might be searching for *her*, even though she told me she was old enough to be my mother." He chuckled, then grew sober once more. "That wasn't quite the case—I wasn't *that* young, nor was she that old—but I digress. Rhea helped me understand that what I was searching for was already here." He held a fist to his chest. "Somehow, that woman led me to truths in only a couple of conversations that years of therapy never could. I owe her a debt. I'll miss her."

Tears streamed down Luxe's face by the end of that one. That story was *so* Rhea. The woman could connect with anyone in any situation. It was a gift, one Luxe envied. The only person Luxe ever truly felt connected to since her parents disappeared was Rhea herself. As far back as Luxe could remember, she always felt on the outside looking in; her aunt was more like the person on the inside, opening the door and coaxing people to join her.

As the gathering wound down, an elderly neighbor, Mr. Hawkins, headed to the exit and stopped to speak with Luxe on his way out. "I know you two only had each other as far as family," he said, patting her on a shoulder. "If you ever need some company, my door is always open."

She smiled—her face hurt from smiling, which seemed an odd side effect of a memorial service—and said, "Thank you, Mr. Hawkins. You're very kind. I appreciate that you came today." That was all true. She chose not to say that she didn't plan to spend her time listening to him complain about "liberal snowflakes" and his son-in-law as he chain-smoked for hours on end. She knew he meant well.

The room was only reserved for three hours, so when there was half an hour left in the time slot, Luxe politely but firmly ushered out the last of the well-wishers so she could clean up. As she stacked the disposable serving trays and dishes from the caterer—a local Greek restaurant her aunt liked—the manager of the apartment complex showed up. Mr. Lind and his wife were decent managers and seemingly kind people, but Luxe really wanted to be done with people in general for the day.

"Hey, Mr. Lind. I'm just getting the mess cleaned up. I'll

be finished soon." She glanced over her shoulder, attempting one more smile.

The thin man in late middle age wore a sympathetic expression. "Actually, I was going to tell you I'll take care of it for you, if you'd rather head home."

"Oh. Really?"

"I imagine you're tired, and cleaning up is the last thing you want to do."

"Well, if you're sure…"

He waved her to the door. "I'm sorry for your loss. Rhea was a good woman. Go get some rest."

She nodded and waved her goodbye, feeling choked up at the sweet gesture. She managed a "Thank you" as she grabbed her bag, then the stack of covered casserole dishes folks brought for her to take home, leaving the community center.

She hurried past her aunt's apartment on the way to her own, gaze averted from the door, angling her head down so that her dark curls physically blocked her side view. She would have to do an estate sale with the furniture and whatever else eventually, but she couldn't even think about that yet. Although she lived in her own one bedroom in the complex now, her aunt's place was the only childhood home she remembered. She wasn't ready to empty it entirely.

As soon as she got home, she kicked off the black high heels she purchased especially for the service before stuffing all the casseroles into the freezer. She already had two partially eaten ones in the fridge that would last for days more. Then she poured a glass of wine and collapsed onto her secondhand, dark red velvet couch. Rhea laughed when Luxe brought it home, because it didn't match anything in her apartment, but Luxe didn't care. She loved the soft, luxurious comfort of the fabric and the old Hollywood aesthetic.

As a bonus, she liked red wine, so any spills were well camouflaged.

Listless, she picked up the book sitting on the coffee table and tried to read. In a couple more weeks, she would start her third semester of grad school, and she wanted to enjoy reading for pleasure as much as possible before she was inundated with psychology textbooks and articles. She gave up quickly, though, and put the cozy, witchy mystery back down after reading the same page at least four times.

She stared unseeing at the wall across from her, which featured several random pieces of art from various thrift stores, and took occasional sips of her wine. What was she supposed to do now? Of course, she would have to work, and attend school, and go grocery shopping, and pay bills. All those things were simple, really. The difficulty existed in the downtime, the seconds and minutes and hours that lay between necessary tasks. The moments when she picked up a book in her aunt's favorite genre and realized she wouldn't be able to talk and laugh about it with Rhea later.

As Luxe entered into adulthood, Rhea transitioned from a parental figure to a best friend—living in the same complex, working in the same shop, enjoying many of the same interests. Luxe never really fit in at school and wasn't in touch with any of her high school or college "friends," aside from the occasional comment on a social media post, nor was she dating anyone; she stopped wasting her time on guys as soon as she knew her aunt was sick.

Now Rhea was gone, and really, *what* was Luxe supposed to do with all of these endless, in between moments?

She sighed, draining the rest of her glass. When in

doubt, sleep sounded like a good plan. The only hard part about sleep was the few moments after waking up, before she remembered her new reality all over again. She knew that, in time, she would wake up with her heart already knowing she was alone in the world, not having to be startled by the remembrance. Out of the two, she wasn't sure which would be better.

It was almost 5 pm, too late for a nap and too early to go to sleep for the night, but Luxe changed into her favorite PJs and crawled into bed anyway. Tomorrow. She would figure out how to deal with the 'in between' moments tomorrow.

Luxe in Between: Chapter Two

CHOWDER THREAT

Luxe dug into her faded and scarred dark brown crossbody bag for the keys to her aunt's shop. She didn't want to go inside, but it was necessary. The shop had been closed for a month already, so although her aunt died only a week ago, she didn't have much choice if she wanted to pay her bills.

She finally felt uneven metal edges with her fingertips, well buried under who knows what. Between nursing Rhea and trying to keep her head above water otherwise, cleaning out her bag was at the bottom of her priority list.

After stepping inside, she relocked the door behind her with a flick of her fingers on the metal handle and stood still for a moment to let her eyes adjust to the dim interior. She breathed in the scents of sage, lavender, and dusty books, willing herself not to cry.

Aunt Rhea opened Hecate's Boutique soon after Luxe came to live with her. They moved to the medium-sized coastal town after Luxe's parents disappeared without a trace almost twenty years earlier, and within the year, Hecate's was up and running. Every single inch of the shop reminded Luxe of her only remaining family member—who no longer remained.

She took a deep breath, released it, and walked to the office, passing by the tarot card case and the crystal display. She used the second key to unlock the door and flipped on the light. Papers crinkled underneath her bag as she set it down on the old, battered wood desk, and she sighed, taking in the organized chaos of the cramped space. She had a lot of catching up to do. Using the elastic around her wrist, she put her dark, curly hair into a messy bun and got to work.

Several hours later, receipts were filed, inventory assessed, and a few new orders called in with the suppliers. Now it was time to send the email. She stared at the screen for far too long before she could will her fingers to type a message to the customers on their mailing list.

Only minutes after hitting send, the computer pinged with responses. She didn't open any of them; she didn't have it in her to read condolences at the moment. It was bad enough that now everyone knew the shop would reopen the following day, and she would need to have those conversations in person with all the customers, especially the long-time patrons of the store. There were a sizable amount of those, given her aunt's propensity to make lifelong friends with whoever happened to be standing in line with her at the grocery store. People always came back; they could buy crystals and incense online but not Rhea's presence.

As Luxe threw her things back into her bag—keys, phone, water bottle—she heard the bell on the shop door chime. She froze. That door was locked. Wasn't it? Her memory wasn't great lately; the brain fog of grief affected all of her functioning.

She poked her head out of the office and saw a silhouette backlit by the light of the setting sun coming through the glass door. She squinted but couldn't make out the person's features.

"We're closed," she said firmly. "The shop will reopen tomorrow."

"I know." The man—she realized it was definitely a man between the deep voice and his height—strolled toward her. "I'm not here to shop. I need to speak with you."

She frowned. "How did you get in here? Do I know you?" Her tone relayed her suspicion, and he stopped walking.

"I'm only here to talk, I promise." He raised his hands, palms facing her in a placating gesture. "I'm not going to harm you. My name is Søren."

"I don't know anyone by that name." She stepped out of the office fully, trying to see him better. He took another step, and the light from the room behind her illuminated his face. He looked vaguely familiar, but she couldn't place him.

Still, there was something about him… She studied him from head to toe. Tall with wide shoulders, he looked like a Viking, if a Viking wore faded designer blue jeans and maintained excellent hygiene and grooming. Maybe a Viking who also surfed and was from a wealthy family. His long, wavy golden blonde hair fell just past his shoulders; his beard was clipped short, leaving a clear impression of a sharply cut jawline. His eyes were startlingly vivid, although she couldn't determine their exact color; they seemed to shift between blue and green. Some part of her brain acknowledged that he was gorgeous, but most of her was too overcome with grief to care about handsome men.

He offered her a small smile as he lowered his hands,

patiently allowing her to take his measure. "I'm only here to talk to you, Niamh. That's all."

"How do you know my name?" She was now even more suspicious. No one called her by her first name—except for her aunt. The thought made her chest hurt and one of her hands rose, unconsciously placing a hand against the ache.

"I'm happy to explain that and more if you'll give me an hour of your time."

"I don't understand. What do you want to talk to me about, exactly? I'm not selling the store." Several real estate vultures reached out in the last weeks while the store was closed to try to convince her to sell; Hecate's was located in a very desirable location in the quaint downtown area of their small city, near many other popular shops and restaurants.

He shook his head. "It's not about the store. It's about your parents."

Her jaw fell open. "Excuse me? What the hell do you know about my parents?"

He gestured to the office. "Can we sit down?"

She considered him for a long moment, eyes narrowed. How would this stranger know anything about her mom and dad? She hadn't seen them since she was four years old. Her aunt always insinuated that they were very likely dead. After going back and forth with herself for several moments, she made a decision.

"I'm not staying here in an empty building with a strange man. I'm not stupid." His expression remained impassive. "I'll meet you out front. I need to get some food, if you want to go to a cafe down the street with me?"

He ducked his chin in acceptance of her offer. "A private conversation would be better, but I understand your caution. I'll wait outside."

He turned and walked away, so she ducked back into the office. Grabbing her bag, she turned off the light and locked the door behind her.

He was waiting as promised, leaning casually against the building. The light from the setting sun seemed to turn him all bronze and gold, tan skin and blond hair glowing. She forced her gaze away from his suddenly very distracting presence and made sure to turn the key all the way to lock up, pulling on the handle to check. She was so sure the door was locked when he waltzed in…

She gave him a tight smile and gestured in the direction of the little cafe, only a block away. Truthfully, she had enough casseroles sitting in her fridge and freezer at home to last six months, gifted from Rhea's friends and neighbors. But she didn't want to go home and be alone with her thoughts quite yet. As difficult as it was to walk into Hecate's earlier, it proved a good distraction. Being busy helped clear the haziness in her head a little.

They walked in silence. Although she didn't specify which cafe she was headed to—there were several in the same direction at varying distances—he stopped in front of her favorite one and opened the door for her. Her gaze cut to him suspiciously as she walked past, but his expression remained passively neutral.

Taking some heed of his mention of privacy, she chose a booth in the back corner, away from the other diners. He slid gracefully onto the brown vinyl bench across from her, and their server popped up immediately to hand them menus. She was relieved that it was no one she knew; that was the downside of frequenting the same businesses all the time. The employees often recognized her, and she didn't want to answer questions or accept condolences.

She ordered soup in a bread bowl; it was still late

summer, but she wanted to indulge in fall comfort food. Besides, this cafe sourced their sourdough bread bowls from the bakery down the street, baked fresh daily, and they were divine. Søren ordered a slice of lemon meringue pie and a coffee.

"Good choice. Their pie is amazing, especially the lemon," she said once the server left to put in their orders. She figured that was an adequate amount of small talk, given the situation. Besides, the lemon pie really was amazing. "Now, you have some explaining to do. How do you know me when I don't know you? What could you possibly know about my parents?" Her dark brown eyes locked onto his blue-green gaze, almost a challenge.

Their server appeared again with a mug and carafe, pouring quickly and neatly. After stirring in one sugar packet, Søren leaned back, holding his coffee in one hand with his other toned arm tossed over the back of the seat. He regarded her for a few beats. "You're different than I imagined," he finally said.

Luxe flicked both brows up, questioning, and waited, foot tapping the worn black and white checkered linoleum under the table.

His head inclined slightly in understanding, and he set the coffee on the table. "Right. To be honest, I'm not sure where to start. This is going to be a lot for you to process." He finally broke eye contact, shifting his gaze to the mug in front of him. "Your first question was how do I know you when you've never met me. The answer to that might seem … alarming, but it's not what it sounds like."

She sniffed, unimpressed. "Spit it out, will you?"

He linked his eyes with hers again and said, "I've known who you are for a very long time, Niamh. Years. I've been … uh, watching you. Watching *over* you, I mean," he hurried to clarify when her eyes grew round. "Keeping an eye out, making sure you were safe. Since you were, oh, maybe eleven or twelve."

Her heart raced. What the fuck was this guy talking about? He had been stalking her for over ten years? Her eyes darted around the restaurant, gauging how fast she could get to the door. Surely, if people saw her run in terror, they would make an effort to stop him from going after her. She inched toward the outside edge of the booth.

He held a hand up. "Calm down. Like I said, it's not what it sounds like, okay? Our fathers know each other. I was asked to find you, and then to keep an eye on you, for your own safety. Until… Well, never mind that for now."

The mention of her father interrupted her urge to run for her life.

Her voice shook when she asked, "Our fathers? You know my father?"

He nodded. A fleeting hint of pain crossed his face before he schooled his expression back to neutrality. "Yes. You'd know him as Cian Knox Finnegan."

"He went by Knox," she whispered. Of course, she actually knew him as 'Daddy.'

"Is that why you also go by your middle name? I always wondered why you chose Luxe over Niamh."

She shook her head. "Not really. None of my teachers or friends could ever spell or pronounce Niamh correctly, that's all. I got tired of explaining my name all the time." She left out the part about being constantly made fun of for her weird name, wild curls, and tiny stature. At some point, many of them realized her aunt owned a witchy store, which didn't help things. Kids could be really mean, and she didn't like to admit how playground taunts affected her confidence long term.

"I see. Which would you like me to call you? I've always thought of you as Niamh, but I'll use whatever you like better."

Her shoulders rose and fell. "Whichever, I honestly don't care. My aunt still called me Niamh. I'm used to both."

He nodded in acceptance. "So, then. Are you going to hear me out?"

She didn't reply but released her grip on her bag and slid back to the middle of the booth seat. As she replayed his words, another question surfaced. "What do you mean, *I* would know him by his name? Of course I would. It's his name."

"Right, about that…" He hesitated. "There's so much to explain. For now, I can tell you that the name you know wasn't the name he was born to."

The space between her brows wrinkled as she tried to figure out what that was supposed to mean. Was her father adopted? If he ever talked about his parents, she was too young to remember. Her aunt certainly never told her anything like that about her dad.

The server arrived with their food, and Luxe eyed her bread bowl full of clam chowder warily, unsure how hungry she felt now.

Søren gestured to her food. "Please, eat. You need the calories." He scanned her critically, and she hunched her shoulders, feeling defensive. She knew how she looked right now: too pale, too thin, and somewhat unkempt. She simply didn't care. A proper diet and exercise and generally taking care of herself wasn't high on her priority list these last couple of months, as the cancer rapidly claimed her aunt's life.

She blew on a spoonful. "I still don't understand. How

do you know my father? Does he know where I am?" Her hand shook as she lifted the spoon to her mouth. This man knew her father and knew where to find her; didn't that mean her father knew where she was? And yet, he wasn't here and hadn't been for so long. She was afraid to even ask about her mother. One absent parent revelation at a time was enough.

"I'm not sure this is the place to get into too many details," Søren hedged, doing a visual sweep around the cafe, which was filling up for the supper rush. "Yes, he knows where you are. He hasn't been able to come to you himself. So my father sent me."

"But he's alive? My aunt thought, maybe…" She trailed off, searching the stranger's face.

Søren gave a single nod. "He is."

"Can I see him? Can you take me to him?" She couldn't help the pleading in her voice. Rhea's loss was so fresh, and Luxe had assumed herself to be entirely alone in the world. To now discover that at least one of her parents was alive somewhere…

Søren shook his head, his expression faintly regretful. "Eventually, I hope you will see him. I can't take you to him yet."

Tears welled in her eyes, but she blinked them back. "What do you want, then? You said you've been watching me for years. Why speak to me now?"

He studied her, giving her a few moments to collect herself. "Again, I'm not sure this is the right place to talk about it." He finally picked up his fork and took a bite of the pie. "Wow, that's pretty good."

She fixed him with an incredulous look, unable to find the words. What the hell was up with this guy? He knew too much about her and her family but was being all mysterious about how and why. She was sick of mystery. Her parents' disappearance was a mystery for most of her life. She wanted answers.

His expression remained impassive, almost blank, as he took another bite of the pie, concentrating on the dessert. She deliberately scooped up a spoonful of chowder … and flung it at him. It splattered across his blue t-shirt and face as his eyes closed, flinching, then opened wide in shock. An employee walking by slowed with a questioning look but hurried away when Luxe glared daggers at him.

"What the fuck was that for?" Søren finally got out as he tried to clean himself off with a paper napkin.

"Tell me what I want to know, or I swear to the goddess I will dump this entire bowl over your head." She gripped the edges of the plate under the bread bowl, meaning every word of her threat.

He was shaking his head and muttering to himself. "I knew I should have waited, but no, Father said it was time. He doesn't understand humans like I do. I knew the grief was still too raw. She's unstable as hell…" He tossed the napkin onto the table and flagged down a server. "Can I please get a box and fork for this pie, one for the soup with a spoon, and the check?"

Finally, he addressed Luxe, who no longer gripped the plate but held a very full spoon of chowder again. The only reason she wasn't letting loose with it was because she was trying to process his comment about "humans" that made it sound like he didn't include himself in that group—and the fact that he called her "unstable."

"I *will* explain everything, but I am telling you, we can't have this conversation here. You'll have to trust me on that." He pulled out his wallet and handed the server a fancy-looking all black credit card in exchange for the to-go boxes. He tossed a twenty-dollar bill on the table as a tip.

Luxe slowly lowered her spoon. He reached across and neatly took it from her and set it next to his plate, then placed her bread bowl in the to-go box along with the set of plasticware. As he transferred his pie to the other box, the server returned the credit card. Søren scribbled a quick signature and stood, grabbing the food. "Come on. Let's find a more private public space, okay?"

She rolled her eyes but maneuvered herself out of the booth, clutching her bag. "Fine. Lead the way." She *would* get answers out of this unemotional, enigmatic, handsome stranger one way or another.

Luxe in Between: Chapter Three

ANYTHING STRANGE

They sat on a bench in the small park near the center of downtown. A few other people strolled amid the grass and trees in twos and threes, enjoying the late summer weather of the Bay area, but none came near the secluded corner Søren chose.

He flipped open the to-go box and made short work of his pie before they spoke. Luxe picked chunks off the side of the bread bowl and dipped them in the lukewarm chowder, chewing slowly as she watched him and waited.

"So," he said, setting the box down next to him. "Can I ask you a question?"

"I think I'm the one who should be asking questions, but okay."

He huffed a laugh. "You'll get your chance." His expression grew serious. "I know your aunt recently passed. I'm sorry for your loss."

She jerked her chin in an affirmative motion, determined not to cry. "That's not a question."

"Right. I'll get to the point. Since she passed, have you experienced anything … new, maybe? Anything strange?"

She gaped at him, a piece of bread forgotten in her hand. "Other than a total stranger walking into my shop, which I swear was locked up, and confessing to stalking me and knowing my father? Nope, not a thing." She swallowed hard, holding in what might become hysterical laughter if she let it out.

He only looked mildly amused. "Very funny. I mean something new or strange within yourself. Like visions, seeing things that aren't really there, maybe peculiar dreams…" He stopped when he saw the look on her face in the waning light.

"What in the actual fuck are you talking about? Are you asking me if I've gone crazy? No, I'm not having hallucinations." She couldn't help but remember he called her "unstable" only twenty minutes before.

He sighed, obviously frustrated. Leaning his head back, he fixed on the darkening sky through the branches. "Well, shit," he muttered, more to himself than her.

"Can you please tell me about my father? Why can't I see him?"

He swung his gaze from the twilight stars back to her, and he pressed his lips into a thin line before he nodded, relenting. "Your father is imprisoned. That's why he can't come to you."

The to-go box tumbled from her hands onto the sidewalk. The remainder of her bread bowl rolled several inches away and landed upside down. She hardly noticed. "*Prison*? Why? How? I don't understand."

He stooped and picked up the mess, placing the bread back inside the box and setting it neatly next to his own empty container.

He opened his mouth to answer, but she cut him off. "This doesn't make any sense! Someone would have told us, contacted us, if he was arrested. What about my mother?" Her voice rose.

"Shhh." His eyes flicked around the park, looking to see if anyone was close by. "Calm down, please. I'm trying to tell you. Will you let me?"

Her mouth snapped shut and she nodded, swallowing back the words that wanted to keep pouring out of her. She was already tired of him telling her to calm down, though; if he said it again, in the midst of delivering information that made staying calm impossible, she could not be held accountable for her reaction.

"He isn't being held here, in this realm. He's in the fae realm, in the queen's prison." He held up a finger as she opened her mouth to interrupt. "Let me get through this, alright? It will all sound weird and hard to believe, but I have evidence for you."

Again, she jerked her head up and down, visibly restraining herself, and he continued. "Your aunt never told you any of this, from what I could gather. I assume she was trying to protect you. But now, you should know. Your mother was a human witch." Her breath caught, hearing the past tense, but she didn't speak. "Your father is fae. High fae. Technically, he is royalty. When he fell in love with your mother, he knew it was forbidden. He knew he was required to marry a high fae and continue the royal line." Here, Søren scrubbed his face with his hands. "He literally had *one* job," he muttered, again speaking more to himself.

Luxe made an impatient noise, and Søren glanced at her. "Right. Sorry. So, he and your mom hid in the human realm. But eventually, his mother—the queen—found him. Well, her spies did. You were only lucky not to be with them at the time. We don't think the queen knows you exist, which is very fortunate."

She couldn't hold back anymore. She stood and faced him, hands on her hips, vibrating with nervous energy. "Hold on one fucking moment. You are sitting here telling me faeries exist, and my father is one of them? What kind of fucked up joke is this?" The park lights flickered on, and she studied his face in the yellowish hue, searching for some hint of whether he was being serious or not. "Tell me the truth."

He threw his hands up. "I *am* telling you the truth!" He stood. "Here. Let me show you." He dug in his pocket and pulled out a small, colorful object. He held it out to her and dropped it in her palm when she put her hand out.

Her breath snagged in her throat when she saw it: a clay keychain in the shape of a heart, handmade by a small child, painted and glitter-glued within an inch of its life, with some signs of wear and tear including a couple of small chips. She made it at preschool for Father's Day. She remembered being so proud when she gave it to her father and he actually attached it to his keys and carried it everywhere. It was one of her last memories of him, sometime in the month before he disappeared.

She gave in to her shaking legs and collapsed back onto the bench. Søren joined her. "I know it's a lot. I'm sorry." His voice was low and sounded genuine, the first hint of emotion he displayed—other than when she threw chowder at him.

Luxe forced her breathing to even out. She still didn't know what to think. "Why now? You said you've been watching me for years, so why are you telling me this now?"

"We assume your aunt didn't tell you much about your parents in order to protect you, to keep you from trying to find them and crossing the queen. We believed, but weren't sure, that Rhea also suppressed your magic for the same reasons. We thought it best to let you live a normal life as long as we could. We certainly didn't wish to involve a youngling in … the situation.

"Once we knew she was so sick, though, Father was sure that, when she passed, your magic would show itself—in which case, first of all, surely you would need someone to explain it to you if she never did. But also, you would possibly be equipped to help your father and his kingdom. To help us." He shook his head. "We could have approached your aunt to ask about your magic, but we didn't, although we were considering it as an option in the next few years… We didn't want to accidentally draw any attention to her from any of our own kind, but especially the queen's spies. So we were forced to make a lot of guesses. It seems we guessed wrong. Although, it's hard to believe…" He trailed off again, looking thoughtful.

"Hard to believe what?" Luxe prompted. To her, it was all hard to believe. Her head spun.

"That you don't have any magic. Surely, any suppression spell by your aunt would have worn off by now. But you said nothing has changed. Your mother was a powerful witch with especially strong psychic ability. Your aunt had that same ability, a little less than your mother, is my understanding. Your father is high fae, as I said, and would have passed down his own powers."

She shrugged. "Sorry to disappoint. Nothing magical about me." She stood, feeling a sudden very strong urge to go home and pretend this entire evening never happened. "I need to go." She grabbed her crossbody and put the strap over her head.

Søren picked up the boxes and tossed them in a nearby

trash can. Luxe was already walking away, and she heard him jog to catch up with her. "Hold on. That's it? You don't want to know anything else?"

"I think I've heard enough for now, thanks."

"Do you want to know about your mother?"

She shook her head firmly. "She's dead, isn't she? What more is there to know?" An ache bloomed in her chest when she said the words, but she stood by them. Her mother was gone. It didn't matter how or when. She would never see her again, nor did it sound like she would ever see her father. And all of this about witches and fae was only making it more difficult for her to process that reality.

"Hey, slow down. Are you alright?" Søren reached out a hand, brushing her forearm with his fingers, and she jerked away. Stopping, she turned and glared at him.

"Of course I'm not *alright*. None of this is *alright*! My mother and aunt are dead, and my father may as well be. I have no family left. There's nothing I can do about any of it. I wish you hadn't told me. Are we done now?"

This time, he firmly grasped her forearm as she tried to turn away. "Give me your phone. I'm adding my number, just in case. Then I'll leave you alone if you want me to."

Scowling, she dug her phone out, unlocked it, and handed it to him. It seemed like it took him way too long to enter his information before he handed it back to her. "If you—"

She didn't wait for him to finish, instead reaching out to snatch the phone back as she turned in the same motion. She walked away and shoved the device back in her bag. He didn't follow.

She wasn't aware of much on the walk, automatically weaving through the other pedestrians out for a stroll. Once back home, about a twenty-minute walk from Hecate's, she tossed her bag down on the couch and headed for the shower. Maybe she could wash away everything from the past hour.

Of course, it didn't work. The rhythm of the water coming down on her seemed to quietly whisper, *"Your mother was a witch, your father is a faery. What does that make you?"* Irritated, she twisted the old chrome knob to turn off the water with more force than necessary.

She padded out to her tiny kitchen once she was dry, hair up in a towel, wearing her favorite pajama shorts and t-shirt. She had worn this set nightly for two weeks now, and they really needed a wash, but she didn't particularly care. A glass of wine was in order, and then some mindless scrolling through social media on her phone seemed like a good distraction.

She sat down on the worn red velvet material of her couch. Setting her cup down—a stainless steel wine tumbler with the words *Hecate's Boutique* above a cauldron graphic—on the side table, she rummaged through her bag for her phone and plugged it into the cord dangling over the arm of the couch. Nestling back into the throw pillows, which were a gift from Rhea when she moved out of her aunt's, she grabbed her wine and opened one of the several social media apps on her phone. Some cute baby animal videos, and maybe some of those hot lumberjack videos, should do the trick.

Instead, the first video that popped up was … Søren. She stared. What was that random man—fae, faery, whatever—doing on her feed? She didn't even listen as he started to speak (because nope), instead flicking her finger to scroll to the next video. Which was … also Søren.

"What the hell?" she muttered. She scrolled to the next, and the next. All were the same handsome, rugged blonde in a t-shirt and designer blue jeans. His surroundings were too dimly lit for her to make out.

She considered turning her phone off—or hell, maybe throwing it out the window—but her curiosity won out. She finally let one of the videos play. Immediately, she recognized the deep, smooth voice. It really was him.

"Niamh. Please listen." She pursed her lips at this. Did she have a choice? "Look, I know it was a lot, everything I told you tonight. I'm sorry for it, but you deserve to know what happened to them. Even if you don't have magic and you can't help us, you deserve that, although I know it's hard to swallow." Here, she gave a snort. "Don't shoot the messenger though, alright? I mean, you can be angry with me if you want, but I'm not the one who took your parents away from you. If you ever want to know more, if you have any questions, you can call me. I won't bother you again unless you reach out, okay?"

She rolled her eyes. That was not going to happen.

"I know you're grieving, Niamh, but please, take care of yourself." He looked like he would maybe say something more, but then he shook his head and the video ended abruptly. A new video popped up of some popular dance trend, but she closed the app and set her phone down. She took a long sip of wine, and then another.

It wasn't all that hard to believe in witches. Her aunt never claimed to have real magic; she said she was simply good at understanding people, and that's why her tarot readings were sought after. But her readings were often disturbingly accurate and specific. Yes, learning that her aunt had some real psychic ability wasn't all that surprising.

But faeries, fae, high fae? Could they be real? She drained the remainder of her wine at the thought. Of course they couldn't, and yet, what reason could Søren have to invent that story? How did he infiltrate her phone? He could be some kind of hacker, she mused. And yet … the keychain. She was convinced he did know her father, and he insisted her father was a fae prince. She set the tumbler down and closed her eyes.

After more thought, she reached a comforting conclusion: it didn't matter. None of it actually affected her life right now. Whoever and whatever her parents were, *she* didn't have magic. Søren said he wouldn't contact her anymore, so the bizarre incident of that evening wouldn't be repeated in any form. She had a store to run, and the fall semester of her grad school classes would start in two weeks.

She felt more at peace as she fell asleep that night, safe in the knowledge that knowing what happened to her parents didn't change what she needed to do tomorrow or the next day. She would keep living her life through the phases of her grief as best she could, and nothing would change.

That night, the first of the dreams came to her.

About the Author

Cara is a native desert dweller in southern Arizona, where she lives with her husband, two children, and their dog MacKenzie. Her biggest dream as a little girl was to be a writer. She has a degree in psychology and creative writing, and has been working with children in many different settings since high school. She is an award winning poet, and she began writing novels in 2022.

A "joyful girl" at her core, she finds inspiration in music, desert skies, and the bittersweet magic of everyday life. Her books blend witchy fantasy stories with themes of healing, identity, and chosen family. When she's not writing or reading, you'll find her listening to various genres of music, soaking in nature, or savoring moments with her kids — always creating, always feeling, always telling stories that matter.

Acknowledgments

As always, my first thanks go to my husband and my two sons. You mean the world to me, and I wouldn't be able to make these author dreams come true without your love and support.

Thank you to Cass; without our "book chats," my stories wouldn't reach their full potential. So grateful to have you in my corner, as well as my bestie Karlene. You both are "my people" and I adore you.

To my beta readers: your feedback is so essential and helpful. I can never thank you enough for spending so much time and effort on my manuscripts. Everyone's feedback was useful and appreciated, but I must give credit to Ash Wren in particular for her contributions to the final version of this story.

To the best editor in the world, Kelly Scriven: my friend, I'm afraid as long as I'm writing books, you're never allowed to retire. Not even if your own books make you super busy and famous. You're stuck with me!

To my ARC and Street Teams: all of you play a key role when it comes to publishing and marketing my stories. I am so incredibly grateful for your continued support. Some of you have been with me since early on in my publishing journey, and I'm thrilled you're still here. Special thanks to Charlotte for putting up with me, as well as helping me and everyone else on the street team stay organized.

To Jane, Sophie, Roxy, Manon, Amber, and everyone

else at Vinci Books: I appreciate all you do. Thanks for giving me the opportunity and for working so hard to give my books their best shot at success.

To my readers: I am forever humbled that you gave my work a chance, and forever grateful for your role in making my wildest dreams come true. (And I'm extra, extra grateful for every single rating/review—they're more important to authors than many realize!) I hope you enjoyed *Deception of Dreams*! Happy reading!

www.ingramcontent.com/pod-product-compliance
Lightning Source LLC
La Vergne TN
LVHW030915080826
845145LV00013B/2901

* 9 7 8 1 0 3 6 7 3 3 7 9 7 *